TIME TRAVELERS

TIME TRAVELERS

FICTION IN THE
FOURTH DIMENSION

Original Title *Timescapes: Stories of Time Travel*

EDITED AND INTRODUCED BY **PETER HAINING**

BARNES
&NOBLE
BOOKS
NEW YORK

CONTENTS

INTRODUCTION

In October 1995 Professor Stephen Hawking, Britain's leading cosmic physicist, amazed the world of science by admitting that a view which he had held for years—that time travel was impossible—might, after all, be wrong. The Cambridge professor and best-selling author of *A Brief History of Time* (1988) confessed, 'If you combine Einstein's general theory of relativity with quantum theory, time travel does begin to seem a possibility.'

His remark came as quite a surprise to scientists and laymen alike: for this was the man who had argued, in a mix of advanced science and ordinary logic, that time travel would allow people to alter their own pasts—murder their ancestors or even prevent their own births. This was clearly ridiculous, he had said, and added, 'The best evidence that time travel will never be possible is that we have not been invaded by hordes of tourists from the future.'

A subsequent rethink, however, led him in the autumn of 1995 to reverse this view. 'One of the consequences of rapid interstellar travel would be that one could also travel back in time,' he said, and then proceeded to launch an appeal for government funding for more research into 'closed time-like curves'—the technical term for time travel. Such research was already going on in a number of universities, said Professor Hawking, including his own and the California Institute of Technology, and it had been the findings of this research that had led to his change of mind.

The arguments about time travel go back a long way—as far back as Sir Isaac Newton in the seventeenth century, who dismissed the concept out of hand, declaring that time and space were fixed and immutable. This remained the received wisdom until 1916, when Albert Einstein proved that time and space *are* closely related and that both are affected by gravity. He also began to theorise that travel at enormous speeds would make it possible to visit the past. This, in turn, has prompted speculation about 'black holes' (collapsed stars) and 'worm-holes' (two black holes linked by a funnel), into which light and matter are sucked at extraordinary rates with the possibility that their gravitational fields are so vast as to actually reverse the flow of time.

Today some scientists are suggesting that a time traveller might enter at one end of a wormhole and emerge from the other in a completely different time. The problem about this is that some people believe that the traveller would collide with himself coming in the reverse direction. However, there is a contrary view which says that nature would not allow him to emerge either near himself or near the place he left. As a consequence, the only place to visit would probably be the other side of the universe.

The paradox of a person being murdered by his own grandchild has been tackled with the help of quantum physics. Research has suggested that if the universe is considered as a 'multiverse' in which all possible histories happen simultaneously, then a time traveller could travel into the past—but *only* into the past of another, parallel universe in which he, as a time traveller who was not born there, kills his grandfather. Of course, everyone involved in speculating about time travel is aware that a time machine would not be easy to build, and that its energy supply would not be easy to find. Some scientists think that the most likely source of fuel is going to be in outer space. And so finding it creates the problem of getting there in the first place.

However, no such problems have confounded the writers of science fiction and fantasy. Time travel has been one of their favourite themes for over a century, ever since the idea was popularised in H. G. Wells' novel, *The Time Machine*, published in 1895. And imagination and invention have powered every traveller's machine, from Wells' ram-shackle contraption to the streamlined conveyances of today. Some of these men and women have also travelled in time paradoxes and time slips; others in time tunnels and time warps. All have gone backwards and forwards into time and—mostly—returned to tell the tale. Their journeys to the past and their histories of the future are what have made this such a rich and varied area of imaginative fiction. It is generally assumed, of course, that people travelling into the past would inevitably want to interfere with history. Indeed, most of us can think of some event in our own lives that we would welcome an opportunity to reverse. But this would almost certainly result in a whole new set of problems.

Notwithstanding the arguments for and against time travel, I am reminded of a formula that was spelled out for me some years ago, which demonstrated that it was possible, no matter how ridiculous it might seem, for a man to *become his own grandfather*. Let me explain how it works.

First, you marry a woman with a pretty daughter. Your father, who has an eye for pretty girls, then sweeps your stepdaughter off her feet and marries her. He becomes your son-in-law, while your stepdaughter becomes your mother since she's your father's wife. Now, your wife gives birth to a son: your son who is also your father's brother-in-law and—as the brother of your stepmother—your uncle. But not to be outdone, your father and new mother have a son, too, and their son is both your brother and your grandchild.

At this point your wife, being your mother's mother, is your grandmother, while you are both her husband and her grandchild. And since your wife's husband would be her grandchild's grandfather you're his *. . . grandfather*!

Is is the challenge of such paradoxes that has helped to make the time travel story such an attraction to writers over the past hundred years. In the pages that follow I have brought together some of the best and most varied tales from the genre, ranging over the past, the present and the future—though not necessarily in that order. They have been assembled as a tribute to the ingenuity of their authors, and especially to H. G. Wells, the man who set the machines rolling.

Professor Hawking has made another significant comment on the link between fact and fiction in time travel. 'There is a two-way trade between science fiction and science,' he said in a reference to the most popular of all TV time travel series, *Star Trek*; 'We may not yet be able to boldly go where no man or woman has gone before, but at least we can do it in the mind.'

Your time capsule awaits!

Peter Haining
May 1997

1

BACK TO THE PRESENT

'The man who came to loathe his own era' —from 'The Reason Is With Us'
by James E. Gunn (*Satellite Science Fiction*, 1958)

A LITTLE SOMETHING FOR US TEMPUNAUTS

Philip K. Dick

When—rather than if—Professor Stephen Hawking's prediction that time travel is possible becomes a reality, the questions to be asked are, first, what might happen on the inaugural flight, and second, could the mission to conquer time repeat the race between the Americans and the Russians to be first in space? These thoughts sparked the imagination of Philip K. Dick and resulted in this opening story of the collection. By 1974, he said, he had become rather weary about the space programme, after the initial thrill of the first moon landing and then the virtual shut-down of the project. 'I wondered, if time travel became a "programme", would it suffer the same fate?' he explained, 'or was there an even worse possibility latent in it, within the very nature of the paradoxes of time travel?' This story is his answer.

Philip Kindred Dick (1928–82) has been called one of the most original and important American writers of sf—Brian W. Aldiss is just one of many major writers who have acknowledged his profound influence on the genre. In a blend of irony and affection, his army of readers and fans have even named themselves 'Dickheads'. Living for much of his life in California, Dick began writing in the Fifties and showed an early interest in 'awareness of reality' themes, drugs and time travel. One of his most highly regarded novels, Now Wait for Last Year *(1966), is about the achievement of time travel by means of a hallucinogen. He used the theme on several occasions, in particular in the short stories 'Breakfast at Twilight' (1953), 'Time Pawn' (1959) and 'All We Marsmen' (1964) and in his novels* Counter-Clock World *(1967) and* Ubik *(1969). His short story 'We can Remember It for You Wholesale' (1966) was memorably filmed in 1990 as* Total Recall, *starring Arnold Schwarzenegger, and launched what has become a whole series of special-effects movie spectaculars. Perhaps one day soon 'A Little Something for Us Tempunauts' (1974) will also catch the eye of an adventurous film-maker?*

*   *   *

Wearily, Addison Doug plodded up the long path of synthetic redwood rounds, step by step, his head down a little, moving as if he were in actual physical pain. The girl watched him, wanting to help him, hurt within her to see how worn and unhappy he was, but at the same time she rejoiced that he was there at all. On and on, towards her, without glancing up, going by feel ... like he's done this many times, she thought suddenly. Knows the way too well. Why?

'Addi,' she called, and ran towards him. 'They said on the TV you were dead. All of you were killed!'

He paused, wiping back his dark hair, which was no longer long; just before the launch they had cropped it. But he had evidently forgotten. 'You believe everything you see on TV?' he said, and came on again, haltingly, but smiling now. And reaching up for her.

God, it felt good to hold him, and to have him clutch at her again, with more strength than she had expected. 'I was going to find somebody else,' she gasped. 'To replace you.'

'I'll knock your head off if you do,' he said. 'Anyhow, that isn't possible; nobody could replace me.'

'But what about the implosion?' she said. 'On re-entry; they said—'

'I forget,' Addison said, in the tone he used when he meant, I'm not going to discuss it. The tone had always angered her before, but not now. This time she sensed how awful the memory was. 'I'm going to stay at your place a couple of days,' he said, as together they moved up the path towards the open front door of the tilted A-frame house. 'If that's okay. And Benz and Crayne will be joining me, later on; maybe even as soon as tonight. We've got a lot to talk over and figure out.'

'Then all three of you survived.' She gazed up into his careworn face. 'Everything they said on TV . . .' She understood, then. Or believed she did. 'It was a cover story. For—political purposes, to fool the Russians. Right? I mean, the Soviet Union'll think the launch was a failure because on re-entry—'

'No,' he said. 'A chrononaut will be joining us, most likely. To help figure out what happened. General Toad said one of them is already on his way here; they got clearance already. Because of the gravity of the situation.'

'Jesus,' the girl said, stricken. 'Then who's the cover story for?'

'Let's have something to drink,' Addison said. 'And then I'll outline it all for you.'

'Only thing I've got at the moment is California brandy.'

Addison Doug said, 'I'd drink anything right now, the way I feel.' He dropped to the couch, leaned back, and sighed a ragged, distressed sigh, as the girl hurriedly began fixing both of them a drink.

The FM-radio in the car yammered, '. . . grieves at the stricken turn of events precipitating out of an unheralded . . .'

'Official nonsense babble,' Crayne said, shutting off the radio. He and Benz were having trouble finding the house, having been there only once before. It struck Crayne that this was a somewhat informal way of convening a conference of this importance, meeting at Addison's chick's pad out here in the boondocks of Ojai. On the other hand, they wouldn't be pestered by the curious. And they probably didn't have much time. But that was hard to say; about that no one knew for sure.

The hills on both sides of the road had once been forests, Crayne observed. Now housing tracts and their melted, irregular, plastic roads marred every rise in sight. 'I'll bet this was nice once,' he said to Benz, who was driving.

'The Los Padres National Forest is near here,' Benz said. 'I got lost in there when I was eight. For hours I was sure a rattler would get me. Every stick was a snake.'

'The rattler's got you now,' Crayne said.

'All of us,' Benz said.

'You know,' Crayne said, 'it's a hell of an experience to be dead.'

'Speak for yourself.'

'But technically—'

'If you listen to the radio and TV.' Benz turned towards him, his big gnome face bleak with admonishing sternness. 'We're no more dead than anyone else on the planet. The difference for us is that our death date is in the past, whereas everyone else's is set somewhere at an uncertain time in the future. Actually, some people have it pretty damn well set, like people in cancer wards; they're as certain as we are. More so. For example, how long can we stay here before we go back? We have a margin, a latitude that a terminal cancer victim doesn't have.'

Crayne said cheerfully, 'The next thing you'll be telling us to cheer us up is that we're in no pain.'

'Addi is. I watched him lurch off earlier today. He's got it psychosomatically—made it into a physical complaint. Like God's kneeling on his neck; you know, carrying a much-too-great burden that's unfair, only he won't complain out loud . . . just points now and then at the nail hole in his hand.' He grinned.

'Addi has got more to live for than we do.'

'Every man has more to live for than any other man. I don't have a cute chick to sleep with, but I'd like to see the semis rolling along Riverside Freeway at sunset a few more times. It's not what you have to live for; it's that you want to live to see it, to be there—that's what is so damn sad.'

They rode on in silence.

In the quiet living room of the girl's house the three tempunauts sat around smoking, taking it easy; Addison Doug thought to himself that the girl looked unusually foxy and desirable in her stretched-tight white sweater and micro-skirt and he wished, wistfully, that she looked a little less interesting. He could not really afford to get embroiled in such stuff, at this point. He was too tired.

'Does she know,' Benz said, indicating the girl, 'what this is all about? I mean, can we talk openly? It won't wipe her out?'

'I haven't explained it to her yet,' Addison said.

'You goddam well better,' Crayne said.

'What is it?' the girl said, stricken, sitting upright with one hand directly between her breasts. As if clutching at a religious artifact that isn't there, Addison thought.

'We got snuffed on re-entry,' Benz said. He was, really, the cruellest of the three. Or at least the most blunt. 'You see, Miss . . .'

'Hawkins,' the girl whispered.

'Glad to meet you, Miss Hawkins.' Benz surveyed her in his cold, lazy fashion. 'You have a first name?'

'Merry Lou.'

'Okay, Merry Lou,' Benz said. To the other two men he observed, 'Sounds like the name a waitress has stitched on her blouse. Merry Lou's my name and I'll be serving you dinner and breakfast and lunch and dinner and breakfast for the next few days or however long it is before you all give up and go back to your own time; that'll be fifty-three dollars and eight cents, please, not including tip. And I hope y'all never come back, y'hear?' His voice had begun to shake; his cigarette too. 'Sorry, Miss Hawkins,' he said then. 'We're all screwed up by the implosion at re-entry. As soon as we got here in ETA we learned about it. We've known longer than anyone else; we knew as soon as we hit Emergence Time.'

'But there's nothing we could do,' Crayne said.

'There's nothing anyone can do,' Addison said to her, and put his arm around her. It felt like a *déja vu* thing but then it hit him. We're in a closed time loop, he thought, we keep going through this again and again, trying to solve the re-entry problem, each time imagining it's the first time, the only time . . . and never succeeding. Which attempt is this? Maybe the millionth; we have sat here a million times, raking the same facts over and over again and getting nowhere. He felt bone-weary, thinking that. And he felt a sort of vast philosophical hate towards all other men, who did not have this enigma to deal with. We all go to one place, he thought, as the Bible says. But . . . for the three of us, we have been there already. Are lying there now. So it's wrong to ask us to stand around on the surface of Earth afterwards and argue and worry about it and try to figure out what malfunctioned. That should be, rightly, for our heirs to do. We've had enough already.

He did not say this aloud, though—for their sake.

'Maybe you bumped into something,' the girl said.

Glancing at the others, Benz said sardonically, 'Maybe we "bumped into something".'

'The TV commentators kept saying that,' Merry Lou said, 'about the hazard in re-entry of being out of phase spatially and colliding right down to the molecular level with tangent objects, any one of which—' She gestured. 'You know. "No two objects can occupy the same space at the same time." So everything blew up, for that reason.' She glanced around questioningly.

'That is the major risk factor,' Crayne acknowledged. 'At least theoretically, as Dr Fein at Planning calculated when they got into the hazard question. But we had a variety of safety locking devices provided that functioned automatically. Re-entry couldn't occur unless these assists had stabilised us spatially so we would not overlap. Of course, all those devices, in sequence, might have failed. One after the other. I was watching my feedback metric scopes on launch, and they agreed, every one of them, that we were phased properly at that time. And I heard no warning tones. Saw none, neither.' He grimaced. 'At least it didn't happen then.'

Suddenly Benz said, 'Do you realise that our next of kin are now rich? All our Federal and commercial life-insurance pay-off. Our "next of kin"—God forbid, that's us, I guess. We can apply for tens of thousands of dollars, cash on the line. Walk into our brokers' offices and say, "I'm dead; lay the heavy bread on me." '

Addison Doug was thinking, The public memorial services. That they have planned, after the autopsies. That long line of black-draped Cads going down Pennsylvania Avenue, with all the government dignitaries and double-domed scientist types—*and we'll be there*. Not once but twice. Once in the oak hand-rubbed brass-fitted flag-draped caskets, but also . . . maybe riding in open limos, waving at the crowds of mourners.

'The ceremonies,' he said aloud.

The others stared at him, angrily, not comprehending. And then, one by one, they understood; he saw it on their faces.

'No,' Benz grated. 'That's—impossible.'

Crayne shook his head emphatically. 'They'll order us to be there, and we will be. Obeying orders.'

'Will we have to *smile*?' Addison said. 'To fucking *smile*?'

'No,' General Toad said slowly, his great wattled head shivering about on his broomstick neck, the colour of his skin dirty and mottled, as if the mass of decoration on his stiff-board collar had started part of him decaying away. 'You are not to smile, but on the contrary are to adopt a properly grief-stricken manner. In keeping with the national mood of sorrow at this time.'

'That'll be hard to do,' Crayne said.

The Russian chrononaut showed no response; his thin beaked face, narrow within its translating earphones, remained strained with concern.

'The nation,' General Toad said, 'will become aware of your presence among us once more for this brief interval; cameras of all major TV networks will pan up to you without warning, and at the same time, the various commentators have been instructed to tell their audiences something like the following.' He got out a piece of typed material, put on his glasses, cleared his throat and said, ' "We seem to be focusing on three figures riding together. Can't quite make them out. Can you?" ' General Toad lowered the paper. 'At this point they'll interrogate their colleagues extempore. Finally they'll exclaim, "Why, Roger", or Walter or Ned, as the case may be, according to the individual network—'

'Or Bill,' Crayne said. 'In case it's the Bufonidae network, down there in the swamp.'

General Toad ignored him. 'They will severally exclaim, "Why Roger I believe we're seeing the three tempunauts themselves! Does this indeed mean that somehow the difficulty—?'' And then the colleague commentator says in his somewhat more sombre voice, ''What we're seeing at this time, I think, David'', or Henry or Pete or Ralph, whichever it is, ''consists of mankind's first verified glimpse of what the technical people refer to as Emergence Time Activity or ETA. Contrary to what might seem to be the case at first sight, these are *not*—repeat, not—our three valiant tempunauts as such, as we would ordinarily experience them, but more likely picked up by our cameras as the three of them are temporarily suspended in their voyage to the future, which we initially had reason to hope would take place in a time continuum roughly a hundred years from now ... but it would seem that they somehow undershot and are here now, at this moment, which of course is, as we know, our present.'' '

Addison Doug closed his eyes and thought, Crayne will ask him if he can be panned up on by the TV cameras holding a balloon and eating cotton candy. I think we're all going nuts from this, all of us. And then he wondered, How many times have we gone through this idiotic exchange?

I can't prove it, he thought wearily. But I know it's true. We've sat here, done this minuscule scrabbling, listened to and said all this crap, many times. He shuddered. Each rinky-dink word ...

'What's the matter?' Benz said acutely.

The Soviet chrononaut spoke up for the first time. 'What is the maximum interval of ETA possible to your three-man team? And how large a per cent has been exhausted by now?'

After a pause Crayne said, 'They briefed us on that before we came in here today. We've consumed approximately one half of our maximum total ETA interval.'

'However,' General Toad rumbled, 'we have scheduled the Day of National Mourning to fall within the expected period remaining to them of ETA time. This required us to speed up the autopsy and other forensic findings, but in view of public sentiment, it was felt ...'

The autopsy, Addison Doug thought, and again he shuddered; this time he could not keep his thoughts within himself and he said, 'Why don't we adjourn this nonsense meeting and drop down to pathology and view a few tissue sections enlarged and in colour, and maybe we'll brainstorm a couple of vital concepts that'll aid medical science in its quest for explanations? Explanations—that's what we need. Explanations for problems that don't exist yet; we can develop the problems later.' He paused. 'Who agrees?'

'I'm not looking at my spleen up there on the screen,' Benz said. 'I'll ride in the parade but I won't participate in my own autopsy.'

'You could distribute microscopic purple-stained slices of your own gut to the mourners along the way,' Crayne said. 'They could provide each of us with a doggy bag; right, General? We can stew tissue sections like confetti. I still think we should smile.'

'I have researched all the memoranda about smiling,' General Toad said, riffling the pages stacked before them, 'and the consensus at policy is that smiling is not in accord with national sentiment. So that issue must be ruled closed. As far as your participating in the autopsical procedures which are now in progress—'

'We're missing out as we sit here,' Crayne said to Addison Doug. 'I always miss out.'

Ignoring him, Addison addressed the Soviet chrononaut. 'Officer N. Gauki,' he said into his microphone, dangling on his chest, 'what in your mind is the greatest terror facing a time traveller? That there will be an implosion due to coincidence on re-entry, such as has occurred in our launch? Or did other traumatic obsessions bother you and your comrade during your own brief but highly successful time flight?'

N. Gauki, after a pause, answered, 'R. Plenya and I exchanged views at several informal times. I believe I can speak for us both when I respond to your question by emphasising our perpetual fear that we had inadvertently entered a closed time loop and would never break out.'

'You'd repeat it for ever?' Addison Doug asked.

'Yes, Mr A. Doug,' the chrononaut said, nodding sombrely.

A fear that he had never experienced before overcame Addison Doug. He turned helplessly to Benz and muttered, 'Shit.' They gazed at each other.

'I really don't believe this is what happened,' Benz said to him in a low voice, putting his hand on Doug's shoulder; he gripped hard, the grip of friendship. 'We just imploded on re-entry, that's all. Take it easy.'

'Could we adjourn soon?' Addison Doug said in a hoarse, strangling voice, half rising from his chair. He felt the room and the people in it rushing in at him, suffocating him. Claustrophobia, he realised. Like when I was in grade school, when they flashed a surprise test on our teaching machines, and I saw I couldn't pass it. 'Please,' he said simply, standing. They were all looking at him, with different expressions. The Russian's face was especially sympathetic, and deeply lined with care. Addison wished—'I want to go home,' he said to them all, and felt stupid.

*   *   *

He was drunk. It was late at night, at a bar on Hollywood Boulevard; fortunately, Merry Lou was with him, and he was having a good time. Everyone was telling him so, anyhow. He clung to Merry Lou and said, 'The great unity in life, the supreme unity and meaning, is man and woman. Their absolute unity; right?'

'I know,' Merry Lou said. 'We studied that in class.' Tonight, at his request, Merry Lou was a small blonde girl, wearing purple bellbottoms and high heels and an open midriff blouse. Earlier she had had a lapis lazuli in her navel, but during dinner at Ting Ho's it had popped out and been lost. The owner of the restaurant had promised to keep on searching for it, but Merry Lou had been gloomy ever since. It was, she said, symbolic. But of what she did not say. Or anyhow he could not remember; maybe that was it. She had told him what it meant, and he had forgotten.

An elegant young black at a nearby table, with an Afro and striped vest and overstuffed red tie, had been staring at Addison for some time. He obviously wanted to come over to their table but was afraid to; meanwhile, he kept on staring.

'Did you ever get the sensation,' Addison said to Merry Lou, 'that you knew exactly what was about to happen? What someone was going to say? Word for word? Down to the slightest detail. As if you had already lived through it once before?'

'Everybody gets into that space,' Merry Lou said. She sipped a Bloody Mary.

The black rose and walked towards them. He stood by Addison. 'I'm sorry to bother you, sir.'

Addison said to Merry Lou, 'He's going to say, "Don't I know you from somewhere? Didn't I see you on TV?"'

'That was precisely what I intended to say,' the black said.

Addison said, 'You undoubtedly saw my picture on page forty-six of the current issue of *Time*, the section on new medical discoveries. I'm the GP from a small town in Iowa catapulted to fame by my invention of a widespread, easily available cure for eternal life. Several of the big pharmaceutical houses are already bidding on my vaccine.'

'That might have been where I saw your picture,' the black said, but he did not appear convinced. Nor did he appear drunk; he eyed Addison Doug intensely. 'May I seat myself with you and the lady?'

'Sure,' Addison Doug said. He now saw, in the man's hand, the ID of the US security agency that had ridden herd on the project from the start.

'Mr Doug,' the security agent said as he seated himself beside Addison, 'you really shouldn't be here shooting off your mouth like this. If I recognised you some other dude might and break out. It's all classified until the Day of Mourning. Technically, you're in violation of a Federal Statute by being here; did you realise that? I should haul you in. But this is a difficult situation; we don't want to do something uncool and make a scene. Where are your two colleagues?'

'At my place,' Merry Lou said. She had obviously not seen the ID. 'Listen,' she said sharply to the agent, 'why don't you get lost? My husband here has been through a gruelling ordeal, and this is his only chance to unwind.'

Addison looked at the man. 'I knew what you were going to say before you came over here.' Word for word, he thought. I am right, and Benz is wrong and this will keep happening, this replay.

'Maybe,' the security agent said, 'I can induce you to go back to Miss Hawkins' place voluntarily. Some info arrived'—he tapped the tiny earphone in his right ear—'just a few minutes ago, to all of us, to deliver to you, marked urgent, if we located you. At the launch-site ruins . . . they've been combing through the rubble, you know?'

'I know,' Addison said.

'They think they have their first clue. Something was brought back by one of you. From ETA, over and above what you took, in violation of all your pre-launch training.'

'Let me ask you this,' Addison Doug said. 'Suppose somebody does see me? Suppose somebody does recognise me? So what?'

'The public believes that even though re-entry failed, the flight into time, the first American time-travel launch, was successful. Three US tempunauts were thrust a hundred years into the future—roughly twice as far as the Soviet launch of last year. That you only went a *week* will be less of a shock if it's believed that you three chose deliberately to remanifest at this continuum because you wished to attend, in fact felt compelled to attend—'

'We wanted to be in the parade,' Addison interrupted. 'Twice.'

'You were drawn to the dramatic and sombre spectacle of your own funeral procession, and will be glimpsed there by the alert camera crews of all major networks. Mr Doug, really, an awful lot of high-level planning and expense have gone into this to help correct a dreadful situation; trust us, believe me. It'll be easier on the public, and that's vital, if there's ever to be another US time shot. And that is, after all, what we all want.'

Addison Doug stared at him. 'We want what?'

Uneasily, the security agent said, 'To take further trips into time. As you have done. Unfortunately, you yourself cannot ever do so again, because of the tragic implosion and death of the three of you. But other tempunauts—'

'We want what? Is that what we want?' Addison's voice rose; people at nearby tables were watching now. Nervously.

'Certainly,' the agent said. 'And keep your voice down.'

'I don't want that,' Addison said. 'I want to stop. To stop for ever. To just lie in the ground, in the dust, with everyone else. To see no more summers—the *same* summer.'

'Seen one, you've seen then all,' Merry Lou said hysterically. 'I think he's right, Addi; we should get out of here. You've had too many drinks, and it's late, and this news about the—'

Addison broke in, 'What was brought back? How much extra mass?'

The security agent said, 'Preliminary analysis shows that machinery weighing about one hundred pounds was lugged back into the time field of the module and picked up along with you. This much mass—' The agent gestured. 'That blew up the pad right on the spot. It couldn't begin to compensate for that much more than had occupied its open area at launch time.'

'Wow!' Merry Lou said, eyes wide. 'Maybe somebody sold one of you a quadraphonic phono for a dollar ninety-eight including fifteen-inch-air-suspension speakers and a lifetime supply of Neil Diamond records.' She tried to laugh, but failed; her eyes dimmed over. 'Addi,' she whispered, 'I'm sorry. But it's sort of—weird. I mean, it's absurd; you all were briefed, weren't you, about your return weight? You weren't even to add so much as a piece of paper to what you took. I even saw Dr Fein demonstrating the reasons on TV. And one of you hoisted a hundred pounds of machinery into that field? You must have been trying to self-destruct, to do that!' Tears slid from her eyes; one tear rolled out on to her nose and hung there. He reached reflexively to wipe it away, as if helping a little girl rather than a grown one.

'I'll fly you to the analysis site,' the security agent said, standing up. He and Addison helped Merry Lou to her feet; she trembled as she stood a moment, finishing her Bloody Mary. Addison felt acute sorrow for her, but then, almost at once, it passed. He wondered why. One can weary even of that, he conjectured. Of caring for someone. If it goes on too long—on and on. For ever. And, at last, even after that, into something no one before, not God Himself, maybe, had ever had to suffer and in the end, for all His great heart, succumb to.

As they walked through the crowded bar towards the street, Addison Doug said to the security agent, 'Which one of us—'

'They know which one,' the agent said as he held the door to the street open for Merry Lou. The agent stood, now, behind Addison, signalling for a grey Federal car to land at the red parking area. Two other security agents, in uniform, hurried towards them.

'Was it me?' Addison Doug asked.

'You better believe it,' the security agent said.

The funeral procession moved with aching solemnity down Pennsylvania Avenue, three flag-draped caskets and dozens of black limousines passing between rows of heavily coated, shivering mourners. A low haze hung over the day, grey outlines of buildings faded into the rain-drenched murk of the Washington March day.

Scrutinising the lead Cadillac through prismatic binoculars, TV's top news and public-events commentator, Henry Cassidy, droned on at his vast unseen audience, '. . . sad recollections of that earlier train among the wheatfields carrying the coffin of Abraham Lincoln back to burial and the nation's capital. And what a sad day this is, and what appropriate weather, with its dour overcast and sprinkles!' In his monitor he saw the zoomar lens pan up on the fourth Cadillac, as it followed those with the caskets of the dead tempunauts.

His engineer tapped him on the arm.

'We appear to be focusing on three unfamiliar figures so far not identified, riding together,' Henry Cassidy said into his neck mike, nodding agreement. 'So far I'm unable to quite make them out. Are your location and vision any better from where you're placed, Everett?' he inquired of his colleague and pressed the button that notified Everett Branton to replace him on the air.

'Why, Henry,' Branton said in a voice of growing excitement, 'I believe we're actually eyewitness to the three American tempunauts as they remanifest themselves on their historic journey into the future!'

'Does this signify,' Cassidy said, 'that somehow they have managed to solve and overcome the—'

'Afraid not, Henry,' Branton said in his slow, regretful voice. 'What we're eyewitnessing to our complete surprise consists of the Western world's first verified glimpse of what the technical people refer to as Emergence Time Activity.'

'Ah, yes, ETA,' Cassidy said brightly, reading it off the official script the Federal authorities had handed to him before air time.

'Right, Henry. Contrary to what *might* seem to be the case at first sight, these are not – repeat *not* – our three brave tempunauts as such, as we would ordinarily experience them—'

'I grasp it now,' Everett,' Cassidy broke in excitedly, since his authorised script read CASS BREAKS IN EXCITEDLY. 'Our three tempunauts have momentarily suspended in their historic voyage to the future, which we believe will span across a time continuum roughly a century from now . . . It would seem that the overwhelming grief and drama of this unanticipated day of mourning has caused them to—'

'Sorry to interrupt, Henry,' Everett Branton said, 'but I think, since the procession has momentarily halted on its slow march forward, that we might be able to—'

'No!' Cassidy said, as a note was handed him in a swift scribble, reading: *Do not interview nauts. Urgent. Dis. previous inst.* 'I don't think we're going to be able to . . .' he continued, '. . . to speak briefly with tempunauts Benz, Crayne and Doug, as you had hoped, Everett. As we had all briefly hoped to.' He wildly waved the boom-mike back; it had already begun to swing out expectantly towards the stopped Cadillac. Cassidy shook his head violently at the mike technician and his engineer.

Perceiving the boom-mike swinging at them Addison Doug stood up in the back of the open Cadillac. Cassidy groaned. He wants to speak, he realised. Didn't they reinstruct *him*? Why am I the only one they get across to? Other boom-mikes representing other networks plus radio station interviewers on foot now were rushing out to thrust up their microphones into the faces of the three tempunauts, especially Addison Doug's. Doug was already beginning to speak, in response to a question shouted up to him by a reporter. With his boom-mike off, Cassidy couldn't hear the question, nor Doug's answer. With reluctance, he signalled for his own boom-mike to trigger on.

'. . . before,' Doug was saying loudly.

'In what manner, "All this has happened before"?' the radio reporter, standing close to the car, was saying.

'I mean,' US tempunaut Addison Doug declared, his face red and strained, 'that I have stood here in this spot and said again and again, and all of you have viewed this parade and our deaths at re-entry endless times, a closed cycle of trapped time which must be broken.'

'Are you seeking,' another reporter jabbered up at Addison Doug, 'for a solution to the re-entry implosion disaster which can be applied in retrospect so that when you do return to the past you will be able to correct the malfunction and avoid the tragedy which cost—or for you three, will cost—your lives?'

Tempunaut Benz said, 'We are doing that, yes.'

'Trying to ascertain the cause of the violent implosion and eliminate the cause before we return,' tempunaut Crayne added, nodding. 'We have learned already that, for reasons unknown, a mass of nearly one hundred pounds of miscellaneous Volkswagen motor parts, including cylinders, the head . . .'

This is awful, Cassidy thought. 'This is amazing!' he said aloud, into his neck mike. 'The already tragically deceased US tempunauts, with a determination that could emerge only from the rigorous training and discipline to which they were subjected—and we wondered why at the time but can clearly see why now—have already analysed the mechanical slip-up responsible, evidently, for their own deaths, and have begun the laborious process of sifting through and eliminating causes of that slip-up so that they can return to their original launch site and re-enter without mishap.'

'One wonders,' Branton mumbled on to the air and into his feedback earphone, 'what the consequences of this alteration of the near past will be. If in re-entry they do *not* implode and are *not* killed, then they will not—well, it's too complex for me, Henry, these time paradoxes that Dr Fein at the Time Extrusion Labs in Pasadena has so frequently and eloquently brought to our attention.'

Into all the microphones available, of all sorts, tempunaut Addison Doug was saying, more quietly now, 'We must not eliminate the cause of re-entry implosion. The only way out of this trip is for us to die. Death is the only solution for this. For the three of us.' He was interrupted as the procession of Cadillacs began to move forward.

Shutting off his mike momentarily, Henry Cassidy said to his engineer, 'Is he nuts?'

'Only time will tell,' his engineer said in a hard-to-hear voice.

'An extraordinary moment in the history of the United States' involvement in time travel,' Cassidy said, then, into his now live mike. 'Only time will tell—if you will pardon the inadvertent pun—whether tempunaut Doug's cryptic remarks, uttered impromptu at this moment of supreme suffering for him, as in a sense of a lesser degree it is for all of us, are the words of a man deranged by grief or an accurate insight into the macabre dilemma that in theoretical terms we knew all along might eventually confront—confront and strike down with its lethal blow—a time-travel launch, either ours or the Russians.'

He segued, then, to a commercial.

'You know,' Branton's voice muttered in his ear, not on the air but just to the control room and to him, 'if he's right they ought to let the poor bastards die.'

'They ought to release them,' Cassidy agreed. 'My God, the way Doug looked and talked, you'd imagine he'd gone through this for a thousand years and then some! I wouldn't be in his shoes for anything.'

'I'll bet you fifty bucks,' Branton said, 'they have gone through this before. Many times.'

'Then we have, too,' Cassidy said.

Rain fell now, making all the lined-up mourners shiny. Their faces, their eyes, even their clothes—everything glistened in wet reflections of broken, fractured light, bent and sparkling, as, from gathering grey formless layers above them, the day darkened.

'Are we on the air?' Branton asked.

Who knows? Cassidy thought. He wished the day would end.

The Soviet chrononaut N. Gauki lifted both hands impassionedly and spoke to the Americans across the table from him in a voice of extreme urgency. 'It is the opinion of myself and my colleague R. Plenya, who for his pioneering achievements in time travel has been certified a Hero of the Soviet People, and rightly so, that based on our own experience and on theoretical material developed both in your own academic circles and in the Soviet Academy of Sciences of the USSR, we believe that tempunaut A. Doug's fears may be justified. And his deliberate destruction of himself and his team-mates at re-entry, by hauling a huge mass of auto back with him from ETA, a violation of his orders, should be regarded as the act of a desperate man with no other means of escape. Of course, the decision is up to you. We have only advisory position in this matter.'

Addison Doug played with his cigarette lighter on the table and did not look up. His ears hummed and he wondered what that meant. It had an electronic quality. Maybe we're within the module again, he thought. But he didn't perceive it; he felt the reality of the people around him, the table, the blue plastic lighter between his fingers. No smoking in the module during re-entry, he thought. He put the lighter carefully away in his pocket.

'We've developed no concrete evidence whatsoever,' General Toad said, 'that a closed time loop has been set up. There's only the subjective feelings of fatigue on the part of Mr Doug. Just his belief that he's done all this repeatedly. As he says, it is very probably psychological in nature.' He rooted, pig-like, among the papers before him. 'I have a report, not disclosed to the media, from four psychiatrists at Yale on his psychological make-up. Although unusually stable, there is a tendency towards cyclothymia on his part, culminating in acute depression. This naturally was taken into account long before the launch, but it was calculated that the joyful qualities of the two others in the team would offset this functionally. Anyhow, that depressive tendency in time is exceptionally high, now.' He held the paper out, but no one at the table accepted it. 'Isn't it true, Dr Fein,' he said, 'that an acutely depressed person experiences time in a peculiar way, that is, circular time, time repeating itself, getting nowhere, round and round? The person gets so psychotic that he refuses to let go of the past. Reruns it in his head constantly.'

'But you see,' Dr Fein said, 'this subjective sensation of being trapped is perhaps all we would have.' This was the research physicist whose basic work had laid the theoretical foundation for the project. 'If a closed loop did unfortunately lock into being.'

'The general,' Addison Doug said, 'is using words he doesn't understand.'

'I researched the one I was unfamiliar with,' General Toad said. 'The technical psychiatric terms . . . know what they mean.'

To Addison Doug, Benz said, 'Where'd you get all those VW parts, Addi?'

'I don't have them yet,' Addison Doug said.

'Probably picked up the first junk he could lay his hands on,' Crayne said. 'Whatever was available, just before we started back.'

'Will start back,' Addison Doug corrected.

'Here are my instructions to the three of you,' General Toad said. 'You are not in any way to attempt to cause damage or implosion or malfunction during re-entry, either by lugging back extra mass or by any other method that enters your mind. You are to return as scheduled and in replica of the prior simulations. This especially applies to you, Mr Doug.' The phone by his right arm buzzed. He frowned, picked up the receiver. An interval passed, and then he scowled deeply and set the receiver back down, loudly.

'You've been overruled,' Dr Fein said.

'Yes, I have,' General Toad said. 'And I must say at this time that I am personally glad because my decision was an unpleasant one.'

'Then we can arrange for implosion at re-entry,' Benz said after a pause.

'The three of you are to make the decision,' General Toad said. 'Since it involves your lives. It's been entirely left up to you. Whichever way you want it. If you're convinced you're in a closed time loop, and you believe a massive implosion at re-entry will abolish it—' He ceased talking, as tempunaut Doug rose to his feet. 'Are you going to make another speech, Doug?' he said.

'I just want to thank everyone involved,' Addison Doug said. 'For letting us decide.' He gazed haggard-faced and wearily around at all the individuals seated at the table. 'I really appreciate it.'

'You know,' Benz said slowly, 'blowing us up at re-entry could add nothing to the chances of abolishing a closed loop. In fact that could do it, Doug.'

'Not if it kills us all,' Crayne said.

'You agree with Addi?' Benz said.

'Dead is dead,' Crayne said. 'I've been pondering it. What other way is more likely to get us out of this? Than if we're dead? What possible other way?'

'You may be in no loop,' Dr Fein pointed out.

'But we may be,' Crayne said.

Doug, still on his feet, said to Crayne and Benz, 'Could we include Merry Lou in our decision-making?'

'Why?' Benz said.

'I can't think too clearly any more,' Doug said. 'Merry Lou can help me; I depend on her.'

'Sure,' Crayne said. Benz, too, nodded.

General Toad examined his wrist-watch stoically and said, 'Gentlemen, this concludes our discussion.'

Soviet chrononaut Gauki removed his headphones and neck mike and hurried towards the three US tempunauts, his hand extended; he was apparently saying something in Russian, but none of them could understand it. They moved away sombrely, clustering close.

'In my opinion you're nuts, Addi,' Benz said. 'But it would appear that I'm the minority now.'

'If he *is* right,' Crayne said, 'if—one chance in a billion—if we are going back again and again for ever, that would justify it.'

'Could we go see Merry Lou?' Addison Doug said. 'Drive over to her place now?'

'She's waiting outside,' Crayne said.

Striding up to stand beside the three tempunauts, General Toad said, 'You know, what made the determination go the way it did was the public reaction to how you, Doug, looked and behaved during the funeral procession. The NSC advisors came to the conclusion that the public would, like you, rather be certain it's over for all of you. That it's more of a relief to them to know you're free of your mission than to save the project and obtain a perfect re-entry. I guess you really made a lasting impression on them, Doug. That whining you did.' He walked away, then, leaving the three of them standing there alone.

'Forget him,' Crayne said to Addison Doug. 'Forget everyone like him. We've got to do what we have to.'

'Merry Lou will explain it to me,' Doug said. She would know what to do, what would be right.

'I'll go get her,' Crayne said, 'and after that the four of us can drive somewhere, maybe to her place, and decide what to do. Okay?'

'Thank you,' Addison Doug said, nodding; he glanced around for her hopefully, wondering where she was. In the next room, perhaps, somewhere close. 'I appreciate that,' he said.

Benz and Crayne eyed each other. He saw that, but did not know what it meant. He only knew that he needed someone, Merry Lou most of all, to help him understand what the situation was. And what to finalise on to get them out of it.

Merry Lou drove them north from Los Angeles in the superfast lane of the freeway towards Ventura, and after that inland to Ojai. The four of them said very little. Merry Lou drove well, as always; leaning against her, Addison Doug felt himself relax into a temporary sort of peace.

'There's nothing like having a chick drive you,' Crayne said, after many miles had passed in silence.

'It's an aristocratic sensation,' Benz murmured. 'To have a woman do the driving. Like you're nobility being chauffeured.'

Merry Lou said, 'Until she runs into something. Some big slow object.'

Addison Doug said, 'When you saw me trudging up to your place . . . up the redwood round path the other day. What did you think? Tell me honestly.'

'You looked,' the girl said, 'as if you'd done it many times. You looked worn and tired and—ready to die. At the end.' She hesitated. 'I'm sorry, but that's how you looked, Addi. I thought to myself, he knows the way too well.'

'Like I'd done it too many times.'

'Yes,' she said.

'Then you vote for implosion,' Addison Doug said.

'Well—'

'Be honest with me,' he said.

Merry Lou said, 'Look in the back seat. The box on the floor.'

With a flashlight from the glove compartment the three men examined the box. Addison Doug, with fear, saw its contents. VW motor parts, rusty and worn. Still oily.

'I got them from behind a foreign-car garage near my place,' Merry Lou said. 'On the way to Pasadena. The first junk I saw that seemed as if it'd be heavy enough. I had heard them say on TV at launch time that anything over fifty pounds up to—'

'It'll do it,' Addison Doug said. 'It did do it.'

'So there's no point in going to your place,' Crayne said. 'It's decided. We might as well head south towards the module. And initiate the procedure for getting out of ETA. And back to re-entry.' His voice was heavy but evenly pitched. 'Thanks for your vote, Miss Hawkins.'

She said, 'You are all so tired.'

'I'm not,' Benz said. 'I'm mad. Mad as hell.'

'At me?' Addison Doug said.

'I don't know,' Benz said. 'It's just—Hell.' He lapsed into brooding silence then. Hunched over, baffled and inert. Withdrawn as far as possible from the others in the car.

At the next freeway junction she turned the car south. A sense of freedom seemed now to fill her, and Addison Doug felt some of the weight, the fatigue, ebbing already.

On the wrist of each of the three men the emergency alert receiver buzzed its warning tone; they all started.

'What's that mean?' Merry Lou said, slowing the car.

'We're to contact General Toad by phone as soon as possible,' Crayne said. He pointed. 'There's a Standard Station over there; take the next exit, Miss Hawkins. We can phone in from there.'

A few minutes later Merry Lou brought her car to a halt beside the outdoor phone booth. 'I hope it's not bad news,' she said.

'I'll talk first,' Doug said, getting out. Bad news, he thought with laboured amusement. Like what? He crunched stiffly across to the phone booth, entered, shut the door behind him, dropped in a dime and dialled the toll-free number.

'Well, do I have news!' General Toad said when the operator had put him on the line. 'It's a good thing we got hold of you. Just a minute—I'm going to let Dr Fein tell you this himself. You're more apt to believe him than me.' Several clicks, and then Dr Fein's reedy, precise, scholarly voice, but intensified by urgency.

'What's the bad news?' Addison Doug said.

'Not bad, necessarily,' Dr Fein said. 'I've had computations run since our discussion, and it would appear—by that I mean it is statistically probable but still unverified for a certainty—that you are right, Addison. You are in a closed time loop.'

Addison Doug exhaled raggedly. You nowhere autocratic mother, he thought. You probably knew all along.

'However,' Dr Fein said excitedly, stammering a little, 'I also calculate—we jointly do, largely through Cal Tech—that the greatest likelihood of maintaining the loop is to implode on re-entry. Do you understand, Addison? If you lug all those rusty VW parts back and implode, then your statistical chance of closing the loop for ever is greater than if you simply re-enter and all goes well.'

Addison Doug said nothing.

'In fact, Addi—and this is the severe part that I have to stress—implosion at re-entry, especially a massive, calculated one of the sort we seem to see shaping up—do you grasp all this, Addi? Am I getting through to you? For Chrissake, Addi? Virtually *guarantees* the locking in of an absolutely unyielding loop such as you've got in mind. Such as we've all been worried about from the start.' A pause. 'Addi? Are you there?'

Addison Doug said, 'I want to die.'

'That's your exhaustion from the loop. God knows how many repetitions there've been already of the three of you—'

'No,' he said and started to hang up.

'Let me speak with Benz and Crayne,' Dr Fein said rapidly. 'Please, before you go ahead with re-entry. Especially Benz; I'd like to speak with him in particular. Please, Addison. For their sake; your almost total exhaustion has—'

He hung up. Left the phone booth, step by step.

As he climbed back into the car, he heard their two alert receivers still buzzing. 'General Toad said the automatic call for us would keep your two receivers doing that for a while,' he said. And shut the car door after him. 'Let's take off.'

'Doesn't he want to talk to us?' Benz said.

Addison Doug said, 'General Toad wanted to inform us that they have a little something for us. We've been voted a special Congressional

Citation for valour or some damn thing like that. A special medal they never voted anyone before. To be awarded posthumously.'

'Well, hell—that's about the only way it can be awarded,' Crayne said.

Merry Lou, as she started up the engine, began to cry.

'It'll be a relief,' Crayne said presently, as they returned bumpily to the freeway, 'when it's over.'

It won't be long now, Addison Doug's mind declared.

On their wrists the emergency alert receivers continued to put out their combined buzzing.

'They will nibble you to death,' Addison Doug said. 'The endless wearing down by various bureaucratic voices.'

The others in the car turned to gaze at him inquiringly, with uneasiness mixed with perplexity.

'Yeah,' Crayne said. 'These automatic alerts are really a nuisance.' He sounded tired. As tired as I am, Addison Doug thought. And, realising this, he felt better. It showed how right he was.

Great drops of water struck the windscreen; it had now begun to rain. That pleased him too. It reminded him of that most exalted of all experiences within the shortness of his life: the funeral procession moving slowly down Pennsylvania Avenue, the flag-draped caskets. Closing his eyes he leaned back and felt good at last. And heard, all around him once again, the sorrow-bent people. And, in his head, dreamed of the special Congressional Medal. For weariness, he thought. A medal for being tired.

He saw, in his head, himself in other parades too, and in the deaths of many. But really it was one death and one parade. Slow cars moving along the street in Dallas and with Dr King as well . . . He saw himself return again and again, in his closed cycle of life, to the national mourning that he could not and they could not forget. He would be there; they would always be there; it would always be, and every one of them would return together again and again for ever. To the place, the moment, they wanted to be. The event which meant the most to all of them.

This was his gift to them, the people, his country. He had bestowed upon the world a wonderful burden. The dreadful and weary miracle of eternal life.

MR STRENBERRY'S TALE

J. B. Priestley

One of the first theorists to discuss the possibility of time travel in the wake of H. G. Wells' novel was J. W. Dunne (1875–1949), a writer and engineer whose books, An Experiment with Time *(1927) and* The Serial Universe *(1934), were as popular in their day as Professor Hawking's* A Brief History of Time. *Likewise, Dunne's work had a profound effect on many contemporary authors, including E. F. Benson, J. B. Priestley and even Wells himself, who wrote in the prologue to* The Shape of Things to Come *(1933), 'Among other gifted and original friends who, at all too rare intervals, honour me by coming along for a gossip is Mr J. W. Dunne, who years ago invented one of the earliest and most "different" aeroplanes, and who has since done a very considerable amount of subtle thinking upon the relationship of time and space.' In his sole novel,* An Experiment with St George *(1939), Dunne featured his theory that time possesses a geography that can be explored.*

John Boynton Priestley (1894–1984), the astute and controversial Yorkshire-born novelist, playwright and critic, is perhaps best-remembered today for his stories of English life, including The Good Companions *(1929),* Angel Pavement *(1930) and* Jenny Villiers *(1947). But he also wrote a number of excellent fantasy stories—including* Adam in Moonshine *(1927) and* The Doomsday Men *(1938)—and an outstanding trio of plays that were all inspired by Dunne's theories:* Time and the Conways *(1937),* I Have Been Here Before *(1937) and* Dangerous Corner *(1932). All three have been regularly and successfully revived for the London and provincial stages in the half-century since they were written. Priestley also used the idea of time travel in a few of his short stories, notably 'Mr Strenberry's Tale', written in 1934 but omitted from his later collected volumes of work. It is ostensibly the story of an everyday encounter in a bar between two men—but the word 'stranger' is barely sufficient to describe one of them. . . .*

*   *   *

'And thank you,' said the landlady, with the mechanical cheerfulness of her kind. She pushed across the counter one shilling and four coppers, which all contrived to get wet on the journey. 'Yes, it's quite enough. Sort of weather to bring them in too, though it's a bit early yet for our lot. Who's in the Private Bar?' She craned her fat little neck, peered across the other side, and then returned, looking very confidential. 'Only one. But he's one of our reg'lars. A bit too reg'lar, if you ask me, Mr Strenberry is.'

I put down my glass, and glanced out, through the open door. All I could see was a piece of wet road. The rain was falling now with that precision which suggests it will go on for ever. It was darker too. 'And who is Mr Strenberry?' I inquired, merely for want of something better to do. It did not matter to me who Mr Strenberry was.

The landlady leaned forward a little. 'He's the schoolmaster from down the road,' she replied, in a delighted whisper. 'Been here—oh, lemme see—it must be four years, might be five. Came from London here. Yes, that's where he came from, London. Sydenham, near the Crystal Palace, that's his home. I know because he's told me so himself, and I've a sister that's lived near there these twenty years.'

I said nothing. There did not seem to be anything to say. The fact that the local schoolmaster came from Sydenham left me as uninterested as it found me. So I merely nodded, took another sip, and filled a pipe.

The landlady glanced at me with a faint reproach in her silly prominent eyes. 'And he's queer is Mr Strenberry,' she added, with something like defiance. 'Oh yes, he's queer enough. Clever, y'know—in a sort of way, book-learning and all that, if you follow my meanin'—but, well—he's queer.'

'In what way is he queer?' It was the least I could do.

She put her hand up to her mouth. 'His wife left him. That's about two years ago. Took their little boy with her too. Gone to stay with relations, it was given out, but we all knew. She left him all right. Just walked out one fine morning and the little boy with her. Nice little boy, too, he was. He lives alone now, Mr Strenberry. And a nice mess, too I'll be bound. Just look at his clothes. He won't be schoolmastering here much longer neither. He's been given a few warnings, that I do know. And you can't blame 'em, can you?'

I replied, with the melancholy resignation that was expected of me, that I could not blame them. Clearly, Mr Strenberry, with his nice mess, his clothes, his general queerness, would not do.

The landlady shook her head and tightened her lips. 'It's the same old trouble now. Taking too much. I don't say getting drunk—because, as far as I can see, he doesn't—but still, taking too much, too reg'lar with it. A lot o' people, temperancers and that sort,' she went on, bitterly, 'think we want to push it down customers' throats. All lies. I never knew anybody that kept a decent house that didn't want people to go steady with it. I've dropped a few hints to Mr Strenberry, but he takes no notice. And what can you do? If he's quiet, behaves himself, and wants it, he's got to have it, hasn't he? We can't stop him. However, I don't want to say too much. And anyhow it isn't just what he takes that makes him queer. It's the way he goes on, and what he says— when he feels like saying anything, and that's not often.'

'You mean, he talks queerly?' I said, casually. Perhaps a man of ideas, Mr Strenberry.

'He might go for a week, he might go a fortnight, and not a word— except "Good evening" or "Thank you", for he's always the gentleman in here, I must say—will you get out of him. Some of the lively ones try to draw him out a bit, pull his leg as you might say—but not a word. Then, all of a sudden, he'll let himself go, talk your head off. And you never heard such stuff. I don't say I've heard much of it myself because I haven't the time to listen to it and I can't be bothered with it, but some of the other customers have told me. If you ask me, it's a bit of a shame, the way they go on, because it's getting to be a case of—' And here she tapped her forehead significantly. 'Mind you, it may have been his queerness that started all his troubles, his wife leaving him and all that. There's several that knows him better than I do will tell you that. Brought it all on himself, they say. But it does seem a pity, doesn't it?'

She looked at me mournfully for about a second and a half, then became brisk and cheerful again. 'He's in there now,' she added, and bustled away to the other side of the bar, where two carters were demanding half-pints.

I went to the outer door and stood there a moment, watching the persistent rain. It looked as if I should not be able to make a move for at least half an hour. So I ordered another drink and asked the landlady to serve it in the Private Bar, where Mr Strenberry was hiding his queerness. Then I followed her and took a seat near the window, only a few feet away from Mr Strenberry.

He was sitting there behind a nearly empty glass, with an unlighted stump of cigarette drooping from a corner of his mouth. Everything about him was drooping. He was a tall, slack, straggling sort of fellow; his thin greying hair fell forward in front; his nose was long, with something pendulous about its reddened tip; his moustache drooped wearily; and even his chin fell away, as if in despair. His eye had that boiled look common to all persevering topers.

'Miserable day,' I told him.

'It is,' he said. 'Rotten day.' He had a high-pitched but slightly husky voice, and I imagined that its characteristic tone would probably be querulous.

There was silence then, or at least nothing but the sound of the rain outside and the murmur of voices from the bar. I stared at the Highlanders and the hunting men who, from various parts of the room, invited you to try somebody's whisky and somebody else's port.

'Got a match?' said Strenberry, after fumbling in his pockets.

I handed him my matchbox and took the opportunity of moving a little nearer. It was obvious that the stump of cigarette would not last him more than half a minute, so I offered him my cigarette case too.

'Very quiet in here,' I remarked.

'For once,' he replied, a kind of weak sneer lighting up his face. 'Lucky for us too. There are more fools in this town than in most, and they all come in here. Lot of loud-mouthed idiots. I won't talk to 'em, won't waste my breath on 'em. They think there's something wrong with me here. They *would*.' He carefully drained his glass, set it down, then pushed it away.

I hastened to finish my glass of bitter. Then I made a pretence of examining the weather. 'Looks as if I shall have to keep under cover for another quarter of an hour or so,' I said carelessly. 'I'm going to have another drink. Won't you join me?'

After a little vague humming and spluttering, he said he would, and thanked me. He asked for a double whisky and a small soda.

'And so you find the people here very stupid?' I said, after we had taken toll of our fresh supply of drink. 'They often are in these small towns.'

'All idiots,' he muttered. 'Not a man with an educated mind amongst them. But then—education! It's a farce, that's all it is, a farce. I come in here—I must go somewhere, you know—and I sit in a corner and say nothing. I know what they're beginning to think. Oh, I've seen them—nudging, you know, giving each other the wink. I don't care. One time I would have cared. Now I don't. It doesn't matter. Nothing matters, really.'

I objected mildly to this pessimism.

'I know,' he went on, looking at me sombrely. 'You needn't tell me, I can see you're an intelligent man, so it's different. But you can't argue with me, and I'll tell you why. You see, you don't know what I know. Oh, I don't care if they do think I'm queer. I *am* queer. And so would you be if you'd seen what I've seen. They wouldn't because they wouldn't have the sense . . .' His voice trailed away. He shrugged his thin sloping shoulders. His face took on a certain obstinate look that you often see on the faces of weak men. Evidently he thought he had said too much.

I was curious now. 'I don't see what you mean,' I began. 'No doubt you've had unpleasant experiences, but then most of us have at some time or other.' I looked at him expectantly.

'I don't mean that,' he said, raising his voice and adding a touch of scorn. 'This is different. You wouldn't understand, unless I told you it all. Even then you mightn't. It's difficult. Oh, what's the use!' He finished his whisky in one quick gulp.

'Well, I wish you'd tell me.'

Doubtfully, mournfully, he examined my face, then he stared about the room, pulling his straggling and drooping moustache. 'Could I have another cigarette?' he asked, finally. When he had lit it, he blew out a cloud of smoke, then looked at me again.

'I've seen something nobody else has seen,' said Mr Strenberry. 'I've seen the end of it all, all this,' he waved a hand and gave a bitter little laugh, 'building houses, factories, education, public health, churches, drinking in pubs, getting children, walking in fields, everything, every mortal blessed thing. That's what I've seen, a glimpse anyhow. Finish! Finish! The End!'

'It sounds like doomsday,' I told him.

'And that's what it was,' cried Mr Strenberry, his face lighting up strangely. 'Anyway, that's what it amounted to. I can't think about anything else. And you couldn't either, if you'd been there. I've gone back to it, thought about it, thought round and round it, oh, thousands of times! Do you know Opperton Heath? You do? Well, that's where it happened, nearly three years ago. That's all, three years ago. I'd gone up there for a walk and to have a look at the birds. I used to be very interested in birds—my God, I've dropped that now—and there are one or two rare kinds up on the Heath there. You know what it's like— lonely. I hadn't met a soul all afternoon. That's the worst of it. If there'd only been somebody else there—'

He broke off, took up his smouldering cigarette, put it down again and stared in front of him. I kept quiet, afraid that a chance word might suddenly shut him up altogether.

'It was a warm afternoon,' he said, beginning again as abruptly as he had stopped, 'and I was lying on the grass, smoking. I remember I was wondering whether to hurry back and get home in time for tea or to stay where I was and not bother about tea. And I wish to God I'd decided to go back, before it happened. But I didn't. There I was, warm, a bit drowsy, just looking at the Heath. Not a soul in sight. Very quiet. If I could write poetry, I'd write a poem about the Heath as I saw it then, before the thing happened. It's all I would write too. The last five minutes there.' He broke off again, and I believe there were tears in his eyes. He looked a figure of maudlin self-pity, but nevertheless it may have been the lost peace and beauty of the world that conjured up those tears. I did not know then. I do not know now.

'Then I saw something,' said Mr Strenberry. 'It was a sort of disturbance in the air, not fifty yards from where I was. I didn't take much notice at first, because you get that flickering on a warm day up there. But this went on. I can't describe it properly, not to make you see it. But in a minute or two, you couldn't help noticing it. Like a thin revolving column of air. A waterspout made of air, if you see what I mean? And there was something dark, something solid, in the centre of it. I thought it must have something to do with a meteor. I got up and went closer, cautiously, you know, taking no chances. It didn't seem to be affecting anything else. There was no wind or anything. Everything was as quiet as it was before. But this column of air was more definite now, though I can't exactly explain how it came to look so definite. But you knew it was there all right, like seeing one piece of glass against another piece. Only there was movement in this, and faster than the fastest piece of machinery you ever set eyes on. And that dark thing in the centre was solider every second. I went closer still. And then the movement inside the column—like a glassy sort of pillar it was, though that doesn't quite give you the idea – stopped, though there was still a flickering and whirling on the outside. I could see that dark thing plainly now. It was a man—a sort of man.'

Mr Strenberry shut his eyes, put his hands up to them, and leaned forward on his elbows. In the quiet that followed, I could hear two fellows laughing in the bar outside. They were shouting something about a litter of pigs.

'He was a lightish greeny-blue in colour, this man,' Mr Strenberry continued, 'and the same all over. He'd no clothes on, but I got the idea that he'd a very tough skin, leathery, y'know. It shone a bit too. He'd no hair on him at all, and didn't look as if he'd shaved it all off but as if he'd never had any. He was bigger than me, bigger than you, but no giant: I should say he was about the size and figure of one of your big heavyweight boxers—except for his head. He'd a tremendous head—and of course as bald as an egg—and a wonderful face. I can see it now. It was flattish, like some of the faces of the Egyptian statues in the British Museum, but what you noticed the minute you saw it, were the eyes. They were more like a beautiful woman's eyes than a man's, very big and soft, y'know, but bigger and softer than any woman's eyes—and such a colour, a kind of dark purple. Full of intelligence too. Blazing with it, I knew that at once. In fact, I could see that this man was as far above me as I am above a Hottentot. More highly developed, y'know. I'm not saying this because of what I learned afterwards. I saw it at once. You couldn't mistake it. This greeny-blue hairless man knew a million things we'd never heard of, and you could see it in his eyes. Well, there he was and he stared at me and I stared at him.'

'Go on,' I said, for Mr Strenberry had stopped and was now busy staring at me.

'This is the part you've got to try and understand,' he cried, excitedly. 'You see, this queer revolving cylinder of air was between us, and if it had been glass two feet thick it couldn't have separated us any better. I couldn't get at him. I don't say I tried very hard at first; I was too surprised and frightened. But I did try to get nearer after a minute or two, but I couldn't, and I can't possibly explain to you—no, not if I tried for a week—how I was stopped. Call it a transparent wall, if you like, but that doesn't give you the idea of it. Anyhow, it doesn't matter about me. The point is, he couldn't get out, and he obviously knew more about it than I did and he was trying desperately hard. He'd got some sort of little instrument in each hand—I could see them flash— and he kept bringing these together. He was terribly agitated. But he couldn't get out. He'd stopped the inside of this column revolving, as I said, but apparently he couldn't stop the outside, which was whirling and whirling just as fast as ever.

'I've asked myself thousands of times,' Mr Strenberry went on, more reflectively now, 'what would have happened if he had got out. Would he have ruled the whole world, knowing so much more than we do? Or would these fools have shoved him into a cage, made a show of him, and finally killed him? Though I don't imagine they could have done that, not with this man. And then again, could he have existed at all once he got out? I don't mean just microbes and things, though they might easily have killed him off, because I don't suppose his body knew anything about such a germ-ridden atmosphere as ours. No, I don't mean that. This is the point. If he'd got out, really burst into this twentieth-century world, he might have stopped existing at all, just vanished into nothing, because after all this twentieth century isn't just a date, it's also a condition, a state of things, and—you see—it doesn't include him. Though, of course, in a sense it does—or it did—because there he was, on the Heath that day.'

'I'm afraid I don't follow all this,' I said. 'But go on, perhaps it will become clearer.'

Mr Strenberry leaned forward and fixed me with his little boiled eyes. 'Don't you see, this man had come from the future? Fellows like H. G. Wells have always been writing about us taking a jump into the future, to have a look at our distant descendants, but of course we don't. We can't; we don't know enough. But what about them, taking a jump into the past, to have a look at *us*? That's far more likely, when you come to think of it. But I don't mean that is what this man was doing. He was trying to do more than that. If you ask me, they'd often taken a peep at us, and at our great-great-grandparents, and for that matter at our great-great-grandchildren too. But he wasn't just doing that. He was trying to get out to escape from his own time altogether.'

I drew in a long breath, then blew it out again, slowly.

'Don't you think I'm merely guessing that,' cried Mr Strenberry, 'because I'm not. I *know*. And I know because he told me. I don't mean to say we talked. As a matter of fact, I did try shouting at him—asking him who he was and where he'd come from, and all that—but I don't think he heard me, and if he did, he certainly didn't understand. But don't make any mistake—he saw me all right. He looked at me just as I looked at him. He made a sign or two, and might have made more if he hadn't been so busy with those instruments and so desperately agitated. He didn't shout at me, never opened his lips. But he *thought* at me. That's the only way I can describe it. Messages from him arrived in my head, and turned themselves into my own words, and even little pictures. And it was horrible—horrible, I tell you. Everything was finished, and he was trying to escape. The only way he could do it was to try and jump back into the past, out of the way. There wasn't much of the world left, fit to live in. Just one biggish island, not belonging

to any of the continents we know—they'd all gone, long ago. I don't
know the date. That never came through, and if it had, I don't suppose
it would have told me much. But it was a long time ahead—perhaps
twenty thousand years, perhaps fifty thousand, perhaps more—I don't
know. What I do know is that this man wasn't anybody very important,
just a sort of minor assistant in some kind of laboratory where they
specialised in time experiments, quite a low-class fellow among his
own kind, though he would have seemed a demigod to me and you.
And I knew that while he was so terrified that he was frantic in his
attempt to escape, at the same time he was ashamed of himself, too—
felt he was a kind of dodger, you see. But even then, what was happening
was so ghastly that he'd never hesitated at all. He had run to the
laboratory or whatever it was, and just had time to jump back through
the ages. He was in terror. He didn't show it as we might, but I tell
you—his mind was *screaming*. Some place—a city, I think it was—
had been entirely destroyed and everything else was going too, everything that had once been human. No words came into my mind to
describe what it was that was destroying everything and terrifying him.
Perhaps I hadn't any words that would fit in. All I got were some little
pictures, very blurred, just like bits of a nightmare. There were great
black things rolling about, just wiping everything out. Not like anything
you've ever seen. You couldn't give them a shape.'

Here Mr Strenberry leaned further forward still, grasped my coat
sleeve, and lowered his voice.

'They weren't beasts or huge insects even,' he whispered. 'They
weren't anything you could put a name to. I don't believe they belonged
to this world at all. And something he thought rather suggested that
too. They came from some other place, from another planet perhaps.
Don't you see, it was all finished here. They were blotting it out, great
rolling black things—oh, horrible! Just imagine what he felt, this man,
who had just managed to escape from them, but now couldn't get out,
into this world and time of ours. Because he couldn't, that was the
awful thing. He tried and tried, but it couldn't be done. And he hadn't
long to try either, I knew that. Because of what was happening at the
other end, you see. I tell you, I stood there, looking at him, with his
thoughts buzzing round my own head, and the sweat was streaming
down my face. I was terrified too, in a panic. And then he was in an
agony of fear, and so was I. It was all up. The inside of that column
of air began revolving again, just as it had done when it first came, and
then I couldn't see him distinctly. Only his eyes. Just those eyes, staring

out of the swirl. And then, I saw something. I swear I did. Something black. Just a glimpse. That's all. A bit of one of those things, getting hold of him—the last man left. That's what it must have been, though how I came to see it, I don't quite know, but I've worked it out this way and that way, and it seems to me—'

'A-ha, who have we here?' cried a loud, cheerful voice. 'How's things, Mr Strenberry?'

Two red-faced men had just entered the room. They grinned at my companion, then winked at one another.

'A nasty day, Mr Strenberry,' said the other fellow. 'What do you say?'

Mr Strenberry, who appeared to have crumpled up at their approach, merely muttered something in reply. Then, giving me a hasty glance, in which shame and despair and scorn were mingled, he suddenly rose and shuffled out of the room.

The two newcomers looked at one another, laughed, and then settled into their corner. The landlady appeared with their drinks. I stood up and looked out of the window. The downpour had dwindled to a few scattered drops, brightening in the sunlight.

'I seen you talking to Mr Strenberry,' the landlady said to me. 'Least, I seen him talking to you. Got him going, too, you did. He's a queer one, isn't he? Didn't I tell you he was a queer one? Telling you one of his tales, I'll be bound. Take no notice of him, mister. You can't believe a single word he says. We found that out long since. That's why he doesn't want to talk to us any more. He knows we've got a pinch of salt ready, Mr Strenberry does.'

ALL THE TIME IN THE WORLD

Arthur C. Clarke

One of the great prophets of the space age, Arthur C. Clarke has long been interested in time travel and the concept of using faster-than-light transportation to permit journeys into the past and future. Recently, to his already impressive list of realised prophecies he has added the suggestions that mankind in the future will be able to wear electronic devices that boost intelligence; will utilise 'microts', tiny robots, to perform mundane household chores; and will take giant 'lifts' into space. Clarke is also convinced that an unlimited source of power— such as might be used to drive a time travel machine—could be generated from vacuum energy.

Arthur Charles Clarke (1917–) was a fan of sf in his youth, but did not start writing the articles and stories about space travel that have made him famous until after the Second World War, during which time he worked as a radar instructor for the RAF. One of his early short stories. 'The Sentinel' (1951), was later to form the basis of the legendary sf film, Stanley Kubrick's 2001: A Space Odyssey *(1968), while his novels including* Rendezvous with Rama *(1973),* The Fountains of Paradise *(1979) and* 2010: Odyssey Two *(1982) have all been best-sellers and won the sf world's top honours. A third book in the 'Odyssey' series,* 3001: The Final Odyssey *(1997), completes what is undoubtedly one of the towering works of imaginative fiction. Although 'All the Time in the World' (1952) is rather more down-to-earth than any of these, in this story of a time distortion machine that is used for some very suspect activities Clarke demonstrates once again his amazing breadth of vision.*

*   *   *

When the quiet knock came on the door, Robert Ashton surveyed the room in one swift, automatic movement. Its dull respectability satisfied

him and should reassure any visitor. Not that he had any reason to
expect the police, but there was no point in taking chances.

'Come in,' he said, pausing only to grab Plato's *Dialogues* from the
shelf beside him. Perhaps this gesture was a little too ostentatious, but
it always impressed his clients.

The door opened slowly. At first, Ashton continued his intent reading,
not bothering to glance up. There was the slightest acceleration of
his heart, a mild and even exhilarating constriction of the chest.
Of course, it couldn't possibly be a flatfoot: someone would have tipped
him off. Still, any unheralded visitor was unusual and thus potentially
dangerous.

Ashton laid down the book, glanced towards the door and remarked
in a non-committal voice: 'What can I do for you?' He did not get up;
such courtesies belonged to a past he had buried long ago. Besides, it
was a woman. In the circles he now frequented, women were accustomed to receive jewels and clothes and money—but never respect.

Yet there was something about this visitor that drew him slowly to
his feet. It was not merely that she was beautiful, but she had a poised
and effortless authority that moved her into a different world from the
flamboyant doxies he met in the normal course of business. There was
a brain and a purpose behind those calm, appraising eyes—a brain,
Ashton suspected, the equal of his own.

He did not know how grossly he had underestimated her.

'Mr Ashton,' she began, 'let us not waste time. I know who you are
and I have work for you. Here are my credentials.'

She opened a large, stylish handbag and extracted a thick bundle of
notes.

'You may regard this,' she said, 'as a sample.'

Ashton caught the bundle as she tossed it carelessly towards him. It
was the largest sum of money he had ever held in his life—at least a
hundred fivers, all new and serially numbered. He felt them between
his fingers. If they were not genuine, they were so good that the difference was of no practical importance.

He ran his thumb to and fro along the edge of the wad as if feeling
a pack for a marked card, and said thoughtfully, 'I'd like to know where
you got these. If they aren't forgeries, they must be hot and will take
some passing.'

'They are genuine. A very short time ago they were in the Bank of
England. But if they are of no use to you throw them in the fire. I
merely let you have them to show that I mean business.'

'Go on.' He gestured to the only seat and balanced himself on the edge of the table.

She drew a sheaf of papers from the capacious handbag and handed it across to him.

'I am prepared to pay you any sum you wish if you will secure these items and bring them to me, at a time and place to be arranged. What is more, I will guarantee that you can make the thefts with no personal danger.'

Ashton looked at the list, and sighed. The woman was mad. Still, she had better be humoured. There might be more money where this came from.

'I notice,' he said mildly, 'that all these items are in the British Museum, and that most of them are, quite literally, priceless. By that I mean that you could neither buy nor sell them.'

'I do not wish to sell them. I am a collector.'

'So it seems. What are you prepared to pay for these acquisitions?'

'Name a figure.'

There was a short silence. Ashton weighed the possibilities. He took a certain professional pride in his work, but there were some things that no amount of money could accomplish. Still, it would be amusing to see how high the bidding would go.

He looked at the list again.

'I think a round million would be a very reasonable figure for this lot,' he said ironically.

'I fear you are not taking me very seriously. With your contacts, you should be able to dispose of these.'

There was a flash of light and something sparkled through the air. Ashton caught the necklace before it hit the ground, and despite himself was unable to suppress a gasp of amazement. A fortune glittered through his fingers. The central diamond was the largest he had ever seen—it must be one of the world's most famous jewels.

His visitor seemed completely indifferent as he slipped the necklace into his pocket. Ashton was badly shaken; he knew she was not acting. To her, that fabulous gem was of no more value than a lump of sugar. This was madness on an unimaginable scale.

'Assuming that you can deliver the money,' he said, 'how do you imagine that it's physically possible to do what you ask? One might steal a single item from this list, but within a few hours the Museum would be solid with police.'

With a fortune already in his pocket, he could afford to be frank. Besides, he was curious to learn more about his fantastic visitor.

She smiled, rather sadly, as if humouring a backward child.

'If I show you the way,' she said softly, 'will you do it?'

'Yes—for a million.'

'Have you noticed anything strange since I came in? Is it not—very quiet?'

Ashton listened. My God, she was right! This room was never completely silent, even at night. There had been a wind blowing over the rooftops; where had it gone now? The distant rumble of traffic had ceased; five minutes ago he had been cursing the engines shunting in the marshalling yard at the end of the road. What had happened to them?

'Go to the window.'

He obeyed the order and drew aside the grimy lace curtains with fingers that shook slightly despite all attempts at control. Then he relaxed. The street was quite empty, as it often was at this time in the midmorning. There was no traffic, and hence no reason for sound. Then he glanced down the row of dingy houses towards the shunting yard.

His visitor smiled as he stiffened with the shock.

'Tell me what you see, Mr Ashton?'

He turned slowly, face pale and throat muscles working.

'What are you?' he gasped. 'A witch?'

'Don't be foolish. There is a simple explanation. It is not the world that has changed—but you.'

Ashton stared again at that unbelievable shunting engine, the plume of steam frozen motionless above it as if made from cotton wool. He realised How that the clouds were equally immobile; they should have been scudding across the sky. All around him was the unnatural stillness of the high-speed photograph, the vivid unreality of a scene glimpsed in a flash of lightning.

'You are intelligent enough to realise what is happening, even if you cannot understand how it is done. Your time scale has been altered: a minute in the outer world would be a year in this room.'

Again she opened the handbag, and this time brought forth what appeared to be a bracelet of some silvery metal, with a series of dials and switches moulded into it.

'You can call this a personal generator,' she said. 'With it strapped about your arm, you are invincible. You can come and go without hindrance—you can steal everything on that list and bring it to me before one of the guards in the Museum has blinked an eyelid. When you have finished, you can be miles away before you switch off the field and step back into the normal world.

'Now listen carefully, and do exactly what I say. The field has a radius of about seven feet, so you must keep at least that distance from any other person. Secondly, you must not switch it off again until you have completed your task and I have given you your payment. *This is most important*. Now, the plan I have worked out is this . . .'

No criminal in the history of the world had ever possessed such power. It was intoxicating—yet Ashton wondered if he would ever get used to it. He had ceased to worry about explanations, at least until the job was done and he had collected his reward. Then, perhaps, he would get away from England and enjoy a well earned retirement.

His visitor had left a few minutes ahead of him, but when he stepped out into the street the scene was completely unchanged. Though he had prepared for it, the sensation was still unnerving. Ashton felt an impulse to hurry, as if this condition couldn't possibly last and he had to get the job done before the gadget ran out of juice. But that, he had been assured, was impossible.

In the High Street he slowed down to look at the frozen traffic, the paralysed pedestrians. He was careful, as he had been warned, not to approach so close to anyone that they came within his field. How ridiculous people looked when one saw them like this, robbed of such grace as movement could give, their mouths half open in foolish grimaces!

Having to seek assistance went against the grain, but some parts of the job were too big for him to handle by himself. Besides, he could pay liberally and never notice it. The main difficulty, Ashton realised, would be to find someone who was intelligent enough not to be scared— or so stupid that he would take everything for granted. He decided to try the first possibility.

Tony Marchetti's place was down a side street so close to the police station that one felt it was really carrying camouflage too far. As he walked past the entrance, Ashton caught a glimpse of the duty sergeant at his desk and resisted a temptation to go inside to combine a little pleasure with business. But that sort of thing could wait until later.

The door of Tony's opened in his face as he approached. It was such a natural occurrence in a world where nothing was normal that it was a moment before Ashton realised its implications. Had his generator failed? He glanced hastily down the street and was reassured by the frozen tableau behind him.

'Well, if it isn't Bob Ashton!' said a familiar voice. 'Fancy meeting you as early in the morning as this. That's an odd bracelet you're wearing. I thought I had the only one.'

'Hello, Aram,' replied Ashton. 'It looks as if there's a lot going on that neither of us knows about. Have you signed up Tony, or is he still free?'

'Sorry. We've a little job which will keep him busy for a while.'

'Don't tell me. It's the National Gallery or the Tate.'

Aram Albenkian fingered his neat goatee. 'Who told you that?' he asked.

'No one. But, after all, you *are* the crookedest art dealer in the trade, and I'm beginning to guess what's going on. Did a tall, very good-looking brunette give you that bracelet and a shopping list?'

'I don't see why I should tell you, but the answer's no. It was a man.'

Ashton felt a momentary surprise. Then he shrugged his shoulders. 'I might have guessed that there would be more than one of them. I'd like to know who's behind it.'

'Have you any theories?' said Albenkian guardedly.

Ashton decided that it would be worth risking some loss of information to test the other's reactions. 'It's obvious they're not interested in money—they have all they want and can get more with this gadget. The woman who saw me said she was a collector. I took it as a joke, but I see now that she meant it seriously.'

'Why do we come into the picture? What's to stop them doing the whole job themselves?' Albenkian asked.

'Maybe they're frightened. Or perhaps they want our—er—specialised knowledge. Some of the items on my list are rather well cased in. My theory is that they're agents for a mad millionaire.'

It didn't hold water, and Ashton knew it. But he wanted to see which leaks Albenkian would try to plug.

'My dear Ashton,' said the other impatiently, holding up his wrist. 'How do you explain this little thing? I know nothing about science, but even I can tell that it's beyond the wildest dreams of our technologies. There's only one conclusion to be drawn from that.'

'Go on.'

'These people are from—somewhere else. Our world is being systematically looted of its treasures. You know all this stuff you read about rockets and spaceships? Well, someone else has done it first.'

Ashton didn't laugh. The theory was no more fantastic than the facts.

'Whoever they are,' he said, 'they seem to know their way around pretty well. I wonder how many teams they've got? Perhaps the Louvre and the Prado are being reconnoitred at this very minute. The world is going to have a shock before the day's out.

They parted amicably enough, neither confiding any details of real importance about his business. For a fleeting moment Ashton thought of trying to buy over Tony, but there was no point in antagonising Albenkian. Steve Regan would have to do. That meant walking about a mile, since of course any form of transport was impossible. He would die of old age before a bus completed the journey. Ashton was not clear what would happen if he attempted to drive a car when the field was operating, and he had been warned not to try any experiments.

It astonished Ashton that even such a nearly certified moron as Steve could take the accelerator so calmly; there was something to be said, after all, for the comic strips which were probably his only reading. After a few words of grossly simplified explanation, Steve buckled on the spare wristlet which, rather to Ashton's surprise, his visitor had handed over without comment. Then they set out on their long walk to the Museum.

Ashton, or his client, had thought of everything. They stopped once at a bench to rest and enjoy some sandwiches and regain their breath. When at last they reached the Museum, neither felt any the worse for the unaccustomed exercise.

They walked together through the gates of the Museum—unable, despite logic, to avoid speaking in whispers—and up the wide stone steps into the entrance hall. Ashton knew his way perfectly. With whimsical humour he displayed his Reading Room ticket as they walked, at a respectful distance, past the statuesque attendants. It occurred to him that the occupants of the greater chamber, for the most part, looked just the same as they normally did, even without the benefit of the accelerator.

It was a straightforward but tedious job collecting the books that had been listed. They had been chosen, it seemed, for their beauty as works of art as much as for their literary content. The selection had been done by someone who knew his job. Had *they* done it themselves, Ashton wondered, or had they bribed other experts as they were bribing him? He wondered if he would ever glimpse the full ramifications of their plot.

There was a considerable amount of panel-smashing to be done, but Ashton was careful not to damage any books, even the unwanted ones.

Whenever he had collected enough volumes to make a comfortable load, Steve carried them out into the courtyard and dumped them on the paving stones until a small pyramid had accumulated.

It would not matter if they were left for short periods outside the field of the accelerator. No one would notice their momentary flicker of existence in the normal world.

They were in the library for two hours of their time, and paused for another snack before passing to the next job. On the way Ashton stopped for a little private business. There was a tinkle of glass as the tiny case, standing in solitary splendour, yielded up its treasure: then the manuscript of *Alice* was safely tucked into Ashton's pocket.

Among the antiquities, he was not quite so much at home. There were a few examples to be taken from every gallery, and sometimes it was hard to see the reasons for the choice. It was as if—and again he remembered Albenkian's words—these works of art had been selected by someone with totally alien standards. This time, with a few exceptions, *they* had obviously not been guided by the experts.

For the second time in history the case of the Portland Vase was shattered. In five seconds, thought Ashton, the alarms would be going all over the Museum and the whole building would be in an uproar. And in five seconds he could be miles away. It was an intoxicating thought, and as he worked swiftly to complete his contract he began to regret the price he had asked. Even now, it was not too late.

He felt the quiet satisfaction of the good workman as he watched Steve carry the great silver tray of the Mildenhall Treasure out into the courtyard and place it beside the now impressive pile. 'That's the lot,' he said. 'I'll settle up at my place this evening. Now let's get his gadget off you.'

They walked out into High Holborn and chose a secluded side street that had no pedestrians near it. Ashton unfastened the peculiar buckle and stepped back from his cohort, watching him freeze into immobility as he did so. Steve was vulnerable again, moving once more with all other men in the stream of time. But before the alarm had gone out he would have lost himself in the London crowds.

When he re-entered the Museum yard, the treasure had already gone. Standing where it had been was his visitor of—how long ago? She was still poised and graceful, but, Ashton thought, looking a little tired. He approached until their fields merged and they were no longer separated by an impassable gulf of silence. 'I hope you're satisfied,' he said. 'How did you move the stuff so quickly?'

She touched the bracelet around her own wrist and gave a wan smile. 'We have many other powers besides this.'

'Then why did you need my help?'

'There were technical reasons. It was necessary to remove the objects we required from the presence of other matter. In this way, we could gather only what we needed and not waste our limited—what shall I call them?—transporting facilities. Now may I have the bracelet back?'

Ashton slowly handed over the one he was carrying, but made no effort to unfasten his own. There might be danger in what he was doing, but he intended to retreat at the first sign of it.

'I'm prepared to reduce my fee,' he said. 'In fact I'll waive all payment—in exchange for this.' He touched his wrist, where the intricate metal band gleamed in the sunlight.

She was watching him with an expression as fathomless as the *Gioconda* smile. (Had *that*, Ashton wondered, gone to join the treasure he had gathered? How much had they taken from the Louvre?)

'I would not call that reducing your fee. All the money in the world could not purchase one of those bracelets.'

'Or the things I have given you.'

'You are greedy, Mr Ashton. You know that with an accelerator the entire world would be yours.'

'What of that? Do you have any further interest in our planet, now you have taken what you need?'

There was a pause. Then, unexpectedly, she smiled. 'So you have guessed I do not belong to your world.'

'Yes. And I know that you have other agents besides myself. Do you come from Mars, or won't you tell me?'

'I am quite willing to tell you. But you may not thank me if I do.'

Ashton looked at her warily. What did she mean by that? Unconscious of his action, he put his wrist behind his back, protecting the bracelet.

'No, I am not from Mars, or any planet of which you have ever heard. You would not understand *what* I am. Yet I will tell you this. I am from the future.'

'The future! That's ridiculous!'

'Indeed? I should be interested to know why.'

'If that sort of thing were possible, our past history would be full of time travellers. Besides, it would involve a *reductio ad absurdum*. Going into the past could change the present and produce all sorts of paradoxes.'

'Those are good points, though not perhaps as original as you suppose. But they only refute the possibility of time travel in general, not in the very special case which concerns us now.'

'What is peculiar about it?' he asked.

'On very rare occasions, and by the release of an enormous amount of energy, it is possible to produce a—*singularity*—in time. During the fraction of a second when that singularity occurs, the past becomes accessible to the future, though only in a restricted way. We can send our minds back to you, but not our bodies.'

'You mean,' said Ashton, 'that you are *borrowing* the body I see?'

'Oh, I have paid for it, as I am paying you. The owner has agreed to the terms. We are very conscientious in these matters.'

Ashton was thinking swiftly. If this story was true, it gave him a definite advantage.

'You mean,' he continued, 'that you have no direct control over matter, and must work through human agents?'

'Yes. Even those bracelets were made here, under our mental control.'

She was explaining too much too readily, revealing all her weaknesses. A warning signal was flashing in the back of Ashton's mind, but he had committed himself too deeply to retreat.

'Then it seems to me,' he said slowly, 'that you cannot force me to hand this bracelet back.'

'That is perfectly true.'

'That's all I want to know.'

She was smiling at him now, and there was something in that smile that chilled him to the marrow.

'We are not vindictive or unkind, Mr Ashton,' she said quietly. 'What I am going to do now appeals to my sense of justice. You have asked for that bracelet; you can keep it. Now I shall tell you just how useful it will be.'

For a moment Ashton had a wild impulse to hand back the accelerator. She must have guessed his thoughts.

'No, it's too late. I insist that you keep it. And I can reassure you on one point. It won't wear out. It will last you' —again that enigmatic smile—'the rest of your life.

'Do you mind if we go for a walk, Mr Ashton? I have done my work here, and would like to have a last glimpse of your world before I leave it for ever.'

She turned towards the iron gates, and did not wait for a reply. Consumed by curiosity, Ashton followed.

They walked in silence until they were standing among the frozen traffic of Tottenham Court Road. For a while she stood staring at the busy yet motionless crowds; then she sighed.

'I cannot help feeling sorry for them, and for you. I wonder what you would have made of yourselves.'

'What do you mean by that?'

'Just now, Mr Ashton, you implied that the future cannot reach back into the past, because that would alter history. A shrewd remark, but, I am afraid, irrelevant. You see, *your* world has no more history to alter.'

She pointed across the road, and Ashton turned swiftly on his heels. There was nothing there except a newsboy crouching over his pile of papers. A placard formed an impossible curve in the breeze that was blowing through this motionless world. Ashton read the crudely lettered words with difficulty:

SUPER-BOMB TEST TODAY

The voice in his ears seemed to come from a very long way off.

'I told you that time travel, even in this restricted form, requires an enormous release of energy—far more than a single bomb can liberate, Mr Ashton. But that bomb is only a trigger—'

She pointed to the solid ground beneath their feet. 'Do you know anything about your own planet? Probably not; your race has learned so little. But even your scientists have discovered that, two thousand miles down, the Earth has a dense, liquid core. That core is made of compressed matter, and it can exist in either of two stable states. Given a certain stimulus, it can change from one of those states to another, just as a seesaw can tip over at the touch of a finger. But that change, Mr Ashton, will liberate as much energy as all the earthquakes since the beginning of your world. The oceans and continents will fly into space; the sun will have a second asteroid belt.

'That cataclysm will send its echoes down the ages, and will open up to us a fraction of a second in your time. During that instant, we are trying to save what we can of your world's treasures. It is all that we can do; even if your motives were purely selfish and completely dishonest, you have done your race a service you never intended.

'And now I must return to our ship, where it waits by the ruins of Earth almost a hundred thousand years from now. You can keep the bracelet.'

The withdrawal was instantaneous. The woman suddenly froze and became one with the other statues in the silent street. He was alone.

Alone! Ashton held the gleaming bracelet before his eyes, hypnotised by its intricate workmanship and by the powers it concealed. He had made a bargain, and he must keep it. He could live out the full span of his life—at the cost of an isolation no other man had ever known. If he switched off the field, the last seconds of history would tick inexorably away.

Seconds? Indeed, there was less time than that. For he knew that the bomb must already have exploded.

He sat down on the edge of the pavement and began to think. There was no need to panic; he must take things calmly, without hysteria. After all, he had plenty of time.

All the time in the world.

THE INSTABILITY

Isaac Asimov

Isaac Asimov is another of the most revered names in sf, and although he has written a number of time travel short stories and a major novel, The End of Eternity *(1955), which chronicles the activities of an inter-temporal elite who oversee the progress of mankind while at the same time weakening man's ability to exercise free will, all his life he retained a sceptical view that such a phenomenon as time travel could exist. In a significant essay, 'Time Travel', written in 1984, he declared that it was a scientific impossibility because of the implausibilities involved, and cited the classic paradox mentioned earlier: 'What if you go back into the past and kill your grandfather when he was still a little boy? In that case, you see, the murderer was never born, so who killed the little boy?' Yet having worked his argument through, Asimov justified his own contributions in these words: 'Time travel stories are too much fun for them to be eliminated merely out of mundane considerations of impracticability, or even impossibility.'*

*Born in Russia, Isaac Asimov (1920–92) went to America as a child and, discovering science fiction in the pages of the Thirties pulp maga-zines, sensed that he had found there his lifetime's inspiration. His most enduring achievements may well be his series of robot stories in which he devised the three laws of robotics—*I, Robot *(1950) and* The Rest of the Robots *(1964)—and the panoramic 'Foundation' series that describes a far-future society. An erudite and ferociously intelligent man, he has also done a great deal to popularise advanced science concepts for general readers and has been an important influence on generations of writers, many of whom he encouraged and published in* Isaac Asimov's Science Fiction Magazine, *which has continued to flourish since his death. 'The Instability', published in the* Observer *in 1989, is a brief yet salutary story of time travel that lacks nothing in verisimilitude despite its author's scepticism about the whole concept!*

*   *   *

Professor Firebrenner had explained it carefully. 'Time perception depends on the structure of the Universe. When the Universe is expanding, we experience time as going forwards; when it is contracting, we would experience it going backwards. If we could somehow force the Universe to be in stasis, neither expanding nor contracting, time would stand still.'

'But you can't put the Universe in stasis,' said Mr Atkins, fascinated.

'I can put a little portion of the Universe in stasis, however,' said the professor. 'Just enough to hold a ship. Time will stand still and we can move forwards or backwards at will, and the entire trip will last less than an instant. But all the parts of the Universe will move while we stand still, nailed to the fabric of the Universe. The Earth moves about the Sun, the Sun moves about the core of the Galaxy, the Galaxy moves about some centre of gravity—*all* the Galaxies move.

'I calculated those motions and I find that 27.5 million years in the future, a red dwarf star will occupy the position that our Sun does now. If we go 27.5 million years into the future, then, in less than an instant, that red dwarf star will be near our space ship and we can come home after studying it a bit.'

Atkins said, 'Can that be done?'

'I've sent experimental animals through time, but I can't make them automatically return. If you and I go, we can manipulate the controls so that we can return.'

'And you want me along?'

'Of course. There should be two. Two people would be more easily believed than one alone. Come—it will be an incredible adventure.'

Atkins inspected the ship. It was a 2217 Glenn-fusion model and looked beautiful.

'Suppose,' he said, 'that it lands *inside* the red dwarf star.'

'It won't, said the professor, 'but if it does, that's the chance we take.'

'But when we get back, the Sun and Earth will have moved on. We'll be in space.'

'Of course, but how far can the Sun and Earth move in the few hours it will take us to observe the star? With this ship we will catch up to our beloved planet—are you ready Mr Atkins?'

'Ready,' sighed Atkins.

Professor Firebrenner made the necessary adjustments and nailed the ship to the fabric of the Universe, while 27.5 million years passed. And then, in less than a flash, time began to move forward again in the usual way, and everything in the Universe moved forward with it . . .

Through the viewing port of their ship, Professor Firebrenner and Mr Atkins could see the small orb of the red dwarf star.

The professor smiled. 'You and I, Atkins,' he said, 'are the first ever to see, close at hand, any star other than our own Sun.'

They remained two and a half hours, during which they photographed the star and its spectrum, made special coronagraphic observations, and tested the chemical composition of the interstellar gas, and then Professor Firebrenner said, rather reluctantly, 'I think we had better go home now.'

Again the controls were adjusted, and again the ship was nailed to the fabric of the Universe. They went 27.5 million years into the past, and in less than a flash they were back where they started.

Space was black. There was nothing. Atkins said, 'What happened? Where are the Earth and the Sun?'

The professor frowned. He said, 'Going *back* in time must be different. The Universe must have moved.'

'Where could it move?'

'I don't know. Other objects shift position within the Universe, but the Universe as a whole must move in an upper-dimensional direction. We are here in the absolute vacuum—in primeval Chaos.'

'But *we're* here. It's not primeval Chaos any more.'

'Exactly. That means we've introduced an instability at this place that we exist, and *that* means . . . ?'

Even as he said 'that', a Big Bang obliterated them. A new Universe came into being and began to expand.

TIME HAS NO BOUNDARIES

Jack Finney

Jack Finney is deservedly famous as the author of Invasion of the Body Snatchers *(1955), the story, filmed twice, of alien spores that take over the inhabitants of a small American town. He has also written one of the most accomplished time travel novels,* Time and Again *(1970). This account of a time traveller who lands in New York in the year 1882 is notable for its authentic picture of the era and for its depiction of the natural bewilderment of a man from a quite different one. Finney's work has frequently been praised for the way the author uses places and situations familiar to readers and then invests them with an aura of mystery and surprise.*

Jack Finney (1911–) was a journalist during his early life, and did not start to write fantasy fiction until he was well into his thirties. His interest in time stories was evident in his first two collections, The Clock of Time *(1958) and* I Love Galesburg in the Springtime: Fantasy and Time Stories *(1963); and following* Time and Again *he wrote* Marion's Wall *(1973), in which a ghost from the Twenties is transported to the present day. 'Time Has No Boundaries', written in 1962 for the* Saturday Evening Post, *introduces us to a man who has perfected a machine to enable law-breakers to make their escape without risk of detection. But what, we may ask, will happen when the law finally catches up with him . . .*

*   *   *

On one of the upper floors of the new Hall of Justice I found the room number I was looking for, and opened the door. A nice-looking girl inside glanced up from her typewriter, switched on a smile, and said, 'Professor Weygand?' It was a question in form only—one glance at me, and she knew—and I smiled and nodded, wishing I'd worn my have-fun-in-San-Francisco clothes instead of my professor's outfit. She said, 'Inspector Ihren's on the phone; would you wait, please?' and I nodded and sat down, smiling benignly the way a professor should.

My trouble is that, although I have the thin, intent, professorial face, I'm a little young for my job, which is assistant professor of physics at a large university. Fortunately I've had some premature grey in my hair ever since I was nineteen, and on campus I generally wear those miserable permanently baggy tweeds that professors are supposed to wear, though a lot of them cheat and don't. These suits, together with round, metal-rimmed, professor-style glasses which I don't really need, and a careful selection of burlap neckties in diseased plaids of bright orange, baboon blue, and gang green (*de rigueur* for gap-pocketed professor suits) complete the image. That's a highly popular word meaning that if you ever want to become a full professor you've got to quit looking like an undergraduate.

I glanced around the little anteroom: yellow plaster walls; a big calendar; filing cabinets; a desk, typewriter, and girl. I watched her the way I inspect some of my more advanced girl students—from under the brows and with a fatherly smile in case she looked up and caught me. What I really wanted to do, though, was pull out Inspector Ihren's letter and read it again for any clue I might have missed about why he wanted to see me. But I'm a little afraid of the police—I get a feeling of guilt just asking a cop a street direction—and I thought rereading the letter just now would betray my nervousness to Miss Candyhips here who would somehow secretly signal the inspector. I knew exactly what it said, anyway. It was a formally polite three-line request, addressed to my office on the campus, to come here and see Inspector Martin O. Ihren, if I would, at my convenience, if I don't mind, please, sir. I sat wondering what he'd have done if, equally politely, I'd refused, when a buzzer buzzed, the smile turned on again, and the girl said, 'Go right in, Professor.' I got up, swallowing nervously, opened the door beside me, and walked into the Inspector's office.

Behind his desk he stood up slowly and reluctantly as though he weren't at all sure but what he'd be throwing me into a cell soon. He put out a hand suspiciously and without a smile saying, 'Nice of you to come.' I answered, sat down before his desk, and I thought I knew what would have happened if I'd refused this man's invitation. He'd simply have arrived in my classroom, clapped on the handcuffs, and dragged me here. I don't mean that his face was forbidding or in any way remarkable; it looked ordinary enough. So did his brown hair and so did his plain grey suit. He was a young-middle-aged man somewhat taller and heavier than I was, and his eyes looked absolutely uninterested in anything in the universe but his work. I had the certain conviction that, except for crime news, he read nothing, not even newspaper headlines; that he was intelligent, shrewd, perceptive, and humourless; and that he probably knew no one but other policemen and didn't think much of most of them. He was an undistinguished formidable man, and I knew my smile looked nervous.

He got right to the point; he was more used to arresting people than dealing with them socially. He said, 'There's some people we can't find, and I thought maybe you could help us.' I looked politely puzzled but he ignored it. 'One of them worked in Haring's Restaurant; you know the place; been there for years. He was a waiter and he disappeared at the end of a three-day weekend with their entire receipts—nearly five thousand bucks. Left a note saying he liked Haring's and enjoyed working there but they'd been underpaying him for ten years and now he figured they were even. Guy with an oddball sense of humour, they tell me.' Ihren leaned back in his swivel chair, and frowned at me. 'We can't find that man. He's been gone over a year now, and not a trace of him.'

I thought he expected me to say something, and did my best. 'Maybe he moved to some other city, and changed his name.'

Ihren looked startled, as though I'd said something even more stupid than he expected. 'That wouldn't help!' he said irritatedly.

I was tired of feeling intimidated. Bravely I said, 'Why not?'

'People don't steal in order to hole up for ever; they steal money to spend it. His money's gone now, he feels forgotten, and he's got a job again somewhere—as a waiter.' I looked sceptical, I suppose, because Ihren said, 'Certainly as a waiter; he won't change jobs. That's all he knows, all he can do. Remember John Carradine, the movie actor? Used to see him a lot. Had a face a foot long, all chin and long jaw; very distinctive.' I nodded, and Ihren turned in his swivel chair to a filing cabinet. He opened a folder, brought out a glossy sheet of paper, and handed it to me. It was a police WANTED poster, and while the photograph on it did not really resemble the movie actor it had the same remarkable long-jawed memorability. Ihren said, 'He could move and he could change his name, but he could never change that face. Wherever he is he should have been found months ago; that poster went everywhere.'

I shrugged, and Ihren swung to the file again. He brought out, and handed me, a large old-fashioned sepia photograph, mounted on heavy grey cardboard. It was a group photo of a kind you seldom see any more—all the employees of a small business lined up on the sidewalk before it. There were a dozen moustached men in this and a woman in a long dress smiling and squinting in the sun as they stood before a small building which I recognised. It was Haring's Restaurant looking not too different than it does now. Inhren said, 'I spotted this on the wall of the restaurant office; I don't suppose anyone has really looked at it in years. The big guy in the middle is the original owner who started the restaurant in 1885 when this was taken; no one knows who anyone else in the picture was but take a good look at the other faces.'

I did, and saw what he meant: a face in the old picture almost identical with the one in the WANTED poster. It had the same astonishing length, the broad chin seeming nearly as wide as the cheekbones, and I looked up at Ihren. 'Who is it? His father? His grandfather?'

Almost reluctantly he said, 'Maybe. It could be, of course. But he sure looks like the guy we're hunting for, doesn't he? And look how he's grinning! Almost as though he'd deliberately got a job in Haring's Restaurant again, and were back in 1885 laughing at me!'

I said, 'Inspector, you're being extremely interesting, not to say down-right entertaining. You've got my full attention, believe me, and I am in no hurry to go anywhere else. But I don't quite see . . .'

'Well, you're a professor, aren't you? And professors are smart, aren't they? I'm looking for help anywhere I can get it. We've got half a dozen unsolved cases like that—people that absolutely should have been found, and found easy! William Spangler Greeson is another one; you ever heard of him?'

'Sure. Who hasn't in San Francisco?'

'That's right, big society name. But did you know he didn't have a dime of his own?'

I shrugged. 'How should I know? I'd have assumed he was rich.'

'His wife is; I suppose that's why he married her, though they tell me she chased him. She's older than he is, quite a lot. Disagreeable woman; I've talked to her. He's a young, handsome, likeable guy, they say, but lazy; so he married her.'

'I've seem him mentioned in Herb Caen's column. Had something to do with the theatre, didn't he?'

'Stage-struck all his life; tried to be an actor and couldn't make it. When they got married she gave him the money to back a play in New York, which kept him happy for a while; used to fly East a lot for rehearsals and out-of-town try-outs. Then he started getting friendly with some of the younger stage people, the good-looking female ones. His wife punished him like a kid. Hustled him back here, and not a dime for the theatre from then on. Money for anything else but he couldn't even buy a ticket to a play any more; he'd been a bad boy. So he disappeared with a hundred and seventy thousand bucks of hers, and not a sign of him since, which just isn't natural. Because he can't— you understand, he *can't*—keep away from the theatre. He should have shown up in New York long since—with a fake name, dyed hair, a moustache, some such nonsense. We should have had him months ago but we haven't; he's gone, too.' Ihren stood up. 'I hope you meant it when you said you weren't in a hurry, because . . .'

'Well as a matter of fact . . .'

'. . . because I made an appointment for both of us. On Powell Street near the Embarcadero. Come on.' He walked out from behind his desk, picking up a large manila envelope lying on one corner of it. There was a New York Police Department return address on the envelope, I saw, and it was addressed to him. He walked to the door without looking back as though he knew I'd follow. Down in front of the building he said, 'We can take a cab; with you along I can turn in a chit for it. When I went by myself I rode the cable car.'

'On a day like this anyone who takes a cab when he can ride the cable car is crazy enough to join the police force.'

Ihren said, 'Okay, tourist', and we walked all the way up to Market and Powell in silence. A cable car had just been swung around on its turntable, and we got an outside seat, no one near us; presently the car began crawling and clanging leisurely up Powell. You can sit outdoors on the cable cars, you know, and it was nice out, plenty of sun and blue sky, a typical late summer San Francisco day. But Ihren might as well have been on the New York subway. 'So where is William Spangler Greeson?' he said as soon as he'd paid our fares. 'Well, on a hunch I wrote the New York police, and they had a man in a few hours for me at the city historical museum.' Ihren opened his manila envelope, pulled out several folded sheets of greyish paper, and handed the top one to me. I opened it; it was a photostatic copy of an old-style playbill, narrow and long. 'Ever hear of that play?' Ihren said, reading over my shoulder. The sheet was headed: TONIGHT & ALL WEEK! SEVEN GALA NIGHTS! Below that, in big type: MABLE'S GREENHORN UNCLE!

'Sure, who hasn't?' I said. 'Shakespeare, isn't it?' We were passing Union Square and the St Francis Hotel.

'Save the jokes for your students, and read the cast of characters.'

I read it, a long list of names; there were nearly as many people in old-time plays as in the audiences. At the bottom of the list it said *Members of the Street Crowd*, followed by a dozen or more names in the middle of which appeared William Spangler Greeson.

Ihren said, 'That play was given in 1906. Here's another from the winter of 1901.' He handed me a second photostat, pointing to another list at the bottom of the cast. *Onlookers at the Big Race*, this one said, and it was followed by a half-inch of names in small type, the third of which was William Spangler Greeson. 'I've got copies of two more playbills,' Ihren said, 'one from 1902, the other from 1904, each with his name in the cast.'

The car swung off Powell, and we hopped off, and continued walking north on Powell. Handing back the photostat, I said, 'It's his grandfather. Probably Greeson inherited his interest in the stage from him.'

'You're finding a lot of grandfathers today, aren't you, Professor?' Ihren was replacing the stats in their envelopes.

'And what are you finding, Inspector?'

'I'll show you in a minute,' he said, and we walked on in silence. We could see the Bay up ahead now, beyond the end of Powell Street, and it looked beautiful in the sun, but Inspector Ihren didn't look at it. We were beside a low concrete building, and he gestured at it with his chin; a sign beside the door read, STUDIO SIXTEEN: COMMERCIAL TV. We walked in, passed through a small office in which no one was present and into an enormous concrete-floored room in which a carpenter was building a set—the front wall of a little cottage. On through the room—the Inspector had obviously been here before—then he pulled open a pair of double doors, and we walked into a tiny movie theatre. There was a blank screen up front, a dozen seats, and a projection booth. From the booth a man's voice called, 'Inspector?'

'Yeah. You ready?'

'Soon as I thread up.'

'Okay.' Ihren motioned me to a seat, and sat down beside me. Conversationally he said, 'There used to be a minor character around town name of Tom Veeley, a sports fan, a nut. Went to every fight, every Giant and Forty-Niners game, every auto race, roller derby, and jai-alai exhibition that came to town—and complained about them all. We knew him because every once in a while he'd leave his wife. She hated sports, she'd nag him, he'd leave, and we'd have to pick him up on her complaint for desertion and non-support; he never got far away. Even when we'd nab him all he'd talk about was how sports were dead, the public didn't care any more and neither did the players, and he wished he'd been around in the really great days of sports. Know what I mean?'

I nodded, the tiny theatre went dark, and a beam of sharp white light flashed out over our heads. Then a movie appeared on the screen before us. It was black and white, square in shape, the motion somewhat more rapid and jerky than we're used to, and it was silent. There wasn't even any music, and it was eerie to watch the movement hearing no sound but the whirr of the projector. The picture was a view of Yankee Stadium taken from far back of third base showing the stands, a man at bat, the pitcher winding up. Then it switched to a close-up—Babe Ruth at the plate, bat on shoulder, wire backstop in the background, fans behind it. He swung hard, hit the ball, and—chin rising as he followed its flight—he trotted forward. Grinning, his fists pumping rhythmically, he jogged around the base. Type matter flashed on to the screen: *The Babe does it again!* it began, and went on to say that this was his fifty-first home run of the 1927 season, and that it looked as though Ruth would set a new record.

The screen went blank except for some meaningless scribbled numbers and perforations flying past, and Ihren said, 'A Hollywood picture studio arranged this for me, no charge. Sometimes they film cops-and-crooks television up here, so they like to co-operate with us.'

Jack Dempsey suddenly appeared on the screen, sitting on a stool in a ring corner, men working over him. It was a poor picture; the ring was outdoors and there was too much sun. But it was Dempsey, all right, maybe twenty-four years old, unshaven and scowling. Around the edge of the ring, the camera panning over them now between rounds, sat men in flat-topped straw hats and stiff collars; some had handker-chiefs tucked into their collars and others were mopping their faces. Then, in the strange silence, Dempsey sprang up and moved out into the ring, crouching very low, and began sparring with an enormous slow-moving opponent: Jess Willard, I imagined. Abruptly the picture ended, the screen illuminated with only a flickering white light. Ihren said, 'I looked through nearly six hours of stuff like this; everything from Red Grange to Gertrude Ederle. I pulled out three shots; here's the last one.'

On the screen the scratched flickering film showed a golfer sighting for a putt; spectators stood three and four deep around the edge of the green. The golfer smiled engagingly and began waggling his putter; he wore knickers well down below his knees and his hair was parted in the middle and combed straight back. It was Bobby Jones, one of the world's great golfers, at the height of his career back in the 1920s. He tapped the ball, it rolled, dropped into the cup and, and Jones hurried after it as the crowd broke on to the green to follow him—all except one man. Grinning, one man walked straight towards the camera, then stopped, doffed his cloth cap in a kind of salute, and bowed from the waist. The camera swung past him to follow Jones who was stooping to retrieve his ball. Then Jones moved on, the man who had bowed to us hurrying after him with the crowd, across the screen and out of sight for ever. Abruptly the picture ended, and the ceiling lights came on.

Ihren turned to face me. 'That was Veeley,' he said, 'and it's no use trying to convince me it was his grandfather, so don't try. He wasn't even born when Bobby Jones was winning golf championships, but just the same that was absolutely and indisputably Tom Veeley, the sports fan who's been missing from San Francisco for six months now.' He sat waiting, but I didn't reply; what could I say to that? Ihren went on, 'He's also sitting just back of home plate behind the screen when Ruth hit the home run, though his face is in shadow. And I think he's one of the men mopping his face at the ringside during the Dempsey fight, though I'm not absolutely certain.'

The projection-booth door opened, the projectionist came out saying, 'That all today, Inspector?' and Ihren said yeah. The projectionist glanced at me, said, 'Hi, Professor,' and left.

Ihren nodded. 'Yeah, he knows you, Professor. He remembers you. Last week when he ran off this stuff for me, we came to the Bobby Jones film. He remarked that he'd run that one off for someone else only a few days before. I asked who it was, and he said a professor from the university named Weygand. Professor, we must be the only two people in the world interested in that one little strip of film. So I checked on you; you were an assistant professor of physics, brilliant and with a fine reputation, but that didn't help me. You had no criminal record, not with us, anyway, but that didn't tell me anything either; most people have no criminal record, and at least half of them ought to. Then I checked with the newspapers, and the *Chronicle* had a clipping about you filed in their morgue. Come on'—Ihren stood up—'let's get out of here.'

Outside, he turned towards the Bay; and we walked to the end of the street, then out on to a wooden pier. A big tanker, her red-painted bottom high out of the water, was sailing past, but Ihren didn't glance at her. He sat down on a piling, motioning me to another beside him, and pulled a newspaper clipping from his breast pocket. 'According to this, you gave a talk before the American-Canadian Society of Physicists in June 1961 at the Fairmont Hotel.'

'Is that a crime?'

'Maybe; I didn't hear it. You spoke of "Some Physical Aspects of Time", the clipping says. But I don't claim I understood the rest.'

'It was a pretty technical talk.'

'I got the idea, though, that you thought it might actually be possible to send a man back to an earlier time.'

I smiled. 'Lots of people have thought so, including Einstein. It's a widely held theory. But that's all, Inspector; just a theory.'

'Then let's talk about something that's more than a theory. For over a year San Francisco has been a very good market for old-style currency; I just found that out. Every coin and stamp dealer in town has had new customers, odd ones who didn't give their names and who didn't care what condition the old money was in. The more worn, dirty and creased—and therefore cheaper—the better they liked it, in fact. One of these customers, about a year ago, was a man with a remarkably long, thin face. He bought bills and a few coins; any kind at all suited him just as long as they were no later than 1885. Another customer was a young, good-looking, agreeable guy who wanted bills no later than the early 1900s. And so on. Do you know why I brought you out on this dock?'

'No.'

He gestured at the long stretch of empty pier behind us. 'Because there's no one within a block of us; no witnesses. So tell me, Professor— I can't use what you say, uncorroborated, as evidence—how the hell did you do it? I think you'd like to tell someone; it might as well be me.'

Astonishingly, he was right; I *did* want to tell someone, very much. Quickly, before I could change my mind, I said, 'I use a little black box with knobs on it, brass knobs.' I stopped, stared for a few seconds at a white Coast Guard cutter sliding into view from behind Angel Island, then shrugged and turned back to Ihren. 'But you aren't a physicist; how can I explain? All I can tell you is that it really *is* possible to send a man into an earlier time. Far easier, in fact, than any of the theorists had supposed. I adjust the knobs, the dials, focusing the black box on the subject like a camera, as it were. Then'—I shrugged again— 'well, I switch on a very faint specialised kind of precisely directed electric current or beam. And while my current is on—how shall I put it? He is afloat, in a manner of speaking; he is actually free of time, which moves on ahead without him. I've calculated that he is adrift, the past catching up with him at a rate of twenty-three years and eleven weeks for every second my current is on. Using a stopwatch, I can send a man back to whatever time he wishes with a plus or minus accuracy of three weeks. I know it works because—well, Tom Veeley is only one example. They all try to do something to show me they arrived safely, and Veeley said he'd do his best to get into the newsreel shot when Jones won the Open Golf Championship. I checked the newsreel last week to make sure he had.'

The inspector nodded. 'All right; now, *why* did you do it? They're criminals, you know; and you helped them escape.'

I said, 'No, I didn't know they were criminals, Inspector. And they didn't tell me. They just seemed like nice people with more troubles than they could handle. And I did it because I needed what a doctor needs when he discovers a new serum—volunteers to try it! And I got them; you're not the only one who ever read that news report.'

'Where'd you do it?'

'Out on the beach not far from the Cliff House. Late at night when no one was around.'

'Why out there?'

'There's some danger a man might appear in a time and place already occupied by something else, a stone wall or building, his molecules occupying the same space. He'd be all mixed in with the other molecules, which would be unpleasant and confining. But there've never been any buildings on the beach. Of course the beach might have been a little higher at one time than another, so I took no chances. I had each of them stand on the lifeguard tower, appropriately dressed for whatever time he planned to enter, and with the right kind of money for the period in his pocket. I'd focus carefully around him so as to exclude the tower, turn on the current for the proper time, and he'd drop on to the beach of fifty, sixty, seventy or eighty years ago.'

For a while the Inspector sat nodding, staring absently at the rough planks of the pier. Then he looked up at me again, vigorously rubbing his palms together. 'All right, Professor, and now you're going to bring them all back!' I began shaking my head, and he smiled grimly and said, 'Oh, yes, you are, or I'll wreck your career! I can do it, you know. I'll bring out everything I've told you, and I'll show the connections. Each of the missing people visited you more than once. Undoubtedly some of them were seen. You may even have been seen on the beach.

Time I'm through, you'll never teach again.' I was still shaking my head, and he said dangerously, 'You mean you won't?'

'I mean I can't, you idiot! How the hell can I reach them? They're back in 1885, 1906, 1927 or whatever; it's absolutely impossible to bring them back. They've escaped you, Inspector—for ever.'

He actually turned white. 'No!' he cried. '*No*; they're criminals and they've got to be punished, *got* to be!'

I was astounded. 'Why? None of them's done any great harm. And as far as we're concerned, they don't exist. Forget them.'

He actually bared his teeth. 'Never,' he whispered, then he roared, 'I *never* forget a wanted man!'

'Okay, Javert.'

'Who?'

'A fictional policeman in a book called *Les Misérables*. He spent half his life hunting down a man no one else wanted any more.'

'Good man; like to have him in the department.'

'He's not generally regarded too highly.'

'He is by me!' Inspector Ihren began slowly pounding his fist into his palm, muttering, 'They've got to be punished, they've got to be punished,' then he looked up at me. 'Get *out* of here,' he yelled, '*fast*! and I was glad to, and did. A block away I looked back, and he was still sitting there on the dock slowly pounding his fist in his palm.

I thought I'd seen the last of him then but I hadn't; I saw Inspector Ihren one more time. Late one evening about ten days later he phoned my apartment and asked me—ordered me—to come right over with my little black box, and I did even though I'd been getting ready for bed; he simply wasn't a man you disobeyed lightly. When I walked up to the big dark Hall of Justice he was standing in the doorway, and without a word he nodded at a car at the kerb. We got in, and drove in silence out to a quiet little residential district.

The streets were empty, the houses dark; it was close to midnight. We parked just within range of a corner street light, and Ihren said, 'I've been doing some thinking since I saw you last, and some research.' He pointed to a mailbox beside the street lamp on the corner a dozen feet ahead. 'That's one of the three mailboxes in the city of San Francisco that has been in the same location for almost ninety years. Not that identical box, of course, but always that location. And now we're going to mail some letters.' From his coat pocket, Inspector Ihren brought out a little sheaf of envelopes, addressed in pen and ink, and stamped for mailing. He showed me the top one, shoving the others into his pocket. 'You see who this is for?'

'The chief of police.'

'That's right; the San Francisco chief of police—in 1885! That's his name, address, and the kind of stamp they used then. I'm going to walk to the mailbox on the corner, and hold this in the slot. You'll focus your little black box on the envelope, turn on the current as I let it go, and it will drop into the mailbox that stood here in 1885!'

I shook my head admiringly; it was ingenious. 'And what does the letter say?'

He grinned evilly. 'I'll tell you what it says! Every spare moment I've had since I last saw you, I've been reading old newspapers at the library. In December 1884 there was a robbery, several thousand dollars missing; there isn't a word in the paper for months afterwards that it was ever solved.' He held up the envelope. 'Well, this letter suggests to the chief of police that they investigate a man they'll find working in Haring's Restaurant, a man with an unusually long thin face. And that if they search his room, they'll probably find several thousand dollars he can't account for. And that he will absolutely *not* have an alibi for the robbery in 1884!' The Inspector smiled, if you could call it a smile. 'That's all they'll need to send him to San Quentin, and mark the case closed; they didn't pamper criminals in those days!'

My jaw was hanging open. 'But he isn't guilty! Not of that crime!'

'He's guilty of another just about like it! And he's got to be punished; I *will* not let him escape, not even to 1885!'

'And the other letters?'

'You can guess. There's one for each of the men you helped get away, addressed to the police of the proper time and place. And you're going to help me mail them all, one by one. If you don't I'll ruin you, and that's a promise, Professor.' He opened his door, stepped out, and walked to the corner without even glancing back.

I suppose there are those who will say I should have refused to use my little black box no matter what the consequences to me. Well, maybe I should have, but I didn't. The Inspector meant what he said and I knew it, and I wasn't going to have the only career I ever had or wanted be ruined. I did the best I could; I begged and pleaded. I got out of the car with my box; the Inspector stood waiting at the mailbox. '*Please* don't make me do this,' I said. '*Please*! There's no need! You haven't told anyone else about this, have you?'

'Of course not; I'd be laughed off the force.'

'Then forget it! Why hound these poor people? They haven't done so much; they haven't really hurt anyone. Be humane! Forgiving! Your ideas are at complete odds with modern conceptions of criminal rehabilitation!'

I stopped for breath, and he said, 'You through, Professor? I hope so, because nothing will ever change my mind. Now, go ahead and use that damn' box!' Hopelessly I shrugged, and began adjusting the dials.

I am sure that the most baffling case the San Francisco Bureau of Missing Persons ever had will never be solved. Only two people— Inspector Ihren and I—know the answer, and we're not going to tell. For a short time there was a clue someone might have stumbled onto, but I found it. It was in the rare photographs section of the public library; they've got hundreds of old San Francisco pictures, and I went through them all and found this one. Then I stole it; one more crime added to the list I was guilty of hardly mattered.

Every once in a while I get it out, and look at it; it shows a row of uniformed men lined up in formation before a San Francisco police station. In a way it reminds me of an old movie comedy because each of them wears a tall helmet of felt with a broad turn-down brim, and long uniform coats to the knees. Nearly every one of them wears a drooping moustache, and holds a long nightstick poised at the shoulder as though ready to bring it down on Chester Conklin's head. Keystone Kops they look like at first glance, but study those faces closely and you change your mind about that. Look especially close at the face of the man at the very end of the row, wearing sergeant's stripes. It looks positively and permanently ferocious, glaring out (or so it always seems) directly at me. It is the implacable face of Martin O. Ihren of the San Francisco police force, back where he really belongs, back where I sent him with my little black box, in the year 1893.

SHE CAUGHT HOLD OF THE TOE

Richard Hughes

Time imagined as a simple object like a reversible stocking is the theme of this curious little story by a writer whose name readers may not immediately associate with tales of fantasy. Richard Hughes is, of course, famous for his tour de force, A High Wind in Jamaica *(1929), in which a number of children play the central role in a tense and exciting sea journey; while his play,* The Sisters' Tragedy *(1922), was described by George Bernard Shaw as 'the finest one-act play in litera- ture'. Yet, he is also highly regarded by lovers of supernatural fiction for his collection of ghost stories,* A Moment of Time *(1926), which includes two minor classics, 'A Night at a Cottage', about a haunted house, and 'Locomotive', the story of a ghost train steaming through the Welsh border country.*

Richard Hughes (1900–1976) was educated at Oxford and after a period spent travelling in the United States, Canada and the West Indies, began to write the poetry and prose which made him one of the leading writers of his generation. His unique ability as a story-teller working in spare, eloquent prose can be seen at its best in 'She Caught Hold of the Toe', written in 1925, in which a little girl finds herself inadvertently turning time backwards . . .

* * *

Joseph was eight, Nellie seven.

Nellie found *Time* hanging on a beech-bough in the wood behind the house. She mistook it for a stocking, and plunged her arm into it to see what was inside. There was nothing: so she caught hold of the toe and turned it inside out.

Just then Joseph came running up. They sat down on the trunk of a tree. Joseph was minded seriously.

'Nellie,' he said, 'we are very young now, only a few years of past remain behind us: what they hold for us I cannot tell: but one thing is certain, at the other end lies Birth.'

Nellie shivered slightly. 'How can you remind me!' she said. 'I swear to you I don't feel a bit younger than I shall at forty. And what is gained by brooding on Birth? One cannot alter the inevitable.'

Joseph smiled. 'Why, Nellie, I swear you look as old to me as when I shall see you for the last time! Ah, I remember as clearly as if it were tomorrow the day of your funeral: a windy, drizzly day—Lord, what a cold I shall catch! I shall die soon after, myself—ah, how it all comes forward to me! Dear, dear! Ah, me! Forty years of happy married life! There is little behind us now, my dear; but what a comfort to the, young is the memory of a happy future!'

'You forget the earlier time twenty years ahead of us. What a struggle we shall have to pay our bills!'

'Well, yes; I suppose it is a symptom of youth, but memory is always clearest of that which is most distant: why, I can recall every detail of the day they will make me Lord Mayor. I remember——'

And so he rambled on.

'But the past, the mysterious past . . .'

'Don't talk about the past, it frightens me!' said Nellie. 'Who can tell, even young as we are, what has happened to him? What misfortune lies behind him?'

'We must trust in God,' said Joseph gently. 'If He thinks fit to bring calamity upon us, that all may have been right in the beginning.'

'Amen, my dear; and yet, if only one's eyes could pierce just a little into the mysterious past, even from one moment to the one before: I should feel less frightened of birth, I think, if I knew just when it had happened: that I might be postpared to meet it.'

'My dear, we are not meant to see the past: we should accept it dutifully, as it goes. Sufficient to the day—why trouble, then, about a yesterday, that once was even as tomorrow?'

Nellie rose and walked over to the tree where *Time* was hanging.

'What are you doing with that stocking?'

'I am turning it right side out,' said Nellie.

THE REASON IS WITH US

James E. Gunn

Time travel has been the subject of a number of television series in recent years: notably the BBC's long-running Doctor Who *(launched in 1963), with eight actors having played the Time Lord to date;* The Time Tunnel *(1966–7), with James Darren and Robert Colbert as two scientists trapped in time because of a malfunctioning time machine; and* Quantum Leap *(1989–93), in which Scott Bakula played a wandering time traveller with only the hologram of a somewhat eccentric colleague (played by Dean Stockwell) to come to his assistance at moments of crisis. James Gunn, the author of the next story, was the creator of* The Immortal, *another TV series, which ran from 1969 to 1971 and recounted the adventures of Ben Richards (played by Christopher George), a man immune to disease and to the ageing process, who moves through time while being relentlessly pursued for the secret of his longevity. It was based on one of his most popular novels,* The Immortals, *published in 1962.*

James Edwin Gunn (1923–) has combined a career as a professor of English and journalism at the University of Kansas with writing sf short stories and critical essays on the genre. His book The Discovery of the Future: The Ways Science Fiction Developed *(1975) was followed by* The New Encyclopedia of Science Fiction *in 1988. Among his best novels are* The Fortress World *(1955),* The Joy Makers *(1961) and* Crisis! *(1986). 'The Reason Is with Us', which was written for the magazine* Satellite Science Fiction *in 1958, is also a story of pursuit through time recounted from the viewpoint of the pursued—in this instance a traveller from the future who has settled in the present day. But now it appears* someone *has caught up with him . . .*

*   *   *

These are the *things you do*: Naked, you arrive inside the warehouse. You are naked, because you can take nothing with you, just as you can leave nothing behind. Those are the two natural rules of time travel.

You choose the warehouse instead of the Centre, because you are no longer an agent of the State, although They do not know it yet. Soon They will know it, and the search will begin. You put on the clothes you have cached in the warehouse. You pocket the few dollars you have managed to put away, one at a time, on your previous trip. You walk confidently along the dark streets, until you come to the rooming house where your room is waiting.

Thus you find a hiding place.

It is not a perfect hiding place, because there are none. There is no place They cannot find you if They want you badly enough. They will want you. Your example is deadly, and you were Their best agent. You know too much about the fulcrums, the pivotal points of history, upon which rests the precarious past—and, hence, the precarious present— of the State. They do not know that you are concerned with only one thing—yourself.

So you find a place where They will have to hunt a long time, hoping They will get tired of hunting before They find you.

You choose the twentieth century. It is a natural choice—it is your speciality. You know it as if you had been born of it, instead of the State. You have lived in it, for years, adding up the durations of all your missions. You were assigned to it as a child of the State. You studied its languages and customs along with your own. You protected the fulcrums from the tampering of enemies of the State. You lectured on it to classes of Leaders, Unrestricted. You perverted it for the history books of the masses. It was your second home.

Slowly, its freedoms began to counteract the poisons of your lifelong indoctrination. Slowly, you began to think for yourself, to compare, to dread your return to the State. Suddenly the balance was broken. You planned your escape.

It is not the best era for concealment. Regimentation has begun. Identity must be certified. Papers must be filed, here and there. And, because it is your speciality, They will search it hardest and longest.

Against that, you weigh your knowledge and your desires. Of the two, perhaps your desires are the heaviest. Technology and art are sufficiently developed to provide you with conveniences and entertain- ment. Freedom is playing its last great role on the stage of decision. The State lurks in the wings. You must be in the audience.

You settle in a large city, in the free half of the world. Strangers are common in large cities. You establish an identity. You get a job as a clerk in a bank, doing sums on a machine that you could do more quickly in your head. It is monotonous and uninspiring, but you do not mind, because you are fully, *really free*, for the first time in your life. The only shadow on your freedom is the knowledge that you are hunted. They are hunting you, up and down the ages of the world. It is a small price to pay.

You live in your room for a few months, but you know that this is only temporary. Single, friendless men are obvious misfits. You must complete the camouflage. You look constantly for a girl. Your task is difficult, not only because you are a stranger, but because there are strategic requirements to be met, psychological problems to be overcome.

Finally, by accident, you meet again the girl from the government office. She is friendly, but not over-curious—pretty but not beautiful. She is modest. She might marry a bank clerk. Her name is Lynn.

You find that your fears were wasted. Physical contact is not distasteful. Lynn's necessary modesty makes her difficult to arouse, but, at last, you are successful. She consents. You are married. You have been frugal. You can afford a down payment on a house.

After a difficult few days, Lynn seems happy. You are happy. Biological mating is not repulsive. On the contrary, you begin to see that the State method of compulsory exogenesis is part of a complex pattern of breaking all ties except those which bind the citizen to the State.

... *Child of the State*, you think, *born from a bottle, reared in a crèche, you have travelled a long strange road, but the destination is in sight.*

As soon as possible, you tell Lynn you want a son.

You relax, just a little. So far, you have not made a mistake. In a few months your camouflage will be complete ...

These are the things you do not do—you do not let your knowledge of the future lead you into any of the simple traps. You have traced others, through seemingly minute political, economic or social perturbations. You are an ordinary citizen of the twentieth-century United States. You act like an ordinary citizen, a timid one.

You do not bet on horse races, boxing matches, football games or elections, even though you know who will win. You do not invent miraculous little gadgets. You do not plagiarise remembered fiction or poetry under a pseudonym. You do not write anonymous letters to statesmen, politicians or newspapers. Your only source of income is your job. You do not lust for money, power or fame. Your only desire is to stay alive and be free.

You do not seem strange, foreign or different. You dress like your neighbours. You speak as they speak. You are pleasant, without inviting close friendships. You laugh at your neighbours' jokes. You echo their opinions on fishing, golf and baseball, on prices and the weather, on the President, foreign policy and the cold war. You do not have opinions of your own.

You do not own a car, a gun or a dog. Immediately after every snow, you shovel your walks carefully. You do not have parties or play your television set loud or sing in the bathtub. You are the last one on or off the subway—if a train is crowded, you wait for the next one. You wait scrupulously for stop lights—only when the street is clear, do you cross.

You do not take chances. You do not walk beside buildings under construction. You do not get into arguments. You do not enter saloons. You do not drink. You do nothing which might bring you into contact with the police.

You do not let your guard down for an instant, not with anyone, not even with Lynn. You do not hint, even by the twitch of an eyebrow, that you are smarter than you seem, that you know more than you should, that you could change the course of history. You are an average clerk, with an average education and average opinions, living in an average house with an average family. No one could be more average.

You do not confide in anyone.

You read the papers and see the fulcrums passing, one by one, fulcrums which lead surely to the State you have fled—but you do not lift a finger to interfere. You are not afraid that your existence is dependent upon that of the State, for you are firmly fixed in the twentieth century. But you know that there are hidden agents around each fulcrum. On some occasions, you were there yourself. The paradox does not disturb you—it is only superficial. You might be successful, but you do not take the chance.

You do not visit a plastic surgeon or a tattoo artist. You are never undressed in front of anyone, not even Lynn, when the light is on. You dress and undress behind a locked bathroom door.

No one ever sees the indelible imprint just under your armpit—TA: 1–4537–A. Lynn's modesty takes a similar form, and she sees nothing strange in your actions.

Always alert, eternally watchful, you do not wonder if what you have is worth what you must pay for it. You know—it is worth it.

And this is what happens to you—one afternoon at work, while you are idly tapping away at the keys of a tabulator, an envelope is dropped in front of you. You glance over your shoulder. Weasel-faced Colbert, the department supervisor, is standing there, frowning at you. You are not supposed to receive mail at the bank. You shrug helplessly at him, and he moves away, muttering soundlessly.

It is a plain envelope with no return address. For some reason, a tremor, quickly stilled, runs down your arm as you pick it up. Your face, however, is only curious. You tear open the end of the envelope calmly and shake out the letter. You open it. It is typewritten. There is no signature. It says—

TA:1–4537–A:
  You are known. Prepare yourself for return. Do not try to escape in any way, or the punishment awaiting you will be even greater.

You snort. 'I'll be damned!' you say. You will indeed.

Someone is breathing in your ear. You glance to your left at Julie Friedman, who is reading the letter over your shoulder. Her dark, pretty face is alive with interest. You shrug at her, puzzled.

'Isn't that funny?' she says.

On your right, Ted Hamm looks up, preoccupied. 'What's the matter?'

'Some practical joker,' you say, and toss the letter to him.

While he reads it, you look around. Colbert is watching, glowering at you. You shrug again and get back to work, but your back is cold, from the nape of your neck to the base of your spine.

But you play your part. You must always play it, as you have decided, clear to the end. You are surprised that you are so calm. It has come, and you are not frightened.

Perhaps, it is because you know that They are not certain. The letter was a mistake. It told you that They were suspicious, and it told you that They weren't certain. Their mistake. You will not jump or run. You will not prove Their suspicions. They do not dare make a mistake. The State is intolerant of mistakes, and the fabric of time is fragile. You, if you are innocent, might be a fulcrum. The limitations on time agents are sharply defined.

You have thought of Them as They, but there is only one. You know that. Agents do not work together—they would be too busy watching one another. And it is unlikely that the agent who suspects you has reported to his superiors. Reporting is a difficult task, at best, and it is not wise to report the possibility of success when there remains a chance of failure. Failure is the State's major crime.

One person remains between you and safety—and he has made a mistake. You know he is watching. If you can get rid of him, it is probable that you will never be bothered again. But, first, you must pick him out. You must make absolutely sure.

Your fingers punch the keys automatically. Three persons were close when you received the letter—Colbert, Julie, Ted. The chances are great that the agent is one of those three. A casual glance could not have pierced your disguise. It had to be someone in frequent contact. You have no friends. *Colbert, Julie, Ted . . .*

Colbert—sour, friendless, always snooping. You have known many like him in the service of the State. But he is middle-aged, and he has spent years with the bank. It is an argument for his innocence, but not a complete one. The State does not balance effort against results. The State would sacrifice twenty loyal agents to get back one stray, and a properly indoctrinated agent would think nothing of putting the welfare of the State above his desires, his distastes, his life.

Julie—the State has women agents. You have heard of them, although you have never met any. Julie does not look like the sexless women of the State you have known, but they would be worthless as agents. From the first, you could not fathom Julie. Sometimes she was friendly, sometimes cold and distant. You had considered Julie as a possible mate—but it would have aroused too much interest in the office. Everyone would have been too friendly. Thinking about it, you shudder. Perhaps, you were that close to proposing to an agent.

Ted—after a moment's consideration, you discard him. He is too frank, too ingenious. He has shown you pictures of his wife and three children, newspaper photographs of himself on the gridiron. Automatically, you checked up on those. It could not be Ted. The wife and the children were positive proof.

The afternoon ends. You pick up the letter and go home. As you come up the front walk, you notice the houses of your neighbours, almost identical to yours, one on each side. Your neighbours, close but not too close. You dismiss them, the Millers on the north, the Brents on the south. Both are young couples like you and Lynn. Possibly the State might assign two agents to work together, but never a man and a woman. Not living in the same house—not with children.

You show Lynn the letter as a curiosity. She reads it and laughs and throws it aside. You sit down to dinner. You think.

'You aren't eating, dear,' Lynn says.

'Oh,' you say. 'I must have been thinking.'

You eat. You try to act natural, but your mind will not rest. Colbert or Julie—Julie or Colbert.

After dinner, you sit and pretend to read. You think of every other person you know, but none of them fit. They have to be in a place where they can watch you. Colbert or Julie—Julie or Colbert.

The evening drags on. Lynn yawns and rises, stretching. She is getting quite round in the belly.

'I get sleepy early these days,' she says pleasantly.

She goes into the bedroom to get ready. By unspoken agreement, you wait until she is in bed.

A little later, you follow, undressing in the bathroom and putting on your pyjamas. When you enter the bedroom, it is dark. You can barely make out Lynn's pale face against the blackness of her hair, spread fan-like on the pillow. You slip into bed.

'Good night,' Lynn says drowsily.

'Good night,' you say.

Soon you know, by her steady breathing, that she is asleep. But you cannot sleep. Your life hangs on a slender thread of recognition.

Colbert or Julie—Julie or Colbert! Around and around they spin, the two faces, the weasel and the minx, blurring as they go faster and faster . . .

You jerk yourself awake. You cannot afford to sleep, not yet.

You hope that it is Colbert. You have never killed a woman. You do not think you would like it. And yet, Colbert is old for the role.

You will not use your carefully tutored powers. With an agent nearby, it would be almost certainly fatal. But there is always the identification under the armpit. If you can trick one of them into giving you a glimpse.

Colbert? Impossible! But you might be able to seduce Julie, or, perhaps, you need not go that far. If she is the agent . . . If not, then it is Colbert. Colbert or Julie—Julie or Colbert. One of the two is the stranger.

Now that you have decided on a course of action, you feel easier. You can sleep. You rise on one elbow and gently pull back a blind to look at your watch. It is midnight. The moonlight streams in brilliantly. It falls gently across Lynn's face.

You look at her. You have become quite fond of Lynn. Of all the things that you would miss, if you were caught and returned, you feel that you might miss Lynn most.

She has one white arm thrown up above her head. Her face is peaceful. Her body is working, even now, to build you the child that will provide the perfect camouflage. They would never suspect a man with a child.

You bend a little closer. The short sleeve of her thin nightgown has slipped down over her shoulder, leaving her arm bare.

Her armpit is smooth. But, just a little lower—is it shadow? No— it is a letter, and another letter, then a number. You decipher them— TA: 1– . . .

Your breath whistles out of you. You look quickly at her face. Her eyes are open, staring into yours, wide and blue, deep with an awful knowledge.

'*You*!' you say hoarsely, and realise that you have given yourself away. But it doesn't matter. You have found the agent, and now it is between you two.

'Me,' Lynn says.

You get up. You slip on a robe and go into the living-room and sit down. You feel cold inside. You have been fond of Lynn.

In a moment, she follows, slipping her arms into a robe. She ties it high, above the swelling. You watch, scornfully.

'No sacrifice is too great,' you say heavily. You want to hurt her, as she has hurt you.

Her eyes flash. 'Not for the State.'

'How did you find me?'

She laughs, derisively. 'The great agent! So clever—so stupid! You had to have clothes and money. You had to return to the period of your last mission. All that was necessary was to get a job in the social security office, here, where it is easy to hide, and check the records. But I didn't even have to do that. You came walking into my arms.'

Papers! You shake your head. They are what you had feared from the start. 'But you were not sure. You couldn't be sure.'

'No.'

'Ah, the sacrifice!' you say. 'It must have been torment to endure my love-making—all for the State.'

Her eyes are fiery. 'Yes.' But her voice falters. 'That is what kept me uncertain. I knew—and yet . . .'

'Ah!' you say.

Her face reddens to match her eyes. 'Not what you think, animal. It seemed impossible that one born of the State, raised by the State, could turn beast so easily.'

'And I never suspected,' you say. 'You are a consummate actress.' You enjoy the look on her face, as she tries to decide whether you are being sarcastic. 'You could not act, of course, before you were sure.'

'Naturally,' she says. 'But now I am sure. I thought that you might remove my doubt by destroying the letter, but it is better this way. Enough of idle talk. You are coming with me.'

You laugh, but laughter fades as she pulls a gun out of her robe pocket. It shoots solid pellets, but it is deadly enough. 'Incredible,' you say. She looks as if she enjoys the expression on your face. 'I might have choked you to death in bed,' you say, 'but I couldn't. Now, perhaps, you can shoot me. You had better. I am not going back.'

'Don't worry,' she says grimly. 'I'll shoot.'

'Shoot now, then. Because if you don't, I am going to leave this era. Goodbye, my dear.'

'Don't be a fool!' she says. 'I will follow you wherever you go. You have no chance now. You will only make it harder on yourself.'

You smile. You start to laugh. 'My dear,' you say, chuckling, 'you have forgotten one of the cardinal rules of time travel. You can take nothing with you from this era.'

'Well,' she says defiantly, but her expression is puzzled.

'Lynn, my dear,' you say gently. 'You have something which is always with you now, which will be with you for a number of months yet.'

She looks down, startled. The gun drops from her hand. You scoop it up.

'Goodbye, again,' you say. But it is difficult to leave. Here, you have had rare moments of happiness. Memories clutch at you, hold you back. Where else will you be as happy?

Slowly Lynn's expression changes. Now it is her turn to laugh. 'Go ahead,' she taunts. 'Leave. Go ahead and try!'

You stiffen. You try. You concentrate upon the time stream with your sharpened time sense. You sweat. But you cannot vary your temporal position by one fraction of a second.

'The great TA: 1–4537–A! They said that you were the most skilful, the cleverest, agent ever to work for the State. But you, also, can forget things. Remember, dear, the other cardinal rule of time travel. You, too, can leave nothing behind.' She sits down complacently smoothing her robe over her lap.

You begin to smile—you laugh. It is true. You are stuck here, both of you, for the rest of your lives.

'Now,' she says, reaching for the telephone, 'all I have to do is call—'

'I wouldn't,' you say, still smiling, gesturing with the gun. 'You can presume, perhaps, on my reluctance to kill you. But do not presume on the State's acceptance of your unorthodox condition. This time, you went too far for the State. Even if They are not horrified, They will not leave you here—alive. And you can never leave.'

Her hand drops from the phone. You laugh. In a little while, you know, she will begin to laugh, too. It is, after all, a most amusing situation. You and Lynn and the little stranger. You have been too timid. Now that you have help you can be bolder. Somehow, you three, working together, will shift a fulcrum and remove the threat to your existence.

'What shall we call it?' you ask, sighing.

'Call *him*!' she says indignantly.

MAN IN HIS TIME

Brian W. Aldiss

This first section began with a topical story and ends with one. Philip K. Dick's tale addressed the problems of the first time travel projects; Brian W. Aldiss focuses on a mission to Mars—which, despite the failure of the Russians' Mars-96 spacecraft in November 1996, is currently the main objective of both America and Russia. 'Man in His Time', a remarkable story of a time slip, deserves comparison with Aldiss' outstanding novel, An Age *(1967), in which time runs backwards—with devastating effect.*

Brian Wilson Aldiss (1925–), a former soldier and bookshop assistant, began writing sf in the mid-Fifties and a decade later was one of the moving forces behind the new wave of British science fiction. His first novel, Non-Stop *(1958), is now regarded as a classic, and he won the first of several awards, a Hugo, for* The Long Afternoon of Earth *in 1962. Aldiss has demonstrated his admiration for the works of H. G. Wells in* The Saliva Tree *(1965) and* Moreau's Other Island *(1980), while* Frankenstein Unbound *(1973) and* Dracula Unbound *(1991) are not parodies of the original novels but cleverly developed time travel fantasies. His trio of* Helliconia *novels (1982–5) have all been bestsellers, and he is widely regarded as one of Britain's leading sf writers. 'Man in His Time', published in 1965, describes the return to Earth from Mars of astronaut Jack Westermark, his crash landing, and the curious limbo in which he then finds himself . . .*

*   *   *

His absence

Janet Westermark sat watching the three men in the office: the administrator who was about to go out of her life, the behaviourist who was about to come into it, and the husband whose life ran parallel to but insulated from her own.

She was not the only one playing a watching game. The behaviourist, whose name was Clement Stackpole, sat hunched in his chair with his ugly strong hands clasped round his knee, thrusting his intelligent and simian face forward, the better to regard his new subject, Jack Westermark.

The administrator of the Mental Research Hospital spoke in a lively and engaged way. Typically, it was only Jack Westermark who seemed absent from the scene.

Your particular problem, restless

His hands upon his lap lay still, but he himself was restless, though the restlessness seemed directed. It was as if he were in another room with other people, Janet thought. She saw that he caught her eye when in fact she was not entirely looking at him, and by the time she returned the glance, he was gone, withdrawn.

'Although Mr Stackpole has not dealt before with your particular problem,' the administrator was saying, 'he has had plenty of field experience. I know—'

'I'm sure we won't,' Westermark said, folding his hands and nodding his head slightly.

Smoothly, the administrator made a pencilled note of the remark, scribbled the precise time beside it, and continued, 'I know Mr Stackpole is too modest to say this, but he is a great man for working in with people—'

'If you feel it's necessary,' Westermark said. 'Though I've seen enough of your equipment for a while.'

The pencil moved, the smooth voice proceeded. 'Good. A great man for working in with people, and I'm sure you and Mr Westermark will soon find you are glad to have him around. Remember, he's there to help both of you.'

Janet smiled, and said from the island of her chair, trying to smile at him and Stackpole, 'I'm sure that everything will work—' She was interrupted by her husband, who rose to his feet, letting his hands drop to his sides and saying, turning slightly to address thin air, 'Do you mind if I say goodbye to Nurse Simmons?'

Her voice no longer wavered

'Everything will be all right, I'm sure,' she said hastily. And Stackpole nodded at her, conspiratorially agreeing to see her point of view.

'We'll all get on fine, Janet,' he said. She was in the swift process of digesting that unexpected use of her Christian name, and the administrator was also giving her the sort of encouraging smile so many people had fed her since Westermark was pulled out of the ocean off Casablanca, when her husband, still having his lonely conversation with the air, said, 'Of course; I should have remembered.'

His right hand went half-way to his forehead—or his heart? Janet wondered—and then dropped, as he added, 'Perhaps she'll come round and see us sometime.' Now he turned and was smiling faintly at another vacant space with just the faintest nod of his head, as if slightly cajoling. 'You'd like that, wouldn't you, Janet?'

She moved her head, instinctively trying to bring her eyes into his gaze as she replied vaguely, 'Of course, darling.' Her voice no longer wavered when she addressed his absent attention.

There was sunlight through which they could see each other

There was sunlight in one corner of the room, coming through the windows of a bay angled towards the sun. For a moment she caught, as she rose to her feet, her husband's profile with the sunlight behind it. It was thin and withdrawn. Intelligent: she had always thought him overburdened with his intelligence, but now there was a lost look there, and she thought of the words of a psychiatrist who had been called in on the case earlier: 'You must understand that the waking brain is perpetually lapped by the unconscious.'

Lapped by the unconscious

Fighting the words away, she said, addressing the smile of the administrator—that smile which must have advanced his career so much—'You've helped me a lot. I couldn't have got through these months without you. Now we'd better go.'

She heard herself chopping her words, fearing Westermark would talk across them, as he did: 'Thank you for your help. If you find anything . . .'

Stackpole walked modestly over to Janet as the administrator rose and said, 'Well, don't either of you forget us if you're in any kind of trouble.'

'I'm sure we won't.'

'And, Jack, we'd like you to come back here to visit us once a month for a personal check-up. Don't want to waste all our expensive equipment, you know, and you are our star—er, patient.' He smiled rather tightly as he said it, glancing at the paper on his desk to check Westermark's answer. Westermark's back was already turned on him, Westermark was already walking slowly to the door, Westermark had said his goodbyes, perched out on the lonely eminence of his existence.

Janet looked helplessly, before she could guard against it, at the administrator and Stackpole. She hated it that they were too professional to take note of what seemed her husband's breach of conduct. Stackpole looked kindly in a monkey way and took her arm with one of his thick hands.

'Shall we be off then? My car's waiting outside.'

Not saying anything, nodding, thinking, and consulting watches

She nodded, not saying anything, thinking only, without the need of the administrator's notes to think it, 'Oh yes, this was when he said, "Do you mind if I say goodbye to Nurse"—who's it?—Simpson?' She was learning to follow her husband's footprints across the broken path of conversation. He was now out in the corridor, the door swinging to behind him, and to empty air the administrator was saying, 'It's her day off today.'

'You're good on your cues,' she said, feeling the hand tighten on her arm. She politely brushed his fingers away, horrid Stackpole, trying to recall what had gone only four minutes before. Jack had said something to her; she couldn't remember, didn't speak, avoided eyes, put out her hand and shook the administrator's firmly.

'Thanks,' she said.

'Au revoir to both of you,' he replied firmly, glancing swiftly: watch, notes, her, the door. 'Of course,' he said. 'If we find anything at all. We are very hopeful . . .'

He adjusted his tie, looking at the watch again.

'Your husband has gone now, Mrs Westermark,' he said, his manner softening. He walked towards the door with her and added, 'You have been wonderfully brave, and I do realise—we all realise—that you will have to go on being wonderful. With time, it should be easier for you;

doesn't Shakespeare say in *Hamlet* that "Use almost can change the stamp of nature"? May I suggest that you follow Stackpole's and my example and keep a little notebook and a strict check on the time?'

They saw her tiny hesitation, stood about her, two men round a personable woman, not entirely innocent of relish. Stackpole cleared his throat, smiled, said, 'He can so easily feel cut off, you know. It's essential that you of all people answer his questions, or he will feel cut off.'

Always a pace ahead

'The children?' she asked.

'Let's see you and Jack well settled in at home again, say for a fortnight or so,' the administrator said, 'before we think about having the children back to see him.'

'That way's better for them and Jack *and* you, Janet,' Stackpole said.

'Don't be glib,' she thought; 'Consolation I need, God knows, but that's too facile.' She turned her face away, fearing it looked too vulnerable these days.

In the corridor, the administrator said, as valediction, 'I'm sure Grandma's spoiling them terribly, Mrs Westermark, but worrying won't mend it, as the old saw says.'

She smiled at him and walked quickly away, a pace ahead of Stackpole.

Westermark sat in the back of the car outside the administrative block. She climbed in beside him. As she did so, he jerked violently back in his seat.

'Darling, what is it?' she asked. He said nothing.

Stackpole had not emerged from the building, evidently having a last word with the administrator. Janet took the moment to lean over and kiss her husband's cheek, aware as she did so that a phantom wife had already, from his viewpoint, done so. His response was a phantom to her.

'The countryside looks green,' he said. His eyes were flickering over the grey concrete block opposite.

'Yes,' she said.

Stackpole came bustling down the steps, apologising as he opened the car door, settled in. He let the clutch back too fast and they shot forward. Janet saw then the reason for Westermark's jerking backwards a short while before. Now the acceleration caught him again; his body was rolled helplessly back. As they drove along, he set one hand fiercely on the side grip, for his sway was not properly counterbalancing the movement of the car.

Once outside the grounds of the Institute, they were in the country, still under a mid-August day.

His theories

Westermark, by concentrating, could bring himself to conform to some of the laws of the time continuum he had left. When the car he was in climbed up his drive (familiar, yet strange with the rhododendrons unclipped and no signs of children) and stopped by the front door, he sat in his seat for three and a half minutes before venturing to open his door. Then he climbed out and stood on the gravel, frowning down at it. Was it as real as ever, as material? Was there a slight glaze on it— as if something shone through from the interior of the earth, shone through all things? Or was it that there was a screen between him and everything else? It was important to decide between the two theories, for he had to live under the discipline of one. What he hoped to prove was that the permeation theory was correct; that way he was merely one of the factors comprising the functioning universe, together with the rest of humanity. By the glaze theory, he was isolated not only from the rest of humanity but from the entire cosmos (except Mars?). It was early days yet; he had a deal of thinking to do, and new ideas would undoubtedly emerge after observation and cogitation. Emotion must not decide the issue; he must be detached. Revolutionary theories could well merge from this—suffering.

He could see his wife by him, standing off in case they happened embarrassingly or painfully to collide. He smiled thinly at her through her glaze. He said, 'I am, but I'd prefer not to talk.' He stepped towards the house, noting the slippery feel of gravel that would not move under his tread until the world caught up. He said, 'I've every respect for the *Guardian*, but I'd prefer not to talk at present.'

Famous Astronaut Returns Home

As the party arrived, a man waited in the porch for them, ambushing Westermark's return home with a deprecatory smile. Hesitant but businesslike, he came forward and looked interrogatively at the three people who had emerged from the car.

'Excuse me, you are Captain Jack Westermark, aren't you?'

He stood aside as Westermark seemed to make straight for him.

'I'm the psychology correspondent for the *Guardian*, if I might intrude for a moment.'

Westermark's mother had opened the front door and stood there smiling welcome at him, one hand nervously up to her grey hair. Her son walked past her. The newspaper man stared after him.

Janet told him apologetically, 'You'll have to excuse us. My husband did reply to you, but he's really not prepared to meet people yet.'

'*When* did he reply, Mrs Westermark? Before he heard what I had to say?'

'Well, naturally not—but his life stream ... I'm sorry, I can't explain.'

'He really is living ahead of time, isn't he? Will you spare me a minute to tell me how you feel now the first shock is over?'

'You really must excuse me,' Janet said, brushing past him. As she followed her husband into the house, she heard Stackpole say, 'Actually, I read the *Guardian*, and perhaps I could help you. The Institute has given me the job of remaining with Captain Westermark. My name's Clement Stackpole—you may know my book, *Persistent Human Relations*, Methuen. But you must not say that Westermark is living ahead of time. That's quite incorrect. What you can say is that some of his psychological and physiological processes have somehow been transposed forward—'

'Ass!' she exclaimed to herself. She had paused by the threshold to catch some of his words. Now she whisked in.

Talk hanging in the air among the long watches of supper

Supper that evening had its discomforts, although Janet Westermark and her mother-in-law achieved an air of melancholy gaiety by bringing two Scandinavian candelabra, relics of a Copenhagen holiday, on to the table and surprising the two men with a gay-looking hors d'oeuvre. But the conversation was mainly like the hors d'oeuvre, Janet thought: little tempting isolated bits of talk, not nourishing.

Mrs Westermark senior had not yet got the hang of talking to her son, and confined her remarks to Janet, though she looked towards Jack often enough. 'How are the children?' he asked her. Flustered by the knowledge that he was waiting a long while for her answer, she replied rather incoherently and dropped her knife.

To relieve the tension, Janet was cooking up a remark on the character of the administrator at the Mental Research Hospital, when Westermark said, 'Then he is at once thoughtful and literate. Commendable and rare in men of his type. I got the impression, as you evidently did, that he was as interested in his job as in advancement. I suppose one might say one even *liked* him. But you know him better, Stackpole; what do you think of him?'

Crumbling bread to cover his ignorance of whom they were supposed to be conversing, Stackpole said, 'Oh, I don't know; it's hard to say really', spinning out time, pretending not to squint at his watch.

'The administrator was quite a charmer, didn't you think, Jack?' Janet remarked—perhaps helping Stackpole as much as Jack.

'He looks as if he might make a slow bowler,' Westermark said, with an intonation that suggested he was agreeing with something as yet unsaid.

'Oh, *him*!' Stackpole said. 'Yes, he seems a satisfactory sort of chap on the whole.'

'He quoted Shakespeare to me and thoughtfully told me where the quotation came from,' Janet said.

'No thank you, Mother,' Westermark said.

'I don't have much to do with him,' Stackpole continued. 'Though I have played cricket with him a time or two. He makes quite a good slow bowler.'

'Are you really?' Westermark exclaimed.

That stopped them. Jack's mother looked helplessly about, caught her son's glazed eye, said, covering up, 'Do have some more sauce, Jack dear', recalled she had already had her answer, almost let her knife slide again, gave up trying to eat.

'I'm a batsman, myself,' Stackpole said, as if bringing an old pneumatic drill to the new silence. When no answer came, he doggedly went on, expounding on the game, the pleasure of it. Janet sat and watched, a shade perplexed that she was admiring Stackpole's performance and wondering at her slight perplexity; then she decided that she had made up her mind to dislike Stackpole, and immediately dissolved the resolution. Was he not on their side? And even the strong hairy hands became a little more acceptable when you thought of them gripping the rubber of a bat handle; and the broad shoulders swinging . . . She closed her eyes momentarily, and tried to concentrate on what he was saying.

A batsman himself

Later, she met Stackpole on the upper landing. He had a small cigar in his mouth, she had two pillows in her arms. He stood in her way.

'Can I help at all, Janet?'

'I'm only making up a bed, Mr Stackpole.'

'Are you not sleeping in with your husband?'

'He would like to be on his own for a night or two, Mr Stackpole. I shall sleep in the children's room for the time being.'

'Then please permit me to carry the pillows for you. And do please call me Clem. All my friends do.'

Trying to be pleasanter, to unfreeze, to recall that Jack was not moving her out of the bedroom permanently, she said, 'I'm sorry. It's just that we once had a terrier called Clem.' But it did not sound as she had wished it to do.

He put the pillows on Peter's blue bed, switched on the bedside lamp, and sat on the edge of the bed, clutching his cigar and puffing at it.

'This may be a bit embarrassing, but there's something I feel I should say to you, Janet.' He did not look at her. She brought him an ashtray and stood by him.

'We feel your husband's mental health may be endangered, although I hasten to assure you that he shows no signs of losing his mental equilibrium beyond what we may call an inordinate absorption in phenomena—and even there, we cannot say, of course we can't, that his absorption is any greater than one might expect. Expect in the totally unprecedented circumstances, I mean. We must talk about this in the next few days.'

She waited for him to go on, not unamused by the play with the cigar. Then he looked straight up at her and said, 'Frankly, Mrs Westermark, we think it would help your husband if you could have sexual relations with him.'

A little taken aback, she said, 'Can you imagine—' Correcting herself, she said, 'That is for my husband to say. I am not unapproachable.'

She saw he had caught her slip. Playing a very straight bat, he said, 'I'm sure you're not, Mrs Westermark.'

With the light out, living, she lay in Peter's bed

She lay in Peter's bed with the light out. Certainly she wanted him: pretty badly, now she allowed herself to dwell on it. During the long months of the Mars expedition, while she had stayed at home and he had got farther from home, while he actually had existence on that other planet, she had been chaste. She had looked after the children and driven round the countryside and enjoyed writing those articles for women's magazines and being interviewed on TV when the ship was reported to have left Mars on its homeward journey. She had been, in part, dormant.

Then came the news, kept from her at first, that there was confusion in communicating with the returning ship. A sensational tabloid broke the secrecy by declaring that the nine-man crew had all gone mad. And the ship had overshot its landing area, crashing into the Atlantic. Her first reaction had been a purely selfish one—no, not selfish, but from the self: He'll never lie with me again. And infinite love and sorrow.

At his rescue, the only survivor, miraculously unmaimed, her hope had revived. Since then, it had remained embalmed, as he was embalmed in time. She tried to visualise love as it would be now, with everything happening first to him, before she had begun to— With his movement of pleasure even before she— No, it wasn't possible! But of course it was, if they worked it out first intellectually; then if she just lay flat ... But what she was trying to visualise, all she could visualise, was not love-making, merely a formal prostration to the exigencies of glands and time flow.

She sat up in bed, longing for movement, freedom. She jumped out and opened the lower window; there was still a tang of cigar smoke in the dark room.

If they worked it out intellectually

Within a couple of days, they had fallen into routine. It was as if the calm weather, perpetuating mildness, aided them. They had to be careful to move slowly through doors, keeping to the left, so as not to bump into each other—a tray of drinks was dropped before they agreed on that. They devised simple knocking systems before using the bathroom. They conversed in bulletins that did not ask questions unless questions were necessary. They walked slightly apart. In short, they made detours round each other's lives.

'It's really quite easy as long as one is careful,' Mrs Westermark senior said to Janet. 'And dear Jack is *so* patient!'

'I even get the feeling he likes the situation.'

'Oh, my dear, how could he *like* such an unfortunate predicament?'

'Mother, you realise how we all exist together, don't you? No, it sounds too terrible—I daren't say it.'

'Now don't you start getting silly ideas. You've been very brave, and this is not the time for us to be getting upset, just as things are going well. If you have any worries, you must tell Clem. That's what he's here for.'

'I know.'

'Well, then!'

She saw Jack walk in the garden. As she looked, he glanced up, smiled, said something to himself, stretched out a hand, withdrew it, and went, still smiling, to sit on one end of the seat on the lawn. Touched, Janet hurried over to the french windows, to go and join him.

She paused. Already, she saw ahead, saw her sequence of actions, for Jack had already sketched them into the future. She would go on to the lawn, call his name, smile, and walk over to him when he smiled back. Then they would stroll together to the seat and sit down, one at each end.

The knowledge drained all spontaneity from her. She might have been working a treadmill, for what she was about to do had already been done as far as Jack was concerned, with his head's start in time. Then if she did not go, if she mutinied, turned back to the discussion of the day's chores with her mother-in-law . . . That left Jack mouthing like a fool on the lawn, indulging in a fantasy there was no penetrating. Let him do that, let Stackpole see; then they could drop this theory about Jack's being ahead of time and would have to treat him for a more normal sort of hallucinatory insanity. He would be safe in Clem's hands.

But Jack's actions proved that she would go out there. It was insane for her not to go out there. Insane? To disobey a law of the universe was impossible, not insane. Jack was not disobeying—he had simply tumbled over a law that nobody knew was there before the first expedition to Mars; certainly they had discovered something more momentous than anyone had expected, and more unforeseen. And she had lost— No, she hadn't lost yet! She ran out on to the lawn, calling to him, letting the action quell the confusion in her mind.

And in the repeated event there was concealed a little freshness, for she remembered how his smile, glimpsed through the window, had held a special warmth, as if he sought to reassure her. What had he said? That was lost. She walked over to the seat and sat beside him.

He had been saving a remark for the statutory and unvarying time lapse.

'Don't worry, Janet,' he said. 'It could be worse.'

'How?' she asked, but he was already answering: 'We could be a day apart. 3.3077 minutes at least allows us a measure of communication.'

'It's wonderful how philosophical you are about it,' she said. She was alarmed at the sarcasm in her tone.

'Shall we have a talk together now?'

'Jack, I've been wanting to have a private talk with you for some time.'

'I?'

The tall beeches that sheltered the garden on the north side were so still that she thought, 'They will look exactly the same for him as for me.'

He delivered a bulletin, staring at his watch. His wrists were thin. He appeared frailer than he had done when they left hospital. 'I am aware, my darling, how painful this must be for you. We are both isolated from the other by this amazing shift of temporal function, but at least I have the consolation of experiencing a new phenomenon, whereas you —'

'I?'

Talking of interstellar distances

'I was going to say that you are stuck with the same old world all of mankind has always known, but I suppose you don't see it that way.' Evidently a remark of hers had caught up with him, for he added inconsequentially, 'I've wanted a private talk with you.'

Janet bit off something she was going to say, for he raised a finger irritably and said, 'Please time your statement, so that we do not talk at cross-purposes. Confine what you have to say to essentials. Really, darling, I'm surprised you don't do as Clem suggests, and make notes of what is said at what time.'

'That — I just wanted — we can't act as if we were a board meeting. I want to know your feelings, how you are, what you are thinking, so that I can help you, so that eventually you will be able to live a normal life again.'

He was timing it so that he answered almost at once, 'I am not suffering from any mental illness, and I have completely recovered my physical health after the crash. There is no reason to foresee that my perceptions will ever lapse back into phase with yours. They have remained an unfluctuating 3.3077 minutes ahead of terrestrial time ever since our ship left the surface of Mars.'

He paused. She thought, 'It is now about 11.03 by my watch, and there is so much I long to say. But it's 11.06 and a bit by *his* time, and he already knows I can't say anything. It's such an effort of endurance, talking across this three and a bit minutes; we might just as well be talking across an interstellar distance.'

Evidently he too had lost the thread of the exercise, for he smiled and stretched out a hand, holding it in the air. Janet looked round. Clem Stackpole was coming out towards them with a tray full of drinks. He set it carefully down on the lawn, and picked up a martini, the stem of which he slipped between Jack's fingers.

'Cheers!' he said, smiling, and, 'Here's your tipple', giving Janet her gin and tonic. He had brought himself a bottle of pale ale.

'Can you make my position clearer to Janet, Clem? She does *not* seem to understand it yet.'

Angrily, she turned to the behaviourist. 'This was meant to be a private talk, Mr Stackpole, between my husband and myself.'

'Sorry you're not getting on too well, then. Perhaps I can help sort you out a bit. It is difficult, I know.'

3.3077

Powerfully, he wrenched the top off the beer bottle and poured the liquid into the glass. Sipping, he said, 'We have always been used to the idea that everything moves forward in time at the same rate. We speak of the course of time, presuming it only as one rate of flow. We've assumed, too, that anything living on another planet in any other part of our universe might have the same rate of flow. In other words, although we've long been accustomed to some oddities of time, thanks to relativity theories, we have accustomed ourselves, perhaps, to certain errors of thinking. Now we're going to have to think differently. You follow me.'

'Perfectly.'

'The universe is by no means the simple box our predecessors imagined. It may be that each planet is encased in its own time field, just as it is in its own gravitational field. From the evidence, it seems that

Mars' time field is 3.3077 minutes ahead of ours on Earth. We deduce this from the fact that your husband and the eight other men with him on Mars experienced no sensation of temporal difference among themselves, and were unaware that anything was untoward until they were away from Mars and attempted to get into communication again with Earth, when the temporal discrepancy at once showed up. Your husband is still living in Mars time. Unfortunately, the other members of the crew did not survive the crash; but we can be sure that if they did, they too would suffer from the same effect. That's clear, isn't it?'

'Entirely. But I still cannot see why this effect, if it is as you say—'

'It's not what *I* say, Janet, but the conclusion arrived at by much cleverer men than I.' He smiled as he said that, adding parenthetically, 'Not that we don't develop and even alter our conclusions every day'

'Then why was a similar effect not noticed when the Russians and Americans returned from the moon?'

'We don't know. There's so much we don't know. We *surmise* that because the moon is a satellite of Earth's, and thus within its gravitational field, there is no temporal discrepancy. But until we have more data, until we can explore further, we know so little, and can only speculate so much. It's like trying to estimate the runs of an entire innings when only one over has been bowled. After the expedition gets back from Venus, we shall be in a much better position to start theorising.'

'*What* expedition to Venus?' she asked, shocked.

'It may not leave for a year yet, but they're speeding up the programme. That will bring us really invaluable data.'

Future time with its uses and abuses

She started to say, 'But after this surely they won't be fool enough—' Then she stopped. She knew they would be fool enough. She thought of Peter saying, 'I'm going to be a spaceman too. *I* want to be the first man on Saturn!'

The men were looking at their watches. Westermark transferred his gaze to the gravel to say, 'This figure of 3.3077 is surely not a universal constant. It may vary—I think it will vary—from planetary body to planetary body. My private opinion is that it is bound to be connected with solar activity in some way. If that is so, then we may find that the men returning from Venus will be perceiving on a continuum slightly in arrears of Earth time.'

He stood up suddenly, looking dismayed, the absorption gone from his face.

'That's a point that hadn't occurred to me,' Stackpole said, making a note. 'If the expedition to Venus is primed with these points beforehand, we should have no trouble about organising their return. Ultimately, this confusion will be sorted out, and I've no doubt that it will eventually vastly enrich the culture of mankind. The possibilities are of such enormity that . . .'

'It's awful! You're all crazy!' Janet exclaimed. She jumped up and hurried off towards the house.

Or then again

Jack began to move after her towards the house. By his watch, which showed Earth time, it was 11.18 and twelve seconds; he thought, not for the first time, that he would invest in another watch, which would be strapped to his right wrist and show Martian time. No, the one on his left wrist should show Martian time, for that was the wrist he principally consulted and the time by which he lived, even when going through the business of communicating with the earth-bound human race.

He realised he was now moving ahead of Janet, by her reckoning. It would be interesting to have someone ahead of *him* in perception; then he would wish to converse, would want to go to the labour of it. Although it would rob him of the sensation that he was perpetually first in the universe, first everywhere, with everything dewy in that strange light—Mars-light! He'd call it that, till he had it classified, the romantic vision preceding the scientific, with a touch of the grand permissible before the steadying discipline closed in. Or then again, suppose they were wrong in their theories, and the perceptual effect was some freak of the long space journey itself; supposing time were quantal . . . Supposing *all* time were quantal. After all, ageing was a matter of steps, not a smooth progress, for much of the inorganic world as for the organic.

Now he was standing quite still on the lawn. The glaze was coming through the grass, making it look brittle, almost tingeing each blade with a tiny spectrum of light. If his perceptual time were further ahead than it was now, would the Mars' light be stronger, the Earth more translucent? How beautiful it would look! After a longer star journey one would return to a cobweb of a world, centuries behind one in perceptual time, a mere embodiment of light, a prism. Hungrily, he visualised it. But they needed more knowledge.

Suddenly he thought, 'If I could get on the Venus expedition! If the Institute's right, I'd be perhaps six, say five and a half—no, one can't say—but I'd be ahead of Venerean time. I *must* go. I'd be valuable to them. I only have to volunteer, surely.'

He did not notice Stackpole touch his arm in cordial fashion and go past him into the house. He stood looking at the ground and through it, to the stoney vales of Mars and the unguessable landscapes of Venus.

The figures move

Janet had consented to ride into town with Stackpole. He was collecting his cricket shoes, which had been restudded; she thought she might buy a roll of film for her camera. The children would like photos of her and Daddy together. Standing together.

As the car ran beside trees, their shadows flickered red and green before her vision. Stackpole held the wheel very capably, whistling under his breath. Strangely, she did not resent a habit she would normally have found irksome, taking it as a sign that he was not entirely at his ease.

'I have an awful feeling you now understand my husband better than I do,' she said.

He did not deny it. 'Why do you feel that?'

'I believe he does not mind the terrible isolation he must be experiencing.'

'He's a brave man.'

Westermark had been home a week now. Janet saw that each day they were more removed from each other, as he spoke less and stood frequently as still as a statue, gazing at the ground raptly. She thought of something she had once been afraid to utter aloud to her mother-in-law; but with Clem Stackpole she was safer.

'You know why we manage to exist in comparative harmony,' she aid. He was slowing the car, half-looking at her. 'We only manage to exist by banishing all events from our lives, all children, all seasons. Otherwise we'd be faced at every moment with the knowledge of how much at odds we really are.'

Catching the note in her voice, Stackpole said soothingly, 'You are every bit as brave as he is, Janet.'

'Damn being brave. What I can't bear is—nothing!'

Seeing the sign by the side of the road, Stackpole glanced into his driving mirror and changed gear. The road was deserted in front as well as behind. He whistled through his teeth again, and Janet felt compelled to go on talking.

'We've already interfered with time too much—all of us, I mean. Time is a European invention. Goodness knows how mixed up in it we are going to get if—well, if this goes on.' She was irritated by the lack of her usual coherence.

As Stackpole spoke next, he was pulling the car into a lay-by, stopping it by overhanging bushes. He turned to her, smiling tolerantly. 'Time was God's invention, if you believe in God, as I prefer to do. We observe it, tame it, exploit it where possible.'

'Exploit it!'

'You mustn't think of the future as if we were all wading knee-deep in treacle or something.' He laughed briefly, resting his hands on the steering wheel. 'What lovely weather it is! I was wondering—on Sunday I'm playing cricket over in the village. Would you like to come and watch the match? And perhaps we could have tea somewhere afterwards.'

All events, all children, all seasons

She had a letter next morning from Jane, her five-year-old daughter, and it made her think. All the letter said was: 'Dear Mummy, Thank you for the dollies. With love from Jane', but Janet knew the labour that had gone into the inch-high letters. How long could she bear to leave the children away from their home and her care?

As soon as the thought emerged, she recalled that during the previous evening she had told herself nebulously that if there was going to be 'anything' with Stackpole, it was as well the children would be out of the way—purely, she now realised, for her convenience and for Stackpole's. She had not thought then about the children; she had thought about Stackpole who, despite the unexpected delicacy he had shown, was not a man she cared for.

'And another intolerably immoral thought,' she muttered unhappily to the empty room, 'what alternative have I to Stackpole?'

She knew Westermark was in his study. It was a cold day, too cold and damp for him to make his daily parade round the garden. She knew he was sinking deeper into isolation, she longed to help, she feared to sacrifice herself to that isolation, longed to stay outside it, in life.

Dropping the letter, she held her head in her hands, closing her eyes as in the curved bone of her skull she heard all her possible courses of action jar together, future lifelines that annihilated each other.

As Janet stood transfixed, Westermark's mother came into the room. 'I was looking for you,' she said. 'You're so unhappy, my dear, aren't you?'

'Mother, people always try and hide from others how they suffer. Does everyone do it?'

'You don't have to hide it from me—chiefly, I suppose, because you can't.'

'But I don't know how much *you* suffer, and it ought to work both ways. Why do we do this awful covering up? What are we afraid of— pity or derision?'

'Help, perhaps.'

'Help! Perhaps you're right . . . That's a disconcerting thought.'

They stood there staring at each other, until the older woman said, awkwardly, 'We don't often talk like this, Janet.'

'No.' She wanted to say more. To a stranger in a train, perhaps she would have done; here, she could not deliver.

Seeing nothing more was to be said on that subject, Mrs Westermark said, 'I was going to tell you, Janet, that I thought perhaps it would be better if the children didn't come back here while things are as they are. If you want to go and see them and stay with them at your parents' house, I can look after Jack and Mr Stackpole for a week. I don't think Jack wants to see them.'

'That's very kind, Mother. I'll see. I promised Clem—well, I told Mr Stackpole that perhaps I'd go and watch him play cricket tomorrow afternoon. It's not important, of course, but I did say—anyhow, I might drive over and see the children on Monday, if you could hold the fort.'

'You've still plenty of time if you feel like going today. I'm sure Mr Stackpole will understand your maternal feelings.'

'I'd prefer to leave it till Monday,' Janet said— a little distantly, for she suspected now the motive behind her mother-in-law's suggestion.

Where the Scientific American *did not reach*

Jack Westermark put down the *Scientific American* and stared at the table top. With his right hand, he felt the beat of his heart. In the magazine was an article about him, illustrated with photographs of him taken at the Research Hospital. This thoughtful article was far removed from the sensational pieces that had appeared elsewhere, the shallow things that referred to him as The Man That Has Done More Than Einstein To Wreck Our Cosmic Picture; and for that very reason it was the more startling, and presented some aspects of the matter that Westermark himself had not considered.

As he thought over its conclusions, he rested from the effort of reading terrestrial books, and Stackpole sat by the fire, smoking a cigar and waiting to take Westermark's dictation. Even reading a magazine represented a feat in space-time, a collaboration, a conspiracy. Stackpole turned the pages at timed intervals, Westermark read when they lay flat. He was unable to turn them when, in their own narrow continuum, they were not being turned; to his fingers, they lay under the jelly-like glaze, that visual hallucination that represented an unconquerable cosmic inertia.

The inertia gave a special shine to the surface of the table as he stared into it and probed into his own mind to determine the truths of the *Scientific American* article.

The writer of the article began by considering the facts and observing that they tended to point towards the existence of 'local times' throughout the universe; and that if this were so, a new explanation might be forthcoming for the recession of the galaxies and different estimates arrived at for the age of the universe (and of course for its complexity). He then proceeded to deal with the problem that vexed other writers on the subject: namely, why, if Westermark lost Earth time on Mars, he had not reciprocally lost Mars time back on Earth. This, more than anything, pointed to the fact that 'local times' were not purely mechanistic but to some extent at least a psychobiological function.

In the table top, Westermark saw himself being asked to travel again to Mars, to take part in a second expedition to those continents of russet sand where the fabric of space-time was in some mysterious and insuperable fashion 3.3077 minutes ahead of Earth norm. Would his interior clock leap forward again? What then of the sheen on things earthly? And what would be the effect of gradually drawing away from the iron laws under which, since its scampering Pleistocene infancy, humankind had lived?

Impatiently he thrust his mind forward to imagine the day when Earth harboured many local times, gleaned from voyages across the vacancies of space; those vacancies lay across time, too, and that little-understood concept (McTaggart had denied its external reality, hadn't he?) would come to lie within the grasp of man's understanding. Wasn't that the ultimate secret, to be able to understand the flux in which existence is staged, as a dream is staged in the primitive reaches of the mind?

And— But— Would not that day bring the annihilation of Earth's local time? That was what he had started. It could only mean that 'local time' was not a product of planetary elements; there the writer of the *Scientific American* article had not dared to go far enough; local time was entirely a product of the psyche. That dark innermost thing that could keep accurate time even while a man lay unconscious was a mere provincial; but it could be educated to be a citizen of the universe. He saw that he was the first of a new race, unimaginable in the wildest mind a few months previously. He was independent of the enemy that, more than Death, menaced contemporary man: Time. Locked within him was an entirely new potential. Superman had arrived.

Painfully, Stackpole stirred in his seat. He sat so wrapt for so long that his limbs grew stiff and dead without his noticing it.

Universal thoughts may occur if one times carefully enough one's circumbendibus about a given table

'Dictation,' he said, and waited impatiently until the command had penetrated backwards to the limbo by the fire where Stackpole sat. What he had to say was so terribly important—yet it had to wait on these people . . .

As was his custom, he rose and began to walk round the table, speaking in phrases quickly delivered. This was to be the testament of the new way of life . . .

'Consciousness is not expendable but concurrent . . . There may have been many time nodes at the beginning of the human race . . . The mentally deranged often revert to different time rates. For some, a day seems to stretch on for ever . . . We know by experience that for children time is seen in the convex mirror of consciousness, enlarged and distorted beyond its focal point . . .' He was momentarily irritated by the scared face of his wife appearing outside the study window, but he brushed it away and continued.

'. . . its focal point . . . Yet man in his ignorance has persisted in pretending time was some sort of uni-directional flow, and homogenous as that . . . despite the evidence to the contrary . . . Our conception of ourselves—no, this erroneous conception has become a basic life assumption . . .'

Daughters of daughters

Westermark's mother was not given to metaphysical speculation, but as she was leaving the room, she turned and said to her daughter-in-law, 'You know what I sometimes think? Jack is so strange, I wonder at nights if men and women aren't getting more and more apart in thought and in their ways with every generation—you know, almost like separate species. My generation made a great attempt to bring the two sexes together in equality and all the rest, but it seems to have come to nothing.'

'Jack will get better,' Janet could hear the lack of confidence in her own voice.

'I thought the same thing—about men and women getting wider apart I mean—when my husband was killed.'

Suddenly all Janet's sympathy was gone. She had recognised a familiar topic drifting on to the scene, knew well the careful tone that ironed away all self-pity as her mother-in-law said, 'Bob was dedicated to speed, you know. That was what killed him really, not the fool backing into the road in front of him.'

'No blame was attached to your husband,' Janet said. 'You should try not to let it worry you still.'

'You see the connection though . . . This progress thing. Bob so crazy to get round the next bend first, and now Jack . . . Oh well, there's nothing a woman can do.'

She closed the door behind her. Absently, Janet picked up the message from the next generation of women: 'Thank you for the dollies.'

The resolves and the sudden risks involved

He was their father. Perhaps Jane and Peter should come back, despite the risks involved. Anxiously, Janet stood there, moving herself with sudden resolve to tackle Jack straight away. He was so irritable, so unapproachable, but at least she could observe how busy he was before interrupting him.

As she slipped into the side hall and made for the back door, she heard her mother-in-law call her. 'Just a minute!' she answered.

The sun had broken through, sucking moisture from the damp garden. It was now unmistakably autumn. She rounded the corner of the house, stepped round the rose bed, and looked into her husband's study.

Shaken, she saw he leaned half over the table. His hands were over his face, blood ran between his fingers and dripped on to an open magazine on the table top. She was aware of Stackpole sitting indifferently beside the electric fire.

She gave a small cry and ran round the house again, to be met at the back door by Mrs Westermark.

'Oh, I was just—Janet, what is it?'

'Jack, Mother! He's had a stroke or something terrible!'

'But how do you know?'

'Quick, we must phone the hospital—I must go to him.'

Mrs Westermark took Janet's arm. 'Perhaps we'd better leave it to Mr Stackpole, hadn't we? I'm afraid—'

'Mother, we must do what we can. I know we're amateurs. Please let me go.'

'No, Janet, we're—it's *their* world. I'm frightened. They'll come if they want us.' She was gripping Janet in her fright. Their wild eyes stared momentarily at each other as if seeing something else, and then Janet snatched herself away. 'I must go to him,' she said.

She hurried down the hall and pushed open the study door. Her husband stood now at the far end of the room by the window, while blood streamed from his nose.

'Jack!' she exclaimed. As she ran towards him, a blow from the empty air struck her on the forehead, so that she staggered aside, falling against a bookcase. A shower of smaller volumes from the upper shelf fell on her and round her. Exclaiming, Stackpole dropped his notebook and ran round the table to her. Even as he went to her aid, he noted the time from his watch: 10.24.

Aid after 10.24 and the tidiness of bed

Westermark's mother appeared in the doorway.

'Stay where you are,' Stackpole shouted, 'or there will be more trouble! Janet, you see what you've done. Get out of here, will you? Jack, I'm right with you—God knows what you've felt, isolated without aid for three and a third minutes!' Angrily, he want across and stood within arm's length of his patient. He threw his handkerchief down on to the table.

'Mr Stackpole—' Westermark's mother said tentatively from the door, an arm round Janet's waist.

He looked back over his shoulder only long enough to say, 'Get towels! Phone the Research Hospital for an ambulance and tell them to be here right away.'

By midday, Westermark was tidily in bed upstairs and the ambulance staff, who had treated him for what after all was only a nosebleed, had left. Stackpole, as he turned from closing the front door, eyed the two women.

'I feel it is my duty to warn you,' he said heavily, 'that another incident such as this might well prove fatal. This time we escaped very lightly. If anything else of this sort happens, I shall feel obliged to recommend to the board that Mr Westermark is moved back to the hospital.'

Current way to define accidents

'He wouldn't want to go,' Janet said. 'Besides, you are being absurd; it was entirely an accident. Now I wish to go upstairs and see how he is.'

'Just before you go, may I point out that what happened was *not* an accident—or not as we generally define accidents, since you saw the results of your interference through the study window before you entered. Where you were to blame—'

'But that's absurd—' both women began to once. Janet went on to say, 'I never would have rushed into the room as I did had I not seen through the window that he was in trouble.'

'What you saw was the result on your husband of your later interference.'

In something like a wail, Westermark's mother said, 'I don't understand any of this. What did Janet bump into when she ran in?'

'She ran, Mrs Westermark, into the spot where her husband had been standing 3.3077 minutes earlier. Surely by now you have grasped this elementary business of time inertia?'

When they both started speaking at once, he stared at them until they stopped and looked at him. Then he said, 'We had better go into the living-room. Speaking for myself, I would like a drink.'

He helped himself, and not until his hand was round a glass of whisky did he say, 'Now, without wishing to lecture to you ladies, I think it is high time you both realised that you are not living in the old safe world of classical mechanics ruled over by a god invented by eighteenth-century enlightenment. All that has happened here is perfectly rational, but if you are going to pretend it is beyond your female understandings—'

'Mr Stackpole,' Janet said sharply. 'Can you please keep to the point without being insulting? Will you tell me why what happened was not an accident? I understand now that when I looked through the study window I saw my husband suffering from a collision that to him had happened three and something minutes before and to me would not happen for another three and something minutes, but at that moment I was so startled that I forgot—'

'No, no, your figures are wrong. The *total* time lapse is only 3.3077 minutes. When you saw your husband, he had been hit half that time— 1.65385 minutes—ago, and there was another 1.65385 minutes to go before you completed the action by bursting into the room and striking him.'

'But she *didn't* strike him!' the older woman cried.

Firmly, Stackpole diverted his attention long enough to reply. 'She struck him at 10.24 Earth time, which equals 10.20 plus about 36 seconds Mars or his time, which equals 9.59 or whatever Neptune time, which equals 156 and a half Sirius time. It's a big universe, Mrs Westermark! You will remain confused as long as you continue to confuse event with time. May I suggest you sit down and have a drink?'

'Leaving aside the figures,' Janet said, returning to the attack— loathsome opportunist the man was—'how can you say that what happened was no accident? You are not claiming I injured my husband deliberately, I hope? What you say suggests that I was powerless from the moment I saw him through the window.'

'"Leaving aside the figures..."' he quoted. 'That's where your responsibility lies. What you saw through the window was the result of your act; it was by then inevitable that you should complete it, for it had already been completed.'

Through the window, draughts of time blow

'I can't understand!' she clutched her forehead, gratefully accepting a cigarette from her mother-in-law, while shrugging off her consolatory 'Don't try to understand, dear!' 'Supposing when I had seen Jack's nose bleeding, I had looked at my watch and thought, "It's 10.20 or whenever it was, and he may be suffering from my interference, so I'd better not go in", and I *hadn't* gone in? Would his nose then miraculously have healed?'

'Of course not. You take such a mechanistic view of the universe. Cultivate a mental approach, try and live in your own century! You could not think what you suggest because that is not in your nature:

just as it is not in your nature to consult your watch intelligently, just as you always "leave aside the figures", as you say. No, I'm not being personal; it's all very feminine and appealing in a way. What I'm saying is that if *before* you looked into the window you had been a person to think, "However I see my husband now, I must recall he has the additional experience of the next 3.3077 minutes", then you could have looked in and seen him unharmed, and you would not have come bursting in as you did.'

She drew on her cigarette, baffled and hurt. 'You're saying I'm a danger to my own husband.'

'*You're* saying that.'

'God, how I hate men!' she exclaimed. 'You're so bloody logical, so bloody smug!'

He finished his whisky and set the glass down on a table beside her so that he leant close. 'You're upset just now,' he said.

'Of course I'm upset! What do you think?' She fought a desire to cry or slap his face. She turned to Jack's mother, who gently took her wrist.

'Why don't you go off straight away and stay with the children for the weekend, darling? Come back when you feel like it. Jack will be all right and I can look after him—as much as he wants looking after.'

She glanced about the room.

'I will. I'll pack right away. They'll be glad to see me.' As she passed Stackpole on the way out, she said bitterly, 'At least *they* won't be worrying about the local time on Sirius!'

'They may,' said Stackpole, imperturbably from the middle of the room, 'have to one day.'

All events, all children, all seasons

2

JOURNEYS TO THE PAST

'She jumped back hastily to avoid the flood of gleaming coins'—from 'The Courtship of 53 Shotl 9 G' by Eric Frank Russell (*Fantastic*, 1954).

THE CLOCK THAT WENT BACKWARDS

Edward Page Mitchell

Although it is generally accepted that H. G. Wells wrote the first time travel story, the distinction rightly belongs to an almost forgotten American newspaperman and pioneer science fiction writer, Edward Page Mitchell (1852–1927). The US fantasy fiction researcher, Sam Moskowitz, who was largely responsible for unearthing Mitchell's mostly anonymous tales in the pages of Scribner's Monthly *magazine and the New York* Sun, *believes that if he had continued the burst of creativity that occurred during the 1870s and early 1880s he might well have gone down in sf history as 'the American H. G. Wells'. As it is, his pioneering stories from that era have been resurrected and their author's reputation assured: they include 'The Tachypomp' (1874), about a humanoid computer; 'The Man without a Body' (1877), featuring matter transmission; 'The Crystal Man' (1881), a story of invisibility which prefigures Wells' famous novel,* The Invisible Man, *published sixteen years later; and 'The Balloon Tree' (1883), one of the earliest tales of a friendly alien.*

Mitchell was born in Bath, Maine, just a few miles up the American East Coast from Portland where, a century later, today's great writer of horror, Stephen King, first saw the light of day. The young Mitchell began writing while still a student, then in 1874 landed the job of editor of the Lewiston Journal. *He had been in the editorial chair only a few months, however, when he was tragically blinded in one eye in a train accident. During his recuperation, with the use of just one eye he taught himself to write again, creating the first of his imaginative stories, 'The Tachypomp.' He sent it to* Scribner's *where it was immediately accepted. Later he began submitting stories to the New York* Sun, *and these so impressed the paper's owner that in 1875 Mitchell was invited to join the staff. He remained with the* Sun *for the remainder of his journalistic career, and though he published several more ground-breaking sf tales in the paper, pressure of work brought this flow to a halt in the mid-1880s and with that any chance of contemporary fame. He wrote 'The Clock that Went Backwards' for the* Sun *in 1881; in addition to being the first time travel story, it is also one of the very earliest time paradox tales.*

*   *   *

A row of Lombardy poplars stood in front of my Great-Aunt Gertrude's house, on the bank of the Sheepscot River. In personal appearance my aunt was surprisingly like one of those trees. She had the look of hopeless anaemia that distinguishes them from fuller-blooded sorts. She was tall, severe in outline, and extremely thin. Her habiliments clung to her. I am sure that had the gods found occasion to impose upon her the fate of Daphne she would have taken her place easily and naturally in the dismal row, as melancholy a poplar as the rest.

Some of my earliest recollections are of this venerable relative. Alive and dead she bore an important part in the events I am about to recount: events which I believe to be without parallel in the experience of mankind.

During our periodical visits of duty to Aunt Gertrude in Maine, my cousin Harry and myself were accustomed to speculate much on her age. Was she sixty, or was she six score? We had no precise information; she might have been either. The old lady was surrounded by old-fashioned things. She seemed to live altogether in the past. In her short half-hours of communicativeness over her second cup of tea, or on the piazza where the poplars sent slim shadows directly towards the east, she used to tell us stories of her alleged ancestors. I say alleged, because we never fully believed that she had ancestors.

A genealogy is a stupid thing. Here is Aunt Gertrude's, reduced to its simplest forms:

Her great-great-grandmother (1599–1642) was a woman of Holland who married a Puritan refugee, and sailed from Leyden to Plymouth in the ship *Ann* in the year of our Lord 1632. This Pilgrim mother had a daughter, Aunt Gertrude's great-grandmother (1640–1718). She came to the Eastern District of Massachusetts in the early part of the last century, and was carried off by the Indians in the Penobscot wars. Her daughter (1680–1776) lived to see these colonies free and independent, and contributed to the population of the coming republic not less than nineteen stalwart sons and comely daughters. One of the latter (1735–

1802) married a Wiscasset skipper engaged in the West India trade, with whom she sailed. She was twice wrecked at sea—once on what is now Seguin Island and once on San Salvador. It was on San Salvador that Aunt Gertrude was born.

We got to be very tired of hearing this family history. Perhaps it was the constant repetition and the merciless persistency with which the above dates were driven into our young ears that made us sceptics. As I have said, we took little stock in Aunt Gertrude's ancestors. They seemed highly improbable. In our private opinion the great-grandmothers and grandmothers and so forth were pure myths, and Aunt Gertrude herself was the principal in all the adventures attributed to them, having lasted from century to century while generations of contemporaries went the way of all flesh.

On the first landing of the square stairway of the mansion loomed a tall Dutch clock. The case was more than eight feet high, of a dark-red wood, not mahogany, and it was curiously inlaid with silver. No common piece of furniture was this. About a hundred years ago there flourished in the town of Brunswick a horologist named Cary, an industrious and accomplished workman. Few well-to-do houses on that part of the coast lacked a Cary timepiece. But Aunt Gertrude's clock had marked the hours and minutes of two full centuries before the Brunswick artisan was born. It was running when William the Taciturn pierced the dikes to relieve Leyden. The name of the maker, Jan Lipperdam, and the date, 1572, were still legible in broad black letters and figures reaching quite across the dial. Cary's masterpieces were plebeian and recent beside this ancient aristocrat. The jolly Dutch moon, made to exhibit the phases over a landscape of windmills and polders, was cunningly painted. A skilled hand had carved the grim ornament at the top, a death's-head transfixed by a two-edged sword. Like all timepieces of the sixteenth century, it had no pendulum. A simple Van Wyck escapement governed the descent of the weights to the bottom of the tall case.

But these weights never moved. Year after year, when Harry and I returned to Maine, we found the hands of the old clock pointing to the quarter past three, as they had pointed when we first saw them. The fat moon hung perpetually in the third quarter, as motionless as the death's-head above. There was a mystery about the silenced movement and the paralysed hands. Aunt Gertrude told us that the works had never performed their functions since a bolt of lightning entered the clock; and she showed us a black hole in the side of the case near the top, with a yawning rift that extended downwards for several feet. This explanation failed to satisfy us. It did not account for the sharpness of her refusal when we proposed to bring over the watchmaker from the village, or for her singular agitation once when she found Harry on a step-ladder, with a borrowed key in his hand, about to test for himself the clock's suspended vitality.

One August night, after we had grown out of boyhood, I was awakened by a noise in the hallway. I shook my cousin. 'Somebody's in the house,' I whispered.

We crept out of our room and on to the stairs. A dim light came from below. We held our breath and noiselessly descended to the second landing. Harry clutched my arm. He pointed down over the banisters, at the same time drawing me back into the shadow.

We saw a strange thing.

Aunt Gertrude stood on a chair in front of the old clock, as spectral in her white nightgown and white nightcap as one of the poplars when covered with snow. It chanced that the floor creaked slightly under our feet. She turned with a sudden movement, peering intently into the darkness, and holding a candle high towards us, so that the light was full upon her pale face. She looked many years older than when I bade her good-night. For a few minutes she was motionless, except in the trembling arm that held aloft the candle. Then, evidently reassured, she placed the light upon a shelf and turned again to the clock.

We now saw the old lady take a key from behind the face and proceed to wind up the weights. We could hear her breath, quick and short. She rested a hand on either side of the case and held her face close to the dial, as if subjecting it to anxious scrutiny. In this attitude she remained for a long time. We heard her utter a sigh of relief, and she half turned towards us for a moment. I shall never forget the expression of wild joy that transfigured her features then.

The hands of the clock were moving; they were moving backwards.

Aunt Gertrude put both arms around the clock and pressed her withered cheek against it. She kissed it repeatedly. She caressed it in a hundred ways, as if it had been a living and beloved thing. She fondled it and talked to it, using words which we could hear but could not understand. The hands continued to move backwards.

Then she started back with a sudden cry. The clock had stopped. We saw her tall body swaying for an instant on the chair. She stretched out her arms in a convulsive gesture of terror and despair, wrenched the minute hand to its old place at a quarter past three, and fell heavily to the floor.

Aunt Gertrude's will left me her bank and gas stocks, real estate, railroad bonds and city sevens, and gave Harry the clock. We thought at the time that this was a very unequal division, the more surprising because my cousin had always seemed to be the favourite. Half in seriousness we made a thorough examination of the ancient timepiece, sounding its wooden case for secret drawers, and even probing the not complicated works with a knitting needle to ascertain if our whimsical relative had bestowed there some codicil or other document changing the aspect of affairs. We discovered nothing.

There was testamentary provision for our education at the University of Leyden. We left the military school in which we had learned a little of the theory of war, and a good deal of the art of standing with our noses over our heels, and took ship without delay. The clock went with us. Before many months it was established in a corner of a room in the Breede Straat.

The fabric of Jan Lipperdam's ingenuity, thus restored to its native air, continued to tell the hour of quarter past three with its odd fidelity. The author of the clock had been under the sod for nearly three hundred years. The combined skill of his successors in the craft at Leyden could make it go neither forwards nor backwards.

We readily picked up enough Dutch to make ourselves understood by the townspeople, the professors, and such of our eight hundred and odd fellow-students as came into intercourse. This language, which looks so hard at first, is only a sort of polarised English. Puzzle over it a little while and it jumps into your comprehension like one of those simple cryptograms made by running together all the words of a sentence and then dividing in the wrong places.

The language acquired and the newness of our surroundings worn off, we settled into tolerably regular pursuits. Harry devoted himself with some assiduity to the study of sociology, with especial reference to the round-faced and not unkind maidens of Leyden. I went in for the higher metaphysics.

Outside of our respective studies, we had a common ground of unfailing interest. To our astonishment, we found that not one in twenty of the faculty or students knew or cared a stiver about the glorious history of the town, or even about the circumstances under which the university itself was founded by the Prince of Orange. In marked contrast with the general indifference was the enthusiasm of Professor Van Stopp, my chosen guide through the cloudiness of speculative philosophy.

This distinguished Hegelian was a tobacco-dried little old man, with a skullcap over features that reminded me strangely of Aunt Gertrude's. Had he been her own brother the facial resemblance could not have been closer. I told him so once, when we were together in the Stadthuis looking at the portrait of the hero of the siege, the Burgomaster Van der Werf. The professor laughed. 'I will show you what is even a more extraordinary coincidence,' said he; and, leading the way across the hall to the great picture of the siege, by Wanners, he pointed out the figure of a burgher participating in the defence. It was true. Van Stopp might have been the burgher's son; the burgher might have been Aunt Gertrude's father.

The professor seemed to be fond of us. We often went to his rooms in an old house in the Rapenburg Straat, one of the few houses remaining that antedate 1574. He would walk with us through the beautiful suburbs of the city, over straight roads lined with poplars that carried us back to the bank of the Sheepscot in our minds. He took us to the top of the ruined Roman tower in the centre of the town, and from the same battlements from which anxious eyes three centuries ago had watched the slow approach of Admiral Boisot's fleet over the submerged polders, he pointed out the great dike of the Landscheiding, which was cut that the oceans might bring Boisot's Zealanders to raise the leaguer and feed the starving. He showed us the headquarters of the Spaniard Valdez at Leyderdorp, and told us how heaven sent a violent northwest wind on the night of the first of October, piling up the water deep where it had been shallow and sweeping the fleet on between Zoeterwoude and Zwieten up to the very walls of the fort at Lammen, the last stronghold of the besiegers and the last obstacle in the way of succour to the famishing inhabitants. Then he showed us where, on the very night before the retreat of the besieging army, a huge breach was made in the wall of Leyden, near the Cow Gate, by the Walloons from Lammen.

'Why!' cried Harry, catching fire from the eloquence of the professor's narrative, 'that was the decisive moment of the siege.'

The professor said nothing. He stood with his arms folded, looking intently into my cousin's eyes.

'For,' continued Harry, 'had that point not been watched, or had defence failed and the breach been carried by the night assault from Lammen, the town would have been burned and the people massacred under the eyes of Admiral Boisot and the fleet of relief. Who defended the breach?'

Van Stopp replied very slowly, as if weighing every word:

'History records the explosion of the mine under the city wall on the last night of the siege; it does not tell the story of the defence or give the defender's name. Yet no man that ever lived had a more tremendous charge than fate entrusted to this unknown hero. Was it chance that sent him to meet that unexpected danger? Consider some of the consequences had he failed. The fall of Leyden would have destroyed the last hope of the Prince of Orange and of the free states. The tyranny of Philip would have been re-established. The birth of religious liberty and of self-government by the people would have been postponed, who knows for how many centuries? Who knows that there would or could have been a republic of the United States of America had there been no United Netherlands? Our university, which has given to the world Grotius, Scaliger, Arminius and Descartes, was founded upon this hero's successful defence of the breach. We owe to him our presence here today. Nay, you owe to him your very existence. Your ancestors were of Leyden; between their lives and the butchers outside the walls he stood that night.'

The little professor towered before us, a giant of enthusiasm and patriotism. Harry's eyes glistened and his cheeks reddened.

'Go home, boys,' said Van Stopp, 'and thank God that while the burghers of Leyden were straining their gaze towards Zoeterwoude and the fleet, there was one pair of vigilant eyes and one stout heart at the town wall just beyond the Cow Gate!'

The rain was splashing against the windows one evening in the autumn of our third year at Leyden, when Professor Van Stopp honoured us with a visit in the Breede Straat. Never had I seen the old gentleman in such spirits. He talked incessantly. The gossip of the town, the news of Europe, science, poetry, philosophy, were in turn touched upon and treated with the same high and good humour. I sought to draw him out on Hegel, with whose chapter on the complexity and interdependency of things I was just then struggling.

'You do not grasp the return of the Itself into Itself through its Otherself?' he said smiling. 'Well, you will, sometime.'

Harry was silent and preoccupied. His taciturnity gradually affected even the professor. The conversation flagged, and we sat a long while without a word. Now and then there was a flash of lightning succeeded by distant thunder.

'Your clock does not go,' suddenly remarked the professor. 'Does it ever go?'

'Never since we can remember,' I replied. 'That is, only once, and then it went backwards. It was when Aunt Gertrude—'

Here I caught a warning glance from Harry. I laughed and stammered, 'The clock is old and useless. It cannot be made to go.'

'Only backwards?' said the professor, calmly, and not appearing to notice my embarrassment. 'Well, and why should not a clock go backwards? Why should not Time itself turn and retrace its course?'

He seemed to be waiting for an answer. I had none to give.

'I thought you Hegelian enough,' he continued, 'to admit that every condition includes its own contradiction. Time is a condition, not an essential. Viewed from the Absolute, the sequence by which future follows present and present follows past is purely arbitrary. Yesterday, today, tomorrow; there is no reason in the nature of things why the order should not be tomorrow, today, yesterday.'

A sharper peal of thunder interrupted the professor's speculations.

'The day is made by the planet's revolution on its axis from west to east. I fancy you can conceive conditions under which it might turn from east to west, unwinding, as it were, the revolutions of past ages. Is it so much more difficult to imagine Time unwinding itself; Time on the ebb, instead of on the flow; the past unfolding as the future recedes; the centuries countermarching; the course of events proceeding towards the Beginning and not, as now, towards the End?'

'But,' I interposed, 'we know that as far as we are concerned the—'

'We know!' exclaimed Van Stopp, with growing scorn. 'Your intelligence has no wings. You follow in the trail of Comte and his slimy brood of creepers and crawlers. You speak with amazing assurance of your position in the universe. You seem to think that your wretched little individuality has a firm foothold in the Absolute. Yet you go to bed tonight and dream into existence men, women, children, beasts of the past or the future. How do you know that at this moment you yourself, with all your conceit of nineteenth-century thought, are anything more than a creature of a dream of the future, dreamed, let us say, by some philosopher of the sixteenth century? How do you know that you are anything more than a creature of a dream of the past, dreamed by some Hegelian of the twenty-sixth century? How do you know, boy, that you will not vanish into the sixteenth century or 2060 the moment the dreamer awakes?'

There was no replying to this, for it was sound metaphysics. Harry yawned. I got up and went to the window. Professor Van Stopp approached the clock.

'Ah, my children,' said he, 'there is no fixed progress of human events. Past, present and future are woven together in one inextricable mesh. Who shall say that this old clock is not right to go backwards?'

A crash of thunder shook the house. The storm was over our heads.

When the blinding glare had passed away, Professor Van Stopp was standing upon a chair before the tall timepiece. His face looked more than ever like Aunt Gertrude's. He stood as she had stood in that last quarter of an hour when we saw her wind the clock.

The same thought struck Harry and myself.

'Hold!' we cried, as he began to wind the works. 'It may be death if you—'

The professor's sallow features shone with the strange enthusiasm that had transformed Aunt Gertrude's.

'True,' he said, 'it may be death; but it may be the awakening. Past, present, future; all woven together! The shuttle goes to and fro, forward and back—'

He had wound the clock. The hands were whirling around the dial from right to left with inconceivable rapidity. In this whirl we ourselves seemed to be borne along. Eternities seemed to contract into minutes while lifetimes were thrown off at every tick. Van Stopp, both arms outstretched, was reeling in his chair. The house shook again under a tremendous peal of thunder. At the same instant a ball of fire, leaving a wake of sulphurous vapour and filling the room with dazzling light, passed over our heads and smote the clock. Van Stopp was prostrated. The hands ceased to revolve.

The roar of the thunder sounded like heavy cannonading. The lightning's blaze appeared as the steady light of a conflagration. With our hands over our eyes, Harry and I rushed into the night.

Under a red sky people were hurrying towards the Stadthuis. Flames in the direction of the Roman tower told us that the heart of the town was afire. The faces of those we saw were haggard and emaciated. From every side we caught disjointed phrases of complaint or despair. 'Horse-flesh at ten schillings the pound,' said one, 'and bread at sixteen schillings.' 'Bread indeed!' an old woman retorted: 'It's eight weeks gone since I have seen a crumb.' 'My little grandchild, the lame one, went last night.' 'Do you know what Gekke Betje, the washerwoman did? She was starving. Her babe died, and she and her man—'

A louder cannon burst cut short this revelation. We made our way on towards the citadel of the town, passing a few soldiers here and there and many burghers with grim faces under their broad-brimmed felt hats.

'There is bread plenty yonder where the gunpowder is, and full pardon, too. Valdez shot another amnesty over the walls this morning.'

An excited crowd immediately surrounded the speaker. 'But the fleet!' they cried.

'The fleet is grounded fast on the Greenway polder. Boisot may turn his one eye seaward for a wind till famine and pestilence have carried off every mother's son of ye, and his ark will not be a rope's length nearer. Death by plague, death by starvation, death by fire and musketry—that is what the burgomaster offers us in return for glory for himself and kingdom for Orange.'

'He asks us,' said a sturdy citizen, 'to hold out only twenty-four hours longer, and to pray meanwhile for an ocean wind.'

'Ah, yes!' sneered the first speaker. 'Pray on. There is bread enough locked in Pieter Adriaanszoon Van der Werf's cellar. I warrant you that is what gives him so wonderful a stomach for resisting the Most Catholic King.'

A young girl, with braided yellow hair, pressed through the crowd and confronted the malcontent. 'Good people,' said the maiden, 'do not listen to him. He is a traitor with a Spanish heart. I am Pieter's daughter. We have no bread. We ate malt cakes and rapeseed like the rest of you till it was gone. Then we stripped the green leaves from the lime trees and willows in our garden and ate them. We have eaten even the thistles and weeds that grew between the stones by the canal. The coward lies.'

Nevertheless, the insinuation had its effect. The throng, now become a mob, surged off in the direction of the burgomaster's house. One ruffian raised his hand to strike the girl out of the way. In a wink the cur was under the feet of his fellows, and Harry, panting and glowing, stood at the maiden's side, shouting defiance in good English at the backs of the rapidly retreating crowd.

With the utmost frankness she put both her arms around Harry's neck and kissed him.

'Thank you,' she said. 'You are a hearty lad. My name is Gertruyd Van der Werf.'

Harry was fumbling in his vocabulary for the proper Dutch phrases, but the girl would not stay for compliments. 'They mean mischief to my father'; and she hurried us through several exceedingly narrow streets into a three-cornered market-place dominated by a church with two spires. 'There he is,' she exclaimed, 'on the steps of St Pancras.'

There was a tumult in the market-place. The conflagration raging beyond the church and the voices of the Spanish and Walloon cannon outside of the walls were less angry than the roar of this multitude of desperate men clamouring for the bread that a single word from their leader's lips would bring them. 'Surrender to the King!' they cried, 'or we will send your dead body to Lammen as Leyden's token of submission.'

One tall man, taller by half a head than any of the burghers confronting him, and so dark of complexion that we wondered how he could be the father of Gertruyd, heard the threat in silence. When the burgomaster spoke, the mob listened in spite of themselves.

'What is it you ask, my friends? That we break our vow and surrender Leyden to the Spaniards? That is to devote ourselves to a fate far more horrible than starvation. I have to keep the oath! Kill me, if you will have it so. I can die only once, whether by your hands, by the enemy's, or by the hand of God. Let us starve, if we must, welcoming starvation because it comes before dishonour. Your menaces do not move me; my life is at your disposal. Here, take my sword, thrust it into my breast, and divide my flesh among you to appease your hunger. So long as I remain alive expect no surrender.'

There was silence again while the mob wavered. Then there were mutterings around us. Above these rang out the clear voice of the girl whose hand Harry still held—unnecessarily, it seemed to me.

'Do you not feel the sea wind? It has come at last. To the tower! And the first man there will see by moonlight the full white sails of the prince's ships.'

For several hours I scoured the streets of the town, seeking in vain my cousin and his companion; the sudden movement of the crowd towards the Roman tower had separated us. On every side I saw evidences of the terrible chastisement that had brought this stout-hearted people to the verge of despair. A man with hungry eyes chased a lean rat along the bank of the canal. A young mother, with two dead babes in her arms, sat in a doorway to which they bore the bodies of her husband and father, just killed at the walls. In the middle of a deserted street I passed unburied corpses in a pile twice as high as my head. The pestilence had been there—kinder than the Spaniard, because it held out no treacherous promises while it dealt its blows.

Towards morning the wind increased to a gale. There was no sleep in Leyden, no more talk of surrender, no longer any thought or care about defence. These words were on the lips of everybody I met: 'Daylight will bring the fleet!'

Did daylight bring the fleet? History says so, but I was not a witness. I know only that before dawn the gale culminated in a violent thunderstorm, and that at the same time a muffled explosion, heavier than the thunder, shook the town. I was in the crowd that watched from the Roman Mound for the first signs of the approaching relief. The concussion shook hope out of every face. 'Their mine has reached the wall!' But where? I pressed forward until I found the burgomaster, who was standing among the rest. 'Quick!' I whispered. 'It is beyond the Cow Gate, and this side of the Tower of Burgundy.' He gave me a searching glance, and then strode away, without making any attempt to quiet the general panic. I followed close at his heels.

It was a tight run of nearly half a mile to the rampart in question. When we reached the Cow Gate this is what we saw:

A great gap, where the wall had been, opening to the swampy fields beyond: in the moat, outside and below, a confusion of upturned faces, belonging to men who struggled like demons to achieve the breach, and who now gained a few feet and now were forced back; on the shattered rampart a handful of soldiers and burghers forming a living wall where masonry had failed; perhaps a double handful of women and girls, serving stones to the defenders and boiling water in buckets, besides pitch and oil and unslaked lime, and some of them quoiting tarred and burning hoops over the necks of the Spaniards in the moat; my cousin Harry leading and directing the men; the burgomaster's daughter Gertruyd encouraging and inspiring the women.

But what attracted my attention more than anything else was the frantic activity of a little figure in black, who, with a huge ladle, was showering molten lead on the heads of the assailing party. As he turned to the bonfire and kettle which supplied him with ammunition, his features came into the full light. I gave a cry of surprise: the ladler of molten lead was Professor Van Stopp.

The burgomaster Van der Werf turned at my sudden exclamation. 'Who is that?' I said. 'The man at the kettle?'

'That,' replied Van der Werf, 'is the brother of my wife, the clockmaker Jan Lipperdam.'

The affair at the breach was over almost before we had had time to grasp the situation. The Spaniards, who had overthrown the wall of brick and stone, found the living wall impregnable. They could not even maintain their position in the moat; they were driven off into the darkness. Now I felt a sharp pain in my left arm. Some stray missile must have hit me while we watched the fight.

'Who has done this thing?' demanded the burgomaster. 'Who is it that has kept watch on today while the rest of us were straining fools' eyes towards tomorrow?'

Gertruyd Van der Werf came forward proudly, leading my cousin. 'My father,' said the girl, 'he has saved my life.'

'That is much to me,' said the burgomaster, 'but it is not all. He has saved Leyden and he has saved Holland.'

I was becoming dizzy. The faces around me seemed unreal. Why were we here with these people? Why did the thunder and lightning forever continue? Why did the clockmaker, Jan Lipperdam, turn always towards me the face of Professor Van Stopp? 'Harry!' I said, 'come back to our rooms.'

But though he grasped my hand warmly his other hand still held that of the girl, and he did not move. Then nausea overcame me. My head swam, and the breach and its defenders faded from sight.

Three days later I sat with one arm bandaged in my accustomed seat in Van Stopp's lecture room. The place beside me was vacant.

'We hear much,' said the Hegelian professor, reading from a notebook in his usual dry, hurried tone, 'of the influence of the sixteenth century upon the nineteenth. No philosopher, as far as I am aware, has studied the influence of the nineteenth century upon the sixteenth. If cause produces effect, does effect never induce cause? Does the law of heredity, unlike all other laws of this universe of mind and matter, operate in one direction only? Does the descendant owe everything to the ancestor, and the ancestor nothing to the descendant? Does destiny, which may seize upon our existence, and for its own purposes bear us far into the future, never carry us back into the past?'

I went back to my rooms in the Breede Straat, where my only companion was the silent clock.

A GUN FOR DINOSAUR

L. Sprague de Camp

After Wells' The Time Machine, *the best novel of time travel is probably* Lest Darkness Fall *by L. Sprague de Camp in which a time traveller finds himself in sixth-century Rome and there tries to avert the onset of the Dark Ages. The story was first published in the legendary sf pulp magazine,* Unknown, *in 1939, and is described in Clute's and Nicholls'* Encyclopedia of Science Fiction *(1993) as 'the most accomplished early excursion into history in magazine sf . . . regarded as a classic'. De Camp returned to this theme of time travel and history in a number of his later short stories, including 'The Glory that Was' (1952), 'Aristotle and the Gun' (1958) and 'A Gun for Dinosaur'.*

Lyon Sprague de Camp (1907–) originally intended to follow a career in aeronautical engineering; he was educated at the California Institute of Technology and then the Stevens Institute of Technology, where he obtained a masters degree in 1933. For several years he worked as a patents engineer and wrote his first book on this subject, before being attracted to the rich fields of scientific speculation in fictional form, then becoming increasingly popular in pulp magazines such as Super Science Stories, Astounding Science-Fiction *and* Unknown. *De Camp's many subsequent works have included the 'Incomplete Enchanter' series (in collaboration with Fletcher Pratt) featuring Harold Shea and his journeys into various alternate worlds, and the 'Gavagan's Bar' series (also with Pratt), humorous tall stories related by space and time travellers. In 'A Gun for Dinosaur', published in* Galaxy Science Fiction *in March 1956, a group of time travellers are taken back to the very earliest period of Earth's history— that bloody and ferocious era when reptile heavyweights ruled the world . . .*

*   *   *

No, Mr Seligman, I won't take you hunting late-Mesozoic dinosaur.

Why not? How much d'you weigh? A hundred and thirty? Let's see, that's under ten stone, which is my lower limit.

I'll take you to any period in the Cenozoic. I'll get you a shot at an entelodont or a titanothere or a uintathere. There've all got fine heads.

I'll even stretch a point and take you to the Pleistocene, where you can try for one of the mammoths or the mastodon.

I'll take you back to the Triassic where you can shoot one of the smaller ancestral dinosaur.

But I will not—will jolly well not—take you to the Jurassic or Cretaceous. You're just too small.

No offence, of course.

What's your weight got to do with it?

Look here, old boy, what did you think you were going to shoot them with?

You hadn't thought, eh?

Well, sit there a minute . . .

Here you are, my own private gun for that work, a Continental .600. Does look like a shotgun, doesn't it? But it's rifled, as you can see by looking through the barrels. Shoots a pair of .600 nitro express cartridges the size of bananas; weighs fourteen and a half pounds and has a muzzle energy of over seven thousand foot-pounds. Costs fourteen hundred and fifty dollars. Lot of money for a gun, what?

I have some spares I rent to the sahibs. Designed for knocking down elephant. Not just wounding them, knocking them base-over-apex: That's why they don't make guns like this in America, though I suppose they will if hunting parties keep going back in time through Prochaska's machine.

I've been guiding hunting parties for twenty years. Guided 'em in Africa until the game gave out there except on the preserves. That just about ended the world's real big-game hunting.

My point is, all that time I've never known a man your size who could handle the six-nought-nought. It knocks 'em over. Even when they stay on their feet, they get so scared of the bloody cannon after a few shots that they flinch. Can't hit an elephant at spitting range. And they find the gun too heavy to drag around rough Mesozoic country. Wears 'em out.

It's true, lots of people have killed elephant with lighter guns: the .500, .475, and .465 doubles, for instance, or even .375 magnum repeaters. The difference is that with a .375 you have to hit something vital, preferably the heart, and can't depend on simple shock power.

An elephant weighs—let's see—four to six tons. You're planning to shoot reptiles weighing two or three times as much as an elephant and with much greater tenacity of life. That's why the syndicate decided to take no more people dinosaur-hunting unless they could handle the .600. We learned the hard way, as you Americans say. There were some unfortunate incidents . . .

I'll tell you, Mr Seligman. It's after seventeen hundred. Time I closed the office. Why don't we stop at the bar on our way out while I tell you the story?

It was about the Raja's and my fifth safari. The Raja? Oh, he's the Aiyar half of Rivers & Aiyar. I call him the Raja because he's the hereditary monarch of Janpur. Means nothing nowadays, of course. Knew him in India and ran into him in New York running the Indian tourist agency. That dark chap in the photograph on my office wall, the one with his foot on the dead sabre-tooth.

Well, the Raja was fed up with handing out brochures about the Taj Mahal and wanted to do a bit of hunting again. I was at loose ends when we heard of Professor Prochaska's time machine at Washington University.

Where is the Raja? Out on safari in the early Oligocene, after titano-there, while I run the office. We take turns about now, but the first few times we went out together.

Anyhow, we caught the next plane to St Louis. To our mortification, we found we weren't the first.

Lord, no! There were other hunting guides and no end of scientists, each with his own idea of the right use for the machine.

We scraped off the historians and archaeologists right at the start.

Seems the bloody machine won't work for periods more recent than 100,000 years ago. From there, up to about a billion years.

Why? Oh, I'm no four-dimensional thinker, but as I understand it, if people could go back to a more recent time, their actions would affect our own history which would be a paradox or contradiction of facts. Can't have that in a well run universe. But before 100,000 BC, more or less, the actions of the expeditions are lost in the stream of time before human history begins. At that, once a stretch of past time has been used, say the month of January, 1,000,000 BC, you can't use that stretch over again by sending another party into it. Paradoxes again.

But the professor isn't worried; with a billion years to exploit, he won't soon run out of eras.

Another limitation of the machine is the matter of size. For technical reasons, Prochaska had to build the transition chamber just big enough to hold four men with their personal gear, plus the chamber-wallah. Larger parties have to be sent through in relays. That means, you see, it's not practical to take jeeps, boats, aircraft or other powered vehicles.

On the other hand, since you're going to periods without human beings, there's no whistling up a hundred native bearers to trot along with your gear on their heads. So we usually take a train of asses—burros, they call them here. Most periods have enough natural forage to get you where you want to go.

As I say, everybody had his own idea for using the machine. The scientists looked down their noses at us hunters and said it would be a crime to waste the machine's time pandering to our sadistic amusements.

We brought up another angle. The machine cost a cool thirty million. I understand this came from the Rockefeller Board and such people, but that only accounted for the original cost, not the cost of operation. And the thing uses fantastic amounts of power. Most of the scientists' projects, while worthy as worthy could be, were run on a shoestring, financially speaking.

Now we guides catered to people with money, a species with which America seems overstocked. No offence, old boy. Most of these could afford a substantial fee for passing through the machine to the past. Thus we could help finance the operation of the machine for scientific purposes, provided we got a fair share of its time.

Won't go into the details, but in the end the guides formed a syndicate of eight members, one member being the partnership of Rivers & Aiyar, to apportion the machine's time.

We had rush business from the start. Our wives—Raja's and mine—raised bloody hell with us. They'd hoped when the big game gave out they'd never have to share us with lions and things again, but you know how women are. Can't realise hunting's not really dangerous if you keep your head and take precautions.

On the fifth expedition, we had two sahibs to wet-nurse: both Americans in their thirties, both physically sound, and both solvent. Otherwise they were as different as different can be.

Courtney James was what you chaps call a playboy: a rich young man from New York who'd always had his own way and didn't see why that agreeable condition shouldn't continue. A big bloke, almost as big as I am; handsome in a florid way, but beginning to run to fat. He was on his fourth wife, and when he showed up at the office with a blonde with 'model' written all over her, I assumed this was the fourth Mrs James.

'Miss Bartram,' she corrected me, with an embarrassed giggle.

'She's not my wife,' James explained. 'My wife is in Mexico, I think, getting a divorce. But Bunny here would like to go along—'

'Sorry,' I said, 'we don't take ladies. At least not to the late Mesozoic.'

This wasn't strictly true, but I felt we were running enough risks, going after a little-known fauna, without dragging in people's domestic entanglements. Nothing against sex, you understand. Marvellous institution and all that, but not where it interferes with my living.

'Oh, nonsense,' said James. 'If she wants to go, she'll go. She skis and flies my airplane, so why shouldn't she—'

'Against the firm's policy.'

'She can keep out of the way when we run up against the dangerous ones.'

'No, sorry.'

'Damn it,' said he, getting red. 'After all, I'm paying you a goodly sum and I'm entitled to take who I please.'

'You can't hire me to do anything against my best judgement,' I said. 'If that's how you feel, get another guide.'

'All right, I will. And I'll tell all my friends you're a goddamn—' Well, he said a lot of things I won't repeat. It ended with my telling him to get out of the office or I'd throw him out.

I was sitting in the office thinking sadly of all that lovely money James would have paid me if I hadn't been so stiff-necked, when in came my other lamb, one August Holtzinger. This was a little slim pale chap with glasses, polite and formal where the other had been breezily self-confident to the point of obnoxiousness.

Holtzinger sat on the edge of his chair and said: 'Uh—Mr Rivers, I don't want you to think I'm here under false pretences. I'm really not much of an outdoorsman and I'll probably be scared to death when I see a real dinosaur. But I'm determined to hang a dinosaur head over my fireplace or die in the attempt.'

'Most of us are frightened at first,' I soothed him, and little by little I got the story out of him.

*   *   *

While James had always been wallowing in money, Holtzinger was a local product who'd only lately come into the real thing. He'd had a little business here in St Louis and just about made ends meet when an uncle cashed in his chips somewhere and left little Augie the pile.

He'd never been married but had a fiancée. He was building a big house, and when it was finished, they'd be married and move into it. And one furnishing he demanded was a ceratopsian head over the fireplace. Those are the ones with the big horned heads with a parrot beak and frill over the neck, you know. You have to think twice about collecting them, because if you put a seven-foot triceratops head into a small living-room, there's apt to be no room left for anything else.

We were talking about this when in came a girl, a small girl in her twenties, quite ordinary-looking, and crying.

'Augie!' she wept. 'You can't! You mustn't! You'll be killed!' She grabbed him round and said to me: 'Mr Rivers, you mustn't take him! He's all I've got! He'll never stand the hardships!'

'My dear young lady,' I said, 'I should hate to cause you distress, but it's up to Mr Holtzinger to decide whether he wishes to retain my services.'

'It's no use, Claire,' said Holtzinger. 'I'm going, though I'll probably hate every minute of it.'

'What's that, old boy?' I asked. 'If you hate it, why go? Did you lose a bet or something?'

'No,' said Holtzinger. 'It's this way. Uh—I'm a completely undistinguished kind of guy. I'm not brilliant or big or strong or handsome. I'm just an ordinary Midwestern small businessman. You never even notice me at Rotary luncheons, I fit in so perfectly. But that doesn't say I'm satisfied. I've always hankered to go to far places and do big things. I'd like to be a glamorous, adventurous sort of guy. Like you, Mr Rivers.'

'Oh, come,' I protested. 'Professional hunting may seem glamorous to you, but to me it's just a living.'

He shook his head. 'Nope. You know what I mean. Well, now I've got this legacy, I could settle down to play bridge and golf the rest of my life and try to act like I wasn't bored. But I'm determined to do something big for once. Since there's no more real big-game hunting, I'm gonna shoot a dinosaur and hang his head over my mantel. I'll never be happy otherwise.'

Well, Holtzinger and his girl, whose name was Roche, argued, but he wouldn't give in. She made me swear to take the best care of her Augie and departed, sniffling.

When Holtzinger had left, who should come in but my vile-tempered friend Courtney James. He apologised for insulting me, though you could hardly say he grovelled.

'I don't actually have a bad temper,' he said, 'except when people won't co-operate with me. Then I sometimes get mad. But so long as they're co-operative, I'm not hard to get along with.'

I knew that by 'co-operate' he meant to do whatever Courtney James wanted, but I didn't press the point. 'How about Miss Bartram?' I asked.

'We had a row,' he said. 'I'm through with women. So if there's no hard feelings, let's go on from where we left off.'

'Absolutely,' I agreed, business being business.

The Raja and I decided to make it a joint safari to eighty-five million years ago: the early upper Cretaceous, or the middle Cretaceous, as some American geologists call it. It's about the best period for dinosaur in Missouri. You'll find some individual species a little larger in the late upper Cretaceous, but the period we were going to gives a wider variety.

Now, as to our equipment, the Raja and I each had a Continental .600 like the one I showed you and a few smaller guns. At this time, we hadn't worked up much capital and had no spare .600s to rent.

August Holtzinger said he would rent a gun, as he expected this to be his only safari and there was no point in spending over a thousand dollars for a gun he'd shoot only a few times. But since we had no spare .600s, his choice was between buying one of those and renting one of our smaller pieces.

We drove into the country to let him try the .600. We set up a target. Holtzinger heaved up the gun as if it weighed a ton and let fly. He missed completely and the kick knocked him flat on his back with his legs in the air.

He got up, looking paler than ever, and handed me back the gun, saying: 'Uh—I think I'd better try something smaller.'

When his shoulder stopped being sore, I tried him out on the smaller rifles. He took a fancy to my Winchester 70, chambered for the .375 magnum cartridge. It's an excellent all-round gun—

What's it like? A conventional magazine rifle with a Mauser-type bolt action. It's perfect for the big cats and bears, but a little light for elephant and very definitely light for dinosaur. I should never have given in, but I was in a hurry and it might have taken months to get him a new .600. They're made to order, you know, and James was getting impatient. James already had a gun, a Holland & Holland .500 double express. With 5,700 foot-pounds of muzzle energy, it's almost in a class with the .600.

Both sahibs had done a bit of shooting, so I didn't worry about their accuracy. Shooting dinosaur is not a matter of extreme accuracy but of sound judgement and smooth co-ordination so you shan't catch twigs in the mechanism of your gun, or fall into holes, or climb a small tree the dinosaur can pluck you out of, or blow your guide's head off.

People used to hunting mammals sometimes try to shoot a dinosaur in the brain. That's the silliest thing you can do, because dinosaur haven't got any. To be exact, they have a little lump of tissue about the size of a tennis ball on the front end of their spines, and how are you going to hit that when it's embedded in a moving six-foot skull?

The only safe rule with dinosaur is—always try for a heart shot. They have big hearts, over a hundred pounds in the largest species, and a couple of .600 slugs through the heart will kill them just as dead as a smaller beast. The problem is to get the slugs through that mountain of muscle and armour around it.

Well, we appeared at Prochaska's laboratory one rainy morning: James and Holtzinger, the Raja and I, our herder Beauregard Black, three helpers, a cook and twelve jacks. Burros, that is.

The transition chamber is a little cubby-hole the size of a small lift. My routine is for the men with the guns to go first in case a hungry theropod might be standing in front of the machine when it arrived. So the two sahibs, the Raja and I crowded into the chamber with our guns and packs. The operator squeezed in after us, closed the door, and fiddled with his dials. He set the thing for April twenty-fourth, 85,000,000 BC, and pressed the red button.

The lights went out, leaving the chamber lit by a little battery-operated lamp. James and Holtzinger looked pretty green, but that may have been the dim lighting. The Raja and I had been through all this before, so the vibration and vertigo didn't bother us.

I could see the little black hands of the dials spinning round, some slowly and some so fast they were a blur. Then they slowed down and stopped. The operator looked at his ground-level gauge and turned a hand-wheel that raised the chamber so it shouldn't materialise underground. Then he pressed another button and the door slid open.

No matter how often I do it, I get a frightful thrill out of stepping into a bygone era. The operator had raised the chamber a foot above ground level, so I jumped down, my gun ready. The others came after. We looked back at the chamber, a big shiny cube hanging in mid-air a foot off the ground, with this little lift-door in front.

'Right-ho,' I told the chamber-wallah, and he closed the door. The chamber disappeared and we looked around. The scene hadn't changed from my last expedition to this era, which had ended, in Cretaceous time, five days before this one began. There wasn't any dinosaur in sight, nothing but lizards.

In this period, the chamber materialises on top of a rocky rise from which you can see in all directions as far as the haze will let you.

To the west, you see the arm of the Kansas Sea that reaches across Missouri and the big swamp around the bayhead where the sauropods live. It used to be thought the sauropods became extinct before the Cretaceous, but that's not so. They were more limited in range because swamps and lagoons didn't cover so much of the world, but there were plenty of them if you knew where to look.

To the north is a low range that the Raja named the Janpur Hills after the little Indian kingdom his forebears had ruled. To the east, the land slopes up to a plateau, good for ceratopsians, while to the south is flat country with more sauropod swamps and lots of ornithopods: duckbills and iguanadonts.

The finest thing about the Cretaceous is the climate: balmy, like the South Sea Islands, with little seasonal change, but not so muggy as most Jurassic climates. We happened to be there in spring, with dwarf magnolias in bloom all over, but the air feels like spring almost any time of year.

A thing about this landscape is that it combines a fairly high rainfall with an open type of vegetation cover. That is, the grasses hadn't yet evolved to the point of forming solid carpets over all open ground, so the ground is thick with laurel, sassafras and other shrubs, with bare ground between. There are big thickets of palmettos and ferns. The trees round the hill are mostly cycads, standing singly and in copses. Most people call them palms, though my scientific friends tell me they're not true palms.

Down towards the Kansas Sea are more cycads and willows, while the uplands are covered with screw-pine and ginkgos.

Now I'm no bloody poet—the Raja writes the stuff, not me—but I can appreciate a beautiful scene. One of the helpers had come through the machine with two of the jacks and was pegging them out, and I was looking through the haze and sniffing the air, when a gun went off behind me—*bang! bang!*

I turned round and there was Courtney James with his .500 and an ornithomime legging it for cover fifty yards away. The ornithomimes are medium-sized running dinosaurs, slender things with long necks and legs, like a cross between a lizard and an ostrich. This kind is about seven feet tall and weighs as much as a man. The beggar had wandered out of the nearest copse and James gave him both barrels. Missed.

I was a bit upset, as trigger-happy sahibs are as much a menace as those who get panicky and freeze or bolt. I yelled:

'Damn it, you idiot, I thought you weren't to shoot without word from me!'

'And who the hell are you to tell me when I'll shoot my own gun?' he demanded.

We had a rare old row until Holtzinger and the Raja got us calmed down.

I explained: 'Look here, Mr James, I've got reasons. If you shoot off all your ammunition before the trip's over, your gun won't be available in a pinch and it's the only one of its calibre. Second, if you empty both barrels at an unimportant target, what would happen if a big theropod charged before you could reload? Finally, it's not sporting to shoot everything in sight. I'll shoot for meat, or for trophies, or to defend myself, but not just to hear the gun go off. If more people had exercised moderation in killing, there'd still be decent sport in our own era. Understand?'

'Yeah, I guess so,' he said. Mercurial sort of bloke.

The rest of the party came through the machine and we pitched our camp a safe distance from the materialising place. Our first task was to get fresh meat. For a twenty-one-day safari like this, we calculate our food requirements closely so we can make out on tinned stuff and concentrates if we must, but we count on killing at least one piece of meat. When that's butchered, we go on a short tour, stopping at four or five camping places to hunt and arriving back at base a few days before the chamber is due to appear.

Holtzinger, as I said, wanted a ceratopsian head, any kind. James insisted on just one head: a tyrannosaur. Then everybody'd think he'd shot the most dangerous game of all time.

Fact is, the tyrannosaur's overrated. He's more a carrion-eater than an active predator, though he'll snap you up if he gets the chance. He's less dangerous than some of the other theropods—the flesh-eaters—such as the big saurophagus of the Jurassic, or even the smaller gorgosaurus from the period we were in. But everybody's read about the tyrant lizard and he does have the biggest head of the theropods.

The one in our period isn't the rex, which is later and a little bigger and more specialised. It's the trionyches with the forelimbs not reduced to quite such little vestiges, though they're too small for anything but picking the brute's teeth after a meal.

When camp was pitched, we still had the afternoon, so the Raja and I took our sahibs on their first hunt. We already had a map of the local terrain from previous trips.

The Raja and I have worked out a system for dinosaur-hunting. We split into two groups of two men and walk parallel from twenty to forty yards apart. Each group consists of one sahib in front and one guide following and telling the sahib where to go.

We tell the sahibs we put them in front so they shall have first shot, which is true, but another reason is they're always tripping and falling with their guns cocked, and if the guide were in front, he'd get shot.

The reason for two groups is that if a dinosaur starts for one, the other gets a good heart shot from the side.

As we walked, there was the usual rustle of lizards scuttling out of the way; little fellows, quick as a flash and coloured like all the jewels in Tiffany's, and big grey ones that hiss and plod off. There were tortoises and a few little snakes. Birds with beaks full of teeth flapped off squawking. And always that marvellous mild Cretaceous air. Makes a chap want to take his clothes off and dance with vine leaves in his hair, if you know what I mean. Not that I'd ever do such a thing, you understand.

Our sahibs soon found that Mesozoic country is cut up into millions of nullahs—gullies, you'd call them. Walking is one long scramble, up and down, up and down.

We'd been scrambling for an hour and the sahibs were soaked with sweat and had their tongues hanging out, when the Raja whistled. He'd spotted a group of bonehead feeding on cycad shoots.

These are the troödonts, small ornithopods about the size of men with a bulge on top of their heads that makes them look quite intelligent. Means nothing, because the bulge is solid bone and the brain is as small as in other dinosaur, hence the name. The males butt each other with these heads in fighting over the females. They munch a shoot, then stand up and look round. They're warier than most dinosaur because they're the favourite food of the big theropods.

People sometimes assume that because dinosaur are so stupid, their senses must be dim, but it's not so. Some, like the sauropods, are pretty dim-sensed, but most have good smell and eyesight and fair hearing. Their weakness is that, having no minds, they have no memories; hence, out of sight, out of mind. When a big theropod comes slavering after you, your best defence is to hide in nullah or behind a bush, and if he can neither see nor smell you, he'll just forget all about you and wander off.

We sneaked up behind a patch of palmetto downwind from the bone-head. I whispered to James: 'You've had a shot already today. Hold your fire until Holtzinger shoots and then shoot only if he misses or if the beast is getting away wounded.'

'Uh-huh,' said James and we separated, he with the Raja and Holtzinger with me. This got to be our regular arrangement. James and I got on each other's nerves, but the Raja, once you forget that Oriental-potentate rot, is a friendly, sentimental sort of bloke nobody can help liking.

Well, we crawled round the palmetto patch on opposite sides and Holtzinger got up to shoot. You daren't shoot a heavy-calibre rifle prone. There's not enough give and the kick can break your shoulder.

Holtzinger sighed round the last few fronds of palmetto. I saw his barrel wobbling and weaving and then off went James' gun, both barrels again. The biggest bonehead went down, rolling and thrashing, and the others ran on their hindlegs in great leaps, their heads jerking and their tails sticking up behind.

'Put your gun on safety,' I said to Holtzinger, who'd started forward. By the time we got to the bonehead, James was standing over it, breaking open his gun and blowing out the barrels. He looked as smug as if he'd inherited another million and he was asking the Raja to take his picture with his foot on the game. His first shot had been excellent, right through the heart. His second had missed because the first knocked the beast down. James couldn't resist that second shot even when there was nothing to shoot at.

I said: 'I thought you were to give Holtzinger first shot.'

'Hell, I waited,' he said, 'and he took so long, I thought something must have gone wrong. If we stood around long enough, they'd see us or smell us.'

There was something in what he said, but his way of saying it got me angry. I said: 'If that sort of thing happens just once more, we'll leave you in camp the next time we go out.'

'Now, gentlemen,' said the Raja. 'After all, Reggie, these aren't experienced hunters.'

'What now?' asked Holtzinger. 'Haul the beast back ourselves or send out the men?'

'I think we can sling him under the pole,' I said. 'He weighs under two hundred.' The pole was a telescoping aluminium carrying pole I had in my pack, with yokes on the ends with sponge-rubber padding. I brought it along because in such eras you can't always count on finding saplings strong enough for proper poles on the spot.

The Raja and I cleaned our bonehead, to lighten him, and tied him to the pole. The flies began to light on the offal by thousands. Scientists say they're not true flies in the modern sense, but they look and act like them. There's one conspicuous kind of carrion fly, a big four-winged insect with a distinctive deep note as it flies.

The rest of the afternoon, we sweated under that pole. We took turns about, one pair carrying the beast while the other two carried the guns. The lizards scuttled out of the way and the flies buzzed round the carcass.

When we got to camp, it was nearly sunset. We felt as if we could eat the whole bonehead at one meal. The boys had the camp running smoothly, so we sat down for our tot of whiskey feeling like lords of creation while the cook broiled bonehead steaks.

Holtzinger said: 'Uh—if I kill a ceratopsian, how do we get his head back?'

I explained: 'If the ground permits, we lash it to the patent aluminium roller-frame and sled it in.'

'How much does a head like that weigh?' he asked.

'Depends on the age and the species,' I told him. 'The biggest weigh over a ton, but most run between five hundred and a thousand pounds.'

'And all the ground's rough like today?'

'Most of it. You see, it's the combination of the open vegetation cover and the high rainfall. Erosion is frightfully rapid.'

'And who hauls the head on its little sled?'

'Everybody with a hand. A big head would need every ounce of muscle in this party and even then we might not succeed. On such a job, there's no place for side.'

'Oh,' said Holtzinger. I could see him wondering whether a ceratopsian head would be worth the effort.

The next couple of days, we trekked round the neighbourhood. Nothing worth shooting; only a herd of fifty-odd ornithomimes who went bounding off like a lot of bloody ballet dancers. Otherwise there were only the usual lizards and pterosaurs and birds and insects. There's a big lace-winged fly that bites dinosaurs, so you can imagine its beak makes nothing of a human skin. One made Holtzinger leap into the air when it bit through his shirt. James joshed him about it, saying: 'What's all the fuss over one little bug?'

The second night, during the Raja's watch, James gave a yell that brought us all out of our tents with rifles. All that had happened was that a dinosaur tick had crawled in with him and started drilling into his armpit. Since it's as big as your thumb even when it hasn't fed, he was understandably startled. Luckily he got it before it had taken its pint of blood. He'd pulled Holtzinger's leg pretty hard about the fly bite, so now Holtzinger repeated: 'What's all the fuss over one little bug, buddy?'

James squashed the tick underfoot and grunted. He didn't like being twitted with his own words.

We packed up and started on our circuit. We meant to take them first to the borders of the sauropod swamp, more to see the wildlife than to collect anything.

From where the transition chamber materialises, the sauropod swamp looks like the couple of hours' walk, but it's an all-day scramble. The first part is easy, as it's downhill and the brush isn't heavy. But as you get near the swamp, the cycads and the willows grow so thickly, you have to worm your way among them.

There was a sandy ridge on the border of the swamp that I led the party to, for it's pretty bare of vegetation and affords a fine view. When we got to the ridge, the sun was about to go down. A couple of crocs slipped off into the water. The sahibs were so exhausted, being soft yet, that they flopped down on the sand as if dead.

The haze is thick round the swamp, so the sun was deep red and distorted by the atmospheric layers—pinched in at various levels. There was a high layer of clouds reflecting the red and gold, too, so altogether it was something for the Raja to write one of his poems about. Only your modern poet prefers to write about a rainy day in a garbage dump. A few little pterosaur were wheeling overhead like bats, only they don't flutter like bats. They swoop and soar after the big night-flying insects.

Beauregard Black collected firewood and lit a fire. We'd started on our steaks, and that pagoda-shaped sun was just slipping below the horizon, and something back in the trees was making a noise like a rusty hinge, when a sauropod breathed out in the water. If Mother Earth were to sigh over the misdeeds of her children, it would sound just about like that.

The sahibs jumped up, waving and shouting: 'Where is he? Where is he?'

I said: 'That black spot in the water, just to the left and this side of that point.'

They yammered while the sauropod filled its lungs and disappeared. 'Is that all?' yelped James. 'Won't we see any more of him?'

Holtzinger said: 'I read they never come out of the water because they're too heavy.'

'No,' I explained. 'They can walk perfectly well and often do, for egg-laying and moving from one swamp to another. But most of the time they spend in the water, like hippopotamus. They eat eight hundred pounds of soft swamp plants a day, all with those little heads. So they wander about the bottoms of lakes and swamps, chomping away, and stick their heads up to breathe every quarter-hour or so. It's getting dark, so this fellow will soon come out and lie down in the shallows to sleep.'

'Can we shoot one?' demanded James.

'I wouldn't,' said I.

'Why not?'

I said: 'There's no point in it and it's not sporting. First, they're even harder to hit in the brain than other dinosaurs because of the way they sway their heads about on those long necks and their hearts are too deeply buried in tissue to reach unless you're awfully lucky. Then, if you kill one in the water, he sinks and can't be recovered. If you kill one on land, the only trophy is that little head. You can't bring the whole beast back because he weighs thirty tons or more. We don't need thirty tons of meat.'

Holtzinger said: 'That museum in New York got one.'

'Yes,' I agreed. 'The American Museum of Natural History sent a party of forty-eight to the early Cretaceous, with a fifty-calibre machine gun. They assembled the gun on the edge of a swamp, killed a sauropod—and spent two solid months skinning it and hacking the carcass apart and dragging it to the time machine. I know the chap in charge of that project and he still has nightmares in which he smells decomposing dinosaur. They also had to kill a dozen big theropods who were attracted by the stench and refused to be frightened off, so they had *them* lying round and rotting, too. And the theropods ate three men of the party despite the big gun.'

Next morning, we were finishing breakfast when one of the helpers called: 'Look, Mr Rivers! Up there!'

He pointed along the shoreline. There were six big duckbill feeding in the shallows. They were the kind called parasaurolophus, with a crest consisting of a long spike of bone sticking out of the back of their heads, like the horn of an oryx, and a web of skin connecting this with the back of their neck.

'Keep your voices down,' I said. The duckbill, like the other ornithopods, are wary beasts because they have no armour or weapons against the theropods. The duckbill feed on the margins of lakes and swamps, and when a gorgosaur rushes out of the trees, they plunge into deep water and swim off. Then when phobosuchus, the super-crocodile, goes for them in the water, they flee to the land. A hectic sort of life, what?

Holtzinger said: 'Uh—Reggie, I've been thinking over what you said about ceratopsian heads. If I could get one of those yonder, I'd be satisfied. It would look big enough in my house, wouldn't it?'

'I'm sure of it, old boy,' I said. 'Now look here. I could take you on a detour to come out on the shore near there, but we should have to plough through half a mile of muck and brush, up to our knees in water, and they'd hear us coming. Or we can creep up to the north end of this sand spit, from which it's four or five hundred yards—a long shot, but not impossible. Think you could do it?'

'With my 'scope sight and a sitting position—yes, I'll try it.'

'You stay here,' I said to James. 'This is Augie's head and I don't want any argument over your having fired first.'

James grunted while Holtzinger clamped his 'scope to his rifle. We crouched our way up the spit, keeping the sand ridge between us and the duckbills. When we got to the end where there was no more cover, we crept along on hands and knees, moving slowly. If you move slowly directly towards or away from a dinosaur, it probably won't notice you.

The duckbills continued to grub about on all fours, every few seconds rising to look round. Holtzinger eased himself into the sitting position, cocked his piece, and aimed through the 'scope. And then—

Bang! bang! went a big rifle back at the camp.

Holtzinger jumped. The duckbill jerked up their heads and leaped for the deep water, splashing like mad. Holtzinger fired once and missed. I took a shot at the last duckbill before it disappeared. I missed, too: the .600 isn't designed for long ranges. Holtzinger and I started back towards the camp, for it had struck us that our party might be in theropod trouble and need reinforcements.

What happened was that a big sauropod, probably the one we'd heard the night before, had wandered down past the camp under water, feeding as it went. Now the water shoaled about a hundred yards offshore from our spit, half-way over to the edge of the swamp on the other side. The sauropod had ambled up the slope until its body was almost all out of water, weaving its head from side to side and looking for anything green to gobble. This kind looks like the well known brontosaurus, but a little bigger. Scientists argue whether it ought to be included in the genus camarasaurus or a separate genus with an even longer name.

When I came in sight of the camp, the sauropod was turning round to go back the way it had come, making horrid groans. It disappeared into deep water, all but its head and ten or twenty feet of neck, which wove about for some time before they vanished into the haze.

When we came up to the camp, James was arguing with the Raja. Holtzinger burst out: 'You bastard! That's the second time you've spoiled my shots!' Strong language for little August.

'Don't be a fool,' said James. 'I couldn't let him wander into camp and stamp everything flat.'

'There was no danger of that,' objected the Raja politely. 'You can see the water is deep offshore. It is just that our trigger-happee Mr James cannot see any animal without shooting.'

I said: 'If it did get close, all you needed to do was throw a stick of firewood at it. They're perfectly harmless.' This wasn't strictly true. When the Comte de Lautrec ran after one for a close shot, the sauropod looked back at him, gave a flick of its tail, and took off the Comte's head as neatly as if he'd been axed in the Tower.

'How was I to know?' yelled James, getting purple. 'You're all against me. What the hell are we on this goddamn trip for except to shoot things? You call yourselves hunters, but I'm the only one who's hit anything!'

I got pretty worthy and said he was just an excitable young skite with more money than brains, whom I should never have brought along.

'If that's how you feel,' he said, 'give me a burro and some food and I'll go back to the base by myself. I won't pollute your air with my loathsome presence!'

'Don't be a bigger ass than you can help,' I snapped. 'That's quite impossible.'

'Then I'll go all alone!' He grabbed his knapsack, thrust a couple of tins of beans and an opener into it, and started off with his rifle.

Beauregard Black spoke up: 'Mr Rivers, we cain't let him go off like that by hisself. He'll git lost and starve or be et by a theropod.'

'I'll fetch him back,' said the Raja and started after the runaway. He caught up as James was disappearing into the cycads. We could see them arguing and waving their hands, but couldn't make out what they said. After a while, they started back with arms around each other's necks like old school pals. I simply don't know how the Raja does it.

This shows the trouble we get into if we make mistakes in planning such a do. Having once got back into the past, we had to make the best of our bargain. We always must, you see.

I don't want to give the impression Courtney James was only a pain in the rump, He had his good points. He got over these rows quickly and next day would be as cheerful as ever. He was helpful with the general work of the camp—when he felt like it, at any rate. He sang well and had an endless fund of dirty stories to keep us amused.

We stayed two more days at that camp. We saw crocodile, the small kind, and plenty of sauropod—as many as five at once—but no more duckbill. Nor any of those fifty-foot super-crocodiles.

So, on the first of May, we broke camp and headed north towards the Janpur Hills. My sahibs were beginning to harden up and were getting impatient. We'd been in the Cretaceous a week and no trophies.

I won't go into details of the next leg. Nothing in the way of a trophy, save a glimpse of a gorgosaur out of range and some tracks indicating a whopping big iguanodont, twenty-five or thirty feet high. We pitched camp at the base of the hills.

We'd finished off the bonehead, so the first thing was to shoot fresh meat. With an eye to trophies, too, of course. We got ready the morning of the third.'

I told James: 'See here, old boy, no more of your tricks. The Raja will tell you when to shoot.'

'Uh-huh, I get you,' he said, meek as Moses. Never could tell how the chap would act.

We marched off, the four of us, into the foothills. We were looking for bonehead, but we'd take an ornithomime. There was also a good chance of getting Holtzinger his ceratopsian. We'd seen a couple on the way up, but mere calves without decent horns.

It was hot and sticky and we were soon panting and sweating like horses. We'd hiked and scrambled all morning without seeing a thing except lizards, when I picked up the smell of carrion. I stopped the party and sniffed. We were in an open glade cut up by these little dry nullahs. The nullahs ran together into a couple of deeper gorges that cut through a slight depression choked with a denser growth, cycad and screw-pine. When I listened, I heard the thrum of carrion flies.

'This way,' I said. 'Something ought to be dead—ah, here it is!'

And there it was: the remains of a huge ceratopsian lying in a little hollow on the edge of the copse. Must have weighed six or eight tons alive; a three-horned variety, perhaps the penultimate species of *Triceratops*. It was hard to tell because most of the hide on the upper surface had been ripped off and many bones had been pulled loose and lay scattered about.

Holtzinger said: 'Oh, hell! Why couldn't I have gotten to him before he died? That would have been a darn fine head.' Associating with us rough types had made little August profane, you'll observe.

I said: 'On your toes, chaps. A theropod's been at this carcass and is probably near by.'

'How d'you know?' James challenged, with the sweat running off his round red face. He spoke in what was for him a low voice, because a nearby theropod is a sobering thought even to the flightiest.

I sniffed again and thought I could detect the distinctive rank odour of theropod. But I couldn't be sure because the stench of the carcass was so strong. My sahibs were turning green at the sight and smell of the cadaver.

I told James: 'It's seldom even the biggest theropod will attack a full-grown ceratopsian. Those horns are too much for them. But they love a dead or dying one. They'll hang round a dead ceratopsian for weeks, gorging and then sleeping their meals off for days as a time. They usually take cover in the heat of the day anyhow, because they can't stand much direct hot sunlight. You'll find them lying in copses like this or in hollows, anywhere there's shade.'

'What'll we do?' asked Holtzinger.

'We'll make our first cast through this copse, in two pairs as usual.

Whatever you do, don't get impulsive or panicky.' I looked at Courtney James, but he looked right back and then merely checked his gun.

'Should I still carry this broken?' he wanted to know.

'No; close it, but keep the safety on till you're ready to shoot,' I said. It's risky carrying a double closed like that, especially in brush, but with a theropod near by, it would have been a greater risk to carry it open and perhaps catch a twig in it when one tried to close it.

'We'll keep closer than usual, to be in sight of each other,' I said. 'Start off at that angle, Raja. Go slowly and stop to listen between steps.'

We pushed through the edge of the copse, leaving the carcass but not its stink behind us. For a few feet, we couldn't see a thing. It opened out as we got in under the trees, which shaded out some of the brush. The sun slanted down through the trees. I could hear nothing but the hum of insects and the scuttle of lizards and the squawks of toothed birds in a tree-top. I thought I could be sure of the theropod smell, but told myself that might be imagination. The theropod might be any of several species, large or small, and the beast itself might be anywhere within a half-mile radius.

'Go on,' I whispered to Holtzinger, for I could hear James and the Raja pushing ahead on my right and see the palm fronds and ferns lashing about as they disturbed them. I suppose they were trying to move quietly, but to me they sounded like an earthquake in a crockery shop.

'A little closer,' I called, and presently they appeared slanting in towards me.

We dropped into a gully filled with ferns and clambered up the other side, then found our way blocked by a big clump of palmetto.

'You go round that side: we'll go round this,' I said, and we started off, stopping to listen and smell. Our positions were exactly the same as on that first day when James killed the bonehead.

I judge we'd gone two-thirds of the way round our half of the palmetto when I heard a noise ahead on our left. Holtzinger heard it and pushed off his safety. I put my thumb on mine and stepped to one side to have a clear field.

The clatter grew louder. I raised my gun to aim at about the height a big theropod's heart would be at the distance it would appear to us out of the greenery. There was a movement in the foliage—and a six-foot-high bonehead stepped into view, walking solemnly across our front from left to right, jerking its head with each step like a giant pigeon.

I heard Holtzinger let out a breath and had to keep myself from laughing. Holtzinger said: 'Uh—'

'Quiet,' I whispered. 'The theropod might still—'

That was as far as I got when that damned gun of James' went off, *bang! bang!* I had a glimpse of the bonehead knocked arsy-versy with its tail and hindlegs flying.

'Got him!' yelled James, and I heard him run forward.

'My God, if he hasn't done it again!' I groaned. Then there was a great swishing, not made by the dying bonehead, and a wild yell from James. Something heaved up and out of the shrubbery and I saw the head of the biggest of the local flesh-eaters, tyrannosaurus trionyches himself.

The scientists can insist that rex is bigger then trionyches, but I'll swear this tyrannosaur was bigger than any rex ever hatched. It must have stood twenty feet high and been fifty feet long. I could see its big bright eye and six-inch teeth and the big dewlap that hangs down from its chin to its chest.

The second of the nullahs that cut through the copse ran athwart our path on the far side of the palmetto clump. Perhaps six feet deep. The tyrannosaur had been lying in this, sleeping off its last meal. Where its back stuck up above ground level, the ferns on the edge of the nullah masked it. James had fired both barrels over the theropod's head and woken it up. Then James, to compound his folly, ran forward without reloading. Another twenty feet and he'd have stepped on the tyranno-saur's back.

James understandably stopped when this thing popped up in front of him. He remembered his gun was empty and he'd left the Raja too far behind to get a clear shot.

James kept his nerve at first. He broke open his gun, took two rounds from his belt and plugged them into the barrels. But in his haste to snap the gun shut, he caught his right hand between the barrels and the action—the fleshy part between his thumb and palm. It was a painful pinch and so startled James that he dropped his gun. That made him go to pieces and he bolted.

His timing couldn't have been worse. The Raja was running up with his gun at high port, ready to snap it to his shoulder the instant he got a clear view of the tyrannosaur. When he saw James running headlong towards him, it made him hesitate, as he didn't want to shoot James. The latter plunged ahead and, before the Raja could jump aside, blundered into him and sent them both sprawling among the ferns. The tyrannosaur collected what little wits it had and crashed after to snap them up.

And how about Holtzinger and me on the other side of the palmettos? Well, the instant James yelled and the tyrannosaur's head appeared, Holtzinger darted forward like a rabbit. I'd brought my gun up for a shot at the tyrannosaur's head, in the hope of getting at least an eye, but before I could find it in my sights, the head was out of sight behind the palmettos. Perhaps I should have shot at where I thought it was, but all my experience is against wild shots.

When I looked back in front of me, Holtzinger had already disappeared round the curve of the palmetto clump. I'm pretty heavily built, but I started after him with a good turn of speed, when I heard his rifle and the click of the bolt between shots: *bang*—click-click—*bang*—click-click, like that.

He'd come up on the tyrannosaur's quarter as the brute started to stoop for James and the Raja. With his muzzle twenty feet from the tyrannosaur's hide, he began pumping .375s into the beast's body. He got off three shots when the tyrannosaur gave a tremendous booming grunt and wheeled round to see what was stinging it. The jaws came open and the head swung round and down again.

Holtzinger got off one more shot and tried to leap to one side. He was standing on a narrow place between the palmetto clump and the nullah. So he fell into the nullah. The tyrannosaur continued its lunge and caught him, either as he was falling or after he struck bottom. The jaws went chomp and up came the head with poor Holtzinger in them, screaming like a doomed soul.

I came up just then and aimed at the brute's face. Then I realised its jaws were full of my friend and I'd be shooting him. As the head went up, like the business end of a big power shovel, I fired a shot at the heart. But the tyrannosaur was already turning away and I suspect the ball just glanced along the ribs.

The beast took a couple of steps away when I gave it the other barrel in the back. It staggered on its next step but kept on. Another step and it was nearly out of sight among the trees, when the Raja fired twice. The stout fellow had untangled himself from James, got up, picked up his gun and let the tyrannosaur have it.

The double wallop knocked the brute over with a tremendous smash. It fell into a dwarf magnolia and I saw one of its hind legs waving in the midst of a shower of incongruously pretty pink and white petals.

Can you imagine the leg of a bird of prey enlarged and thickened until it's as big round as the leg of an elephant?

But the tyrannosaur got up again and blundered off without even dropping its victim. The last I saw of it was Holtzinger's legs dangling out one side of its jaws (by now he'd stopped screaming) and its big tail banging against the tree trunks as it swung from side to side.

The Raja and I reloaded and ran after the brute for all we were worth. I tripped and fell once, but jumped up again and didn't notice my skinned elbow till later. When we burst out of the copse, the tyrannosaur was already at the far end of the glade. I took a quick shot, but probably missed, and it was out of sight before I could fire another.

We ran on, following the tracks and spatters of blood, until we had to stop from exhaustion. Their movements look slow and ponderous, but with those tremendous legs, they don't have to step very fast to work up considerable speed.

When we'd finished gasping and mopping our foreheads, we tried to track the tyrannosaur, on the theory that it might be dying and we should come up to it. But the spoor faded out and left us at a loss. We circled round hoping to pick it up, but no luck.

Hours later, we gave up and went back to the glade, feeling very dismal.

Courtney James was sitting with his back against a tree, holding his rifle and Holtzinger's. His right hand was swollen and blue where he'd pinched it, but still usable.

His first words were: 'Where the hell have you been? You shouldn't have gone off and left me; another of those things might have come along. Isn't it bad enough to lose one hunter through your stupidity without risking another one?'

I'd been preparing a pretty warm wigging for James, but his attack so astonished me, I could only bleat: '*We* lost—?'

'Sure,' he said. 'You put us in front of you, so if anybody gets eaten, it's us. You sent a guy up against these animals under-gunned. You—'

'You stinking little swine,' I began and went on from there. I learned later he'd spent his time working out an elaborate theory according to which this disaster was all our fault—Holtzinger's, the Raja's and mine. Nothing about James' firing out of turn or panicking or Holtzinger's saving his worthless life. Oh, dear, no. It was the Raja's fault for not jumping out of his way, etcetera.

Well, I've led a rough life and can express myself quite eloquently. The Raja tried to keep up with me, but ran out of English and was reduced to cursing James in Hindustani.

I could see by the purple colour on James' face that I was getting home. If I'd stopped to think, I should have known better than to revile a man with a gun. Presently James put down Holtzinger's rifle and raised his own, saying: 'Nobody calls me things like that and gets away with it. I'll just say the tyrannosaur ate you, too.'

The Raja and I were standing with our guns broken open, under our arms, so it would take a good part of a second to snap them shut and bring them up to fire. Moreover, you don't shoot a .600 holding it loosely in your hands, not if you know what's good for you. Next thing, James was setting the butt of his .500 against his shoulder, with the barrels pointed at my face. Looked like a pair of blooming vehicular tunnels.

The Raja saw what was happening before I did. As the beggar brought his gun up, he stepped forward with a tremendous kick. Used to play football as a young chap, you see. He knocked the .500 up and it went off so the bullet missed my head by an inch and the explosion jolly well near broke my eardrums.

The butt had been punted away from James' shoulder when the gun went off, so it came back like the kick of a horse. It spun him half round.

The Raja dropped his own gun, grabbed the barrels and twisted it out of James' hands, nearly breaking the bloke's trigger finger. He meant to hit James with the butt, but I rapped James across the head with my own barrels, then bowled him over and began punching the stuffing out of him. He was a good-sized lad, but with my sixteen stone, he had no chance.

When his face was properly discoloured, I stopped. We turned him over, took a strap out of his knapsack and tied his wrists behind him. We agreed there was no safety for us unless we kept him under guard every minute until we got him back to our time. Once a man has tried to kill you, don't give me another opportunity. Of course he might never try again, but why risk it?

We marched James back to camp and told the crew what we were up against. James cursed everybody and dared us to kill him.

'You'd better, you sons of bitches, or I'll kill you some day,' he said. 'Why don't you? Because you know somebody'd give you away, don't you? Ha-ha!'

The rest of that safari was dismal. We spent three days combing the country for that tyrannosaur. No luck. It might have been lying in any of those nullahs, dead or convalescing, and we should never see it unless we blundered on top of it. But we felt it wouldn't have been cricket not to make a good try at recovering Holtzinger's remains, if any.

After we got back to our main camp, it rained. When it wasn't raining, we collected small reptiles and things for our scientific friends. When the transition chamber materialised, we fell over one another getting into it.

The Raja and I had discussed the question of legal proceedings by or against Courtney James. We decided there was no precedent for punishing crimes committed eighty-five million years before, which would presumably be outlawed by the statute of limitations. We therefore untied him and pushed him into the chamber after all the others but us had gone through.

When we came out in the present, we handed him his gun—empty—and his other effects. As we expected, he walked off without a word, his arms full of gear. At that point, Holtzinger's girl, Claire Roche, rushed up crying: 'Where is he? Where's August?'

I won't go over the painful scene except to say it was distressing in spite of the Raja's skill at that sort of thing.

We took our men and beasts down to the old laboratory building that Washington University has fitted up as a serai for expeditions to the past. We paid everybody off and found we were nearly broke. The advance payments from Holtzinger and James didn't cover our expenses and we should have damned little chance of collecting the rest of our fees from James or from Holtzinger's estate.

And speaking of James, d'you know what that blighter was doing all this time? He went home, got more ammunition and came back to the university. He hunted up Professor Prochaska and asked him:

'Professor, I'd like you to send me back to the Cretaceous for a quick trip. If you can work me into your schedule right now, you can just about name your own price. I'll offer five thousand to begin with. I want to go to April twenty-third, 85,000,000 BC.'

Prochaska answered: 'Vot do you vant to go back again so soon so badly for?'

'I lost my wallet in the Cretaceous,' said James. 'I figure if I go back to the day before I arrived in that era on my last trip, I'll watch myself when I arrived on that trip and follow myself till I see myself lose the wallet.'

'Five thousand is a lot for a vallet.'

'It's got some things in it I can't replace. Suppose you let me worry about whether it's worth my while.'

'Vell,' said Prochaska, thinking, 'the party that vas supposed to go out this morning has phoned that they vould be late, so maybe I can vork you in. I have alvays vondered vot vould happen vhen the same man occupied the same time tvice.'

So James wrote out a cheque and Prochaska took him to the chamber and saw him off. James' idea, it seems, was to sit behind a bush a few yards from where the transition chamber would appear and pot the Raja and me as we emerged.

Hours later, we'd changed into our street clothes and phoned our wives to come get us. We were standing on Forsythe Boulevard waiting for them when there was a loud crack, like an explosion or a close-by clap of thunder, and a flash of light not fifty feet from us. The shock-wave staggered us and broke windows in quite a number of buildings.

We ran towards the place and got there just as a policeman and several citizens came up. On the boulevard, just off the kerb, lay a human body. At least it had been that, but it looked as if every bone in it had been pulverised and every blood vessel burst. The clothes it had been wearing were shredded, but I recognised an H. & H. .500 double-barrelled express rifle. The wood was scorched and the metal pitted, but it was Courtney James' gun. No doubt whatever.

Skipping the investigations and the milling about, what had happened was this: nobody had shot us as we emerged on the twenty-fourth and that, of course, couldn't be changed. For that matter, the instant James started to do anything that would make a visible change in the world of 85,000,000 BC, the space-time forces would snap him forward to the present to prevent a paradox.

Now that this is better understood, the professor won't send anybody to a period less than five hundred years *prior to* the time that some traveller has already explored, because it would be too easy to do some act, like chopping down a street or losing some durable artificat, that would affect the later world. Over long periods, he tells me, such changes average out and are lost in the stream of time.

We had a bloody rough time after that, with the bad publicity and all, though we did collect a fee from James' estate. The disaster hadn't been entirely James' fault. I shouldn't have taken him when I knew what a spoiled, unstable sort he was. And if Holtzinger could have used a heavy gun, he'd probably have knocked the tyrannosaur down, even if he didn't kill it, and so given the rest of us a chance to finish it.

So that's why I won't take you to that period to hunt. There are plenty of other eras, and if you think them over, I'm sure you'll find—

Good Lord, look at the time! Must run, old boy; my wife'll skin me. Good-night!

THE DEADLY MISSION OF
PHINEAS SNODGRASS

Frederik Pohl

This ingenious little tale was inspired by Sprague de Camp's time travel stories, especially the Roman saga Lest Darkness Fall, *which Fred Pohl read while in his teens and has remembered all his life as 'a wonderful novel'. His own contributions to the genre are a number of highly rated novels, including* Slave Ship *(1957) about the use of animals to fight wars,* A Plague of Pythons *(1965) dealing with mental transference from body to body, and* The World at the End of Time *(1990) featuring the meeting of a group of humans with an omnipotent alien. He also co-wrote the classic* The Space Merchants *(initially serialised as* Gravy Planet, *1952) with C. M. Kornbluth, of whom more later.*

Frederik Pohl (1919–), born in New York, was a member of the Futurians, and it was in collaboration with other enthusiasts belonging to that pioneer sf fan group that he wrote some of his earliest short stories. His subsequent career included working as an editor at Astounding Stories, Super Science Stories *and* Galaxy Science Fiction, *followed during the Fifties and Sixties by a lengthy period as agent to a number of the leading genre writers. In the last decade, Pohl has returned to writing novels and short stories with all his earlier verve and imagination. Commenting on how he came to write 'The Deadly Mission of Phineas Snodgrass' (which originally appeared in* Galaxy *in 1962 as 'The Time Machine of Phineas Snodgrass'), Pohl says, 'It is both a sort of belated rejoinder to de Camp and a snap at the heels of the pronatalists and other sweet, dangerous people who believe that there is some way of dealing with the world's ills that does not include population limitation.'*

*   *   *

This is the story of Phineas Snodgrass, inventor. He built a time machine.

He built a time machine and in it he went back some two thousand years, to about the time of the birth of Christ. He made himself known to the Emperor Augustus, his lady Livia and other rich and powerful Romans of the day and, quickly making friends, secured their co-operation in bringing abut a rapid transformation of Year One living habits. (He stole the idea from a science-fiction novel by L. Sprague de Camp, called *Lest Darkness Fall*.)

His time machine wasn't very big, but his heart was, so Snodgrass selected his cargo with the plan of providing the maximum immediate help for the world's people. The principal features of ancient Rome were dirt and disease, pain and death. Snodgrass decided to make the Roman world healthy and to keep its people alive through twentieth-century medicine. Everything else could take care of itself, once the human race was free of its terrible plagues and early deaths.

Snodgrass introduced penicillin and aureomycin and painless dentistry. He ground lenses for spectacles and explained the surgical techniques for removing cataracts. He taught anaesthesia and the germ theory of disease, and showed how to purify drinking water. He built Kleenex factories and taught the Romans to cover their mouths when they coughed. He demanded, and got, covers for the open Roman sewers, and he pioneered the practice of the balanced diet.

Snodgrass brought health to the ancient world, and kept his own health, too. He lived to more than a hundred years. He died, in fact, in the year AD 100, a very contented man.

When Snodgrass arrived in Augustus' great palace on the Palatine Hill, there were some 250,000,000 human beings alive in the world. He persuaded the principate to share his blessings with all the world, benefiting not only the hundred million subjects of the Empire, but the other one hundred millions in Asia and the tens of millions in Africa, the Western Hemisphere and all the Pacific islands.

Everybody got healthy.

Infant mortality dropped at once, from ninety deaths in a hundred to fewer than two. Life expectancies doubled immediately. Everyone was well, and demonstrated their health by having more children, who grew in health to maturity and had more.

It is a feeble population that cannot double itself every generation if it tries.

These Romans, Goths and Mongols were tough. Every thirty years

the population of the world increased by a factor of two. In the year
A D 30, the world population was a half billion. In A D 60, it was a full
billion. By the time Snodgrass passed away, a happy man, it was as
large as it is today.

It is too bad that Snodgrass did not have room in his time machine for
the blueprints of cargo ships, the texts on metallurgy to build the tools
that would make the reapers that would harvest the fields—for the
triple-expansion steam turbines that would generate the electricity that
would power the machines that would run the cities—for all the technology that 2,000 subsequent years had brought about.

But he didn't.

Consequently, by the time of his death conditions were no longer
quite perfect. A great many were badly housed.

On the whole, Snodgrass was pleased, for all these things could
surely take care of themselves. With a healthy world population, the
increase of numbers would be a mere spur to research. Boundless nature,
once its ways were studied, would surely provide for any number of
human beings.

Indeed it did. Steam engines on the Newcomen design were lifting
water to irrigate fields to grow food long before his death. The Nile was
damned at Aswan in the year 55. Battery-powered street-cars replaced
ox-carts in Rome and Alexandria before A D 75, and the galley slaves
were freed by huge, clumsy diesel outboards that drove the food ships
across the Mediterranean a few years later.

In the year A D 200 the world had now something over twenty billion
souls, and technology was running neck-and-neck with expansion.
Nuclear-driven ploughs had cleared the Teutoburg Wald, where Varus'
bones were still mouldering, and fertiliser made from ion-exchange
mining of the sea produced fantastic crops of hybrid grains. In A D 300
the world population stood at a quarter of a trillion. Hydrogen fusion
produced fabulous quantities of energy from the sea; atomic transmuta-
tion converted any matter into food. This was necessary, because there
was no longer any room for farms. The Earth was getting crowded. By
the middle of the sixth century the 60,000,000 square miles of land
surface on the Earth were so well-covered that no human being standing
anywhere on dry land could stretch out his arms in any direction without
touching another human being standing beside him.

But everyone was healthy, and science marched on. The seas were
drained, which immediately tripled the available land area. (In fifty

years the sea bottoms were also full.) Energy which had come from the fusion of marine hydrogen now came by the tapping of the full energy output of the Sun, through gigantic 'mirrors' composed of pure force. The other planets froze, of course; but this no longer mattered, since in the decades that followed they were disintegrated for the sake of the energy at their cores. So was the Sun. Maintaining life on Earth on such artificial standards was prodigal of energy consumption; in time every star in the Galaxy was transmitting its total power output to the Earth, and plans were afoot to tap Andromeda, which would care for all necessary expansion for—thirty years.

At this point a calculation was made.

Taking the weight of the average man at about a hundred and thirty pounds—in round numbers, 6×10^4 grammes—and allowing for a continued doubling of population every thirty years (although there was no such thing as a 'year' any more, since the Sun had been disintegrated; now a lonely Earth floated aimlessly towards Vega), it was discovered that by the year 1970 the total mass of human flesh, bone and blood would be 6×10^{27} grammes.

This presented a problem. The total mass of the Earth itself was only 5.98×10^{27} grammes. Already, humanity lived in burrows penetrating crust and basalt and quarrying into the congealed nickel-iron core; by 1970 all the core itself would have been transmuted into living men and women, and their galleries would have to be tunnelled through masses of their own bodies, a writhing, squeezed ball of living corpses drifting through space.

Moreover, simple arithmetic showed that this was not the end. In finite time the mass of human beings would equal the total mass of the Galaxy; and in some further time it would equal and exceed the total mass of *all* galaxies everywhere.

This state of affairs could no longer be tolerated, and so a project was launched.

With some difficulty resources were diverted to permit the construction of a small but important device. It was a time machine. With one volunteer aboard (selected from the 900 trillion who applied) it went back to the year 1. Its cargo was only a hunting rifle with one cartridge, and with that cartridge the volunteer assassinated Snodgrass as he trudged up the Palatine.

To the great (if only potential) joy of some quintillions of never-to-be-born persons, Darkness blessedly fell.

OF TIME AND KATHY BENEDICT

William F. Nolan

This next contribution takes us to a more recent past—the turn of the twentieth century, to be exact—in a tale that combines a trip through time, some fascinating motoring history and a truly moving love story. The author, William F. Nolan, is one of America's most versatile authors: he has written stories in many genres, including science fiction, horror, crime, fantasy and Westerns, and on themes such as aviation, sport, auto racing and show business. This, though, is his only fictional excursion into romance, and fifteen years after being committed to paper both it and Kathy Benedict herself remain among his favourites.

William Francis Nolan (1928–) was co-author with George Clayton Johnson of Logan's Run (1967), which inspired a film and a TV series; it has since been continued in two sequels, Logan's World (1977) and Logan's Search (1980), both by Nolan alone. A former commercial artist and racing driver, he has written for films and TV as well as recently launching a series of mystery novels in which the trio of famous hardboiled writers Dashiell Hammett, Raymond Chandler and Erle Stanley Gardner appear as private eyes solving crimes instead of writing about them. 'Of Time and Kathy Benedict' (1984) is unique not only within Nolan's work but also among time travel stories, and no one is better suited to introduce it than the author himself. 'The automotive background to the story is totally authentic,' he says, 'and the primary race described in these pages is accurate to the smallest detail. It really happened exactly as I have written it—I simply added Kathy Benedict, a special lady of whom I grew fond as I fashioned this account of her strange adventures. There is darkness here, and fantasy, but the primary ingredient is emotion, the deep bonding of two very different people from very different worlds.'

*   *   *

Now that she was on the lake, with the Michigan shoreline lost to her, and with the steady cat-purr of the outboard soothing her mind, she could think about the last year, examine it thread by thread like a dark tapestry.

Dark. That *was* the word for it. Three dark, miserable love affairs in twelve dark, miserable months. First, with Glenn, the self-obsessed painter from the Village who had worshipped her body but refused to consider the fact that a brain went with it. And Tony, the smooth number she'd met at the new disco off Park Avenue, with his carefully tailored Italian suits and his neurotic need to dominate his women. Great dancer. Terrific lover. Lousy human being. And, finally, the wasted months with Rick, God's gift to architecture, who promised to name a bridge after her if she'd marry him and raise his kids—three of them from his last divorce. She had tried to make him understand that as an independent woman, with a going career in research, she wasn't ready for instant motherhood at twenty-one. And there was the night, three months into their relationship, when Rick drunkenly admitted he was bisexual and actually preferred males to females. He'd taken a cruel pleasure in explaining this preference to her, and that was the last time they'd seen each other. Which was . . . when? Over two months ago. Early October now, and they'd split in late July.

She looked ahead, at the wide, flat horizon of the lake as the small boat sliced cleanly through the glittering skin of water.

Wide. Timeless. Serene.

What had Hemingway called it? The last 'free place'. The sea. She smiled. Lake St Clair wasn't exactly what he'd been talking about, but for her, at this moment, it would do just fine. She did feel free out here, alone on the water, with the cacophonous roar of New York no longer assaulting her mind and body. The magic peace of the lake surrounded her like a pulsing womb, feeding her hunger for solitude and silence. This assignment in Michigan had been a true blessing, offering her the chance to escape the ceaseless roar of the city . . .

'Dearborn? Where's that?'

'Where the museum is . . . in Detroit. You can check out everything at the museum. They've got the car there.'

Her boss referred to '999'—the cumbersome, flat-bodied, tiller-steered vehicle designed by Henry Ford and first raced here at Grosse Pointe, just east of Detroit, late in 1902. The newspaper she worked for was planning a special feature piece celebrating the anniversary of this historic event. Old 999 was the car that launched the Henry Ford Motor Company, leading to the mass-production American automobile.

'The museum people restored it, right down to the original red paint. It's supposed to look exactly like it did back in 1902,' Kathy's boss had told her. 'You go check it out, take some shots of it, dig up some fresh info, then spend a few days at Grosse Pointe . . . get the feel of the place.'

She'd been delighted with the assignment. Autumn in Michigan. Lakes and rivers and hills . . . Trees all crimson and gold . . . Sun and clear blue sky . . . Into Detroit, out to the Henry Ford Museum in Dearborn, a look at Ford's birthplace, a long talk with the curator, some pictures of ridiculous old 999 ('. . . and they named her after the New York Central's record-breaking steam locomotive') and on out to Grosse Pointe and this lovely, lonely, soothing ride on the lake. Just what she'd been needing. Balm for the soul.

As a little girl, she'd vacationed with her parents in Missouri and Illinois, in country much like this—and the odours of crushed leaves, of clean water, of hills rioting in autumn colours came back to her sharply here on the lake. It was a reunion, a homecoming. Emotionally, she *belonged* here, not in the rush and rawness of New York. Maybe, she told herself, when I save enough I can come here to live, meet a man who loves lakes and hills and country air . . .

Something was wrong. Suddenly, disturbingly wrong.

The water was gradually darkening around the boat; she looked up to see an ugly, bloated mass of grey-black clouds filling the lake sky. It seemed as if they had instantly materialised there. And, just as suddenly, a cold wind was chopping at her.

Kathy recalled the warning from the old man at the boathouse: 'Wouldn't go too far out if I was you, miss. Storm can build up mighty fast on the lake. You get some mean ones this time of year. Small boat like this is no good in a storm . . . engine can flood out . . . lotsa things can go wrong.'

The clouds rumbled—an ominous sound—and rain stung her upturned face. A patter at first, then heavier. The cold drops bit into her skin through her skirt and light sweater. Lucky thing she'd taken her raincoat along 'just in case'. Kathy quickly pulled the coat on, buttoning it against the wind-blown rain.

Time to head back, before the full storm hit. She swung the boat around towards shore, adjusting the throttle for maximum speed.

The motor abruptly sputtered and died. Too much gas. *Damn*! She jerked at the start rope. No luck. Again. And again. Wouldn't start. Forget it; she was never any good with engines. There were oars and she could row herself in. Shore wasn't far, and she could use the exercise. Good for her figure.

So row. Row, row, row your boat . . .

As a child, she'd loved rowing. Now she found it it was tougher than she'd remembered. The water was heavy and thick; it seemed to resist the oars, and the boat moved sluggishly.

The storm was increasing in strength. Rain stabbed at her, slashing against her face, and the wind slapped at the boat in ice-chilled gusts. God, but it was cold! Really, really cold. The coat offered no warmth; her whole body felt chilled, clammy.

Now the lake surface was erupting under the storm's steadily increasing velocity; the boat rocked and pitched violently. Kathy could still make out the broken shoreline through the curtaining rain as she laboured at the oars, but it grew dimmer with each passing minute. Her efforts were futile: she was rowing *against* the wind, and whenever she paused for breath the shoreline fell back, with the wind forcing her out into the heart of the lake.

She felt compelled to raise her head, to scan the lake horizon. Something huge was out there. Absolutely monstrous! Coming for her. Rushing towards the boat.

A wave.

How could such a mountain of water exist here? This ravening mammoth belonged in Melville's wild sea—not here in a Michigan lake. Impossible, she told herself; I'm not really seeing it. An illusion, created by freak storm conditions, unreal as a desert mirage.

Then she heard the roar. Real. Horribly, undeniably real.

The wave exploded over her, a foam-flecked beast that tossed her up and over in its watery jaws—flinging her from the boat, taking her down into the churning depths of the lake.

Into blackness.

And silence.

'You all right, miss?'

'Wha—what?'

'I asked if you're all right. Are you hurt? Leg broken or anything? I could call a doctor.'

She brought the wavering face above her into focus.

Male. Young. Intense blue eyes. Red hair. A nice, firm, handsome face.

'Well, ma'am, *should* I?'

'Should you what?' Her voice sounded alien to her.

'Call a doctor! I mean, you were unconscious when I found you, and I—'

'No. No doctor. I'm all right. Just a little . . . dizzy.'

With his help, she got to her feet, swayed weakly against him. 'Oops! I'm not too steady!'

He gripped her arm, supporting her. 'I've gotcha, miss.'

Kathy looked around. Beach. Nothing but water and beach. The sky was cloudless again as the sun rode down its western edge, into twilight.

'Guess the storm's over.'

'Beg your pardon, miss?'

'The wave . . . a really *big* one . . . must have carried me in.'

For the first time, she looked at this young man clearly—at his starched shirt with its detachable collar and cuffs, at his striped peg-top trousers and yellow straw hat.

'Are they doing a film here?'

'I don't follow you, miss.'

She brushed sand from her hair. One sleeve of her raincoat was ripped, and her purse was missing. Gone with the boat. 'Wow, I'm a real mess. Do I look terrible?'

'Oh . . . not at all,' he stammered. 'Fact is, you're as pretty as a Gibson Girl.'

She giggled. 'Well, I see that your compliments are in keeping with your attire. What's your name?'

'McGuire, ma'am,' he said, removing his hat. 'William Patrick McGuire. Folks call me Willy.'

'Well, I'm Katherine Louise Benedict—and I give up. If you're *not* acting in a film here then what *are* you doing in that get-up?'

'Get-up?' He looked down at himself in confusion. 'I don't—'

She snapped her fingers. 'Ha! Got it! A party at the hotel! You're in *costume*!' She looked him over very carefully. 'Lemme try and guess the year. Ummmm . . . turn of the century . . . ah, I'd guess 1902, *right*?'

Young McGuire was frowning. 'I don't mean to be offensive, Miss Benedict, but what has this year to do with how I'm dressed?'

'*This* year?'

'You said 1902, and this *is* 1902.'

She stared at him for a long moment. Then she spoke slowly and

distinctly: 'We *are* on the beach at Lake St Clair, Grosse Pointe, Michigan, United States of America, right?'

'We sure as heck are.'

'And what, exactly, is the month and the year?'

'It's October 1902,' said Willy McGuire.

For another long moment Kathy didn't speak. Then, slowly, she
turned her head towards the water, gazing out at the quiet lake. The
surface was utterly calm.

She looked back at Willy. 'That wave—the one that hit my boat—
did you see it?'

'Afraid not, ma'am.'

'What about the storm? Was anyone else caught in it?'

'Lake's been calm all day,' said Willy, speaking softly. 'Last storm
we had out here was two weeks back.'

She blinked at him.

'You positive *certain* you're all right, ma'am? I mean, when you fell
here on the beach you could have hit your head . . . fall could have
made you kinda dizzy and all.'

She sighed. 'I *do* feel a little dizzy. Maybe you'd better walk me
back to the hotel.'

What Kathy Benedict encountered as she reached the lobby of the
Grosse Pointe Hotel was emotionally traumatic and impossible to deny.
The truth of her situation was here in three-dimensional reality: the
clip-clopping of horse-and-carriage traffic; women in wide feathered
hats and pinch-waisted floor-length skirts; men in bowlers with canes
and high-button shoes; a gaudy board-fence poster announcing the forthcoming Detroit appearance of Miss Lillian Russell—and the turn-of-the-
century hotel itself, with its polished brass spittoons, ornate bevelled
mirrors, cut-velvet lobby furniture and massive wall portrait of a toothily
grinning, walrus-moustached gentleman identified by a flag-draped
plaque as 'Theodore Roosevelt, President of the United States'.

She knew this was no movie set, no costume party.

There was no longer any doubt in her mind: the wave at Lake St Clair
had carried her backwards eighty years, through a sea of time, to the
beach at Grosse Pointe, 1902.

People were staring. Her clothes were alien.

Had she not been wearing her long raincoat she would have been
considered downright indecent. As it was, she was definitely a curiosity
standing beside Willy McGuire in the lobby of the hotel.

She touched Willy's shoulder. 'I—need to lie down. I'm really very tired.'

'There's a doctor in the hotel. Are you sure you don't want me to—'

'Yes, I'm sure,' she said firmly. 'But you *can* do something else for me.'

'Just name it, Miss Benedict.'

'In the water . . . I lost my purse. I've no money, Mr McGuire. I'd like to borrow some. Until I can . . . get my bearings.'

'Why, yes, of course. I surely do understand your plight.' He took out his wallet, hesitated. 'Uh . . . how much would be required?'

'Whatever you can spare. I'll pay you back as soon as I can.'

Kathy knew that she'd have to find work—but just where did a 1982 female research specialist find a job in 1902?

Willy handed her a folded bill. 'Hope this is enough. I'm a mechanic's helper, so I don't make a lot—an' payday's near a week off.'

Kathy checked the amount. Ten dollars! How could she possibly do *anything* with ten dollars? She had to pay for a hotel room, buy new clothes, food . . . Then she broke into giggles, clapping a hand to her mouth to stop the laughter.

'Did I say something funny?' Willy looked confused.

'Oh no. No, I was just . . . thinking about the price of things.'

He shook his head darkly. 'Begging your pardon, Miss Benedict, but I don't see how *anybody* can laugh at today's prices. Do you know sirloin steak's shot up to twenty-four cents a pound? And bacon's up to twelve and a half ! The papers are calling 'em ''Prices That Stagger Humanity!'' '

Kathy nodded, stifling another giggle. 'I know. It's absolutely frightful.'

In preparing the Henry Ford story, she'd thoroughly researched this period in America—and now realised that Willy's ten dollars would actually go a long way in a year when coffee was a nickel a cup, when a turkey dinner cost twenty cents and a good hotel room could be had for under a dollar a night.

With relief, she thanked him, adding: 'And I *will* pay it back very soon, Mr McGuire!'

'Uh, no hurry. But . . . now that I've done you a favour, *I'd* like to ask one.'

'Surely.'

He twisted the straw hat nervously in his hands. 'I'd mightily appreciate it—if you'd call me Willy.'

* * *

It took her a long while to fall asleep that night. She kept telling herself: Believe it . . . it's real . . . it isn't a dream . . . you're really here . . . this *is* 1902 . . . believe it, believe it, *believe* it . . .

Until she drifted into an exhausted sleep.

The next morning Kathy went shopping. At a 'Come in and Get to Know Us' sale in a new dry-goods store for ladies she purchased an ostrich-feather hat, full skirt, chemise, shoes, shirtwaist and a corset— all for a total of six dollars and twenty-one cents.

Back in her hotel room she felt ridiculous (and more than a little breathless) as a hotel maid laced up her corset. But every decent woman wore one, and there was no way she could eliminate the damnable thing!

Finally, standing in front of the mirror, fully dressed from heels to hat, Kathy began to appreciate the style and feminine grace of this earlier American period. She had coiled her shining brown hair in a bun, pinning it under the wide-brimmed, plumed hat and now she turned to and fro, in a rustle of full skirts, marvelling at her tiny cinched waist and full bosom.

'Kathy, girl,' she said, smiling at her mirror image, 'with all due modesty, you are an *elegant* young lady!'

That same afternoon, answering a no-experience-required job ad for office help in down-town Detroit, she found herself in the offices of Dodd, Stitchley, Hanneford and Leach, Attorneys at Law.

Kathy knew she could not afford to be choosy; right now, any job would do until she could adjust to this new world. Later, given her superior intelligence and natural talents, she could cast about for a suitable profession.

'Are you familiar with our needs, young lady?' asked the stout, matronly woman at the front desk.

'Not really,' said Kathy. 'Your ad specified "Office Help Female".'

The woman nodded. 'We need typewriters.'

'Oh!' Kathy shrugged. 'Maybe I copied the wrong address. I don't sell them.'

'You don't sell what?' The woman leaned forward, staring at Kathy through tiny, square glasses.

'Typewriters,' said Kathy. Suddenly she remembered that in 1902 typists were called 'lady typewriters'. There was so *much* to remember about this period!

'Frankly, miss, I do not understand what you are talking about.' The buxom woman frowned behind her glasses. '*Can* you operate a letter-typing machine or can't you?'

'Yes, I can,' nodded Kathy. 'I really can.' She smiled warmly. 'And I *want* the job!'

Which is how Kathy Benedict, a 28,000-dollar-a-year research specialist from New York City, became an 8.00-dollars-per-week office worker with the firm of Dodd, Stitchley, Hanneford and Leach in Detroit, Michigan, during October of 1902.

With her first week's pay in hand, Kathy marched up the steps of Mrs O'Grady's rooming house on Elm Street and asked to see Mr William McGuire.

'Why, Miss Benedict!' Willy seemed shocked to see her there in the hallway outside his room. He stood in the open door, blinking at her. The left half of his face was covered with shaving cream.

'Hello, Willy,' she said. 'May I come in?'

'I don't think that would be proper. Not after dark and all. I mean, you are a single lady and these are bachelor rooms and it just isn't done!'

Kathy sighed. Again, she had failed to consider the period's strict rules of public conduct for unaccompanied females. She didn't want to cause Willy any embarrassment.

'Then could we meet downstairs . . . in the lobby?'

'Of course.' He touched at his lathered cheek. 'Soon as I finish shaving. I do it twice a day. Heavy beard if I don't.'

'Fine,' she said. 'See you down there.'

Waiting for Willy McGuire in the lobby of the Elm Street rooming house, Kathy reviewed the week in her mind. A sense of peace had entered her life; she felt cool and tranquil in this new existence. No television. No rock concerts. No disco. Life had the flavour of vintage wine. The panic and confusion of the first day here had given away to calm acceptance. She was taking this quaint, charming period on its own terms.

Willy joined her and they sat down on a high-backed red velvet couch. Willy looked fresh-scrubbed and glad to see her.

'Here's the first half of what I owe you,' she told him, handing over the money. 'I'll have the rest next week.'

'I didn't expect any of it back this soon,' he said.

'It was very kind of you to trust a stranger the way you did,' Kathy smiled.

'I'd surely like to know you better, Miss Benedict. I hope we can be friends.'

'Not if you keep calling me Miss Benedict.'

'All right, then . . .' He grinned. 'Kate.'

'*Kate*?'

'Aye,' said Willy. 'Or would you prefer Katherine?'

'Nope. Kate will do fine. It's just that—nobody's called me that since I was six. Hmmmmm . . .' She nodded. 'Willy and Kate. Has a certain *ring* to it!'

And, at that precise moment, looking at the handsome, red-haired young Irishman seated beside her, she realised that she had met a totally decent human being, full of warmth and honesty and manly virtue.

She decided to investigate the possibility of falling in love with him.

They rode in Willy's carriage through the quiet suburbs of Detroit that Sunday, savouring the briskness of the autumn air and the fire-coloured woods. Sunlight rippled along the dark flanks of their slow-trotting horse and the faint sounds of a tinkling piano reached them from a passing farmhouse.

'I love horses,' said Kathy. 'I used to ride them all the time in Missouri.'

'They're too slow for my taste,' Willy declared. 'I like to work with machines . . . Cycles, for instance. That's how I got started in this business. Bought me a motor-tandem last year. Filed down the cylinder, raised the compression, then piped the exhaust around the carburettor. She went like Billy Blue Blazes!'

'I don't much care for motor-cycles. People get hurt on them.'

'You can fall off a horse, too! Heck, I admit I've had me some spills on the two-wheelers, but nothin' serious. Hey—how'd you like to see where I work?'

'Love to,' she said.

'Giddy-up, Teddy!' Willy ordered, snapping the reins. He grinned over at Kathy. 'He's named after the President!'

Willy stopped the carriage in front of a small shop at 81 Park Place— where she was introduced to a gaunt, solemn-faced man named Ed 'Spider' Huff.

'Spider's our chief mechanic, and I'm his assistant,' Willy explained. 'We work together here in the shop.'

'On cycles?'

'Not hardly, ma'am,' said Huff in a rasping, humourless voice. 'This here is the age of the horseless carriage. Do you know we've already got almost two hundred miles of paved road in this country? In New York State alone, they got darn near a thousand automobiles registered.'

'I assume, then, that you are working on automobiles?'

'We sure are,' Huff replied. 'But the plain truth of it is there ain't no other automobile anywhere on this whole round globe to match what we got inside—a real thoroughbred racing machine!'

'Spider's right for dang sure!' nodded Willy.

She was suddenly very curious. 'Could I see it?'

Huff canted his head, squinting at her. He rubbed a gaunt hand slowly along his chin. 'Wimminfolk don't cotton to racing automobilies. Too much noise. Smoke. Get grease on your dress.'

'Truly, I'd *like* to see it.'

Willy clapped Huff in the shoulder. 'C'mon, Spider—she's a real good sport. Let's show her.'

'All rightie,' nodded Huff, 'but I'll wager she won't favour it none.'

They led Kathy through the office to the shop's inner garage. A long bulked shape dominated the floor area, draped in an oil-spattered blanket.

'We keep her tucked in like a sweet babe when we ain't workin' on her,' Huff declared.

'So I see,' nodded Kathy.

'Well, dang it, Willy!' growled Huff. 'If you're gonna show her, then *show* her!'

Willy peeled off the blanket. 'There she is!' he said, with obvious pride in his tone.

Kathy stared at the big, square, red-painted racing machine, with its front-mounted radiator, nakedly exposed engine, and high, wire-spoked wheels. In place of a steering wheel an iron tiller bar with raised hand-grips was installed for control—and the driver sat in an open bucket seat. There was no windscreen or body panelling.

'It's 999!' Kathy murmured.

The two men blinked in shock.

'How'd *you* know we call her that?' Huff demanded.

'Uh . . . rumour's going around town that there's a racing car here in Detroit named after the New York Central's locomotive. Some of the typewriters were talking about it at work.'

'Good thing she's about ready to race,' declared Willy. 'Guess when you got a rig this fast word just leaks out.'

'Anyway, it's a wonderful name for her. Who's the owner?'

'Our boss, Tom Cooper,' said Huff. 'Had a lot of troubles with 999

out at the track on the test runs an' old Hank got fed up and sold out
to Tom. They came into this as partners—but Hank's out now.'

'Hank?'

'Yeah,' said Willy. 'Hank Ford. Him an' Tom designed her together.'

'And not an extra pound of weight anywhere on 'er,' said Huff.
'That's why the engine's mounted on a stripped chassis. She's got
special cast-iron cylinder walls, giving a seven-inch bore and stroke.
And that, ma'am, is *power!*'

'Yep,' nodded Willy. 'She's the biggest four-cylinder rig in the States.
Separate exhaust pipes for each cylinder. We can squeeze upward of
seventy horse out of her! That means, with the throttle wide open, on
a watered-down track, she'll do close to a mile a minute—better'n *fifty*
miles an hour!'

Kathy was excited; her assignment to research a race eighty years in
the past had become a present-day reality. 'And you've entered her
against Alex Winton for the Manufacturers' Challenge Cup at Grosse
Pointe on October 25!'

They both stared at her.

'But how—' Willy began.

'Rumour,' she added quickly. 'That's the rumour I heard.'

'Well, you heard right,' declared Huff. 'Ole Alex Winton thinks that
Bullet of his can't be beat. Him with his big money and his fancy
reputation. He's got a surprise comin' right enough!'

Kathy smiled. 'Indeed he has, Mr Huff. Indeed he has.'

Each afternoon after work Kathy began dropping by the shop on Park
Place to watch the preparations on 999. She was introduced to the car's
owner, Tom Cooper—and to a brash, dark-haired young man from
Ohio named Barney, an ex-bicycle racer who had been hired to tame
the big red racing machine.

Of course she recognised him instantly, since he was destined to
become as legendary as 999 itself. His full name was Berna Eli 'Barney'
Oldfield, the barnstorming daredevil whose racing escapades on the dirt
tracks of America would earn him more fame and glory than any driver
of his era. In March of 1910, at Daytona Beach, he would become the
official 'Speed King of the World' by driving a 'Lightning' Benz for
a new land speed record of 131 miles per hour. But here, in this moment
in time, he was just a raw-looking twenty-four-year-old youth on the
verge of his first automobile race.

Kathy asked him if he smoked cigars.

'No, ma'am, I don't,' said Oldfield.

And the next day she brought him one. He looked confused; ladies didn't offer cigars to gentlemen.

'Barney,' she said. 'I want you to have this for the race. It's important.'

'But I told you, ma'am, I don't smoke cheroots!'

'You don't have to smoke it, just *use* it.'

'You've lost me, ma'am.'

'Horse tracks are bumpy, full of ruts and potholes. A cigar between your teeth will act to cushion the road shocks. Just do me a personal favour . . . try it!'

Oldfield slipped the fat, five-cent cigar into his coverall pocket. 'I'll try it, Miss Benedict, because when a pretty lady asks me a favour I don't say no.'

Kathy felt a current of excitement shiver along her body. When she'd been researching Oldfield, as part of her 999 assignment, she had difficulty in tracing the origin of Barney's cigar, his famed trademark during the course of his racing career. Finally, she'd uncovered an interview with Oldfield, given a month before his death in 1946, in which a reporter had asked: 'Just where *did* you get your first cigar?'

And Barney had replied: 'From a lady I met just prior to my first race. But I'll tell you the truth, son—I don't recall her name.'

Kathy now realised that *she* was the woman whose name Barney had long since forgotten. The unique image of Barney Oldfield, hunched over a racing wheel, a cigar clenched between his teeth, began with Kathy Benedict.

They arrived at the Grosse Pointe track on Friday, October 24, a full day before the race, for test runs: Willy, Spider Huff, Cooper and Oldfield. Kathy had taken sick leave from the office to be with them.

'We'll need all the practice time we can get,' Willy told her. 'Still some bugs to get out.'

'McGuire!' yelled Tom Cooper. 'You gonna stand there all day gab- bin' your fool head off—or are you gonna crank her up? Now, *jump*!'

And Willy jumped.

Cooper was a square-bodied, gruff-looking man wearing a fleece-lined jacket over a plaid cowboy shirt—and he had made it clear that he didn't think women belonged around racing cars. Privately, Cooper had told Willy that he felt Kate Benedict would bring them bad luck in the race, but that he'd let her hang around so long as she 'kept her place' and stayed out of their way.

Tom Cooper had always had strong ideas about what a 'good woman' should be: 'She ought to be a first-rate cook, be able to sing and play the piano, know how to raise kids and take care of a house, mind her manners, dress cleanly, be able to milk cows, feed chickens, tend the garden—know how to shop, be able to sew and knit, churn butter, make cheese, pickle cucumbers and drive cattle.'

He had ended this incredible list with a question: 'And just how many of these talents do *you* possess, Miss Benedict?'

She lifted her chin, looking him squarely in the eye. 'The only thing I'm really good at, Mr Cooper, is independent thinking.'

Then she'd turned on her heel and stalked away.

In practice around the mile dirt oval, Barney found that 999 was a savage beast to handle at anything approaching full throttle.

'She's got the power, all right, but she's wild,' he said after several runs. 'Open her up and she goes for the fence. Dunno if I can keep her on the track.'

'Are you willing to try?' asked Cooper. 'You'll have to do better than fifty out there tomorrow to beat Winton's Bullet. Can you handle her at that speed?'

Oldfield squinted down from his seat behind the tiller. 'Well,' he grinned, 'this damn chariot may kill me—but they will have to say afterwards that I was goin' like hell when she took me through the rail!' He looked down sheepishly at Kathy: 'And I beg yer pardon for my crude way of expression.'

The morning of October 25, 1902, dawned chill and grey, and by noon a gust of wind-driven rain had dampened the Grosse Pointe oval.

The popular horse track had originally been laid out over a stretch of low-lying marshland bordering the Detroit River, and many a spirited thoroughbred had galloped its dusty surface. On this particular afternoon, however, the crowd of two thousand excited citizens had come to see horsepower instead of horses, as a group of odd-looking machines lined up behind the starting tape. Alexander Winton, the millionaire founder of the Winton Motor Carriage Company and the man credited with the first commercial sale of an auto in the United States in 1898, was the odds-on favourite in his swift, flat-bodied Winton Bullet. Dapper and handsomely moustached, he waved a white-gloved hand to the crowd. They responded with cheers and encouragement: 'Go get 'em, Alex!'

Winton's main competition was expected to come from the powerful Geneva Steamer, Detroit's largest car, with its wide wheelbase, four massive boilers, and tall stack—looking more like a land-bound ship than a racing automobile. A Winton Pup, a White Steamer, and young Oldfield at the tiller of 999 filled out the five-car field.

Kathy spotted Henry Ford among the spectators in the main grandstand, looking tense and apprehensive; Ford was no longer the legal owner of 999, but the car *had* been built to his design, and he was anxious to see it win. In 1902, Ford was thirty-nine, with his whole legendary career as the nation's auto king ahead of him. His empire was still a dream.

Kathy's heart was pounding; she felt flushed, almost dizzy with excitement. The race she'd spent weeks reading about was actually going to happen in front of her; she was a vital, breathing part of the history she'd so carefully researched. At the starting line, she overheard Tom Cooper's last-minute words to Oldfield.

'All the money's on Winton,' he was saying. 'But we're betting you can whup him! What do you say, lad?'

'I say let him eat my dust. Nobody's gonna catch me out there on that track today.'

'Do you think he can do it, Kate?' asked Willy, gripping her elbow as they stood close to the fence. 'Do you think Barney can beat Winton? The Bullet's won a lot of races!'

'We'll just have to wait and see,' she said, with a twinkle in her eyes. 'But I can guarantee one thing—this race will go down in history!'

At the drop of the starter's flag all five cars surged forward, the high, whistling kettle-boil scream of the steamers drowned by the thunderpistoned roar of 999 and the Winton Bullet.

Sliding wide as he throttled the bouncing red hell wagon around the first turn, Barney immediately took the lead away from Winton. But could he *hold* it?

'Winton's a fox!' declared Willy as they watched the cars roar into the back stretch. 'He's given Barney some room just to find out what 999 can do. See! He's starting his move now!'

Which was true. It was a five-mile event, and by the end of the first mile Alex Winton had Oldfield firmly in his sights, and was closing steadily with the Bullet as the two steamers and the Pup dropped back.

It was a two-care race.

Barney knew he was in trouble. He was getting a continuous oil bath from the exposed crankshaft, and almost lost control as his goggles filmed with oil. He pushed them up on his forehead, knowing they were useless. But there was a greater problem: bouncing over the ruts and deep-gouged potholes, the car's rigid ashwood-and-steel chassis was giving Oldfield a terrible pounding, and he was losing the sharp edge of concentration needed to win. On some of the rougher sections of the track the entire car became airborne.

Watching the Bullet's relentless progress, as Winton closed the gap between himself and Oldfield, Kathy experienced a sharp sense of frustration. At this rate, within another mile the Bullet would overhaul 999 and take the lead.

But that must not happen, she told herself. It *could* not happen. The pattern of the race was already fixed in history!

Suddenly, she had the answer.

'He forgot it!' she yelled to Willy.

'Forgot what?'

'Never mind! Just wait here. I'll be back.'

And she pushed through the spectators, knocking off a fat man's bowler and dislodging several straw boaters; she had a destination and there was no time to waste in getting there.

When Oldfield neared the far turn, at the end of the back stretch, each new wheel hole in the track's surface rattling his teeth, he saw Kathy Benedict straddling the fence.

She was waving him closer to the rail, pointing to something in her hand, yelling at him, her voice without sound in the Gatling-gun roar of 999's engine.

Closer. And yet closer. What in the devil's name did this mad girl want with him?

Then she tossed something—and he caught it. By damn!

The cigar!

It was *just* what he needed—and he jammed the cushioning cheroot between his teeth, lowered his body over the iron control bar, and opened the throttle. In a whirling plume of yellow dust, 999 hurtled forward.

Now let old Winton try and catch him!

'Look at that!' shouted Willy when Kathy was back with him at the fence. 'He's pullin' away!'

Oldfield was driving brilliantly now, throwing the big red wagon into each turn with fearless energy, sliding wide, almost clipping the fence, yet maintaining that hairline edge of control at the tiller. The blast from the red car's four open exhausts was deafening—and the crowd cheered wildly as 999 whipped past the main grandstand in a crimson blur.

By the third mile, Alex Winton was out, his overstrained engine misfiring as the Bullet slowed to a crawl in Barney's dust.

And when Oldfield boomed under the finish flag, to a sea of cheering from the stands, he had lapped the second-place Geneva Steamer and left the other competitors far, far behind.

Willy jumped up and down, hugged Kathy, lifting her from the ground and spinning her in a circle, yelling out his delight.

Sure enough, just as she'd promised it would be, this one had been a race for the history books.

The morning papers proclaimed 999's triumph in bold black headlines: WINTON LOSES! OLDFIELD WINS! And the lurid copy described Barney as 'hatless, his long, tawny hair flying out behind him with the speed of his mount, seeming a dozen times on the verge of capsize, he became a human comet behind the tiller of his incredible machine.'

Reporters asked Barney what it was like to travel at a truly astonishing fifty miles per hour! How could mortal man stand the bullet-like speed?

Oldfield was quoted in detail: 'You have every sensation of being hurled through space. The machine is throbbing under you with its cylinders beating a drummer's tattoo, and the air tears past you in a gale. In its maddening dash through the swirling dust the machine takes on the attributes of a sentient thing ... I tell you, gentlemen, no man can drive faster and live!'

Henry Ford was quick to claim credit for the design and manufacture of 999, and the nation's papers headlined his name next to Oldfield's, touting the victory at Grosse Pointe as 'the real beginning of the Auto Age'.

Within a month, riding the crest of public acclaim, Hank Ford laid the foundations for his Ford Motor Company—already planning for the day when his 'tin lizzies' would swarm the highways of America.

The victory of 999 also benefited Willy McGuire. 'I want you and Spider to work for me from now on, Willy,' Hank Ford had told him. 'Cooper just doesn't appreciate you. And, for a start, I'll *double* your salary!'

*   *   *

During the days following the race at Grosse Pointe, Kathy fell deeply in love with the happy, red-haired Irishman. He was totally unlike any man she'd ever known: honest, kind, strong, gentle and attentive. And he loved her as a *complete* woman—mind and body. For the first time in her life, she had found real emotional fulfilment.

His question was inevitable: 'Will you marry me, Kate?'

And her reply came instantly: 'Yes, yes, yes! Oh, *yes*, Willy, I'll marry you!'

As they embraced, holding one another tightly, Kathy knew that she was no longer afraid of anything. The old life was gone.

'Nothing frightens me now that I'm with you,' she told him.

'Not even the lake?' he suddenly asked, his blue eyes intense.

She was startled by the question. 'I never said that I was afraid of the lake.'

'It's been obvious. We do everything together. Ride . . . skate . . . picnic . . . attend band concerts. But you never want to go boating with me on the lake.'

'I don't like boating. I told you that.'

His eyes were steady on hers. 'Then why were you on the lake alone the day I found you? What made you go out there?'

She sighed, lowering her eyes. 'It's a long, long story and someday, when I'm sure you'll understand, I'll tell you all about it. I swear I will.'

'It's a fine day, Kate. Sky's clear. No wind. No clouds. I think we ought to go out on the lake. Together.'

'But why?'

'To put that final fear of yours to rest. It's like climbing back on a horse once he's bucked you off. If you don't, you never ride again. The fear is always there.'

A strained moment of silence.

'I'm *not* afraid of the lake, Willy,' she said in a measured tone.

'Then prove you're not! Today. Now. Show me, Kate!'

And she agreed. There was nothing to fear out there on the quiet water. She kept telling herself that over and over . . .

Nothing to fear.

Nothing.

Nothing.

Nothing.

The weather was ideal for boating—and Willy handled the oars with practised ease, giving Kathy a sense of confidence and serenity.

She *did* feel serene out here on the placid lake. She enjoyed the pleasant warmth of the afternoon sun on her shoulders as she twirled the bright red parasol Willy had bought her just for this occasion.

The water was spangled with moving patterns of sunlight, glittering diamond shapes, shifting and breaking and re-forming in complex designs around the boat as Willy rowed steadily away from the shore.

In this calming aura of peace and natural beauty she wondered why she had been so afraid of the lake. It was lovely here, and there was certainly nothing to fear. The bizarre circumstances of that fateful afternoon in 1982 were unique; a freak storm had created some kind of time gate through which she had passed. And no harm had been done to her. In fact, she was grateful for the experience; it had brought her across a bridge of years to the one man she could truly love and respect.

She reached out to touch his shoulder gently. 'Mr McGuire, I love you.'

He grinned at her. 'And I love *you*, Miss Benedict!'

Willy laid aside the oars to take her into his arms. They stretched out next to one another in the bottom of the easy-drifting boat. The sky above them was a delicate shade of pastel blue (like Willy's eyes, she thought) and a faint breeze carried the perfume of deep woods out on to the water.

'It's an absolutely perfect moment,' she said. 'I wish we could put it in a bottle and open it whenever we get sad!'

'Don't need to,' said Willy softly. 'We've got a lifetime of perfect moments ahead of us, Kate.'

'No.' She shook her head. 'Life is never perfect.'

'*Ours* will be,' he said, running a finger along the side of her sun-warm cheek, tracing the curve of her chin. 'I'll make it perfect—and that's a promise.'

She kissed him, pressing her lips deeply into his.

He sat up.

'Hey,' she protested, opening her eyes. 'Where'd you go? We were just getting started.' And she giggled.

'Sky's darkening,' he said, looking upwards, shading his eyes. 'I'd better row us in. A lake storm can—'

'*Storm!*' She sat up abruptly, staring at him, at the sky and water. 'No! Oh, God, no!'

'Whoa there, you're shaking!' he said, holding her. 'There's nothing to get worried over. We'll be back on shore in a few minutes.'

'But you weren't *there* ... you don't understand!' she said, a desperate tone in her voice. 'That's just how the other storm came along—out of nowhere. And the wind . . .'

It was there, suddenly whipping at the lake surface.

He was rowing strongly now, with the boat cutting towards the shoreline. 'Be on the beach in a jiffy. You'll see. Trust me, Kate.'

But the wind was building rapidly, blowing against them, neutralising Willy's efforts.

Kathy looked fearfully at the sky. Yes, there they were, the same ugly mass of grey-black clouds.

It began to rain.

'Hurry, Willy! Row faster!'

'I'm trying . . . but this wind's really strong!'

She sat in a huddled position in the stern of the boat, head down now, hands locked around her legs as the rain struck at her in blown gusts.

'Never seen a storm build up this fast,' Willy grunted, rowing harder. 'Freak weather, that's for sure.'

How could he understand that she'd seen it all before, in a world eighty years beyond him? Clouds, wind, rain and—

And . . .

She knew when she looked up, slowly raising her head, that it would be there, at the horizon, coming for them.

The wave.

Willy stopped rowing at her scream. He looked towards the horizon. 'God A'amighty!'

Then, in the blink of a cat's eye, it was upon them—blasting their senses, an angry, falling mountain of rushing water that split their boat asunder and pitched them into the seething depths of the lake.

Into blackness.

And silence.

Kathy opened her eyes.

She was alone on the beach. Somehow, without any visible proof, she knew she had returned to 1982.

And Willy was gone.

The thought tore through her, knife-sharp, filling her with desperate anguish.

Willy has gone!

She had lost him to the lake. It had given him to her and now it had taken him away.

For ever.

A husky lifeguard in orange swim trunks was running towards her across the sand.

I don't *want* to be saved, she told herself; I want to go back into the lake and die there, as Willy had died. There's no reason to go on living. No reason at all.

'You all right, miss?'

Same words! Same voice!

She looked up—into the face of her beloved. The blue eyes. The red hair. The gentle, intense features.

'Willy!' she cried, suddenly hugging him. 'Oh, God, Willy, I thought I'd lost you! I thought you were—'

She hesitated as the young man pulled back.

'Afraid you've made a mistake,' he said. 'My name's Tom.'

She stared at him, and then she knew who he was. No doubt of it. Kathy *knew*.

'What about your middle name?'

'It's William,' he told her. And then grinned. 'Oh, I see what you mean—but nobody ever calls me Willy. Not since I was a kid.'

'I know your last name,' she said softly.

'Huh?'

'It's McGuire.'

He blinked at her. 'Yeah. Yeah, it *is*.'

'Thomas William McGuire,' she said, smiling at him. 'Please . . . sit down here, next to me.'

With a small sigh, he did so. She intrigued him.

'When were you born?'

'In 1960.'

'And who was your father? What was *his* name?'

'Timothy McGuire.'

'Born? . . . The year?'

'My Dad was born in 1929.'

'And your grandfather . . . What was *his* name and when was he born?'

'Patrick McGuire. Born in 1904.'

Kathy's eyes were shining. She blinked back the wetness. 'And his father, your great-grandfather—'

He started to speak, but she touched his lips with a finger to stop the words.

'He was William Patrick McGuire,' she said, 'and he was born in 1880, right?'

The young man was amazed. He nodded slowly. 'Yeah. Right.'

'And he survived a boating accident late in 1902, on *this* lake, didn't he?'

'He sure did, miss.'

'Who was your great-grandmother?' Kathy asked.

'Her name was Patricia Hennessey. They met after the accident, that Christmas. They say he kind of—'

'Kind of what?'

'Kind of married her on the rebound. Seems he lost the girl he *was* going to marry in the boating accident. My great-grandma was what I guess you'd call a second choice.'

Then he grinned (Willy's grin!), shaking his head. 'I just can't figure how you knew about him . . . Are you a friend of the family?'

'No.' She shook her head.

'And we've never met before, have we?'

She looked into the deep lake-blue of his eyes. 'No, Willy, we've never met.' She smiled. 'But we're going to be friends . . . very, very good friends.'

And she kissed him gently, softly, under the serene sky of a sun-bright Michigan afternoon on the shore of a placid lake in the autumn of a very special year.

PRODUCTION PROBLEM

Robert F. Young

*One of the opportunities to be gained from travelling into the past—
or even into the future, for that matter—is perhaps to take advantage
of the creative achievements for one's own time. The concept intrigued
Robert F. Young and inspired his story 'Production Problem', first
published in* Venture SF *in November 1964. He also wrote about time
travel in several other stories, including 'When Time Was New' (1964)
about a journey into prehistory, which he expanded twenty years later
into a novel entitled* Eridahn *(1983); and the moving romantic tale,
'One Love Have I' (1969), which is not unlike the previous story by
William F. Nolan.*

*Robert Franklin Young (1915–1986) once described his early career
as 'a series of menial jobs' before his natural ability as a writer,
combined with a fine imagination, enabled him to make a living contribution to a whole range of publications—from the* Saturday Evening
Post *to several science fiction magazines, including the* Magazine of
Fantasy and Science Fiction, *in which he quickly built up a loyal following. The best of his early sf stories were collected in* The Worlds of
Robert F. Young *(1965) and* A Glass of Stars *(1968) and, despite the
comparative success of his novels, including* Starfinder *(1980) and* The
Last Yggdrasil *(1982), it is for his satirical and occasionally acerbic
short work that he will be best remembered. 'Production Problem' is
amusingly typical of his style.*

*   *   *

'The man from Timesearch, Inc. is here, sir.'

'Show him in,' Bridgemaker told the robutler.

The man from Timesearch halted just within the doorway. Nervously
he shifted the oblong package he was carrying from one hand to the
other. 'Good morning, Honourable Bridgemaker.'

'Did you find the machine?' Bridgemaker demanded.

'I—I'm afraid we failed again, sir. But we did locate another one of its products.' The man handed Bridgemaker the package.

Bridgemaker waved his arm in an angry gesture that included the whole room. 'But you've brought me hundreds of its products!' he shouted. 'What I want is the machine itself so I can make my own products!'

'I'm afraid, Honourable Bridgemaker, that the machine never existed. Our field men have explored the Pre-Technological Age, the First Technological Age, and the early years of our own age; but even though they witnessed some of the ancient technicians at work, they never caught a glimpse of the machine.'

'But if the ancient technicians could create something without a machine, *I* could too,' Bridgemaker said. 'And since I can't, the machine *had* to exist. Go back at once!'

'Yes, Honourable Bridgemaker.' The man bowed and withdrew.

Bridgemaker tore open the package. He glanced at the product, then set the controls on his Language Adjuster, Duplicator and Alterator machine.

While he waited, he brooded on the irony of his life. Ever since he was a small boy he had hungered hopelessly for one vocation. Now that success in a totally different vocation had made him financially independent, he had focused all his energies into the attainment of his first love. But all he'd got for his trouble was a roomful of ancient products, and even though he'd increased his financial independence by duplicating and distributing those products, the basic frustration still remained: he was a second-hand artist and he wanted desperately to be a first-hand artist.

He went over to one of the shelves that wainscoted the room and glanced at some of his vicarious creations: *Farewell to Arms*, by Chamfer Bridgemaker . . . *Five Little Peppers and How They Grew*, by Chamfer Bridgemaker . . . *The Odyssey*, by Chamfer Bridgemaker . . . *Ivanhoe*, by Chamfer Bridgemaker—

There was a loud *plop!* as the first copy of *Tom Swift and His Electric Locomotive* came out of the Language Adjuster, Duplicator and Alterator machine.

Bridgemaker sat down to read his latest masterpiece.

I HEAR YOU CALLING

Eric Frank Russell

The theories that Charles Fort developed earlier this century from his huge collection of cuttings about inexplicable events all over the world and which led him to the conclusion that human beings may be the 'property' of aliens, was one of the formative influences on Eric Frank Russell. Renewed interest in Fort's books and theories has been instrumental in generating the current fascination with strange phenomena, typified by the huge success of the TV series The X-Files, *and has again focused interest on Russell's stories, which utilise similar material. His novel,* Sinister Barrier *(1943), for example, about alien entities that have been 'feeding' on man's emotions and thereby caused much human conflict, was primarily responsible for making his reputation, along with the 'Jay Score' series about an interplanetary crew of explorers and their heroic robot, which has recently been cited as a forerunner of* Star Trek.

Eric Frank Russell (1905–78) was the son of an Army instructor and spent much of his childhood travelling all over the world. He briefly served in the Army himself, then tried a variety of jobs before making his mark as a writer of science fiction. His quirky imagination made him popular with American readers, and his was one of the foremost British names to appear in US sf magazines during the Fifties and Sixties. 'The Waitabits', written in 1955, and dealing with a group of aliens for whom time moves exceedingly slowly, is perhaps Russell's best known story to feature time travel. The comical 'The Courtship of 53 Shotl 9 G', about a man from the future discovering love in the little Irish backwater of Ballykilljoy, was published a year earlier. 'I Hear You Calling', which appeared in Science Fantasy *in December 1954, is different again: a grim little vignette about the dangers of inadvertently summoning a traveller from the far future . . .*

*   *   *

A frightened town, dark and deadly. A minor name on a vast map. Formerly noteworthy for nothing save the idle rumour that a flying saucer had landed nearby. That had been a month ago and proved baseless. Police and pressmen scoured the outskirts. No saucer.

This event faded, lost significance as hunters took off in pursuit of something else, something weightier and more urgent that cleared the streets by night. On the main stem a few dusty, neglected neons glowed over empty bars while cops lurked in shadowy doorways, watched cats playing leapfrog and jumping low.

Widgey Bullock knew nothing of this. To him the town had its virtues. That was why he had just arrived there. It was forty miles from port, devoid of naval patrols, officers, pickpockets and the same old bunch of painted trollops. A new landfall. A place where a naval stoker first-class could roll the boat without getting tossed into the brig.

Entering a likely bar, he shoved his pork-pie on to the back of his head, said, 'I'm in the mood, Mac. Give me an Atom bomb.'

'What might that be?' inquired the barman. He was a fat simple, pasty-faced with too little sun, too little sleep.

'I should have to tell you?' Widgey hitched his lean bulk on a stool, rubbed blue jowls. 'Equal parts rum, tequila and vodka. Add a pinch of red pepper and shake.'

'God!' said the other. He slopped it together, vibrated it, slid it across. Then he watched warily as if awaiting the mushroom cloud.

Widgey poured some down. He twitched his scalp and the cap jerked with it.

'What a joint,' he commented, staring around. 'No juke-box, no dames, no company, nobody but you and me. Where's everybody?'

'Home,' said the barman. He nodded toward the wall-clock. 'Ten thirty and it's dark.'

'Mean to say the town's closed down?' Widgey tipped the cap over his eyes, stared incredulously. 'Ten thirty's the time for things to start livening up. The police should get jumping around midnight.'

'Not here,' said the barman. His gaze drifted toward the door, came back. He didn't seem to know what might enter next but obviously didn't want it, not at any price.

'What's wrong with here?' demanded Widgey, ignoring the door.

'Folk are getting themselves killed.'

'How's that? Somebody feuding?'

'They just lie around dead,' said the barman. 'Dead and empty.'

'Empty?'

'No blood,' said the barman.

'Give me another,' Widgey ordered, poking his glass. He got it, took a deep gulp, coughing with the fire of it. 'Now let's have this straight. Who's being killed?'

'One here, one there,' the other said. 'Mostly strangers.'

'I'm a stranger myself,' Widgey pointed out. 'Does that put me on the list?'

'Wouldn't be surprised.'

'What a dump!' Widgey complained. 'Forty miles I come for bright lights and freedom. What do I get? A hick town heading for bed and a barkeep measuring my corpse.'

'Sorry,' said the other, 'But you might as well know.' He waves a hand to emphasize the sheer emptiness of the place. 'This is just the way it's been every night for the last three weeks. When I go home I keep close by the wall and wear my eyes in my pants the whole way. I keep my door locked twice over.'

'What are the cops doing about it?'

'Looking,' said the barman. 'What else can they do?'

'This sounds like a bar-yarn to me,' observed Widgey, suspiciously. 'Are you figuring on getting rid of me and shutting shop early?'

'Dead wrong,' the barman told him. 'It's all in the papers. A dry stiff every other night.' He eyed the door again. 'Besides, I can't close up when I like and I need the company.'

'I'll say you do.' Widgey assured. 'Fellow your weight will have buckets of blood. You're a major target.'

'Shut up!' said the barman, looking sick.

'I'm not worrying,' Widgey went on. 'Just one night here and back to the ship tomorrow. After that, you can have this lousy town and welcome.' He took a long swig, smacked his lips. 'Know of any other joint where there'd be more than two of us?'

'No. Not at this time.'

'Well, d'you know of an address where I can knock three times and ask for Mabel?'

'Think I'm a pimp?' asked the barman, frowning.

'I think you ought to know your way around seeing this is your own stamping ground.'

'It isn't mine. I've been here only a couple of months.' He wiped the back of his neck, peered towards the street. 'That's what scares me. I rank as a stranger too.'

'Take it easy,' Widgey advised. 'When you're dead and empty you won't know it even if you look like a slack sack.' He poked the glass again. 'Make it a double. If you can't give me an address I'll have to do without. Maybe I can drink myself beyond what I have in mind.'

The barman said, 'Any more you'd better take with you. This is where I shut shop.'

Widgey pointed to a yellow bottle. 'I'll take that.' He fumbled clumsily in a pocket, dug out money and paid. A couple of coins fell to the floor. He teetered as he picked them up.

'It's working on you,' said the barman.

'Which is all that is,' said Widgey.

Pocketing the bottle he rolled out with a decided list to starboard. The street was a mess of greys and blacks, the neons gone. A thin sliver of moon rode above bulging clouds.

He headed uncertainly for the crummy hotel where he'd booked a room. A leering tomcat slunk across his path, wanting the same as he did. Hidden in the dark entrance to an alley a policeman watching his passing, made no sound to betray his presence. On the other side of the road a woman hurried along, wary and fearful.

'Hi, Babe!' he hoarsed across, not caring whether she were hot or cold, young or old.

She broke into a near-run, her heels making a fast and urgent *clip-clop*. Widgey stood watching her and swearing under his breath. The policeman emerged from the alley, kept an eye on both of them. The woman stopped two hundred yards down, frantically stabbed a key at a door, went into a house. The slam of the door sounded like the crack of doom.

'Bet they say their prayers, too,' scoffed Widgey.

Alcoholically aggrieved, he lurched onward, found the hotel, climbed upstairs. Savagely he flung his cap across the room, pulled off his jacket and shied it the same way, kicked his shoes under the bed. He spent a minute examining himself in the mirror over the washbasin, pawing his ears and making faces at himself. Then he went to the window and looked out at the night.

There was another woman on the road below. She drifted along in a strange unhurried manner, an undulating glide like that of a column of grey smoke wafted by a gentle breeze. She was blurry as if draped and veiled. A lot of things look blurry when a man has heavy cargo under the hatches.

But a woman is a woman. One who travels late and without haste is always a good prospect, thought Widgey. Slipping the catch, he opened the window and leaned out. No cops were visible. Nobody but the vague figure.

'Yoohoo!'

It achieved nothing. Perhaps she hadn't heard.

'*Yoohoo!*'

The figure stopped. Moonlight was too poor to show which way she was looking but at least her halt was encouraging.

'YOOHOO!' bawled Widgey, bending farther out and throwing discretion to the winds. He waved an energetic arm.

The figure made a vague gesture, crossed the road towards the hotel. Closing the window, Widgey delightedly tried a slow soft shoe routine but his balance had gone to pot. Seas were rough tonight.

He left his door a couple of inches ajar so she would know which room was which. Hurriedly he cleaned a couple of glasses by sloshing water around them, put them on the bedside table along with the yellow bottle.

A timid knock sounded.

'Come in!' He spat on his hands, used them to brush back his hair, fixed a welcoming grin on his face.

The knocker came in.

Widgey backed away fast, then more slowly as strength flowed out of his legs. His grin had vanished and he'd gone cold sober in one-fifth of a second. He wanted to yell bloody murder but couldn't emit a squeak.

The edge of the bed caught behind his retreating knees. He flopped backward, lay on the bed with chest and throat exposed. He couldn't do a thing to save himself, not a damn thing.

It glided soundlessly to the bedside, bent over and looked at him with eyes that were black pinheads set deeply in green fluff. Its long, elastic mouth came out and pouted like the nozzle of a fire-hose. The last that Widgey heard was a whisper from a million miles away.

'*I am Yuhu. You called me.*'

THE MEN WHO MURDERED MOHAMMED

Alfred Bester

This next story has been described by sf historian Peter Nicholls as 'perhaps the most concentratedly witty twist on the time-paradox story ever written.' It concerns a great mathematician, Professor Henry Hassel, who returns home one day to find his wife in another man's arms and decides on a most unusual punishment—he will build a time machine and venture into the past to take revenge on his unfaithful spouse's ancestors. But, as you will discover, the peculiar nature of time has some unexpected surprises in store for the professor.

Alfred Bester (1913–87), who was born in New York and spent much of his life there, did not produce a large body of sf, concentrating more on TV scripts and on his job as an editorial member of the staff of Holiday *magazine. This said, his novel* The Demolished Man *(1953), a brilliant murder mystery set in a world where the ruling class possesses telepathic skills, won a Hugo award and is now considered a classic, while his short stories were influential on such emerging talents as James Blish, Samuel R. Delany and Michael Moorcock. 'The Men Who Murdered Mohammed' (1958) is among the very best of these shorter works, clever in concept and, as admirers of Alfred Bester would expect, quite unlike any other time travel story in this collection.*

*   *   *

There was a man who mutilated history. He toppled empires and uprooted dynasties. Because of him Mount Vernon should not be a national shrine, and Columbus, Ohio, should be called Cabot, Ohio. Because of him the name Marie Curie should be cursed in France, and no one should swear by the beard of the Prophet. Actually, these realities did not happen, because he was a mad professor; or, to put it another way, he only succeeded in making them unreal for himself.

Now, the patient reader is too familiar with the conventional mad professor, undersized and overbrowed, creating monsters in his laboratory which invariably turn on their maker and menace his lovely daughter. This story isn't about that sort of make-believe man. It's about Henry Hassel, a genuine mad professor in a class with such better-known men as Ludwig Boltzmann (*see* Ideal Gas Law), Jacques Charles and André Marie Ampère (1775–1836).

Everyone ought to know that the electrical ampere was so named in honour of Ampère. Ludwig Boltzmann was a distinguished Austrian physicist, as famous for his research on black-body radiation as on Ideal Gases. You can look him up in Volume Three of the *Encyclopaedia Britannica*, BALT to BRAI. Jacques Alexandre César Charles was the first mathematician to become interested in flight, and he invented the hydrogen balloon. These were real men.

They were also real mad professors. Ampère, for example, was on his way to an important meeting of scientists in Paris. In his taxi he got a brilliant idea (of an electrical nature, I assume) and whipped out a pencil and jotted the equation on the wall of the hansom cab. Roughly, it was: $dH = ipdl/r^2$ in which p is the perpendicular distance from P to the line of the element dl; or $dH = i \sin \emptyset \ dl/r^2$. This is sometimes known as Laplace's Law, although he wasn't at the meeting.

Anyway, the cab arrived at the Académie. Ampère jumped out, paid the driver and rushed into the meeting to tell everybody about his idea. Then he realised he didn't have the note on him, remembered where he'd left it, and had to chase through the streets of Paris after the taxi to recover his runaway equation. Sometimes I imagine that's how Fermat lost his famous 'Last Theorem', although Fermat wasn't at the meeting either, having died some two hundred years earlier.

Or take Boltzmann. Giving a course in Advanced Ideal Gases, he peppered his lectures with involved calculus, which he worked out quickly and casually in his head. He had that kind of head. His students had so much trouble trying to puzzle out the maths by ear that they couldn't keep up with the lectures, and they begged Boltzmann to work out his equations on the blackboard.

Boltzmann apologised and promised to be more helpful in the future. At the next lecture he began, 'Gentlemen, combining Boyle's Law with the Law of Charles, we arrive at the equation $pv = p_o v_o(1 + at)$. Now, obviously, if $_aS^b = f(x)dx \ \emptyset(a)$, then $pv = RT$ and $_vS \ f \ (x,y,z,) \ dV = 0$.

It's as simple as two plus two equals four.' At this point Boltzmann remembered his promise. He turned to the blackboard, conscientiously chalked $2 + 2 = 4$, and then breezed on, casually doing the complicated calculus in his head.

Jacques Charles, the brilliant mathematician who discovered Charles' Law (sometimes known as Gay-Lussac's Law), which Boltzmann mentioned in his lecture, had a lunatic passion to become a famous palaeographer—that is, a discoverer of ancient manuscripts. I think that being forced to share credit with Gay-Lussac may have unhinged him.

He paid a transparent swindler named Vrain-Lucas 200,000 francs for holograph letters purportedly written by Julius Caesar, Alexander the Great, and Pontius Pilate. Charles, a man who could see through any gas, ideal or not, actually believed in these forgeries despite the fact that the maladroit Vrain-Lucas had written them in modern French on modern notepaper bearing modern watermarks. Charles even tried to donate them to the Louvre.

Now, these men weren't idiots. They were geniuses who paid a high price for their genius because the rest of their thinking was other-world. A genius is someone who travels to truth by an unexpected path. Unfortunately, unexpected paths lead to disaster in everyday life. This is what happened to Henry Hassel, professor of Applied Compulsion at Unknown University in the year 1980.

Nobody knows where Unknown University is or what they teach there. It has a faculty of some two hundred eccentrics, and a student body of two thousand misfits—the kind that remain anonymous until they win Nobel prizes or become the First Man on Mars. You can always spot a graduate of UU when you ask people where they went to school. If you get an evasive reply like: 'State', or 'Oh, a fresh-water school you never heard of', you can bet they went to Unknown. Someday I hope to tell you more about this university, which is a centre of learning only in the Pickwickian sense.

Anyway, Henry Hassel started home from his office in the Psychotic Psenter early one afternoon, strolling through the Physical Culture arcade. It is not true that he did this to leer at the nude co-eds practising Arcane Eurythmics; rather, Hassel liked to admire the trophies displayed in the arcade in memory of great Unknown teams which had won the sort of championships that Unknown teams win—in sports like Strabismus, Occlusion and Botulism. (Hassel had been Frambesia singles champion three years running.) He arrived home uplifted, and burst gaily into the house to discover his wife in the arms of a man.

There she was, a lovely woman of thirty-five, with smoky red hair and almond eyes, being heartily embraced by a person whose pockets were stuffed with pamphlets, microchemical apparatus and a patella-reflex hammer—a typical campus character of UU, in fact. The embrace was so concentrated that neither of the offending parties noticed Henry Hassel glaring at them from the hallway.

Now, remember Ampère and Charles and Boltzmann. Hassel weighed 190 pounds. He was muscular and uninhibited. It would have been child's play for him to have dismembered his wife and her lover, and thus simply and directly achieved the goal he desired—the end of his wife's life. But Henry Hassel was in the genius class; his mind just didn't operate that way.

Hassel breathed hard, turned and lumbered into his private laboratory like a freight engine. He opened a drawer labelled DUODENUM and removed a .45-calibre revolver. He opened other drawers, more interestingly labelled, and assembled apparatus. In exactly 7½ minutes (such was his rage), he put together a time machine (such was his genius).

Professor Hassel assembled the time machine around him, set a dial for 1902, picked up the revolver and pressed a button. The machine made a nose like defective plumbing and Hassel disappeared. He reappeared in Philadelphia on June 3, 1902, went directly to no. 1218 Walnut Street, a red-brick house with marble steps, and rang the bell. A man who might have passed for the third Smith Brother opened the door and looked at Henry Hassel.

'Mr Jessup?' Hassel asked in a suffocated voice.

'Yes?'

'You are Mr Jessup?'

'I am.'

'You will have a son, Edgar? Edgar Allan Jessup—so named because of your regrettable admiration for Poe?'

The third Smith Brother was startled. 'Not that I know of,' he said. 'I'm not married yet.'

'You will be,' Hassel said angrily. 'I have the misfortune to be married to your son's daughter, Greta. Excuse me.' He raised the revolver and shot his wife's grandfather-to-be.

'She will have ceased to exist,' Hassel muttered, blowing smoke out of the revolver. 'I'll be a bachelor. I may even be married to somebody else . . . Good God! Who?'

Hassel waited impatiently for the automatic recall of the time machine to snatch him back to his own laboratory. He rushed into his living-room. There was his red-beaded wife, still in the arms of a man.

Hassel was thunderstruck.

'So that's it,' he growled. 'A family tradition of faithlessness. Well, we'll see about that. We have ways and means.' He permitted himself a hollow laugh, returned to his laboratory, and sent himself back to the year 1901, where he shot and killed Emma Hotchkiss, his wife's maternal grandmother-to-be. He returned to his own home in his own time. There was his red-headed wife, still in the arms of another man.

'But I *know* the old hag was her grandmother,' Hassel muttered. 'You couldn't miss the resemblance. What the hell's gone wrong?'

Hassel was confused and dismayed, but not without resources. He went to his study, had difficulty picking up the phone, but finally managed to dial the Malpractice Laboratory. His finger kept oozing out of the dial holes.

'Sam?' he said. 'This is Henry.'

'Who?'

'Henry.'

'You'll have to speak up.'

'Henry Hassel!'

'Oh, good-afternoon, Henry.'

'Tell me all about time.'

'Time? Hmmm . . .' The Simplex-and-Multiplex Computer cleared its throat while it waited for the data circuits to link up. 'Ahem Time. (1) Absolute. (2) Relative. (3) Recurrent. (1) Absolute: period, contingent, duration, diurnity, perpetuity—'

'Sorry, Sam. Wrong request. Go back. I want time, reference to succession of, travel in.'

Sam shifted gears and began again. Hassel listened intently. He nodded. He grunted. 'Uh huh. Uh huh. Right. I see. Thought so. A continuum, eh? Acts performed in past must alter future. Then I'm on the right track. But act must be significant, eh? Mass-action effect. Trivia cannot divert existing phenomena streams. Hmmm. But how trivial is a grandmother?'

'What are you trying to do, Henry?'

'Kill my wife,' Hassel snapped. He hung up. He returned to his laboratory. He considered, still in a jealous rage.

'Got to do something significant,' he muttered. 'Wipe Greta out. Wipe it all out. All right, by God! I'll show 'em.'

Hassel went back to the year 1775, visited a Virginia farm and shot a young colonel in the brisket. The colonel's name was George Washington, and Hassel made sure he was dead. He returned to his own time and his own home. There was his red-headed wife, still in the arms of another.

'Damn!' said Hassel. He was running out of ammunition. He opened a fresh box of cartridges, went back in time, and massacred Christopher Columbus, Napoleon, Mohammed, and half a dozen other celebrities. 'That ought to do it, by God!' said Hassel.

He returned to his own time, and found his wife as before.

His knees turned to water; his feet seemed to melt into the floor. He went back to his laboratory, walking through nightmare quicksands.

'What the hell is significant?' Hassel asked himself painfully. 'How much does it take to change futurity? By God, I'll really change it this time. I'll go for broke.'

He travelled to Paris at the turn of the twentieth century and visited a Madame Curie in an attic workshop near the Sorbonne. 'Madame,' he said in his execrable French, 'I am a stranger to you of the utmost, but a scientist entire. Knowing of your experiments with radium—Oh? You haven't got to radium yet? No matter. I am here to teach you all of nuclear fission.'

He taught her. He had the satisfaction of seeing Paris go up in a mushroom of smoke before the automatic recall brought him home. 'That'll teach women to be faithless,' he growled. 'Guhhh!' The last was wrenched from his lips when he saw his red-headed wife still— But no need to belabour the obvious.

Hassel swam through fogs to his study and sat down to think. While he's thinking I'd better warn you that this is not a conventional time story. If you imagine for a moment that Henry is going to discover that the man fondling his wife is himself, you're mistaken. The viper is not Henry Hassel, his son, a relation, or even Ludwig Boltzmann (1844–1906). Hassel does not make a circle in time, ending where the story begins—to the satisfaction of nobody and the fury of everybody—for the simple reason that time isn't circular, or linear, or tandem, discoid, syzygous, longinquitous or pandiculated. Time is a private matter, as Hassel discovered.

'Maybe I slipped up somehow,' Hassel muttered. 'I'd better find out.' He fought with the telephone, which seemed to weigh a hundred tons, and at last managed to get through to the library.

'Hello, Library? This is Henry.'

'Who?'

'Henry Hassel.'

'Speak up, please.'

'HENRY HASSEL!'

'Oh. Good afternoon, Henry.'

'What have you got on George Washington?'

Library clucked while her scanners sorted through her catalogues. 'George Washington, first President of the United States, was born in—'

'First President? Wasn't he murdered in 1775?'

'Really, Henry. That's an absurd question. Everybody knows that George Wash—'

'Doesn't anybody know he was shot?'

'By whom?'

'Me.'

'When?'

'In 1775.'

'How did you manage to do that?'

'I've got a revolver.'

'No, I mean, how did you do it two hundred years ago?'

'I've got a time machine.'

'Well, there's no record here,' Library said. 'He's still doing fine in my files. You must have missed.'

'I did not miss. What about Christopher Columbus? Any record of his death in 1489?'

'But he discovered the New World in 1492.'

'He did not. He was murdered in 1489.'

'How?'

'With a forty-five slug in the gizzard.'

'You again, Henry?'

'Yes.'

'There's no record here,' Library insisted. 'You must be one lousy shot.'

'I will not lose my temper,' Hassel said in a trembling voice.

'Why not, Henry?'

'Because it's lost already,' he shouted. 'All right! What about Marie Curie? Did she or did she not discover the fission bomb which destroyed Paris at the turn of the century?'

'She did not. Enrico Fermi—'

'She did.'

'She didn't.'

'I personally taught her. Me. Henry Hassel.'

'Everybody says you're a wonderful theoretician, but a lousy teacher, Henry. You—'

'Go to hell, you old biddy. This has got to be explained.'

'Why?'

'I forget. There was something on my mind, but it doesn't matter now. What would you suggest?'

'You really have a time machine?'

'Of course I've got a time machine.'

'Then go back and check.'

Hassel returned to the year 1775, visited Mount Vernon, and interrupted the spring planting. 'Excuse me, Colonel,' he began.

The big man looked at him curiously. 'You talk funny, stranger,' he said. 'Where are you from?'

'Oh, a fresh-water school you never heard of.'

'You look funny too. Kind of misty, so to speak.'

'Tell me, Colonel, what do you hear from Christopher Columbus?'

'Not much,' Colonel Washington answered. 'Been dead two, three hundred years.'

'When did he die?'

'Year fifteen hundred some-odd, near as I remember.'

'He did not. He died in 1489.'

'Got your dates wrong, friend. He discovered America in 1492.'

'Cabot discovered America. Sebastian Cabot.'

'Nope. Cabot came a mite later.'

'I have infallible proof!' Hassel began, but broke off as a stocky and rather stout man, with a face ludicrously reddened by rage, approached. He was wearing baggy grey slacks and a tweed jacket two sizes too small for him. He was carrying a .45 revolver. It was only after he had stared for a moment that Henry Hassel realised that he was looking at himself and not relishing the sight.

'My God!' Hassel murmured. 'It's me, coming back to murder Washington that first time. If I'd made this second trip an hour later, I'd have found Washington dead. Hey!' he called. 'Not yet. Hold off a minute. I've got to straighten something out first.'

Hassel paid no attention to himself; indeed, he did not appear to be aware of himself. He marched straight up to Colonel Washington and shot him in the gizzard. Colonel Washington collapsed, emphatically dead. The first murderer inspected the body, and then, ignoring Hassel's attempt to stop him and engage him in dispute, turned and marched off, muttering venomously to himself.

'He didn't hear me,' Hassel wondered. 'He didn't even feel me. And why don't I remember myself trying to stop me the first time I shot the colonel? What the hell is going on?'

Considerably disturbed, Henry Hassel visited Chicago and dropped into the Chicago University squash courts in the early 1940s. There, in a slippery mess of graphite bricks and graphite dust that coated him, he located an Italian scientist named Fermi.

'Repeating Marie Curie's work, I see, *dottore*?' Hassel said.

Fermi glanced about as though he had heard a faint sound.

'Repeating Marie Curie's work, *dottore*?' Hassel roared.

Fermi looked at him strangely. 'Where you from, *amico*?'

'State.'

'State Department?'

'Just State. It's true, isn't it, *dottore*, that Marie Curie discovered nuclear fission back in nineteen ought ought?'

'No! No! No!' Fermi cried. 'We are the first, and we are not there yet. Police! Police! Spy!'

'This time I'll go on record,' Hassel growled. He pulled out his trusty .45, emptied it into Dr Fermi's chest,.and awaited arrest and immolation in newspaper files. To his amazement, Dr Fermi did not collapse. Dr Fermi merely explored his chest tenderly and, to the men who answered his cry, said, 'It is nothing. I felt in my within a sudden sensation of burn which may be a neuralgia of the cardiac nerve, but is most likely gas.'

Hassel was too agitated to wait for the automatic recall of the time machine. Instead he returned at once to Unknown University under his own power. This should have given him a clue, but he was too possessed to notice. It was at this time that I (1913–75) first saw him—a dim figure tramping through parked cars, closed doors and brick walls, with the light of lunatic determination on his face.

He oozed into the library, prepared for an exhaustive discussion, but could not make himself felt or heard by the catalogues. He went to the Malpractice Laboratory, where Sam, the Simplex-and-Multiplex Computer, has installations sensitive up to 10,700 angstroms. Sam could not see Henry, but managed to hear him through a sort of wave-interference phenomenon.

'Sam,' Hassel said, 'I've made one hell of a discovery.'

'You're always making discoveries, Henry,' Sam complained. 'Your data allocation is filled. Do I have to start another tape for you?'

'But I need advice. Who's the leading authority on time, reference to succession of, travel in?'

'That would be Israel Lennox, spatial mechanics, professor of, Yale.'

'How do I get in touch with him?'

'You don't, Henry. He's dead. Died in '75.'

'What authority have you got on time, travel in, living?'

'Wiley Murphy.'

'Murphy? From our own Trauma Department? That's a break. Where is he now?'

'As a matter of fact, Henry, he went over to your house to ask you something.'

Hassel went home without walking, searched through his laboratory and study without finding anyone, and at last floated into the living-room, where his red-headed wife was still in the arms of another man. (All this, you understand, had taken place within the space of a few moments after the construction of the time machine; such is the nature of time and time travel.) Hassel cleared his throat once or twice and tried to tap his wife on the shoulder. His fingers went through her.

'Excuse me, darling,' he said. 'Has Wiley Murphy been in to see me?'

Then he looked closer and saw that the man embracing his wife was Murphy himself.

'Murphy!' Hassel exclaimed. 'The very man I'm looking for. I've had the most extraordinary experience.' Hassel at once launched into a lucid description of his extraordinary experience, which went something like this: 'Murphy, $u - v = (u^{\frac{1}{2}} - v^{\frac{1}{4}}) (u^a + u^x v^y + v^b)$ but when George Washington $F(x) y^2 \phi dx$ and Enrico Fermi $F(u^{\frac{1}{2}})$ dxdt one half of Marie Curie, then what about Christopher Columbus times the square root of minus one?'

Murphy ignored Hassel, as did Mrs Hassel. I jotted down Hassel's equations on the hood of a passing taxi.

'Do listen to me, Murphy,' Hassel said. 'Greta dear, would you mind leaving us for a moment? I— For heaven's sake, will you two stop that nonsense? This is serious.'

Hassel tried to separate the couple. He could no more touch them than make them hear him. His face turned red again, and he became quite choleric as he beat at Mrs Hassel and Murphy. It was like beating an Ideal Gas. I thought it best to interfere.

'Hassel!'

'Who's that?'

'Come outside a moment. I want to talk to you.'

He shot through the wall. 'Where are you?'

'Over here.'

'You're sort of dim.'

'So are you.'

'Who are you?'

'My name's Lennox. Israel Lennox.'

'Israel Lennox, spatial mechanics, professor of, Yale?'

'The same.'

'But you died in '75.'

'I disappeared in '75.'

'What d'you mean?'

'I invented a time machine.'

'By God! So did I,' Hassel said. 'This afternoon. The idea came to me in a flash—I don't know why—and I've had the most extraordinary experience. Lennox, time is not a continuum.'

'No?'

'It's a series of discrete particles—like pearls on a string.'

'Yes?'

'Each pearl is a "Now". Each "Now" has its own past and future. But none of them relate to any others. You see? If $a = a_1 + a_2ji + \text{\o}ax(b_1)$—'

'Never mind the mathematics, Henry.'

'It's a form of quantum transfer of energy. Time is emitted in discrete corpuscles or quanta. We can visit each individual quantum and make changes within it, but no change in any one corpuscle affects any other corpuscle. Right?'

'Wrong,' I said sorrowfully.

'What d'you mean—"Wrong"?' he said, angrily gesturing through the cleavage of a passing co-ed. 'You take the trochoid equations and—'

'Wrong,' I repeated firmly. 'Will you listen to me, Henry?'

'Oh, go ahead,' he said.

'Have you noticed that you've become rather insubstantial? Dim? Spectral? Space and time no longer affect you?'

'Yes.'

'Henry, I had the misfortune to construct a time machine back in '75.'

'So you said. Listen, what about power input? I figure I'm using about 7.3 kilowatts per—'

'Never mind the power input, Henry. On my first trip into the past, I visited the Pleistocene. I was eager to photograph the mastodon, the giant ground sloth, and the sabre-tooth tiger. While I was backing up to get a mastodon fully in the field of view at f/6.3 at 1/100th of a second, or on the LVS scale—'

'Never mind the LVS scale,' he said.

'While I was backing up, I inadvertently trampled and killed a small Pleistocene insect.'

'Aha!' said Hassel.

'I was terrified by the incident. I had visions of returning to my world to find it completely changed as a result of this single death. Imagine my surprise when I returned to my world to find that nothing had changed.'

'Oho!' said Hassel.

'I became curious. I went back to the Pleistocene and killed the mastodon. Nothing was changed in 1975. I returned to the Pleistocene and slaughtered the wildlife—still with no effect. I ranged through time, killing and destroying, in an attempt to alter the present.'

'Then you did it just like me,' Hassel exclaimed. 'Odd we didn't run into each other.'

'Not odd at all.'

'I got Columbus.'

'I got Marco Polo.'

'I got Napoleon.'

'I thought Einstein was more important.'

'Mohammed didn't change things much—I expected more from *him*.'

'I know. I got him too.'

'What do you mean, you got him too?' Hassel demanded.

'I killed him September 16, 599. Old Style.'

'Why, I got Mohammed January 5, 598.'

'I believe you.'

'But how could you have killed him after I killed him?'

'We both killed him.'

'That's impossible.'

'My boy,' I said, 'time is entirely subjective. It's a private matter— a personal experience. 'There is no such thing as objective time, just as there is no such thing as objective love, or an objective soul.'

'Do you mean to say that time travel is impossible? But we've done it.'

'To be sure, and many others, for all I know. But we each travel into our own past, and no other person's. There is no universal continuum, Henry. There are only billions of individuals, each with his own continuum; and one continuum cannot affect the other. We're like millions of strands of spaghetti in the same pot. No time traveller can ever meet another time traveller in the past or future. Each of us must travel up and down his own strand alone.'

'But we're meeting each other now.'

'We're no longer time travellers, Henry. We've become the spaghetti sauce.'

'Spaghetti sauce?'

'Yes. You and I can visit any strand we like, because we've destroyed ourselves.'

'I don't understand.'

'When a man changes the past he only affects his own past—no one else's. The past is like memory. When you erase a man's memory, you wipe him out, but you don't wipe out anybody else. You and I have erased our past. The individual worlds of the others go on, but we have ceased to exist.' I paused significantly.

'What d'you mean—"ceased to exist"?'

'With each act of destruction we dissolved a little. Now we're all gone. We've committed chronicide. We're ghosts. I hope Mrs Hassel will be vary happy with Mr Murphy ... Now let's go over to the Académie. Ampère is telling a great story about Ludwig Boltzmann.'

TIME INTERVENING

Ray Bradbury

It is a curious fact that Ray Bradbury, who has probably written more short stories about time travel than anyone else, actually prefers the slowest *forms of transport. He hates flying, has never learned to drive a car, and by choice will travel by rail or sea. Yet this is the man whose imagination has travelled headlong around the galaxy, visited Mars time and again, and devised every kind of excursion through time. Among the most anthologised of these stories are 'The Black Ferris' (1948), 'Forever and the Earth' (1954), 'A Sound of Thunder' (1952), 'Time in Thy Flight' (1953), 'A Scent of Sarsaparilla' (1953), 'The Time Machine' (1955) and 'The Toynbee Convector' (1988).*

Raymond Douglas Bradbury (1920–) is one of today's most gifted writers, almost effortlessly, apparently, creating the kind of original fantasy, science fiction, horror and mystery stories that have put him at the forefront of these genres while at the same time earning him an honoured place among mainstream writers. His classic novels The Martian Chronicles *(1950),* The Illustrated Man *(1951), and* Fahrenheit 451 *(1953) have all been filmed, and many of his short stories have been adapted for popular television series. Recently, he has added two exceptional crime novels to his* oeuvre, Death Is a Lonely Business *(1985) and* A Graveyard for Lunatics *(1990). 'Time Intervening' is a rarity among Bradbury's works, a sombre and moving time story originally published under the title 'Interim' in the Fall 1947 issue of Cornell University's magazine* Epoch. *It has not so far appeared in his collected works, and should not be confused with his other story called 'Interim', which appeared in the July 1947 issue of* Weird Tales *and subsequently in his collection,* Dark Carnival *(1947).*

*   *   *

Very late on this night, the old man came from his house with a flashlight in his hand and asked of the little boys the object of their frolic. The little boys gave no answer, but tumbled on in the leaves.

The old man went into his house and sat down and worried. It was three in the morning. He saw his own pale small hands trembling on his knees. He was all joints and angles, and his face, reflected above the mantel, was no more than a pale cloud of breath exhaled upon the mirror.

The children laughed softly outside, in the leaf piles.

He switched out his flashlight quietly and sat in the dark. Why he should be in any way bothered by playing children he could not know. But it was late for them to be out, at three in the morning, playing. He was very cold.

There was a sound of a key in the door and the old man arose to go see who could possibly be coming into his house. The front door opened and a young man entered with a young woman. They were looking at each other softly and tenderly, holding hands, and the old man stared at them and cried, 'What are you *doing* in my house?'

The young man and the young woman replied, 'What are *you* doing in *our* house?' The young man said, 'Here now, get on out.' And took the old man by the elbow and shoved him out of the door and closed and locked it after searching him to see if he had stolen something.

'This is *my* house, you *can't* lock me out.' The old man beat upon the door. He stood in the dark morning air. Looking up he saw the lights illumine the warm inside windows and rooms upstairs and then, with a move of shadows, go out.

The old man walked down the street and came back and still the small boys rolled in the dark icy morning leaves, not looking at him. He stood before the house and as he watched the lights turned on and turned off more than a thousand times. He counted softly under his breath.

A young boy of about fourteen ran by to the house, a football in his hand. He opened the door without even trying to unlock it, and went in. The door closed.

Half an hour later, with the morning wind rising, the old man saw a car pull up and a plump woman got out with a little boy three years old. They walked across the dark lawn and went into the house after the woman had looked at the old man and said, 'Is that *you*, Mr Terle?'

'Yes,' said the old man, automatically, for somehow he didn't wish to frighten her. But it was a lie. He knew he was not Mr Terle at all. Mr Terle lived down the street.

The lights glowed on and off a thousand more times.

The children rustled softly in the dark leaves.

A seventeen-year-old boy bounded across the street, smelling faintly of the smudged lipstick on his cheek, almost knocked the old man down, cried, 'Sorry!' and leaped up the steps. Fitting a key to the lock he went in.

The old man stood there with the town lying asleep on all sides of him; the unlit windows, the breathing rooms, the stars all through the trees, liberally caught and held on winter branches, so much snow suspended glittering on the cold air.

'That's my house; who are all those people going in it!' cried the old man to the wrestling children.

The wind blew, shaking the empty trees.

In the year which was 1923 the house was dark, a car drove up before it, the mother stepped from the car with her son William who was three. William looked at the dark morning world and saw his house and as he felt his mother lead him towards the house he heard her say, 'Is that *you*, Mr Terle?' and in the shadows by the great wind-filled oak tree an old man stood and replied, 'Yes.' The door closed.

In the year which was 1934 William came running in the summer night, feeling the football cradled in his hands, feeling the dark street pass under his running feet, along the sidewalk. He smelled, rather than saw, an old man, as he ran past. Neither of them spoke. And so on into the house.

In the year 1937 William ran with antelope boundings across the street, a smell of lipstick on his face, a smell of someone young and fresh upon his cheeks; all thoughts of love and deep night. He almost knocked the stranger down, cried, 'Sorry!' and ran to fit a key to the front door.

In the year 1947 a car drew up before the house, William relaxed, his wife beside him. He wore a fine tweed suit, it was late, he was tired, they both smelled faintly of so many drinks offered and accepted. For a moment they both heard the wind in the trees. 'Is that a light in our house?' asked the wife. William felt uneasy. 'Yes,' he said. They got out of the car and let themselves into the house with a key. An old man came from the living-room and cried, 'What are you *doing* in my house?'

'Your house?' said William. 'Here now, old man, get on out.' And William, feeling faintly sick to his stomach, for there was something to the old man that made him feel all water and nothing, searched the old man and pushed him out of the door and closed and locked it. From outside the old man cried, 'This is *my* house, you *can't* lock me out!'

They went up to bed and turned the lights out.

In the year 1928, William and the other small boys wrestled on the lawn, waiting for the time when they would leave to watch the circus come chuffing in to the dawn-pale railroad station on the blue metal tracks. In the leaves they lay and laughed and kicked and fought. An old man with a flashlight came across the lawn. 'Why are you playing here on my lawn at this time of morning?' asked the old man. 'Who are you?' replied William looking up a moment from the tangle.

The old man stood over the tumbling children a long moment. Then he dropped his flashlight. 'Oh my dear boy, I know now, now I know!' He bent to touch the boy. 'I am you, and you are me. I love you, my dear boy, with all of my heart! Let me tell you what will happen to you in the years to come! If you *knew*! I am you, and you were once me! My name is William, so is yours! And all those people going into the house, they are William, they are you, they are me!' The old man shivered. 'Oh, all the dark years and the passing of time!'

'Go away,' said the boy. 'You're crazy.'

'But,' said the old man.

'You're crazy. I'll call my father!'

The old man turned and walked away.

There was a flickering of the house lights, on and off. The boys wrestled quietly and secretly in the rustling leaves. The old man stood on the dark lawn.

Upstairs, in his bed, William Latting did not sleep on his bed in the year 1947. He sat up, lit a cigarette, and looked out of the window. His wife was awake. 'What's wrong?' she asked.

'That old man,' said William Latting. 'I think he's still down there, under the oak tree.'

'Oh, he couldn't be,' she said.

'I can't see very well, but I think he's there. I can barely make him out, it's so dark.'

'He'll go away,' she said.

William Latting drew quietly on his cigarette. He nodded. 'Who are those kids?'

From her bed his wife said, 'What *kids*?'

'Playing on the lawn out there, what a hell of a time of night to be playing in the leaves.'

'Probably the Moran boys.'

'Doesn't look like them.'

He stood by the window. 'You hear something?'

'What?'

'A baby crying. Way off.'

'I don't hear anything,' she said.

She lay listening. They both thought they heard running footsteps on the street, a key to the door. William Latting went to the hall and looked down the stairs but saw nothing.

In the year 1937, coming in the door, William saw a man in a dressing-gown at the top of the stairs looking down, a cigarette in his hand. 'That *you*, Dad?' No answer. The man sighed and went back into some room. William went to the kitchen to raid the ice-box.

The children wrestled in the soft dark leaves of morning.

William Latting said, 'Listen.'

He and his wife listened.

'It's the old man,' said William. 'Crying.'

'Why should he be crying?'

'I don't know. Why does anybody cry? Maybe he's unhappy.'

'If he's still down there in the morning,' said his wife, in the dark room, 'call the police.'

William Latting went away from the window, put out his cigarette and lay in the bed, his eyes closed. 'No,' he said quietly. 'I won't call the police. Not for him, I won't.'

'Why not?'

His voice was certain. 'I wouldn't want to do that. I just wouldn't.'

They both lay there and faintly there was a sound of crying and the wind blew and William Latting knew that all he had to do if he wanted to watch the boys wrestling in the dark cool leaves of morning would be reach out with his hand and lift the shade and look, and there they would be, far below, wrestling and wrestling as dawn came pale in the eastern sky.

3

HISTORY OF THE FUTURE

'As I stared at this sinister apparition, I felt a tickling on my cheeks...' —
from *The Time Machine* by H. G. Wells (*Famous Fantastic Mysteries*, 1950).

THE GREY MAN

H. G. Wells

H. G. Wells' stroke of genius in The Time Machine *was to devise a machine in which the narrator is free to cross the frontiers of time and journey far into the future. It was a concept that was not long in being imitated: the Frenchman Alfred Jarry's 'How to Construct a Time Machine' (1900)—curiously, still untranslated into English—was the first and, as this collection demonstrates, the idea has continued to fascinate writers ever since.*

Herbert George Wells (1866–1946) became absorbed with science during his schooldays and in 1888 began writing a serial story entitled The Chronic Argonauts *for a student magazine,* The Science Schools Journal, *published by the Royal College of Science. Set in the little Welsh village of Llyddwdd, it recounted the experiments of a certain Dr Nebogipfel who wanted to travel in time and who soon earned himself the label, among the superstitious locals, of 'necromancer'. By turns comic and ingenious—if rather amateurish—the serial ran for three months during that summer and ended inconclusively with Nebogipfel disappearing from view in 'a thunderous roar like the bursting forth of a great fountain of water'. However, the theme continued to haunt its young author and, seven years later, having developed his art in journalism and short stories, he made it the basis of his first novel,* The Time Machine, *which he subtitled 'An Invention'. Wells' career and reputation never looked back. The novel itself has never been out of print in the intervening century, and* The Chronic Argonauts *has been reprinted a number of times in anthologies.*

What is not generally known, however, is that before The Time Machine *was published as a book by William Heinemann Ltd it was serialised in Heinemann's own monthly magazine, the* New Review, *edited by W. E. Henley. And in the May 1895 issue a curious thing occurred. What was then Chapter 11, entitled 'The Further Vision', featured an episode in which the time traveller had a rather brutal confrontation with a 'grotesque monster' of the future resembling a centipede. When, several months later, the complete book was issued this episode had been excised—and has never been reinstated. Why was the story of 'The Grey Man' (my title) cut from* The Time Machine? *Did Wells or his publisher decide that it was too unpleasant for sensitive Victorian readers? The mystery may never be solved—but here is the tale. The first paragraph will be found in any reprint of the novel, but the narrative then continues without the tale presented here . . .*

* * *

I have already told you of the sickness and confusion that comes with time travelling. And this time I was not seated properly in the saddle, but sideways and in an unstable fashion. For an indefinite time I clung to the machine as it swayed and vibrated, quite unheeding how I went, and when I brought myself to look at the dials again I was amazed to find where I had arrived. One dial records days, another thousands of days, another millions of days, and another thousands of millions. Now, instead of reversing the levers I had pulled them over so as to go forward with them, and when I came to look at these indicators I found that the thousands hand was sweeping round as fast as the seconds hands of a watch—into futurity.

Very cautiously, for I remembered my former headlong fall, I began to reverse my machine's motion. Slower and slower went the circling hands until the thousands one seemed motionless and the daily one was no longer a mere mist upon its scale. Still slower, until the grey haze around me became distincter and dim outlines of an undulating waste grew visible.

I stopped. I was on a bleak moorland, covered with a sparse vegetation, and grey with a thin hoar-frost. The time was midday, the orange sun, shorn of its effulgence, brooded near the meridian in a sky of drabby grey. Only a few black bushes broke the monotony of the scene. The great buildings of the decadent men among whom, it seemed to me, I had been so recently, had vanished and left no trace: not a mound even marked their position. Hill and valley, sea and river—all, under the wear and work of the rain and frost, had melted into new forms. No doubt, too, the rain and snow had long since washed out the Morlock tunnels. A nipping breeze stung my hands and face. So far as I could see there were neither hills, nor trees, nor rivers: only an uneven stretch of cheerless plateau.

Then suddenly a dark bulk rose out of the moor, something that gleamed like a serrated row of iron plates, and vanished almost immediately in a depression. And then I became aware of a number of faint-grey things, coloured to almost the exact tint of the frost-bitten soil, which were browsing here and there upon its scanty grass, and running to and fro. I saw one jump with a sudden start, and then my eye detected perhaps a score of them. At first I thought they were rabbits, or some small breed of kangaroo. Then, as one came hopping near me, I perceived that it belonged to neither of these groups. It was plantigrade, its hind legs rather the longer; it was tailless, and covered with a straight greyish hair that thickened about the head into a Skye terrier's mane. As I had understood that in the Golden Age man had killed out almost all the other animals, sparing only a few of the more ornamental, I was naturally curious about the creatures. They did not seem afraid of me, but browsed on, much as rabbits would do in a place unfrequented by men; and it occurred to me that I might perhaps secure a specimen.

I got off the machine, and picked up a big stone. I had scarcely done so when one of the little creatures came within easy range. I was so lucky as to hit it on the head, and it rolled over at once and lay motionless. I ran to it at once. It remained still, almost as if it were killed. I was surprised to see that the thing had five feeble digits to both its fore- and hind-feet—the fore-feet, indeed, were almost as human as the fore-feet of a frog. It had, moreover, a roundish head, with a projecting forehead and forward-looking eyes, obscured by its lank hair. A disagreeable apprehension flashed across my mind. As I knelt down and seized my capture, intending to examine its teeth and other anatomical points which might show human characteristics, the metallic-looking object, to which I have already alluded, reappeared above a ridge in the moor, coming towards me and making a strange clattering sound as it came. Forthwith the grey animals about me began to answer with a short, weak yelping—as if of terror—and bolted off in a direction opposite to that from which this new creature approached. They must have hidden in burrows or behind bushes and tussocks, for in a moment not one of them was visible.

I rose to my feet, and stared at this grotesque monster. I can only describe it by comparing it to a centipede. It stood about three feet high, and had a long segmented body, perhaps thirty feet long, with curiously overlapping greenish-black plates. It seemed to crawl upon a multitude of feet, looping its body as it advanced. Its blunt round head, with a polygonal arrangement of black eye spots, carried two flexible, writhing, horn-like antennae. It was coming along, I should judge, at a pace of about eight or ten miles an hour, and it left me little time for thinking. Leaving my grey animal, or grey man, whichever it was, on the ground, I set off for the machine. Half-way I paused, regretting that abandonment, but a glance over my shoulder destroyed any such regret. When I gained the machine the monster was scarce fifty yards away. It was certainly not a vertebrated animal. It had no snout, and its mouth was fringed with jointed dark-coloured plates. But I did not care for a nearer view.

I traversed one day and stopped again, hoping to find the colossus gone and some vestige of my victim; but, I should judge, the giant centipede did not trouble itself about bones. At any rate both had vanished. The faintly human touch of these little creatures perplexed me greatly. If you come to think, there is no reason why a degenerate humanity should not come at last to differentiate into as many species as the descendants of the mud fish who fathered all the land vertebrates. I saw no more of any insect colossus, as to my thinking the segmented creature must have been. Evidently the physiological difficulty that at present keeps all the insects small had been surmounted at last, and this division of the animal kingdom had arrived at the long-awaited supremacy which its enormous energy and vitality deserve. I made several attempts to kill or capture another of the greyish vermin, but none of my missiles were so successful as my first; and, after perhaps a dozen disappointing throws, that left my arm aching, I felt a gust of irritation at my folly in coming so far into futurity without weapons or equipment. I resolved to run on for one glimpse of the still remoter future—one peep into the deeper abysm of time—and then to return to you and my own epoch. Once more I remounted the machine, and once more the world grew hazy and grey . . .

FLUX

Michael Moorcock

Among the many admirers of H. G. Wells' work, the Englishman Michael Moorcock has on a number of occasions utilised his mentor's concepts as the starting-point for innovative storytelling. Time travel, especially, features in several of his works, notably the trio of novels The Warlord of the Air *(1971),* The Land Leviathan *(1974) and* The Steel Tsar *(1981), known collectively as 'The Nomad of Time', which feature the adventures of Captain Oswald Bastable, a Victorian soldier who is transported from the North East Frontier of 1902 to the very different world of 1973. The trilogy is widely recognised as one of the leading 'steampunk' sagas. Another novel,* Behold The Man *(1966), also deals with time travel—in this case, back to the era of Christ.*

Michael Moorcock (1939–), a former journalist, comic strip writer and long-time fan of sf, during the Sixties edited one of the most important 'new wave' magazines, New Worlds, *before establishing himself among the influential contemporary writers in the genre. His novels about the amoral antihero Jerry Cornelius, who travels from the present day to the far future in a series of dizzying adventures, have also enjoyed great popularity; they have been adapted for a cartoon strip and inspired a movie,* The Final Programme *(1973), starring Jon Finch. In 'Flux', written in 1963 for* New Worlds Science Fiction, *Moorcock takes up another enduring Wellsian theme, strife between European nations, and recounts the mission of time traveller Max File to the future, in search of a solution—a journey that is full of unexpected problems for the man and his machine . . .*

*　　*　　*

Max File leaned forward, addressing an impatient question towards the driving compartment: 'How long now before we get there?'

Then he remembered that his car had no driver. Usually, as Marshalin-Chief of the European Defensive Nuclear Striking Force, he allowed himself the luxury of a chauffeur; but today his destination was secret and known not even to himself.

The plan of his route lay safely locked away in the computer of the car's automatic controller.

He settled back in his seat, deciding that it was useless to fret.

The car left the Main Way about half a mile before it met up with the central traffic circuit which flung vehicles and goods into the surrounding urban system like a gigantic whirling wheel. The car was making for the older parts of the city, nearest the ground. For this, File was grateful, though he did not overtly admit it to himself. Above him, the horizon-wide drone and vibrating murmur of this engineer's paradise still went on, but at least it was more diffuse. The noise was just as great, but more chaotic, and therefore more pleasing to File's ear. Twice the car was forced to pause before dense streams of pedestrians issuing from public pressure-train stations, faces set and sweating as they battled their way to work.

File sat impassively through the delay, though already he was late for the meeting. What did it mean, he wondered, this Gargantua which sat perpetually bellowing athwart the whole continent? It never slept; it never ceased proudly to roar out its own power. And however benevolent it was towards its hundreds of millions of inhabitants, there was no denying that they were, every one, its slaves.

How had it arisen? What would become of it? It was already so overgrown internally that only with difficulty human beings found themselves room to live in it. If it were seen from out in space, he thought, no human beings would be visible; it would seem to be only a fast-moving machine of marvellous power but no purpose.

Max File did not have much faith in the European Economic Community's ability to prolong its life infinitely. It had grown swiftly, but it had grown by itself, without the benefit of proper human design. Already, he thought, he could detect the seeds of inevitable collapse.

Patiently, the car eased forward through the crowd, found an unobstructed lane, and then continued on its complicated route. Eventually it made its way through a tangle of signs, directions and crossovers, before stopping in front of a small ten-storey building bearing a grim but solid stamp of authority.

There were guards at the entrance, betokening the gravity of the emergency. File was escorted to a suite on the fifth floor. Here, he was ushered into a windowless chamber with panelled wood walls and a steady, quiet illumination. At the oval table, the government of the European Economic Community had already convened and was waiting silently for his arrival. The ministers looked up as he entered.

They made an oddly serene and formal group, with their uniformly dark conservative dress and the white notepaper lying unmarked in neat squares before them. An air of careful constraint prevailed in the room. Most of the ministers gave File only distant nods as he entered and then cast their eyes primly downward as before. File returned the nods. He was acquainted with them all, but not closely. For some reason they always tended to keep their distance from him, in spite of the high position he held—and for which he seemed to have been destined since childhood.

Only Prime Minister Strasser rose to welcome him.

'Please be seated, File,' he said. File shook the old man's proffered hand, then made his way to his place. Strasser began to speak at once, clearly intending to make the meeting brief and to the point.

'As we all know,' he began, 'the situation in Europe has reached the verge of civil war. However, most of us also know that we are not here today to discuss a course of action—I speak now for your benefit, File. We are here to understand our position, and to propose a mission.'

Strasser sat down and nodded perfunctorily to the man on his left. Standon, pale and bony, inclined his head toward's File and spoke:

'When we first sat down to deal with this problem, we thought it differed from no other crisis in history—that we would first consider the aims and intentions of the quarrelling economic and political factions, decide which to back and which to fight. It was not long before we discovered our error.

'First, we realised that Europe is only a political entity and not a national entity, obviating the most obvious basis for action. Then we tried to comprehend the entire system which we think of as Europe—and failed. As an industrial economy, Europe passes comprehension!'

He paused, and a strange emotion seemed to well just beneath the surface of his face. He moved his body uneasily, then continued in a stronger tone:

'We are the first government in history which is aware, and will admit, that it does not know how to control events. The continent in our charge has become the most massive, complex, high-pressured phenomenon ever to appear on the face of this planet. We no more know how to control it than we know how to control the mechanism governing the growth of an actual living organism. Some of us are of the opinion that European industry has in fact become a living organ-

ism—but one without the sanity and certainty of proper development
that a natural organism has. It began haphazardly, and then followed
its own laws. There is one of us'—he indicated stern Brown-Gothe
across the table—'who equates it with a cancer.'

File mused on the similarity of the ministers' conclusions to his own
thoughts of only a few minutes before.

'Europe suffers from compression,' Standon continued. 'Everything
is so pressurised, energies and processes abut so solidly on one another,
that the whole system has massed together in a solid plenum. Politically
speaking, there just isn't room to move around. Consequently, we are
unable to apprehend the course of events either by computation or by
common sense, and we are unable to say what will result from any
given action. In short, we are in complete ignorance of the future,
whether we participate in it or not.'

File looked up and down the table. Most of the ministers still gazed
passively at their notepads. One or two, with Strasser and Standon,
were looking at him expectantly.

'I had been coming to the same conclusion myself,' he said. 'But
you must have decided upon something.'

'No,' said Standon forcefully. 'This is the essence of the matter. If
things were that clear-cut there would not be this problem—we should
simply choose a side. But there are not two factions—there are three
or four, with others in the background. The very idea of what is best
loses meaning when we do not know what is going to happen. Logically,
destruction of the community is the only criterion of what is undesirable,
but even then, who knows? Perhaps we have grown so monstrous that
there is no possibility of our further existence. There are no ideals to
guide us. And in any case, there is no longer deliberate direction as far
as Europe is concerned.'

Standon took his eyes off File and seemed to withdraw for a moment.
'I might add,' he said, 'that after having had several weeks to think
about it, we are of the opinion that this has always been the case in
political affairs: only the fact that there was space to move around in
gave the statesmen of the past the illusion that they were free to determine events. Now there is no empty space, the illusion has vanished,
and we are aware of our helplessness. At the same time, everything is
much more frightening.'

He shrugged. 'For instance, Europe, because of its massiveness, could
absorb a large number of nuclear fusion explosions and still keep functioning. I need hardly add that at the present time such weapons are

available to any large-scale corporation. We even think there are some small-yield bombs in the hands of minority groups.'

File reflected as calmly as he could. Suddenly the crisis had slid over the edge of practical considerations into the realm of philosophy. It sounded absurd, but there was no denying the fact.

He appreciated the caution of these very self-composed men. Like them, he had a fear of tyranny, but history provided many warnings against hasty preventive measures. It was to avert tyranny that the conspirators murdered Caesar, yet within hours the consequences of their foolish deed had plunged the state into a reign of terror even worse than anything they had imagined. The ministers were right: there was no such thing as free will, and a state was manageable only if it was uncomplicated enough not to go off the rails in any case.

He said, 'I presume everything has been done to try to analyse events? Cybernetics . . . ?'

Standon gave him a tolerant smile. 'Everything has been done.'

As if this were a cue, a third man spoke. Appeltoft, whose special province was science and technology, was younger than the others and somewhat more emotional. He looked up to address File:

'Our only hope lies in discovering how events are organised in time— this might sound highly speculative for such a serious and practical matter, but this is what things have come to. In order to take effective action in the present, we must first know the future. This is the mission we have in mind for you. The Research Complex at Geneva has found a way to deposit a man some years in the future and bring him back. You will be sent ten years forward to find out what will happen and how it will come about. You will then return, report your findings to us, and we will use this information to guide our actions, and also— scientifically—to analyse the laws governing the sequence of time. This is how we hope to formulate a method of human government for use by future ages, and, perhaps, remove the random element from human affairs.'

File was impressed by the striking, unconventional method the Cabinet had adopted to resolve its dilemma.

'You leave immediately,' Appeltoft told him, breaking in on his thoughts. 'After this conference, you and I will fly to Geneva where the technicians have the apparatus in readiness.' A hint of bitterness came into his voice. 'I had wished to go myself, but . . .' He shrugged and made a vague, disgusted gesture which took in the rest of the Cabinet.

'That's a point,' File said. 'Why have you chosen me?'

The ministers looked at one another shiftily. Strasser spoke up.

'The reason lies in your education, Max,' he said diffidently. 'The difficulties facing us now were beginning to show themselves over a generation ago. The government of the time decided to bring up a small number of children according to a new system of education. The idea was to develop people capable of comprehending in detail the massiveness of modern civilisation, by means of forced learning in every subject. The experiment failed. All your schoolfellows lost their sanity. You survived, but did not turn into the product we had hoped for. To prevent any later derangement of your mind, a large part of the information which had been pressured into it was removed by hypnotic means. The result is yourself as you are—a super-dilettante, with an intense curiosity and a gift for management. We gave you the post you now hold and forgot about you. Now you are ideal for our purpose.'

Inwardly, File underwent a jolt—even more so because the account agreed well with his own suspicions concerning his origins. He pulled himself together before he could become introspective.

'I was the only one to make it, eh? I wonder why.'

Standon regarded File steadily in the dim light. Once again that strange layer of emotion seemed to stir in him, lying somewhere below his features but not affecting the muscles or skin.

'Because of your determination, Mr File. Because whatever happens, somehow, you have the capacity to find a way out.'

File left the building even more aware of his speculations than before. Appeltoft came with him, and the car whined smoothly towards the nearest air centre.

He had a peg to hang his thoughts on now. The sequence of time ... Yes, there was no doubt that the explanation of the titanic phenomena through which he was being driven lay in the sequence of time.

Looking around him, he saw how literally true were the statements just given him by the ministers.

After the formation of the Economic Community, into which all the European countries were finally joined, the continent's capacity had accelerated fantastically. Economic development had soared so high that eventually it became necessary to buttress up the whole structure from underneath. Stage by stage, the buttresses had become more massive, until the Community was tied to the ground, a rigid unchangeable monster, humming and roaring with energy.

Even the airy architectural promise of the previous century had not materialised. The constructions wheeling past the car had an appearance of Wagnerian heaviness, blocking out the sunlight.

He turned to Appeltoft. 'So in an hour I'll be ten years in the future. Ridiculous statement!'

Appeltoft laughed, as though to show he appreciated the paradox.

'But tell me,' File continued, 'are you really so ignorant about time's nature, and yet you can effect travel in it?'

'We are not so ignorant about its nature, as about its structure and organisation,' Appeltoft told him. 'The equations which enable us to transmit through time give no clue to that—in fact they say that time has no sequence at all, which can hardly be possible.'

Appeltoft paused. His manner towards File gave the latter cause to think that the scientist still resented not being allowed to be the first time traveller, though he was trying to hide it. File didn't blame him. When a man has worked fanatically for something, it must be a blow to see a complete stranger take over the fruits of it.

'There are two theories extant,' Appeltoft eventually went on. 'The first, and the one I favour, is the common-sense view—past, present, future, proceeding in an unending line and each even having a definite position on the line. Unfortunately the idea has not lent itself to any mathematical formulation.

'The other idea, which some of my co-workers hold, goes like this: that time isn't really a forward-moving flow at all. It exists as a constant: all things are actually happening at once, but human beings haven't got the built-in perceptions to see it as such. Imagine a circular stage with a sequence of events going on round it, representing, say, periods in one man's life. In that case they would be played by different actors, but in the actuality of time the same man plays all parts. According to this, an alteration in one scene has an effect on all subsequent scenes all the way round back to the beginning.'

'So that time is cyclic—what you do in the future may influence your future past, as it were?'

'If the theory is correct. Some formulations have been derived, but they don't work very well. All we really know, is that we can deposit you into the future and probably bring you back.'

'Probably! You've had failures?'

'Thirty-three per cent of our test animals don't return,' Appeltoft said blithely.

Once they were at the air centre, it took them less than an hour to reach the Geneva Research Complex. From the air receptor on the roof,

Appeltoft conducted him nearly half a mile down to the underground laboratories. Finally, he pulled an old-fashioned key chain from the pocket, attached to which was a little radio key. As he pressed the stud a door swung open a few yards ahead.

They entered a blue-painted chamber whose walls were lined with what looked like computer-program inlets. A number of white-robed technicians sat about, waiting.

Occupying the centre of the room was a chair, mounted on a pedestal. A swivel arm held a small box with instrument dials on the external surfaces; but the most notable feature was the three translucent rods which seemed to ray out from just behind the chair, one going straight up and the other two at right angles, one on either side.

The floor was covered with trestles supporting a network of helices and semiconductor electron channels, radiating out from the chair like a spider's web. File found himself trying to interpret the set-up in the pseudoscientific jargon which was his way of understanding contemporary technology. Electrons . . . indeterminacy . . . what would the three rods be for?

'This is the time-transmission apparatus,' Appeltoft told him without preamble. 'The actual apparatus itself will remain here in the present time. Only that chair, with you sitting in it, will make the time transference itself.'

'So you will control everything from here?'

'Not exactly. It will be a "powered flight", so to speak, and you will carry the controls. But the power unit will remain here. We might be able to do something if the mission goes wrong—perhaps not. We probably won't even know.

'The three rods accompanying the chair represent the three spatial dimensions. As these rotate out of true space, time-motion will begin.'

Stepping carefully across the trestles, they walked nearer to the chair. Appeltoft explained the controls and instruments. 'This is your speed gauge—you've no way of controlling that, it's all automatic. This switch here is Stop and Start—it's marked, you'll notice. And this one gives the point in time you occupy, in years, days, hours and seconds. Everything else is programmed for you. As you see, it reads Nil now. When you arrive, it will read Ten Years.'

'Point in time, eh?' File mused. 'That could have two meanings according to what you've just told me.'

Appeltoft nodded. 'You're astute. Pragmatically, my own view of straight-line time is closest to the operation of the time transmitter. It's the easiest to grasp, anyway.'

File studied the apparatus for nearly a minute without speaking. The silence dragged on. Though he wasn't aware of it, strain was growing.

'Well, don't just stand there,' Appeltoft snapped with sudden ferocity. 'Get on the damned thing! We haven't got all day!'

File gave him a look of surprised reproof.

Appeltoft sagged. 'Sorry. If you know—how jealous I am of you. To be the first man with a chance to discover the secret of time! It's the secret to the universe itself!'

Well, File thought to himself, as he watched the young minister's lean, intense face, *if I had his determination I might have been a scientist and made discoveries for myself, instead of being a jacked-up dilettante.* 'A dilettante,' he muttered aloud.

'Eh?' Appeltoft said. 'Well, come on, let's get it done.'

File climbed into the seat built into the back of the chair. Camera lenses peered over his shoulders. 'You know what to look for?' Appeltoft asked finally.

'As much as anybody. Besides—I want to go as much as you do.'

'All right then. Capacity's built up. Press the switch to Start. It will automatically revert to Stop at the end of the journey.'

File obeyed. At first, nothing happened. Then he got the impression that the translucent rods, which he could see out of the corners of his eyes, were rotating clockwise, though they didn't seem to change their positions. At the same time, the room appeared to spin in the opposite direction—again, it was movement without change of position.

The effect was entirely like having drunk too much, and File felt dizzy. He pulled his eyes to the speed gauge. One minute per minute— marking time! One and a half, two . . .

With a weird flickering effect the laboratory vanished. He was in a neutral grey fog, left only with sensation.

The first sensation was that he was taking part in the rotating movement—being steadily canted to the left. As his angle to the vertical increased, the second sensation increased: a rushing momentum, a gathering speed towards a nameless destination.

000001.146.15.0073—the numbers slipped into place, swiftly towards the right-hand side, slowly towards the left. 000002 . . . 3 . . . 4 . . . 5 . . . 6 . . . 7 . . .

Then the nausea returned, the feeling of being spun round—the other way, now. Light dazzled his eyes.

000010.000.00.0000.

When he grew used to it, the light was really dim. He was still in the laboratory, but it was deserted, illuminated by emergency lights glowing weakly in the ceiling. It was not in ruins, and there was no sign of violence, but the place had obviously been empty for some time.

Climbing down from the chair, he went to the door, used the radio key which Appeltoft had given him, went through, and closed it behind him. He walked along the corridor and through the other departments.

The whole complex shouldn't be deserted after only ten years. Something drastic must have happened.

He frowned, annoyed at himself. Of course it had. That was why he was here.

The high-level streets of Geneva were equally deserted. He could see the tops of mountains in the distance, poking between metallic roadways. The drone of the city was missing. There was some noise to be heard, but it was muted and irregular.

As he mounted an interlevel ramp he saw one or two figures, mostly alone. He had never seen so few people. Perhaps the quickest way to find out what was going on would be to locate the library and read up some recent history. It might give a clue, anyway.

He reached the building which pushed up through several layers of deserted street. A huge black sign hung over the main entrance. It said: MEN ONLY.

Puzzled, File entered the cool half-light and approached the wary young man at the inquiry desk.

'Excuse me,' he said, and jumped as the man produced a squat gun from under the counter and levelled it at him.

'What do you want?'

'I've come to consult recent texts dealing with the development of Europe in the last ten years,' File said.

The young man grinned with his thin lips. The gun held steady, he said, 'Development?'

'I'm a serious student—all I want to do is look up some information.'

The young man put away the gun and with one hand pressed the buttons of an index system. He took two cards out and handed them to File.

'Fifth floor, room 543. Here's the key. Lock the door behind you. Last week a gang of women broke through the barricades and tried to burn us down. They like their meat pre-cooked, eh?'

File frowned at him but said nothing. He went to the elevator. The young man called, 'For a student you don't know much about this library. That elevator hasn't worked for four years. The women control all the main power sources these days.'

Still in a quandary, File walked up to the fifth floor, found the room he wanted, unlocked the door, entered, and locked it behind him.

Seating himself before the viewer, he pressed the appropriate buttons on the panel before him, and the pages started to appear on the screen.

Hmmm . . . Let's see . . . Investigations of Dalmeny Foundation members. Paper VII: PARTIAL RESULTS OF THE BAVARIAN EXPERIMENT . . .

—Civil war imminent, the Council temporarily averted it by promising that thorough research would be made into every claim for a solution to the problems of over-compression. This, as we know now, was a stonewalling action since they later admitted they had been incapable of predicting the outcome of any trend. The faction, one of the most powerful headed by the late Stefan Untermeyer, demanded that they be allowed to conduct a controlled experiment.

—Unable to stall any longer, the Council reluctantly agreed, and a large part of Bavaria was set aside so that the plans of the Untermeyer faction could be implemented. This plan necessitated sexual segregation. Men and women were separated and each given an intensive psycho conditioning to hate the opposite sex. Next, acts were passed making contact with the opposite sex punishable by death. This act had to be enforced frequently, although not as frequently as originally had been thought. Ironically, Untermeyer was one of the first to be punished under the act.

—It is difficult these days, to make a clear assessment of the results of this experiment (which so quickly got out of hand and resulted in the literal war between the sexes, which now exists with cannibalism so prevalent, each sex regarding it as lawful to eat a member of the other) but it is obvious that measures for reassimilation have so far met with little success and that, since this creed has now spread through Germany, Scandinavia and elsewhere, an incredible depletion of life in Northern Europe is likely. In the long run, of course, repopulation will result as the roving hordes from France and Spain press northwards. Europe, having collapsed, is ready for conquest, and when the squabblings of America and the United East are ended, either by bloodshed or peaceful negotiation, Europe's only salvation may be in coming under the sway of one of these powers. However, as we know, both these powers have similar problems to those of Europe in its last days of sanity.

File pursed his lips, consulted the other card and pressed a fresh series of buttons.

Nobody could have predicted this. But by the look of it there's more to come. Let's see what this is . . . FINDINGS OF THE VINER COMMITTEE FOR THE INVESTIGATION OF SOCIAL DISINTE-GRATION IN SOUTHERN EUROPE . . .

—The terms of reference of the Committee were as follows: to investigate the disintegration of the pre-experimental European society in Southern Europe and to suggest measures for reorganising the society into an operating whole.

—Briefly, as is generally known, the European Council gave permission for the Population Phasing Group to conduct an experiment in Greece. This Group, using the principles of suspended animation discovered a few years earlier by Batchovski, instituted total birth control and placed three-quarters of the population of Greece into suspended animation, the other quarter being thought sufficient to run public and social services and so on, reasoning, quite rationally it seemed, that in this way further population explosion would be averted, less overcrowding would result and the pace of our society could be relaxed. After a given time, the first quarter would go into suspended animation and be replaced by the next quarter and so on. This phasing process did seem to be the most reasonable solution to the Problem of Europe, as it was called.

—However, in ridding the population of claustrophobia, the system produced an effect of extreme agoraphobia. The people, being used to living close together, became restless, and the tension which had preceded the introduction of the PPG Experiment was turned into new channels. Mobs, exhibiting signs of extreme neurosis, completely insensate and deaf to all reason, attacked what was called the SA Vaults and demanded the release of their relatives and friends. The authorities attempted to argue with them but, in the turmoil which followed, were either killed or forced to flee. Unable to operate the machines keeping the rest of the population in suspended animation, the mobs destroyed them, killing the people they had intended to reawaken.

—When the Committee reached Southern Europe, they found a declining society. Little attempt had been made to retrieve the situation, people were living in the vast depopulated connurbations in little groups, fighting off the influx of roaming bands from France, Spain and Italy, where earlier a religious fanatic had, quite unexpectedly, started a jehad against the automated, but workable, society. This 'back to nature' movement snowballed. Power installations were destroyed, and millions of tons of earth were imported from Africa to spread over the ruins. In the chaos which ensued, people fought and squabbled over what little food could be grown in the unproductive earth where it had been imported and in the Holiday Spaces. Britain, already suffering from the effects of this breakdown and unable to obtain sufficient supplies to feed its own population properly, had begun sending aid but had been forced to give up this measure and look to its own problems—the sudden spread of an unknown disease, similar to typhus, which was found to have come from Yugoslav refugees who had themselves suffered badly from the introduction of a synthetic food product which contained the germs. By the time we reached Southern Europe, the social services all over the continent had disintegrated and only the Dalmeny Foundation (which had commissioned us) and half a dozen less well organised groups were managing to maintain any kind of academic activity . . .

As File read on through the depressing texts, he felt the blood leave his face. At length he had checked and rechecked the documents; he sat back and contemplated.

The blundering nature of the experiments appalled him. Nothing could be a better confirmation of what he had been told at the Cabinet Meeting, and it made him doubt, now, that anything at all could be done to avert the calamity. If men were so blind and foolish, could even Appeltoft's incisive mind save them? Even supposing he succeeded in making a clear, workable analysis of the science of events from the information File had obtained . . .

That part of it was out of his hands, he realised, and perhaps Appeltoft's confidence stood for something. Impatiently he rushed back to the laboratory, mounted the chair of the time machine, and pressed the switch to Start. 000009.000.00.0003 . . .

Soon there was a grey mist surrounding him as before. Rotation and momentum began to impress themselves on his senses.

Then his gauges jigged and danced, clicked and tumbled insanely. 009000.100.02.0000 . . . . 000175.000.03–0800 . . . . 630946.020.44.1125 . . .

Something had gone wrong. Desperately he tried to stop the machine and inspect the controls. Every dial registered noughts now.

But the laboratory was gone. He was surrounded by darkness.

He was in limbo.

000000.000.00.0000.

File did not know how long he sped through the emptiness. Gradually, the mistiness began to return, then, after what seemed an interminable time, a flurry of impressions spun round his eyes.

At last, the time machine came to a halt, but he did not pause to see what was around him. He pressed the Start switch again.

Nothing happened. File inspected all the dials in turn, casting a long look at one which, as Appeltoft had told him, registered the machine's 'time-potential'—that is, its capacity to travel through time.

The hand was at zero. He was stranded.

Thirty-three per cent of our test animals don't return. Appeltoft's remark slipped sardonically into his memory.

The cameras behind his shoulders were humming almost imperceptibly as they recorded the screen on microtape. Bleakly, File lifted his head and took stock of his surroundings.

The sight was beautiful but alien. The landscape consisted of sullen orange dust, over which roamed what looked like clouds—purple masses rolling and drifting over the surface of the desert. On the horizon of this barren scene, the outlines of grotesque architecture were visible. Or were they just natural formations?

He glanced upwards. There were no clouds in the sky; evidently they were too dense to float in free air. A small sun hung low, red in a deep-blue sky where stars were faintly visible.

His heart was beating rapidly; as he noticed this, he realised that he was breathing more deeply than usual, every third breath almost a gasp. Was he so far removed from his own time that even the atmosphere was different?

Skrrak! The sound came with a brittle, frail quality over the thin air. File turned his head, startled.

A group of bipeds was advancing; straggling on bony, delicate limbs through knee-deep strata of purple clouds which rolled in masses a few hundred yards away. They were humanoid, but skeletal, ugly, and clearly not human. The leader, who was over seven feet tall, was shouting and pointing at File and the machine.

Another waved his hands: '*Sa Skrrak—dek svala yaal!*'

The group, about ten in number, carried long slim spears, and their torsos and legs were covered with scrubby hair. Their triangular heads had huge ridges of bone over and under the eyes so that they seemed to be wearing helmets. Thin hair swirled around their heads as they came closer, proceeding cautiously as if in slow motion.

As they approached, File saw that some of them carried curious rifle-like weapons, and the leader bore a box-shaped instrument with a lens structure on one side, which he was pointing in his direction.

File felt the warmth of a pale-green beam and tried to dodge it. But the alien creature skilfully kept it trained on him.

After a second or two, a buzzing set up in his brain; fantastic colours engulfed his mind, separating out into waves of white and gold. Then geometric patterns flared behind his eyes. Then words—at first in his brain and then in his ears.

'Strange one, what is your tribe?'

He was hearing the guttural language of the alien—and understanding it. The creature touched a switch on the top of the box, and the beam flicked off.

'I am from another time,' File said without emphasis.

The warriors shifted their weapons uneasily. The leader nodded, a stiff gesture, as if his bone structure did not permit easy movement. 'That would be an explanation.'

'Explanation?'

'I am conversant with all the tribes, and you do not correspond to any of them.' The warrior shifted his great head to give the horizon a quick scrutiny. 'We are the Yulk. Unless you intend to depart immediately, you had best come with us.'

'But my machine . . .'

'That also we will take. You will not wish it to be destroyed by the Raxa, who do not permit the existence of any creature or artifact save themselves.'

File debated for some moments. The chair and its three rods were easily portable, but was it wise to move them?

Idly, he moved the useless Start switch again. Damn! Since the machine no longer worked, what difference did it make if he moved it to the Moon? And yet to go off with these alien creatures when his only objective was to return to the Geneva Complex seemed the most obvious absurdity.

A sick feeling of failure came over him. He was beginning to realise that he was never going to get back to Geneva. The scientists had known that there was some fault in their time-transmission methods; now, he knew, the chair with its three rods had lost all touch with the equipment in the laboratory. It was, in fact, no longer a time machine, and that meant he was doomed to stay here for the rest of his life.

Helplessly he gave his consent. A quartet of warriors picked up the chair, and the party set off across the ochre desert, glancing warily about it as they travelled.

They skirted round the moving clouds wherever they could, but sometimes the banks of purple vapour swept over them, borne by the wide movements of the travelling breeze, and they stumbled through a vermilion fog. File noticed that the alien beings kept a tight hold on their weapons when this happened. What was it they feared? Even in this desolated and near-empty world, strife and dramas played themselves out.

An hour's journey brought them to a settlement of tents clustered on a low hillside. A carefully cultivated plot of some wretched vegetation grew over about half the hill, as though only just managing to maintain itself in the sterile desert. Tethered over the camp were five floating vessels, each about a hundred feet long, graceful machines with stubby, oblate sterns and tapered bows. A short open deck projected aft atop each vessel and the forward parts were laced with windows.

File's gaze lingered on these craft. They contrasted oddly with the plainly nomadic living quarters below, cured animal hides with weak fires flickering among them.

A meal had just been prepared. File's time machine was taken to an empty tent, and he was invited to eat with the chief. As he entered the largest tent of the settlement and saw the nobility of this small tribe gathered round a vegetable stewpot with their weapons beside them, he knew what it was they reminded him of.

Lizards.

They began to eat from glass bowls. It seemed these people knew how to work the silicates of the desert as well as build flying ships— if they had not stolen them from some more advanced people.

In the course of the meal, File also discovered that the machine the warrior had trained on him in the desert was 100 per cent efficient. He had been completely re-educated to talk and think in another language, even though he could, if he chose, detach himself slightly, hear the strangeness of the sounds which came from both his mouth and those of the Yulk.

The chief's name was Gzerhtcak, an almost impossible sound to European ears. As they ate, he answered File's questions in unemotional tones.

From what he was told, he imagined that this was an Earth in old age, an Earth millions, perhaps billions of years ahead of his own time, and it was nearly all desert. There were about eight tribes living within a radius of a few hundred miles, and when they were not squabbling among themselves they were fighting a never-ending struggle for existence both with the ailing conditions of a dying world, and with the Raxa, creatures who were not organic life at all but consisted of mineral crystals conglomerated into geometrical forms, and, in some mysterious way, endowed both with sentience and the property of mobility.

'Fifty generations ago,' the Yulk chief told him, 'the Raxa had no existence in the world; then they began to grow. They thrive in the dead desert, which is all food for them, while we steadily die. There is nothing we can do, but fight.'

Furthermore, the atmosphere of the Earth was becoming unbreathable. Little fresh oxygen was being produced, since there was no vegetation except at the plantations. Besides this, noxious vapours were being manufactured by a chemical-geological action in the ground, and by slow volcanic processes which drifted through the sand from far below. Only in a few places, such as this region where the tribes lived, was the atmosphere still suitable for respiration, and that only because of the relative stillness of the atmosphere which discouraged the separate gases from mixing.

It was a despairing picture of courage and hopelessness which gradually unfolded to File. Was this the final result of man's inability to control events, or was the collapse of the European Economic Community an insignificant happening which had been swallowed up by a vaster history? He tended to think that this was so; for he felt sure that the creatures who sat and ate with him were not even descended from human stock.

Lizards. The old order of the world of life had died away. Men had gone. Only these fragments remained—lizards elevated to a man-like state, attempting to retain a foothold in a world which had changed its mind. Probably the other tribes the Yulk spoke of were also humanoids who had evolved from various lower animals.

'Tomorrow is the great battle,' the Yulk chief said. 'We throw all our resources against the Raxa, who advance steadily to destroy the last plantations on which we depend. After tomorrow, we shall know in our hearts how long we have to live.'

Max File clenched his hands impotently. His fate was sealed. Eventually he too would take his place alongside the Yulk warriors in the last stand against humanity's enemy.

*   *   *

Appeltoft spread his hands impassively and looked at Strasser. What could he do? He had done all he could.

'What happened?' said the Prime Minister.

'We tracked him ten years into the future. We got him on the start of his journey back, and then quite suddenly—gone. Nothing. I told you we lost thirty-three per cent of our experimental animals in the same way. I warned you of the risk.'

'I know—but have you tried everything? You know what it will mean if he doesn't return . . .'

'We have been trying, of course. We are searching now, trying to pick him up, but outside the Earth's time track all is chaotic to our instruments—some defect in our understanding of time. We can probe out—but really, a needle in a haystack is nothing compared—'

'Well, keep trying. Because if you don't get him back soon we shall be forced to allow the Untermeyer people to go ahead in Bavaria, and we have no means of predicting the result.'

Appeltoft sighed wearily and returned to his laboratory.

When he had left the chamber, Standon said, 'Poor devil.'

'There's a time and a place for sentimentality, Standon,' Strasser said guiltily.

The Earth still rotated in the same period, and after a sleep of about eight hours, File left his tent and stretched his limbs in the thin air, aroused by the sound of clinking metal. It was just after dawn, and the fighting males of the tribe were setting out to battle. The females and children, shivering, watched as their menfolk went off in procession into the desert. A few rode reptile-like horses, precious cosseted animals, all of whom had been harnessed for the battle. Twenty feet above their heads the five aircraft floated patiently, following the direction given by the chief below.

File hung around the camp, apprehensive and edgy. About an hour after sunset, the remnants of the forces returned.

It was defeat. A third of the men had survived. None of the aircraft returned, and File had learned the night before that although the tribe retained the knowledge and skill to build more, it was an undertaking that strained their resources to the utmost, and the construction of another would almost certainly never begin.

Humanity's strength was depleted beyond revival point. The mineral intelligences called the Raxa would continue their implacable advance with little to stop them.

The Yulk chief was the last man in. Bruised, bleeding, and scorched by near misses from energy beams, he submitted to the medications of the women, and then called the nobles together as usual for their evening meal.

One by one, the wearied warriors took their leave and made their ways to their tents, until File was left alone with Gzerhtcak.

He looked directly into the old man's eyes. 'There is no hope,' he said bluntly.

'I know. But there is no need for you to remain.'

'I have no choice.' He sighed. 'My machine has broken down. I must throw in my lot with you.'

'Perhaps we can repair your machine. But you will be plunging into the unknown . . .'

File made a gesture with his hands. 'What could you possibly do to repair my machine?'

The chief rose and led the way to the tent where the machine lay. A brief command into the night produced a boy with a box of tools. The chief studied File's machine, lifting a panel to see behind the instruments. Finally, he made adjustments, adding a device which took him about twenty minutes to make with glowing bits of wire. The time-potential meter began to lift above zero.

File stared in surprise.

'Our science is very ancient and very wise,' the chief said, 'though these days we know it only by rote. Still, I, as father of the tribe, know enough so that when a man like yourself tells me that he has stranded himself in time, I know what the reason is.'

File was astounded by the turn of events. 'When I get home–' he began.

'*You will never get home.* Neither will your scientists ever analyse time. Our ancient science has a maxim: No man understands time. Your machine travels under its own power now. If you leave here, you simply escape this place and take your chance elsewhere.'

'I must make the attempt,' File said. 'I cannot remain here while there is a hope of getting back.'

But still he lingered.

The chief seemed to guess his thoughts. 'Do not fear that you desert us,' he said. 'Your position is clear, as is ours. There is no help for either of us.'

File nodded and stepped up to the chair of the machine. As he cleaned off the grime and dust with his shirt sleeves, it occurred to him to look at the date register—he had not bothered to read the figures on his arrival. He did not expect it to make sense, for it had too few digits to account for the present antiquity of the Earth.

But when he read the dial he received a shock. 000008–324.01.7954. Less than nine years after his departure from the Geneva Complex!

He seated himself on the time machine and pressed the switch.

Internal rotation clockwise . . . external rotation anticlockwise . . . then the forward rushing. He plunged into the continuum of Time.

Minutes passed, and no sign came that he would emerge automatically from his journey. Taking a chance, he pressed the switch to Stop.

With a residual turning of the translucent rods, the machine deposited itself into normal space-time orientation. About him, the landscape was more mind-shaking than anything he had ever dreamed.

Was it crystal? The final victory of the crystalline Raxa? For a moment the fantastic landscape, with its flashing, brilliant, mathematical overgrowth, deluded him into thinking it was so. But then he saw that it could not be—or if it was, the Raxa had evolved beyond their mineral heritage.

It was a world of geometrical form, but it was also a world of constant movement—or rather, since the movement was all so sudden as to be instantaneous, of constant transformation. Flashing extensions and withdrawals, all on the vertical and horizontal planes, dazzled his eyes. When he looked closer, he saw that in fact *three-dimensional form was nowhere present*. Everything consisted of two-dimensional shapes, which came together transitorily to give the *illusion* of form.

The colours, too—they underwent transformations and graduations which bespoke the action of regular mathematical principles, like the prismatic separation into the ideal spectrum. But here the manifestations were infinitely more subtle and inventive, just as subtle, tenuous music, using fifty instruments, can be made out of the seven tones of the diatonic scale.

File looked at the date register. It told him he was now fifteen years away from Appeltoft, anxiously awaiting his return in the Geneva Complex.

He tried again.

A lush world of lustrous vegetation swayed and rustled in a hot breeze. A troup of armadillo-like animals, but the size of horses, paraded through the clearing where File's machine had come to rest. Without pausing, the leader swung its head to give him a docile, supercilious inspection, then turned to grunt something to the followers. They also gave him a cursory glance and then they had passed through a screen of wavy grass-trees. He heard their motions through the forest for some distance.

Again.

Barren rock. The sky hung with traceries of what were obviously dust clouds. Here the ground was clean of even the slightest trace of dust, but a strong cold wind blew. Presumably it swept the dust into the atmosphere and prevented it from precipitating, scouring the rock to a sparkling, ragged surface. He could hardly believe that this scrubbed shining landscape was actually the surface of a planet. It was like an exhibit.

Again.

Now he was in space, protected by some field the time machine seemed to create around itself. Something huge as Jupiter hung where Earth should have been.

Again.

Space again. A scarlet sun pouring bloody light over him. On his left, a tiny, vivid star, like a burning magnesium flare, lanced at his eyes. An impossible three-planet triune rotated majestically above him, with no more distance between them than from the Earth to the Moon.

He looked at the date register again. Twenty-odd years from departure.

Where was the sequence? Where was the progression he had come to find? How was Appeltoft to make sense out of this?

How was he going to find Appeltoft?

Desperately, he set the machine in motion again. His desperation seemed to have some effect: he picked up speed, rushing with insensate energy, and now he was not just in limbo but could see something of the universe through which he was passing.

After a while he got the impression that he was still, that it was the machine that was static while time and space were not. The universe poured around him, a disordered tumult of forces and energies, lacking direction, lacking purpose . . .

On he sped, hour after hour, as if he were trying to flee from some fact he could not face. But at last he could hide from it no longer. As he observed the chaos around him he *knew*.

Time *had* no sequence! It was *not* a continuous flowing. It had no positive direction. It went neither forwards, backwards, nor in a circle; neither did it stay still. *It was totally random.*

The universe was bereft of logic. It was nothing but chaos.

It had no purpose, no beginning, no end. It existed only as a random mass of gases, solids, liquids, fragmentary accidental patterns. Like a kaleidoscope, it occasionally formed itself into patterns, so that it *seemed* ordered, *seemed* to contain laws, *seemed* to have form and direction.

But, in fact, there was nothing but chaos, nothing but a constant state of flux—the only thing that was constant. There *were* no laws governing time! Appeltoft's ambition was impossible!

The world from which he had come, or any other world for that matter, could dissipate into its component elements at any instant, *or could have come into being at any previous instant, complete with everybody's memories*! Who would be the wiser? The whole of the European Economic Community might have existed only for the half-second which it had taken him to press the starting switch of the time machine. No wonder he couldn't find it!

Chaos, flux, eternal death. All problems were without solution. As File realised these facts he howled with the horror of it. He could not bring himself to stop. In proportion to his despair and fear, his speed increased, faster and faster, until he was pouring madly through turmoil.

Faster, farther . . .

The formless universe around him began to vanish as he went to an immense distance and beyond the limits of speed. Matter was breaking up, disappearing. Still he rushed on in terror, until the time machine fell away beneath him, and the matter of his body disintegrated and vanished.

He was a bodiless intelligence, hurtling through the void. Then his emotions began to vanish. His thoughts. His identity. The sensation of movement dropped away. Max File was gone. Nothing to see, hear, feel, or know.

He hung there, nothing but consciousness. He did not think—he no longer had any apparatus to think with. He had no name. He had no memories. No qualities, attributes, or feelings. He was just *there*. Pure ego.

The same as nothing.

There was no time. A split second was the same as a billion ages.

So it would not have been possible for File, later, to assign any period to his interlude in unqualified void. He only became aware of anything when he began to emerge.

At first, there was only a vague feeling, like something misty. Then more qualities began to attach themselves to him. Motion began. Chaotic matter became distantly perceptible—disorganised particles, flowing energies and wavy lines.

A name impinged on his consciousness: Max File. Then the thought: That's me.

Matter gradually congregated round him, and soon he had a body again and a complete set of memories. He could accept the existence of an unorganised universe now. He sighed. At the same moment the time machine formed underneath him.

All he could do now was to try to return to Geneva, however remote the possibility. How strange, to think that the whole of Europe, with all its seriously taken problems, was nothing more than a chance coming-together of random particles! But at least it was home—even if it only existed for a few seconds.

And if he could only rejoin those few seconds, he thought in agonised joyousness, he would be dissolved along with the rest of it and be released from this hideous extension of life he had escaped into.

And yet, he thought, how could he get back? Only by searching, only by searching . . .

He reckoned (though of course his calculations were liable to considerable error) that he spent several centuries searching through mindless turmoil. He grew no older; he felt no hunger or thirst; he did not breathe—how his heart kept beating without breath was a mystery to him, but it was on this, the centre of his sense of time, that he based his belief about the duration of the search. Occasionally he came upon other brief manifestations, other transient conglomerations of chaos. But now he was not interested in them, and he did not find Earth at the time of the EEC.

It was hopeless. He could search for ever.

In despair, he began to withdraw again, to become a bodiless entity and find oblivion, escape from his torments in the living death. It was while he was about to dispense with the last vestige of identity that he discovered his unsuspected power.

He happened to direct his mind to a grouping of jostling particles some distance away. Under the impact of his will, it moved!

Interested, he halted his withdrawal, but did not try to emerge back into his proper self—he had the feeling that as Max File he was impotent. As an almost unqualified ego, perhaps . . .

He allowed an image to form in his mind—it happened to be that of a woman—and directed it at the formless chaos. Instantly, against dark flux, lit by random flashes of light, a woman was formed out of chaotic matter. She moved, looked at him, and gave a languorous smile.

There was no doubt about it. She was not just an image. She was alive, perfect, and aware.

Amazed, he automatically let go of the mental image and transmitted a cancellation. The woman vanished, replaced by random particles and energies as before. The cloud lingered for a moment, then dispersed.

It was a new-found delight. He could make anything! For ages he experimented, creating everything he could think of. Once a whole world formed beneath him, complete with civilisations, a tiny sun, and rocket-ships probing out.

He cancelled it at once. It was enough to know that his every intention, even his vaguest and grandest thought, was translated into detail.

Now he had a means to return home—and now he could solve the government's problem for good and all.

For if he could not find Europe, could he not create it over again? Would that not be just as good? In fact, it was a point of philosophy whether it would not be in fact the same Europe. This was Nietzsche's belief, he remembered—his hope of personal immortality. Since, in the boundless universe, he was bound to recur—File's discoveries had reinforced this view, anyhow—he would not die. Two identical objects shared the same existence.

And in this second Europe, why should he not solve the government's dilemma for them? Was there any reason why he should not create a community which did not contain the seeds of destruction? An economic community with stability, which the prototype had lacked?

He began to grow excited. It would defeat Flux, stand against the chaos of the rest of the universe, containing a structure which would last. Otherwise, it would be the same in every detail . . .

He set to work, summoning up thoughts, memories and images, impinging them on the surrounding chaos. Matter began to form. He set the time machine in motion, travelling on to the world he was creating . . .

Suddenly he was in mistiness again. Rotating . . . rotation without change of position . . . rushing forward . . .

The numbers clicked off his dial: 000008 . . . 7 . . . 6 . . . 5 . . . 4 . . .

Then everything steadied around him as the machine came to a stop. He was in Appeltoft's laboratory in Geneva. Technicians prowled the outskirts of the room, beyond the barriers of trestles. The time machine, its translucent rods pointing dramatically in three directions, rested on a rough wooden pedestal.

File moved, stiff, aching and dusty, in the grimy seat. Appeltoft rushed forward, helping him down anxiously and delightedly.

'You're back on the dot, old man! As a test flight it was perfect—from our end.' He flicked his finger over his shoulder. 'Bring brandy for the man! You look done in, Max. Come and clean up; then you can tell us how it went . . .'

File nodded, smiling wordlessly. It was almost perfect . . . but he had not realised just how efficiently he had been taught a new language.

Appeltoft had spoken to him in the voice-torturing tongue of the Yulk.

THE GREATEST TELEVISION SHOW ON EARTH

J. G. Ballard

The idea of time travel being used by the media to capture history as it happened, or the future as it may be, has been the theme of a number of stories. These include 'History in Reverse' by Lee Laurence (1939), featuring a film crew journeying back in time to film the events described in H. G. Wells' famous work, The Outline of History; *Robert Silverberg's 'What We Learned from this Morning's Newspaper' (1972), about the ability of the press to change the course of events; and the following story by J. G. Ballard, which focuses on the power of television, and particularly the medium's relish for controversy and disaster—facets of life that are all too familiar to Ballard, who has regularly been embroiled in arguments about his work: most recently the David Cronenberg version of his novel,* Crash, *about a group of people who find car crashes and the resulting injuries sexually arousing.*

James Graham Ballard (1930–) was born in Shanghai and spent several of his formative years in a Japanese POW camp during the Second World War. At the end of hostilities he came to England and worked in advertising and films before starting to write for New Worlds, *then being edited by his friend, Michael Moorcock. Ballard's stories of physical and mental disintegration marked him out as a unique voice, and his popularity has grown with each passing year. He has written a number of stories about time travel, including 'The Voices of Time' (1960), 'The Garden of Time' (1962) and 'The Gentle Assassin' (1967), in which a man from the future interferes fatally in the attempted assassination of a monarch. 'The Greatest Television Show on Earth', written for* Ambit *in 1976, is perhaps even more thought-provoking than any of these—and certainly all too chillingly possible.*

*   *   *

The discovery in the year 2001 of an effective system of time travel had a number of important repercussions, nowhere greater than in the field of television. The last quarter of the twentieth century had seen the spectacular growth of television across every continent on the globe, and the programmes transmitted by the huge American, European and Afro-Asian networks each claimed audiences of a billion viewers. Yet despite their enormous financial resources the television companies were faced with a chronic shortage of news and entertainment. Vietnam, the first TV War, had given viewers all the excitement of live transmissions from the battlefield, but wars in general, not to mention newsworthy activity of any kind, had died out as the world's population devoted itself almost exclusively to watching television.

At this point the discovery of time travel made its fortunate appearance.

As soon as the first spate of patent suits had been settled (one Japanese entrepreneur almost succeeded in copyrighting history; time was then declared 'open' territory) it became clear that the greatest obstacle to time travel was not the laws of the physical universe but the vast sums of money needed to build and power the installations. These safaris into the past cost approximately a million dollars a minute. After a few brief journeys to verify the Crucifixion, the signing of Magna Carta and Columbus' discovery of the Americas, the government-financed Einstein Memorial Time Center at Princeton was forced to suspend operations.

Plainly, only one other group could finance further explorations into the past—the world's television corporations. Their eager assurances that there would be no undue sensationalism convinced government leaders that the educational benefits of these travelogues through time outweighed any possible lapses in taste.

The television companies, for their part, saw in the past an inexhaustible supply of first-class news and entertainment—all of it, moreover, free. Immediately they set to work, investing billions of dollars, rupees, roubles and yen in duplicating the great chronotron at the Princeton Time Center. Task forces of physicists and mathematicians were enrolled as assistant producers. Camera crews were sent to key sites—London, Washington and Peking—and shortly afterwards the first pilot programmes were transmitted to an eager world.

These blurry scenes, like faded newsreels, of the coronation of Queen Elizabeth II, the inauguration of Franklin Delano Roosevelt and the funeral of Mao Tse-tung triumphantly demonstrated the feasibility of

Time Vision. After this solemn unveiling—a gesture in the direction of the government watchdog committees—the television companies began seriously to plan their schedules. The winter programmes for the year 2002 offered viewers the assassination of President Kennedy ('live', as the North American company tactlessly put it), the D-Day landings and the Battle of Stalingrad. Asian viewers were given Pearl Harbor and the fall of Corregidor.

This emphasis on death and destruction set the pace for what followed. The success of the programmes was beyond the planners' wildest dreams. These fleeting glimpses of smoke-crossed battlegrounds, with their burnt-out tanks and landing craft, had whetted an enormous appetite. More and more camera crews were readied, and an army of military historians deployed to establish the exact time at which Bastogne was relieved, the victory flags hoisted above Mount Suribachi and the Reichstag.

Within a year a dozen programmes each week brought to three billion viewers the highlights of World War II and the subsequent decades, all transmitted as they actually occurred. Night after night, somewhere around the world, John F. Kennedy was shot dead in Dealey Plaza, atom bombs exploded over Hiroshima and Nagasaki, Adolf Hitler committed suicide in the ruins of his Berlin bunker.

After this success the television companies moved back to the 1914–18 War, ready to reap an even richer harvest of audience ratings from the killing grounds of Passchendaele and Verdun. To their surprise, however, the glimpses of this mud- and shell-filled universe were a dismal failure compared with the great technological battles of World War II being transmitted live at the same time on rival channels from the carrier decks of the Philippine Sea and the thousand-bomber raids over Essen and Düsseldorf.

One sequence alone from World War I quickened the viewers' jaded palates—a cavalry charge by Uhlans of the German Imperial Army. Riding over the barbed wire on their splendid mounts, white plumes flying above the mud, these lance-wielding horsemen brought to a billion war-weary TV screens the magic of pageantry and costume. At a moment when it might have faltered, Time Vision was saved by the epaulette and the cuirass.

Immediately, camera crews began to travel back into the nineteenth century. World Wars I and II faded from the screen. Within a few months viewers saw the coronation of Queen Victoria, the assassination of Lincoln and the siege of the Alamo.

As a climax to this season of instant history, the great Time Vision corporations of Europe and North America collaborated on their most spectacular broadcast to date— a live coverage of the defeat of Napoleon Bonaparte at the Battle of Waterloo.

While making their preparations the two companies made a discovery that was to have far-reaching consequences for the whole history of Time Vision. During their visits to the battle (insulated from the shot and fury by the invisible walls of their time capsules) the producers found that there were fewer combatants actually present than described by the historians of the day. Whatever the immense political consequences of the defeat of Napoleonic France, the battle itself was a disappointing affair, a few thousand march-wearied troops engaged in sporadic rifle and artillery duels.

An emergency conference of programme chiefs discussed this failure of Waterloo to live up to its reputation. Senior producers revisited the battlefield, leaving their capsules to wander in disguise among the exhausted soldiery. The prospect of the lowest audience ratings in the history of Time Vision seemed hourly more imminent.

At this crisis point some nameless assistant producer came up with a remarkable idea. Rather than sit back helplessly behind their cameras, the Time Vision companies should step in themselves, he suggested, lending their vast expertise and resources to heightening the drama of the battle. More extras—that is, mercenaries recruited from the nearby farming communities—could be thrown into the fray, supplies of powder and shot distributed to the empty guns, and the entire choreography of the battle revamped by the military consultants in the editorial departments. 'History,' he concluded, 'is just a first-draft screenplay.'

This suggestion of remaking history to boost its audience appeal was seized upon. Equipped with a lavish supply of gold coinage, agents of the television companies moved across the Belgian and North German plains, hiring thousands of mercenaries (at the standard rate for TV extras of fifty dollars per day on location, regardless of rank, seventy-five dollars for a speaking part). The relief column of the Prussian General Blücher, reputed by historians to be many thousand strong and to have decisively turned the battle against Napoleon, was in fact found to be a puny force of brigade strength. Within a few days thousands of eager recruits flocked to the colours, antibiotics secretly administered to polluted water supplies cured a squadron of cavalry hunters suffering from anthrax, and a complete artillery brigade threatened with typhus was put on its feet by a massive dose of chloromycetin.

The Battle of Waterloo, when finally transmitted to an audience of over one billion viewers, was a brilliant spectacle more than equal to its advance publicity of the past two hundred years. The thousands of mercenaries fought with savage fury, the air was split by non-stop artillery barrages, waves of cavalry charged and recharged. Napoleon himself was completely bewildered by the way events turned out, spending his last years in baffled exile.

After the success of Waterloo the Time Vision companies realised the advantages of preparing their ground. From then onwards almost all important historical events were rescripted by the editorial departments. Hannibal's army crossing the Alps was found to contain a mere half-dozen elephants—two hundred more were provided to trample down the dumbfounded Romans. Caesar's assassins numbered only two—five additional conspirators were hired. Famous historical orations, such as the Gettysburg Address, were cut and edited to make them more stirring. Waterloo, meanwhile, was not forgotten. To recoup the original investment the battle was sublet to smaller TV contractors, some of whom boosted the battle to a scale resembling Armageddon. However, these spectacles in the De Mille manner, in which rival companies appeared on the same battlefield, pouring in extras, weapons and animals, were looked down on by more sophisticated viewers.

To the annoyance of the television companies, the most fascinating subject in the whole of history remained barred to them. At the stern insistence of the Christian Churches the entire events surrounding the life of Christ were kept off the screen. Whatever the spiritual benefits of hearing the Sermon on the Mount transmitted live might be, these were tempered by the prospect of this sublime experience being faded out between beatitudes for the commercial breaks.

Baulked here, the programmers moved further back in time. To celebrate the fifth anniversary of Time Vision, preparations began for a stupendous joint venture—the flight of the Israelites from Egypt and the crossing of the Red Sea. A hundred camera units and several thousand producers and technicians took up their positions in the Sinai Peninsula. Two months before the transmission it was obvious that there would now be more than two sides in this classic confrontation between the armies of Egypt and the children of the Lord. Not only did the camera crews outnumber the forces of either side, but the hiring of Egyptian extras, additional wave-making equipment and the prefabricated barrage built to support the cameras might well present the Israelites from getting across at all. Clearly, the powers of the Almighty would be severely tested in his first important confrontation with the ratings.

A few forebodings were expressed by the more old-fashioned clerics, printed under ironic headlines such as 'War against Heaven?', 'Sinai Truce Offer rejected by TV Producers Guild'. At bookmakers throughout Europe and the United States the odds lengthened against the Israelites. On the day of transmission, January 1st, 2006, the audience ratings showed that 98 per cent of the Western world's adult viewers were by their sets.

The first pictures appeared on the screens. Under a fitful sky the fleeing Israelites plodded into view, advancing towards the invisible cameras mounted over the water. Originally three hundred in number, the Israelites now formed a vast throng that stretched with its baggage train for several miles across the desert. Confused by the great press of camp-followers, the Israelite leaders paused on the shore, uncertain how to cross this shifting mass of unstable water. Along the horizon the sabre-wheeled chariots of Pharaoh's army raced towards them.

The viewers watched spellbound, many wondering whether the television companies had at last gone too far.

Then, without explanation, a thousand million screens went blank.

Pandemonium broke loose. Everywhere switchboards were jammed. Priority calls at intergovernmental level jammed the Comsat relays, the Time Vision studios in Europe and America were besieged.

Nothing came through. All contacts with the camera crews on location had been broken. Finally, two hours later, a brief picture appeared, of racing waters swilling over the shattered remains of television cameras and switchgear. On the near bank, the Egyptian forces turned for home. Across the waters, the small band of Israelites moved towards the safety of Sinai.

What most surprised the viewers was the eerie light that illuminated the picture, as if some archaic but extraordinary method of power were being used to transmit it.

No further attempts to regain contact succeeded. Almost all the world's Time Vision equipment had been destroyed, its leading producers and technicians lost for ever, perhaps wandering the stony rocks of Sinai like a second lost tribe. Shortly after this débâcle, these safaris into the past were eliminated from the world's TV programmes. As one priest with a taste for ironic humour remarked to his chastened television congregation: 'The big channel up in the sky has its ratings too.'

THROUGH TIME AND SPACE WITH FERDINAND FEGHOOT

Grendel Briarton

Despite the success of The Time Machine, *Wells never returned to the theme of time travel again. Several of his successors, however, have created whole series around such men and their machines, including Poul Anderson with his critically acclaimed 'Time Patrol' novellas about a group of far-future custodians of intergalactic law; Larry Niven, with his similar long stories of Hanville Svetz, an intrepid time traveller; and Reginald Bretnor, writing as Grendel Briarton, whose comic gems feature the master of space, time and the punning catch-phrase, Ferdinand Feghoot. From the mid-Fifties until just before his death, the author delighted readers of sf magazines—in particular those of* Fantasy and Science Fiction—*with his vignettes about this witty traveller whose mission is to move effortlessly around the galaxy solving problems. Invariably ending in a comic punch line, these tales are universally and affectionately remembered as 'Feghoots'.*

Reginald Bretnor (1911–92), like Isaac Asimov, was born in Russia but emigrated to the USA with his family while he was still a child. As a writer, he had both a serious and a humorous side, producing a number of critical works on the development of sf, collectively known as The Craft of Science Fiction *(1976), as well as two major comic series, the 'Papa Schimmelhorn' fantasy stories and the tales of Ferdinand Feghoot. The following episode—written in 1961—in which the composer Richard Wagner is taken by Ferdinand into the far future to answer a charge of plagiarism, is one of the most hilarious in the entire series. It is, as Grendel Briarton proudly boasted by way of introduction, a 'Super-Feghoot'!*

*   *   *

It was because of an argument with Ferdinand Feghoot that Richard Wagner was convicted of plagiarism in 2867. On a visit to Bayreuth, Feghoot had told him about the planet Madamabutterfry in the Twenty-Ninth Century, and how the natives believed that every grand opera idea had been stolen from them, and how they invariably proved it. Instantly, Wagner flew into a fury. 'Only Teutonic ideas are goot for Grand Opera!' he stormed. 'The rest iss all rubbish! Get your mazhine for shpace-time. Ve go to your planet. I vill show you!'

On Madamabutterfry, the customs officials asked whether Wagner had anything to declare—any operas, acts, scenes or arias—and he sneeringly gave them a list. Within minutes, they had him arrested, and a police official was offering to show him the themes he had pilfered.

Right at the spaceport, he was led to a vast, ancient tree with eye-buds and tentacle-tendrils. Every leaf drooped; its bark was dull, dry and scaly; it rustled hopelessly at them. Near it was a pile of used spaceship parts and a sign saying:

ROOTBOTTOM STANLEY, THE EARTHMAN'S FRIEND!
BEST DEAL IN THE GALAXY!! ABSOLUTELY *NO* BEING
UNDERSELLS ME!!!
GARFINKLES, TOP QUALITY 17.95! TODAY *ONLY* 8.95!
NEVER AGAIN! *1.97*!!!

Near by was a little booth manned by a small, mole-like people; its sign said simply:

GARFINKLES, SIX FOR A DIME

'So tragic,' murmured the policeman, 'such a valuable theme.'
'But vodt could I have written aboudt it?' roared Wagner.
'That's obvious,' Feghoot said. '*Tree Stan Undersold.*'
They went on to a cook-shop, where their escort showed them an enormous jar full of jam. Stretched over its top was a flat, rubbery organism with two mournful eyes and a mouth in the middle.
'Such a sadness,' lamented the policeman, dabbing away at a tear. 'With hunger he grasps at the jar, and so does his work. But if he is fed, then he will let go and sleep.'
'Can't I *please* have some jam?' called a thin little voice. 'Just a nibble, just one. Oh, how I long for it!'

'I suspect,' remarked Feghoot before Wagner could speak, 'that this is the *Nibble-longing Lid.*'

Finally they were brought to the edge of an odorous bog, where a huge, frog-like person was unhappily tying oysters to strings and dropping them into the water to marinate them. His topknot glowed fitfully with a faint, sickly light.

'This is most tragic of all,' said the policeman. 'Very artistic, nice to steal. No one buys now his bivalves. That is why his light-on-top cannot shine.'

'*An oudraitch!*' screamed Wagner, leaping and frothing and tearing his hair. 'It iss ridiculous! Vot iss this to me?'

'*Dim Oyster Sinker,*' said Ferdinand Feghoot.

TIME BUM

C. M. Kornbluth

'Time Police' patrolling the future with occasional forays into our present is another theme that has been well used by writers. The Fifties are generally regarded as the heyday of the operations of these law men and secret agents, and this next story, which appeared in the January–February 1953 issue of Fantastic, remains a model of its kind and has rarely been equalled. What makes the tale special is that Kornbluth has managed to combine, in a way that is wholly convincing, a character from the pages of Damon Runyon with a fantasy theme. When you've read it, just hope that the ending is pure fiction!

Cyril M. Kornbluth (1923–58) was an adept writer of fantasy and science fiction whose developing talent was cut short by his premature death. A fan turned writer after his distinguished military service during the Second World War, Kornbluth nurtured an interest in time travel that surfaced in one of his earliest short stories, 'The Little Black Bag' (1950), about a medical bag from the future which arrives in the present and is sadly misused. His novel Gunner Cade (1952), about a future where war has been turned into a spectator sport, attracted a wide readership on both sides of the Atlantic, and was followed by the equally impressive The Space Merchants (1953), which he wrote in collaboration with Frederik Pohl. The book inspired a whole decade of novels predicting worlds dominated by media groups. The Syndic (1953) was a brilliant satire on the America of the future, where society is being run by almost benevolent organised criminals. Harry Twenty-Third Street, the 'time bum' of this story, is on the wrong side of the law, too, and has come up with a new con trick. The result is a Runyonesque caper that would surely have delighted the master.

*   *   *

Harry Twenty-Third Street suddenly burst into laughter. His friend and sometime roper Farmer Brown looked inquisitive.

'I just thought of a new con,' Harry Twenty-Third Street said, still chuckling.

Farmer Brown shook his head positively. 'There's no such thing, my man,' he said. 'There are only new switches on old cons. What have you got—a store con? Shall you be needing a roper?' He tried not to look eager as a matter of principle, but everybody knew the Farmer needed a connection badly. His girl had two-timed him on a badger game, running off with the chump and marrying him after an expensive, month-long build-up.

Harry said, 'Sorry, old boy. No details. It's too good to split up. I shall rip and tear the suckers with this con for many a year, I trust, before the details become available to the trade. Nobody, but nobody, is going to call copper after I take him. It's beautiful and it's mine. I will see you around, my friend.'

Harry got up from the booth and left, nodding cheerfully to a safe-blower here, a fixer there, on his way to the locked door of the hang-out. Naturally he didn't nod to such small fry as pickpockets and dope peddlers. Harry had his pride.

The puzzled Farmer sipped his lemon squash and concluded that Harry had been kidding him. He noticed that Harry had left behind him in the booth a copy of a magazine with a spaceship and a pretty girl in green bra and pants on the cover.

'A furnished . . . bungalow?' the man said hesitantly, as though he knew what he wanted but wasn't quite sure of the word.

'Certainly, Mr Clurg,' Walter Lachlan said. 'I'm sure we can suit you. Wife and family?'

'No,' said Clurg. 'They are . . . far away.' He seemed to get some secret amusement from the thought. And then, to Walter's horror, he sat down calmly in empty air beside the desk and, of course, crashed to the floor looking ludicrous and astonished.

Walter gaped and helped him up, sputtering apologies and wondering privately what was wrong with the man. There wasn't a chair there. There was a chair on the other side of the desk and a chair against the wall. But there just wasn't a chair where Clurg had sat down.

Clurg apparently was unhurt; he protested against Walter's apologies, saying: 'I should have known, Master Lachlan. It's quite all right; it was all my fault. What about the bang—the bungalow?'

Business sense triumphed over Walter's bewilderment. He pulled out his listings and they conferred on the merits of several furnished bungalows. When Walter mentioned that the Curran place was especially nice, in an especially nice neighbourhood—he lived up the street himself—Clurg was impressed. 'I'll take that one,' he said. 'What is the ... feoff?'

Walter had learned a certain amount of law for his real-estate licence examination; he recognised the word. 'The *rent* is seventy-five dollars,' he said. 'You speak English very well, Mr Clurg.' He hadn't been certain that the man was a foreigner until the dictionary word came out. 'You have hardly any accent.'

'Thank you,' Clurg said, pleased. 'I worked hard at it. Let me see—seventy-five is six twelves and three.' He opened one of his shiny-new leather suitcases and calmly laid six heavy little paper rolls on Walter's desk. He broke open a seventh and laid down three mint-new silver dollars. 'There I am,' he said. 'I mean, there you are.'

Walter didn't know what to say. It had never happened before. People paid by cheque or in bills. They just didn't pay in silver dollars. But it was money—why shouldn't Mr Clurg pay in silver dollars if he wanted to? He shook himself, scooped the rolls into his top desk drawer and said: 'I'll drive you out there if you like. It's nearly quitting-time anyway.'

Walter told his wife Betty over the dinner-table: 'We ought to have him in some evening. I can't imagine where on Earth he comes from. I had to show him how to turn on the kitchen range. When it went on he said, "Oh, yes—electricity!" and laughed his head off. And he kept ducking the question when I tried to ask him in a nice way. Maybe he's some kind of a political refugee.'

'Maybe ...' Betty began dreamily, and then shut her mouth. She didn't want Walter laughing at her again. As it was, he made her buy her science fiction magazines down-town instead of at neighbourhood news-stands. He thought it wasn't becoming for his wife to read them. He's so eager for success, she thought sentimentally.

That night, while Walter watched a television variety show, she read a story in one of her magazines. (Its cover, depicting a space ship and a girl in green bra and shorts, had been prudently torn off and thrown away.) It was about a man from the future who had gone back in time, bringing with him all sorts of marvellous inventions. In the end the Time Police punished him for unauthorised time travelling. They had come back and got him, brought him back to his own time. She smiled. It *would* be nice if Mr Clurg, instead of being a slightly eccentric foreigner, were a man from the future with all sorts of interesting stories to tell and a satchelful of gadgets that could be sold for millions and millions of dollars.

After a week they did have Clurg over for dinner. It started badly. Once more he managed to sit down in empty air and crash to the floor. While they were brushing him off he said fretfully: 'I *can't* get used to not—' and then said no more.

He was a picky eater. Betty had done one of her mother's specialities, veal cutlet with tomato sauce, topped by a poached egg. He ate the egg and sauce, made a clumsy attempt to cut up the meat, and abandoned it. She served a plate of cheese, half a dozen kinds, for dessert, and Clurg tasted them uncertainly, breaking off a crumb from each, while Betty wondered where that constituted good manners. His face lit up when he tried a ripe cheddar. He popped the whole wedge into his mouth and said to Betty: 'I will have that, please.'

'Seconds?' asked Walter. 'Sure. Don't bother, Betty. I'll get it.' He brought back a quarter-pound wedge of the cheddar.

Walter and Betty watched silently as Clurg calmly ate every crumb of it. He sighed. 'Very good. Quite like—' The word, Walter and Betty later agreed, was *see-mon-joe*. They were able to agree quite early in the evening, because Clurg got up after eating the cheese, said warmly, 'Thank you so much!' and walked out of the house.

Betty said, '*What—on—Earth!*'

Walter said uneasily, 'I'm sorry, doll. I didn't think he'd be quite that peculiar—'

'—But after *all!*'

'—Of course he's a foreigner. What was that word?'

He jotted it down.

While they were doing the dishes Betty said, 'I think he was drunk. Falling-down drunk.'

'No,' Walter said. 'it's exactly the same thing he did in my office. As though he expected a chair to come to him instead of him going to a chair.' He laughed and said uncertainly, 'Or maybe he's royalty. I read once about Queen Victoria never looking around before she sat down, she was so sure there'd be a chair there.'

'Well, there isn't any more royalty, not to speak of,' she said angrily, hanging up the dish towel. 'What's on TV tonight?'

'Uncle Miltie. But . . . uh . . . I think I'll read. Uh . . . where do you keep those magazines of yours, doll? Believe I'll give them a try.'

She gave him a look that he wouldn't meet, and she went to get him some of her magazines. She also got a slim green book which she hadn't looked at for years. While Walter flipped uneasily through the magazines she studied the book.

After about ten minutes she said: 'Walter. *Seemonjoe.* I think I know what language it is.'

He was instantly alert. 'Yeah? What?'

'It should be spelled c-i-m-a-n-g-o, with little jiggers over the c and g. It means "universal food" in Esperanto.'

'Where's Esperanto?' he demanded.

'Esperanto isn't anywhere. It's an artificial language. I played around with it a little once. It was supposed to end war and all sorts of things. Some people called it "the language of the future".' Her voice was tremulous.

Walter said, 'I'm going to get to the bottom of this.'

He saw Clurg go into the neighbourhood movie for the matinée. That gave him about three hours.

Walter hurried to the Curran bungalow, remembered to slow down and tried hard to look casual as he unlocked the door and went in. There wouldn't be any trouble—he was a good citizen, known and respected—he could let himself into a tenant's house and wait for him to talk about business if he wanted to.

He tried not to think of what people would think if he should be caught rifling Clurg's luggage, as he intended to do. He had brought along an assortment of luggage keys. Surprised by his own ingenuity, he had got them at a locksmith's by saying his own key was lost and he didn't want to haul a heavy packed bag down-town.

But he didn't need the keys. In the bedroom closet the two suitcases stood, unlocked.

There was nothing in the first except uniformly new clothes, bought locally at good shops. The second was full of the same. Going through a rather extreme sports jacket, Walter found a wad of paper in the breast pocket. It was a newspaper page. A number had been pencilled on a margin; apparently the sheet had been torn out and stuck into the pocket and forgotten. The date-line on the paper was July 18th, 2403.

Walter had some trouble reading the stories at first, but found it was easy enough if he read them aloud and listened to his voice.

One said:

There was an advertisement on the other side:

Underneath it another ad asked:

Walter's heart pounded. Gold—to avoid tiresome polishing! Six-inch
diamonds—for long wear!

And Clurg must be a time policeman. 'Only in the Time Police can
you see the pageant of the ages!' What did a time policeman do? he
wasn't quite clear about that. But what they *didn't* do was let anybody

else—anybody earlier—know that the Time Police existed. He, Walter Lachlan of the Twentieth Century, held in the palm of his hand Time Policeman Clurg of the Twenty-Fifth Century—the Twenty-Fifth Century where gold and diamonds were common as steel and glass in this!

He was there when Clurg came back from the matinée.

Mutely, Walter extended the page of newsprint. Clurg snatched it incredulously, stared at it and crumpled it in his fist. He collapsed on the floor with a groan. 'I'm done for!' Walter heard him say.

'Listen, Clurg,' Walter said. 'Nobody ever needs to know about this—*nobody*.'

Clurg looked up with sudden hope in his eyes. 'You will keep silent?' he asked wildly. 'It is my life!'

'What's it worth to you?' Walter demanded with brutal directness. 'I can use some of those diamonds and some of that gold. Can you get it into this century?'

'It would be missed. It would be over my mass-balance,' Clurg said. 'But I have a Duplix. I can copy diamonds and gold for you; that was how I made my feoff money.'

He snatched an instrument from his pocket—a fountain pen, Walter thought. 'It is low in charge. It would Duplix about five kilograms in one operation—'

'You mean,' Walter demanded, 'that if I brought you five kilograms of diamonds and gold you could duplicate it? And the originals wouldn't be harmed? Let me see that thing. Can I work it?'

Clurg passed over the 'fountain pen'. Walter saw that within the case was a tangle of wires, tiny tubes, lenses—he passed it back hastily. Clurg said, 'That is correct. You could buy or borrow jewellery and I could duplix it. Then you could return the originals and retain the copies. You swear by your contemporary God that you would say nothing?'

Walter was thinking. He could scrape together a good 30,000 dollars by pledging the house, the business, his own real estate, the bank account, the life insurance, the securities. Put it all into diamonds, of course, and then—*doubled*! *Overnight*!

'I'll say nothing,' he told Clurg. 'If you come through.' He took the sheet from the twenty-fifth century newspaper from Clurg's hands and put it securely in his own pocket. 'When I get those diamonds duplicated,' he said, 'I'll burn this and forget the rest. Until then, I want you to stay close to home. I'll come round in a day or so with the stuff for you to duplicate.'

Clurg nervously promised.

The secrecy, of course, didn't include Betty. He told her when he got home and she let out a yell of delight. She demanded the newspaper, read it avidly, and then demanded to see Clurg.

'I don't think he'll talk,' Walter said doubtfully. 'But if you really want to . . .'

She did, and they walked to the Curran bungalow. Clurg was gone, lock, stock and barrel, leaving not a trace behind. They waited for hours, nervously.

At last Betty said, 'He's gone back.'

Walter nodded. 'He wouldn't keep his bargain, but by God I'm going to keep mine. Come along. We're going to the *Enterprise*.'

'Walter,' she said. 'You wouldn't—would you?'

He went alone, after a bitter quarrel.

At the *Enterprise* office he was wearily listened to by a reporter, who wearily looked over the twenty-fifth century newspaper. 'I don't know what you're peddling, Mr Lachlan,' he said, 'but we like people to buy their ads in the *Enterprise*. This is a pretty bare-faced publicity grab.'

'But—' Walter sputtered.

'Sam, would you please ask Mr Morris to come up here if he can?' the reporter was saying into the phone. To Walter he explained, 'Mr Morris is our press-room foreman.'

The foreman was a huge, white-haired old fellow, partly deaf. The reporter showed him the newspaper from the twenty-fifth century and said, 'How about this?'

Mr Morris looked at it and smelled it and said, showing no interest in the reading matter: 'American Type Foundry Futura number nine, discontinued about ten years ago. It's been hand-set. The ink—hard to say. Expensive stuff, not a news ink. A book ink, a job-printing ink. The paper, now, I know. A nice linen rag that Benziger jobs in Philadelphia.'

'You see, Mr Lachlan? It's a fake.' The reporter shrugged.

Walter walked slowly from the city room. The press-room foreman *knew*. It was a fake. And Clurg was a faker. Suddenly Walter's heels touched the ground after twenty-four hours and stayed there. Good God, the diamonds! Clurg was a conman! He would have worked a package switch! He would have had thirty thousand dollars' worth of diamonds for less than a month's work!

He told Betty about it when he got home and she laughed unmercifully. 'Time Policeman' was to become a family joke between the Lachlans.

Harry Twenty-Third Street stood, blinking, in a very peculiar place. Peculiarly, his feet were firmly encased, up to the ankles, in a block of clear plastic.

There were odd-looking people and a big voice was saying: 'May it please the court. The People of the Twenty-Fifth Century versus Harold Parish, alias Harry Twenty-Third Street, alias Clurg, of the Twentieth Century. The charge is impersonating an officer of the Time Police. The Prosecutor's Office will ask for the death penalty in view of the heinous nature of the offence, which threatens the whole fabric—'

'ALL YOU ZOMBIES—'

Robert A. Heinlein

*Robert Heinlein was for several decades the most important writer of
science fiction in the world, his reputation built on the creation of
stories with totally convincing backgrounds. Many of Heinlein's books
and short stories fall into a category that he labelled 'Future History',
and the idea of time travel in this future was one in which he fully
believed. As early as 1941 he wrote a story about people caught in a
time loop, 'By His Bootstraps', which was published under one of his
pen-names, Anson MacDonald, and then in 1957 he produced a full-
length time travel novel,* The Door into Summer, *which has remained
in print ever since. To his countless admirers Heinlein was a guide to
the new directions that time travel stories might take, just as Wells had
been in inaugurating the genre.*

*Born in Missouri, Robert Anson Heinlein (1907–88) served with
distinction as an officer in the US Navy before ill-health forced him to
abandon his career and turn to writing science fiction—inspired by the
books of Wells and Jules Verne which he had read as a youngster.
Short stories first brought him to the attention of sf readers, but it was
his novels that made him an international best-seller, in particular the
classic,* Stranger in a Strange Land *(1961) which won a Hugo award
and rapidly became one of the cult books of the Sixties. Several of his
novels have been filmed, and in 1975 he was given the First Grand
Master Nebula award. 'All You Zombies—' (published in the* Magazine
of Fantasy and Science Fiction *in 1959) features a character who moves
forwards and backwards in time on the kind of genetic mission only
Heinlein could have dreamed up. It has been described by Brian Ash
in his* Who's Who in Science Fiction *(1976) as 'a paradoxical time-
travel tale yet to be surpassed'.*

*   *   *

2217 – Time Zone V (EST) – 7 Nov 1970 – NYC – 'Pop's Place': I was polishing a brandy snifter when the Unmarried Mother came in. I noted the time—10.17 p.m. zone five, or eastern time, November 7, 1970. Temporal agents always notice time and date; we must.

The Unmarried Mother was a man twenty-five years old, no taller than I am, childish features and a touchy temper. I didn't like his looks—I never had—but he was a lad I was here to recruit, he was my boy. I gave him my best barkeeper's smile.

Maybe I'm too critical. He wasn't swish; his nickname came from what he always said when some nosy type asked him his line: 'I'm an unmarried mother.' If he felt less than murderous he would add: '—at four cents a word. I write confession stories.'

If he felt nasty, he would wait for somebody to make something of it. He had a lethal style of infighting, like a female cop—one reason I wanted him. Not the only one.

He had a load on and his face showed that he despised people more than usual. Silently I poured a double shot of Old Underwear and left the bottle. He drank it, poured another.

I wiped the bar top. 'How's the "Unmarried Mother" racket?'

His fingers tightened on the glass and he seemed about to throw it at me; I felt for the sap under the bar. In temporal manipulation you try to figure everything, but there are so many factors that you never take needless risks.

I saw him relax that tiny amount they teach you to watch for in the Bureau's training school. 'Sorry,' I said. 'Just asking. "How's business?" Make it "How's the weather?"'

He looked sour. 'Business is okay. I write 'em, they print 'em, I eat.'

I poured myself one, leaned towards him. 'Matter of fact,' I said, 'you write a nice stick—I've sampled a few. You have an amazingly sure touch with the woman's angle.'

It was a slip I had to risk; he never admitted what pen-names he used. But he was boiled enough to pick up only the last: 'Woman's angle!' he repeated with a snort. 'Yeah, I know the woman's angle. I should.'

'So?' I said doubtfully. 'Sisters?'

'No. You wouldn't believe me if I told you.'

'Now, now,' I answered mildly, 'bartenders and psychiatrists learn that nothing is stranger than truth. Why, son, if you heard the stories I do—well, you'd make yourself rich. Incredible.'

'You don't know what "incredible" means!'

'So? Nothing astonishes me. I've always heard worse.'

He snorted again. 'Want to bet the rest of the bottle?'

'I'll bet a full bottle.' I placed one on the bar.

'Well—' I signalled my other bartender to handle the trade. We were at the far end, a single-stool space that I kept private by loading the bar top by it with jars of pickled eggs and other clutter. A few were at the other end watching the fights and somebody was playing the juke-box—private as a bed where we were.

'Okay,' he began, 'to start with, I'm a bastard.'

'No distinction around here,' I said.

'I mean it,' he snapped. 'My parents weren't married.'

'Still no distinction,' I insisted. 'Neither were mine.'

'When—' He stopped, gave me the first warm look I ever saw on him. 'You mean that?'

'I do. A one hundred per cent bastard. In fact,' I added, 'no one in my family ever marries. All bastards.'

'Then what's that?' he indicated at my hand.

'Oh, that.' I showed it to him. 'It just looks like a wedding ring: I wear it to keep women off.' It is an antique I bought in 1985 from a fellow-operative—he had fetched it from pre-Christian Crete. 'The Worm Ouroboros . . . The World Snake that eats its own tail, for ever without end. A symbol of the Great Paradox.'

He barely glanced at it. 'If you're really a bastard, you know how it feels. When I was a little girl—'

'Wups!' I said. 'Did I hear you correctly?'

'Who's telling this story? Look, ever hear of Christine Jorgensen? Or Roberta Cowell?'

'Uh, sex-change cases? You're trying to tell me—'

'Don't interrupt or swelp me, I won't talk. I was a foundling, left at an orphanage in Cleveland in 1945 when I was a month old. When I was a little girl, I envied kids with parents. Then, when I learned about sex—and, believe me, Pop, you learn fast in an orphanage—'

'I know.'

'—I made a solemn vow that any kid of mine would have both a pop and a mom. It kept me "pure", quite a feat in that vicinity—I had to learn to fight to manage it. Then I got older and realised I stood darn little chance of getting married—for the same reason I hadn't been adopted.' He scowled. 'I was horse-faced and buck-toothed, flat-chested and straight-haired.'

'You don't look any worse than I do.'

'Who cares how a barkeeper looks? Or a writer? But people wanting to adopt pick little blue-eyed golden-haired morons. Later on, the boys want bulging breasts, a cuté face, and an Oh-you-wonderful-male manner.' He shrugged. 'I couldn't compete. So I decided to join the W.E.N.C.H.E.S.'

'Eh?'

'Women's Emergency National Corps, Hospitality and Entertainment Section, what they now call "Space Angels"—Auxiliary Nursing Group, Extraterrestrial Legions.'

I knew both terms, once I had them chronised. We use still a third name, it's that elite military service corps: Women's Hospitality Order Refortifying and Encouraging Spacemen. Vocabulary shift is the worst hurdle in time jumps—did you know that 'service station' once meant a dispensary for petroleum fractions? Once on an assignment in the Churchill Era, a woman said to me, 'Meet me at the service station next door'—which is not what it sounds; a 'service station' (then) wouldn't have a bed in it.

He went on: 'It was when they first admitted you can't send men into space for months and years and not relieve the tension. You remember how the wowsers screamed? That improved my chance, since volunteers were scarce. A gal had to be respectable, preferably a virgin (they liked to train them from scratch), above average mentally, and stable emotionally. But most volunteers were old hookers, or neurotics who would crack up ten days off Earth. So I didn't need looks; if they accepted me, they would fix my buck teeth, put a wave in my hair, teach me to walk and dance and how to listen to a man pleasingly, and everything else—plus training for the prime duties. They would even use plastic surgery if it would help—nothing too good for Our Boys.

'Best yet, they made sure you didn't get pregnant during your enlistment—and you were almost certain to marry at the end of your hitch. Same way today, A.N.G.E.L.S. marry spacers—they talk the language.

'When I was eighteen I was placed as a "mother's helper". This family simply wanted a cheap servant but I didn't mind as I couldn't enlist till I was twenty-one. I did housework and went to night school—pretending to continue my high-school typing and shorthand but going to charm class instead, to better my chances for enlistment.

'Then I met this city slicker with his hundred-dollar bills.' He scowled. 'The no-good actually did have a wad of hundred-dollar bills. He showed me one night, told me to help myself.

'But I didn't. I liked him. He was the first man I ever met who was nice to me without trying games with me. I quit night school to see him oftener. It was the happiest time of my life.

'Then one night in the park the games began.'

He stopped. I said, 'And then?'

'And then *nothing*! I never saw him again. He walked me home and told me he loved me—and kissed me good-night and never came back.' He looked grim. 'If I could find him, I'd kill him!'

'Well,' I sympathised, 'I know how you feel. But killing him—just for doing what comes naturally—hmm . . . Did you struggle?'

'Huh? What's that got to do with it?'

'Quite a bit. Maybe he deserves a couple of broken arms for running out on you, but—'

'He deserves worse than that! Wait till you hear. Somehow I kept anyone from suspecting and decided it was all for the best. I hadn't really loved him and probably would never love anybody—and I was more eager to join the W.E.N.C.H.E.S. than ever. I wasn't disqualified, they didn't insist on virgins. I cheered up.

'It wasn't until my skirts got tight that I realised.'

'Pregnant?'

'He had me higher 'n a kite! Those skinflints I lived with ignored it as long as I could work—then kicked me out and the orphanage wouldn't take me back. I landed in a charity ward surrounded by other big bellies and trotted bedpans until my time came.

'One night I found myself on an operating table, with a nurse saying, "Relax. Now breathe deeply."

'I woke up in bed, numb from the chest down. My surgeon came in. "How do you feel?" he says cheerfully.

' "Like a mummy."

' "Naturally. You're wrapped like one and full of dope to keep you numb. You'll get well—but a Caesarean isn't a hangnail."

' "Caesarean," I said. "Doc—*did I lose the baby?*"

' "Oh, no. Your baby's fine."

' "Oh. Boy or girl?"

' "A healthy little girl. Five pounds, three ounces."

'I relaxed. It's something, to have made a baby. I told myself I would go somewhere and tack "Mrs" on my name and let the kid think her papa was dead—no orphanage for *my* kid!

'But the surgeon was talking. "Tell me, uh—" he avoided my name "—did you ever think your glandular set-up was odd?"

'I said, "Huh? of course not. What are you driving at?"

'He hesitated. "I'll give you this in one dose, then a hypo to let you sleep off your jitters. You'll have 'em."

' "Why?" I demanded.

' "Ever hear of that Scottish physician who was female until she was thirty-five?—then had surgery and became legally and medically a man? Got married. All okay."

' "What's that got to do with me?"

' "That's what I'm saying. You're a man."

'I tried to sit up. *"What?"*

' "Take it easy. When I opened you, I found a mess. I sent for the Chief of Surgery while I got the baby out, then we held a consultation with you on the table—and worked for hours to salvage what we could. You had two full sets of organs, both immature, but with the female set well enough developed for you to have a baby. They could never be any use to you again, so we took them out and rearranged things so that you can develop properly as a man." He put a hand on me. 'Don't worry. You're young, your bones will readjust, we'll watch your glandular balance—and make a fine young man out of you."

'I started to cry. "What about my *baby*?"

' "Well, you can't nurse her, you haven't milk enough for a kitten. If I were you, I wouldn't see her—put her up for adoption.'

' "*No!*"

'He shrugged. "The choice is yours; you're her mother—well, her parent. But don't worry now; we'll get you well first."

'Next day they let me see the kid and I saw her daily—trying to get used to her. I had never seen a brand-new baby and had no idea how awful they look—my daughter looked like an orange monkey. My feeling changed to cold determination to do right by her. But four weeks later that didn't mean anything.'

'Eh?'

'She was snatched.'

'Snatched?'

The Unmarried Mother almost knocked over the bottle we had bet. 'Kidnapped—stolen from the hospital nursery!' He breathed hard. 'How's that for taking the last a man's got to live for?'

'A bad deal,' I agree. 'Let's pour you another. No clues?'

'Nothing the police could trace. Somebody came to see her, claimed to be her uncle. While the nurse had her back turned, he walked out with her.'

'Description?'

'Just a man, with a face-shaped face, like yours or mine.' He frowned. 'I think it was the baby's father. The nurse swore it was an older man but he probably used make-up. Who else would swipe my baby? Childless women pull such stunts—but whoever heard of a man doing it?'

'What happened to you then?'

'Eleven more months of that grim place and three operations. In four months I started to grow a beard; before I was out I was shaving regularly . . . and no longer doubted that I was male.' He grinned wryly. 'I was staring down nurses' necklines.'

'Well,' I said, 'seems to me you came through okay. Here you are, a normal man, making good money, no real troubles. And the life of a female is not an easy one.'

He glared at me. 'A lot you know about it!'

'So?'

'Ever hear the expression "a ruined woman"?'

'Mmmm, years ago. Doesn't mean much today.'

'I was as ruined as a woman can be; that bum *really* ruined me—I was no longer a woman . . . and I didn't know *how* to be a man.'

'Takes getting used to, I suppose.'

'You have no idea. I don't mean learning how to dress, or not walking into the wrong rest room; I learned those in the hospital. But how could I *live*? What job could I get? Hell, I couldn't even drive a car. I didn't know a trade; I couldn't do manual labour—too much scar tissue, too tender.

'I hated him for having ruined me for the W.E.N.C.H.E.S., too, but I didn't know how much until I tried to join the Space Corps instead. One look at my belly and I was marked unfit for military service. The medical officer spent time on me just from curiosity; he had read about my case.

'So I changed my name and came to New York. I got by as a fry cook, then rented a typewriter and set myself up as a public stenographer—what a laugh! In four months I typed four letters and one manuscript. The manuscript was for *Real-Life Tales* and a waste of paper, but the goof who wrote it, sold it. Which gave me an idea; I bought a stack of confession magazines and studied them.' He looked cynical: 'Now you know how I get the authentic woman's angle on an unmarried-mother story . . . through the only version I haven't sold—the true one. Do I win the bottle?'

I pushed it towards him. I was upset myself, but there was work to do. I said, 'Son, you still want to lay hands on that so-and-so?'

His eyes lighted up—a feral gleam.

'Hold it!' I said. 'You wouldn't kill him?'

He chuckled nastily. 'Try me.'

'Take it easy. I know more about it than you think I do. I can help you. I know where he is.'

He reached across the bar. '*Where is he*?'

I said softly, 'Let go my shirt, sonny—or you'll land in the alley and we'll tell the cops you fainted.' I showed him the sap.

He let go. 'Sorry. But where is he?' He looked at me. 'And how do you know so much?'

'All in good time. There are records—hospital records, orphanage records, medical records. The matron of your orphanage was Mrs Fetherage—right? She was followed by Mrs Gruenstein—right? Your name, as a girl, was "Jane"—right? And you didn't tell me any of this—right?'

I had him baffled and a bit scared. 'What's this? You trying to make trouble for me?'

'No indeed. I've your welfare at heart. I can put this character in your lap. You do to him as you see fit—and I guarantee that you'll get away with it. But I don't think you'll kill him. You'd be nuts to—and you aren't nuts. Not quite.'

He brushed it aside. 'Cut the noise. *Where is he*?'

I poured him a short one; he was drunk but anger was offsetting it. 'Not so fast. I do something for you—you do something for me.'

'Uh . . . what?'

'You don't like your work. What would you say to high pay, steady work, unlimited expense account, your own boss on the job, and lots of variety and adventure?'

He stared. 'I'd say, "Get those goddamn reindeer off my roof!" Shove it, Pop—there's no such job.'

'Okay, put it this way: I hand him to you, you settle with him, then try my job. If it's not all I claim—well, I can't hold you.'

He was wavering; the last drink did it. 'When d'yuh d'liver 'im?' he said thickly.

'If it's a deal—*right now*!'

He shoved out his hand. 'It's a deal!'

I nodded to my assistant to watch both ends, noted the time—2300—started to duck through the gate under the bar—when the juke-box blared out: 'I'm My Own Granpaw!' The service man had orders to load it with old Americana and classics because I couldn't stomach the 'music' of 1970, but I hadn't known that tape was in it. I called out, 'Shut that off! Give the customer his money back.' I added, 'Store-room, back in a moment', and headed there with my Unmarried Mother following.

It was down the passage across from the johns, a steel door to which no one but my day manager and myself had a key; inside was a door to an inner room to which only I had a key. We went there.

He looked blearily around at windowless walls. 'Where is 'e?'

'Right away.' I opened a case, the only thing in the room; it was a USFF Co-ordinates Transformer Field Kit, series 1992, Mod. II—a beauty, no moving parts, weight twenty-three kilos fully charged, and shaped to pass as a suitcase. I had adjusted it precisely earlier that day; all I had to do was to shake out the metal net which limits the transformation field.

Which I did. 'Wha's that?' he demanded.

'Time machine,' I said and tossed the net over us.

'Hey!' he yelled and stepped back. There is a technique to this; the net has to be thrown so that the subject will instinctively step back *on to* the metal mesh, then you close the net with both of you inside completely—else you might leave shoe soles behind or a piece of foot, or scoop up a slice of floor. But that's all the skill it takes. Some agents con a subject into the net; I tell the truth and use that instant of utter astonishment to flip the switch. Which I did.

1030 – VI – 3 April 1963 – Cleveland, Ohio-Apex Bldg: 'Hey!' he repeated. 'Take this damn thing off!'

'Sorry,' I apologised and did so, stuffed the net into the case, closed it. 'You said you wanted to find him.'

'But—you said that was a time machine!'

I pointed out of a window. 'Does that look like November? Or New York?' While he was gawking at new buds and spring weather, I reopened the case, took out a packet of hundred-dollar bills, checked that the numbers and signatures were compatible with 1963. The Temporal Bureau doesn't care how much you spend (it costs nothing) but they don't like unnecessary anachronisms. Too many mistakes, and a general court-martial will exile you for a year in a nasty period, say 1974, with its strict rationing and forced labour. I never make such mistakes, the money was okay.

He turned round and said, 'What happened?'

'He's here. Go outside and take him. Here's expense money.' I shoved it at him and added, 'Settle him, then I'll pick you up.'

Hundred-dollar bills have a hypnotic effect on a person not used to them. He was thumbing them unbelievingly as I eased him into the hall, locked him out. The next jump was easy, a small shift in era.

7100 – VI – 10 March 1964 – Cleveland – Apex Bldg: There was a notice under the door saying that my lease expired next week; otherwise the room looked as it had a moment before. Outside, trees were bare and snow threatened; I hurried, stopping only for contemporary money and a coat, hat and top-coat I had left there when I leased the room. I hired a car, went to the hospital. It took twenty minutes to bore the nursery attendant to the point where I could swipe the baby without being noticed. We went back to the Apex Building. This dial setting was more involved as the building did not yet exist in 1945. But I had precalculated it.

0010 – VI – 20 Sept 1945 – Cleveland-Skyview Motel: Field kit, baby and I arrived in a motel outside town. Earlier I had registered as 'Gregory Johnson, Warren, Ohio', so we arrived in a room with curtains closed, windows locked and doors bolted, and the floor cleared to allow for waver as the machine hunts. You can get a nasty bruise from a chair where it shouldn't be—not the chair of course, but backlash from the field.

No trouble. Jane was sleeping soundly; I carried her out, put her in a grocery box on the seat of a car I had provided earlier, drove to the orphanage, put her on the steps, drove two blocks to a 'service station' (the petroleum products sort) and phoned the orphanage, drove back in time to see them taking the box inside, kept going and abandoned the car near the motel—walked to it and jumped forward to the Apex Building in 1963.

1100 – VI – 24 April 1963 – Cleveland-Apex Bldg: I had cut the time rather fine—temporal accuracy depends on span, except on return to zero. If I had it right, Jane was discovering, out in the park this balmy spring night, that she wasn't quite as 'nice' a girl as she had thought. I grabbed a taxi to the home of these skinflints, had the hackie wait around a corner while I lurked in shadows.

Presently I spotted them down the street, arms around each other. He took her up on the porch and made a long job of kissing her good-night—longer than I thought. Then she went in and he came down the walk, turned away. I slid into step and hooked an arm in his. 'That's all, son,' I announced quietly. 'I'm back to pick you up.'

'*You!*' He gasped and caught his breath.

'Me. Now you know who *he* is—and after you think it over you'll know who you are . . . and if you think hard enough, you'll figure out who the baby is . . . and who *I* am.'

He didn't answer, he was badly shaken. It's a shock to have it proved to you that you can't resist seducing yourself. I took him to the Apex Building and we jumped again.

2300 – VII – 12 Aug 1985 – Sub Rockies Base: I woke the duty sergeant, showed my ID, told the sergeant to bed my companion down with a happy pill and recruit him in the morning. The sergeant looked sour, but rank is rank, regardless of era; he did what I said—thinking, no doubt, that the next time we met he might be the colonel and I the sergeant: which can happen in our corps. 'What name?' he asked.

I wrote it out. He raised his eyebrows. 'Like so, eh? *Hmm*—'

'You just do your job, Sergeant.' I turned to my companion.

'Son, your troubles are over. You're about to start the best job a man ever held—and you'll do well. *I know.*'

'That you will!' agreed the sergeant. 'Look at me—born in 1917—still around, still young, still enjoying life.' I went back to the jump room, set everything on preselected zero.

2301 – V – 7 Nov 1970 – NYC – 'Pop's Place': I came out of the store-room carrying a fifth of Drambuie to account for the minute I had been gone. My assistant was arguing with the customer who had been playing 'I'm My Own Granpaw!' I said, 'Oh, let him play it, then unplug it.' I was very tired.

It's rough, but somebody must do it and it's very hard to recruit anyone in the later years, since the Mistake of 1972. Can you think of a better source than to pick people all fouled up where they are and give them well paid, interesting (even though dangerous) work in a necessary cause? Everybody knows now why the Fizzle War of 1963 fizzled. The bomb with New York's number on it didn't go off, a hundred other things didn't go as planned—all arranged by the likes of me.

But not the Mistake of '72; that one is not our fault—and can't be undone; there's no paradox to resolve. A thing either is, or it isn't, now and for ever amen. But there won't be another like it; an order dated. '1992' takes precedence any year.

I closed five minutes early, leaving a letter in the cash register telling my day manager that I was accepting his offer to buy me out, to see my lawyer as I was leaving on a long vacation. The Bureau might or might not pick up his payments, but they want things left tidy. I went to the room at the back of the storeroom and forward to 1993.

2200 – VII – 12 Jan 1993 – Sub Rockies Annex – HQ Temporal DOL: I checked in with the duty officer and went to my quarters, intending to sleep for a week. I had fetched the bottle we bet (after all, I won it) and took a drink before I wrote my report. It tasted foul and I wondered why I had ever liked Old Underwear. But it was better than nothing; I don't like to be cold sober, I think too much. But I don't really hit the bottle either; other people have snakes—I have people.

I dictated my report; forty recruitments all okayed by the Psych Bureau—counting my own, which I knew would be okayed. I was here, wasn't I? Then I taped a request for assignment to operations; I was sick of recruiting. I dropped both in the slot and headed for bed.

My eye fell on 'The By-laws of Time', over my bed:

> Never Do Yesterday What
> Should Be Done Tomorrow.
> If At Last You Do Succeed,
> Never Try Again.
> A Stitch in Time Saves Nine
> Billion.
> A Paradox May Be Paradoc-
> tored.
> It Is Earlier When You Think.
> Ancestors Are Just People.
> Even Jove Nods.

They didn't inspire me the way they had when I was a recruit; thirty subjective years of time-jumping wears you down. I undressed and when I got down to the hide I looked at my belly. A Caesarean leaves a big scar but I'm so hairy now that I don't notice it unless I look for it.

Then I glanced at the ring on my finger.

The Snake That Eats Its Own Tail, For Ever and Ever . . . I *know* where *I* came from—*but where did all you zombies come from?*

I felt a headache coming on, but a headache powder is one thing I do not take. I did once—and you all went away.

So I crawled into bed and whistled out the light.

You aren't really there at all. There isn't anybody but me—Jane—here alone in the dark.

I miss you dreadfully!

THE GERNSBACK CONTINUUM

William Gibson

William Gibson, the author of this next story, is a writer of amazing invention who has become associated with the 'cyberpunk' style of contempory fiction—he is credited by some with inventing the genre, an allegation he strongly denies—and is seen as the finest sf writer of his generation. His pictures of a computer-organised near-future society where high tech exists alongside slum dwellings and street-wise citizens have struck a chord with readers all over the world, and the sales of his books are now phenomenal.

Although born in the USA, since the late Sixties William Ford Gibson (1948–) has lived in Canada, where he moved in protest at the Vietnam War. His first novel, Neuromancer *(1984), about the burned-out software cowboy Case hired to break into cyberspace, brilliantly combined the old hardboiled school of Raymond Chandler and Ross Macdonald with the new worlds of computers and virtual reality. Subsequent works—including* Count Zero *(1986),* Mona Lisa Overdrive *(1988) and, most recently,* Idoru *(1996)—according to the* Sunday Times *have earned him the stature of 'guru of the new cybernetic world order' and 'the new George Orwell'. 'The Gernsback Continuum', written in 1981, is highly topical, featuring the current obsessions with UFOs and assorted phenomena in the story of a man travelling to find 'the tomorrow that never was'.*

*   *   *

Mercifully, the whole thing is starting to fade, to become an episode. When I do still catch the odd glimpse, it's peripheral; mere fragments of mad-doctor chrome, confining themselves to the corner of the eye. There was that flying-wing liner over San Francisco last week, but it was almost translucent. And the shark-fin roadsters have got scarcer, and freeways discreetly avoid unfolding themselves into the gleaming eighty-lane monsters I was forced to drive last month in my rented Toyota. And I know that none of it will follow me to New York; my vision is narrowing to a single wavelength of probability. I've worked hard for that. Television helped a lot.

I suppose it started in London, in that bogus Greek tavern in Battersea Park Road, with lunch on Cohen's corporate tab. Dead steam-table food and it took them thirty minutes to find an ice bucket for the retsina. Cohen works for Barris-Watford, who publish big, trendy 'trade' paperbacks: illustrated histories of the neon sign, the pinball machine, the wind-up toys of Occupied Japan. I'd gone over to shoot a series of shoe ads; California girls with tanned legs and frisky Day-Glo jogging shoes had capered for me down the escalators of St John's Wood and across the platforms of Tooting Bec. A lean and hungry young agency had decided that the mystery of London Transport would sell waffle-tread nylon runners. They decide; I shoot. And Cohen, whom I knew vaguely from the old days in New York, had invited me to lunch the day before I was due out of Heathrow. He brought along a very fashionably dressed young woman named Dialta Downes, who was virtually chinless and evidently a noted pop-art historian. In retrospect, I see her walking in beside Cohen under a floating neon sign that flashes THIS WAY LIES MADNESS in huge sans-serif capitals.

Cohen introduced us and explained that Dialta was the prime mover behind the latest Barris-Watford project, an illustrated history of what she called 'American Streamlined Modern'. Cohen called it 'raygun Gothic'. Their working title was *The Airstream Futuropolis: The Tomorrow That Never Was.*

There's a British obsession with the more baroque elements of American pop culture, something like the weird cowboys-and-Indians fetish of the West Germans or the aberrant French hunger for old Jerry Lewis films. In Dialta Downes this manifested itself in a mania for a uniquely American form of architecture that most Americans are scarcely aware of. At first I wasn't sure what she was talking about, but gradually it began to dawn on me. I found myself remembering Sunday morning television in the Fifties.

Sometimes they'd run old eroded newsreels as filler on the local station. You'd sit there with a peanut-butter sandwich and a glass of milk, and a static-ridden Hollywood baritone would tell you that there was A Flying Car in Your Future. And three Detroit engineers would putter around with this big old Nash with wings, and you'd see it rumbling furiously down some deserted Michigan runway. You never actually saw it take off, but it flew away to Dialta Downes' never-never land, true home of a generation of completely uninhibited technophiles. She was talking about those odds and ends of 'futuristic' Thirties and Forties architecture you pass daily in American cities without noticing: the movie marquees ribbed to radiate some mysterious energy, the dime stores faced with fluted aluminium, the chrome-tube chairs gathering dust in the lobbies of transient hotels. She saw these things as segments of a dreamworld, abandoned in the uncaring present; she wanted me to photograph them for her.

The Thirties had seen the first generation of American industrial designers; until the Thirties, all pencil sharpeners had looked like pencil sharpeners—your basic Victorian mechanism, perhaps with a curlicue of decorative trim. After the advent of the designers, some pencil sharpeners looked as though they'd been put together in wind tunnels. For the most part, the change was only skin-deep; under the streamlined chrome shell, you'd find the same Victorian mechanism. Which made a certain kind of sense, because the most successful American designers had been recruited from the ranks of Broadway theatre designers. It was all a stage set, a series of elaborate props for playing at living in the future.

Over coffee, Cohen produced a fat manila envelope full of glossies. I saw the winged statues that guard the Hoover Dam, forty-foot concrete hood ornaments leaning steadfastly into an imaginary hurricane. I saw a dozen shots of Frank Lloyd Wright's Johnson's Wax Building, juxtaposed with the covers of old *Amazing Stories* pulps, by an artist named Frank R. Paul; the employees of Johnson's Wax must have felt as though they were walking into one of Paul's spray-paint pulp utopias. Wright's building looked as though it had been designed for people who wore white togas and Lucite sandals. I hesitated over one sketch of a particularly grandiose prop-driven airliner, all wing, like a fat symmetrical boomerang with windows in unlikely places. Labelled arrows indicated the locations of the grand ballroom and two squash courts. It was dated 1936.

'This thing couldn't have flown . . . ?' I looked at Dialta Downes.

'Oh, no, quite impossible, even with those twelve giant props; but they loved the look, don't you see? New York to London in less than two days, first-class dining-rooms, private cabins, sun decks, dancing to jazz in the evening . . . The designers were populists, you see; they were trying to give the public what it wanted. What the public wanted was the future.'

*   *   *

I'd been in Burbank for three days, trying to suffuse a really dull-looking rocker with charisma, when I got the package from Cohen. It is possible to photograph what isn't there; it's damned hard to do, and consequently a very marketable talent. While I'm not bad at it, I'm not exactly the best, either, and this poor guy strained my Nikon's credibility. I got out, depressed because I do like to do a good job, but not totally depressed, because I did make sure I'd got the cheque for the job, and I decided to restore myself with the sublime artiness of the Barris-Watford assignment. Cohen had sent me some books on Thirties design, more photos of streamlined buildings, and a list of Dialta Downes' fifty favourite examples of the style in California.

Architectural photography can involve a lot of waiting; the building becomes a kind of sundial, while you wait for a shadow to crawl away from a detail you want, or for the mass and balance of the structure to reveal itself in a certain way. While I was waiting, I thought myself into Dialta Downes' America. When I isolated a few of the factory buildings on the ground glass of the Hasselblad, they came across with a kind of sinister totalitarian dignity, like the stadiums Albert Speer built for Hitler. But the rest of it was relentlessly tacky: ephemeral stuff extruded by the collective American subconscious of the Thirties, tending mostly to survive along depressing strips lined with dusty motels, mattress wholesalers, and small used-car lots. I went for the gas stations in a big way.

During the high point of the Downes Age, they put Ming the Merciless in charge of designing California gas stations. Favouring the architecture of his native Mongo, he cruised up and down the coast erecting raygun emplacements in white stucco. Lots of them featured superfluous central towers ringed with those strange radiator flags that were a signature motif of the style, and made them look as though they might generate potent bursts of raw technological enthusiasm, if you could only find the switch that turned them on. I shot one in San Jose an hour before the bulldozers arrived and drove right through the structural truth of plaster and lathing and cheap concrete.

'Think of it,' Dialta Downes had said, 'as a kind of alternative America: a 1980 that never happened. An architecture of broken dreams.'

And that was my frame of mind as I made the stations of her convoluted socio-architectural cross in my red Toyota—as I gradually tuned in to her image of a shadowy America-that-wasn't, of Coca-Cola plants like beached submarines, and fifth-run movie houses like the temples of some lost sect that had worshipped blue mirrors and geometry. And as I moved among these secret ruins, I found myself wondering what the inhabitants of that lost future would think of the world I lived in. The Thirties dreamed white marble and slipstream chrome, immortal crystal and burnished bronze, but the rockets on the covers of the Gernsback pulps had fallen on London in the dead of night, screaming. After the war, everyone had a car—no wings for it—and the promised superhighway to drive it down, so that the sky itself darkened, and the fumes ate the marble and pitted the miracle crystal . . .

And one day, on the outskirts of Bolinas, when I was setting up to shoot a particularly lavish example of Ming's martial architecture, I penetrated a fine membrane, a membrane of probability . . .

Ever so gently, I went over the Edge—

And looked up to see a twelve-engined thing like a bloated boomerang, all wing, thrumming its way east with an elephantine grace, so low that I could count the rivets in its dull silver skin, and hear—maybe—the echo of jazz.

I took it to Kihn.

Merv Kihn, a free-lance journalist with an extensive line in Texas pterodactyls, redneck UFO contactees, bush-league Loch Ness monsters, and the Top Ten conspiracy theories in the loonier reaches of the American mass mind.

'It's good,' said Kihn, polishing his yellow Polaroid shooting glasses on the hem of his Hawaiian shirt, 'but it's not *mental*; lacks the true quill.'

'But I saw it, Mervyn.' We were seated poolside in brilliant Arizona sunlight. He was in Tucson waiting for a group of retired Las Vegas civil servants whose leader received messages from Them on her microwave oven. I'd driven all night and was feeling it.

'Of course you did. Of course you saw it. You've read my stuff; haven't you grasped my blanket solution to the UFO problem? It's simple, plain and country simple: people' —he settled the glasses carefully on his long hawk nose and fixed me with his best basilisk glare—'*see* . . . things. People see these things. Nothing's there, but people *see* them anyway. Because they need to, probably. You've read Jung, you should know the score . . . In your case, it's so obvious: you admit you were thinking about this crackpot architecture, having fantasies . . . Look, I'm sure you've taken your share of drugs, right? How many people survived the Sixties in California without having the odd hallucination? All those nights when you discovered that whole armies of Disney technicians had been employed to weave animated holograms of Egyptian hieroglyphs into the fabric of your jeans, say, or the times when—'

'But it wasn't like that.'

'Of course not. It wasn't like that at all; it was "in a setting of clear reality", right? Everything normal, and then there's the monster, the mandala, the neon cigar. In your case, a giant Tom Swift airplane. It happens *all the time*. You aren't even crazy. You know that, don't you?' He fished a beer out of the battered foam cooler beside his deckchair.

'Last week I was in Virginia. Grayson County. I interviewed a six-teen-year-old girl who'd been assaulted by a *bar hade*.'

'A what?'

'A bear head. The severed head of a bear. This *bar hade*, see, was floating around on its own little flying saucer, looked kind of like the hub-caps on cousin Wayne's vintage Caddy. Had red, glowing eyes like two cigar stubs and telescoping chrome antennas poking up behind its ears.' He burped.

'It assaulted her? How?'

'You don't want to know; you're obviously impressionable. "It was cold" '—he lapsed into his bad southern accent—' "and metallic". It made electronic noises. Now that is the real thing, the straight goods from the mass unconscious, friend; that little girl is a witch. There's just no place for her to function in this society. She'd have seen the devil, if she hadn't been brought up on *The Bionic Man* and all those *Star Trek* reruns. She is clued into the main vein. And she knows that it happened to her. I got out ten minutes before the heavy UFO boys showed up with the polygraph.'

I must have looked pained, because he set his beer down carefully beside the cooler and sat up.

'If you want a classier explanation, I'd say you saw a semiotic ghost. All these contactee stories, for instance, are framed in a kind of sci-fi imagery that permeates our culture. I could buy aliens, but not aliens that look like Fifties comic art. They're semiotic phantoms, bits of deep cultural imagery that have split off and taken on a life of their own, like the Jules Verne airships that those old Kansas farmers were always seeing. But you saw a different kind of ghost, that's all. That plane was part of the mass unconscious, once. You picked up on that, somehow. The important thing is not to worry about it.'

I did worry about it, though.

Kihn combed his thinning blond hair and went off to hear what They had had to say over the radar range lately, and I drew the curtains in my room and lay down in air-conditioned darkness to worry about it. I was still worrying about it when I woke up. Kihn had left a note on my door; he was flying up north in a chartered plane to check out a cattle-mutilation rumour ('muties', he called them; another of his journalistic specialities).

I had a meal, showered, took a crumbling diet pill that had been kicking around in the bottom of my shaving kit for three years, and headed back to Los Angeles.

The speed limited my vision to the tunnel of the Toyota's headlights. The body could drive, I told myself, while the mind maintained. Maintained and stayed away from the weird peripheral window-dressing of amphetatmine and exhaustion, the spectral, luminous vegetation that grows out of the corners of the mind's eye along late-night highways. But the mind had its own ideas, and Kihn's opinion of what I was already thinking of as my 'sighting' rattled endlessly through my head in a tight, lopsided orbit. Semiotic ghosts. Fragments of the Mass Dream, whirling past in the wind of my passage. Somehow this feedback loop aggravated the diet pill, and the speed vegetation along the road began to assume the colours of infra-red satellite images, glowing shreds blown apart on the Toyota's slipstream.

I pulled over, then, and a half-dozen aluminium beer cans winked good-night as I killed the headlights. I wondered what time it was in London, and tried to imagine Dialta Downes having breakfast in her Hampstead flat, surrounded by streamlined chrome figurines and books on American culture.

Desert nights in that country are enormous; the moon is closer. I watched the moon for a long time and decided that Kihn was right. The main thing was not to worry. All across the continent, daily, people who were more normal than I'd ever aspired to be saw giant birds, Bigfeet, flying oil refineries; they kept Kihn busy and solvent. Why should I be upset by a glimpse of the 1930s pop imagination loose over Bolinas? I decided to go to sleep, with nothing worse to worry about than rattlesnakes and cannibal hippies, safe amid the friendly roadside garbage of my own familiar continuum. In the morning I'd drive down to Nogales and photograph the old brothels, something I'd intended to do for years. The diet pill had given up.

*   *   *

The light woke me, and then the voices.

The light came from somewhere behind me and threw shifting shadows inside the car. The voices were calm, indistinct, male and female, engaged in conversation.

My neck was stiff and my eyeballs felt gritty in their sockets. My leg had gone to sleep, pressed against the steering wheel. I fumbled for my glasses in the pocket of my work shirt and finally got them on.

Then I looked behind me and saw the city.

The books on Thirties design were in the trunk; one of them contained sketches of an idealised city that drew on *Metropolis* and *Things to Come*, but squared everything, soaring up through an architect's perfect clouds to zeppelin docks and mad neon spires. That city was a scale model of the one that rose behind me. Spire stood on spire in gleaming ziggurat steps that climbed to a central golden temple tower ringed with the crazy radiator flangers of the Mongo gas stations. You could hide the Empire State Building in the smallest of those towers. Roads of crystal soared between the spires, crossed and recrossed my smooth silver shapes like beads of running mercury. The air was thick with ships: giant wing-liners, little darting silver things (sometimes one of the quicksilver shapes from the sky bridges rose gracefully into the air and flew up to join the dance), mile-long blimps, hovering dragonfly things that were gyrocopters . . .

I closed my eyes tight and swung around in the seat. When I opened them, I willed myself to see the mileage meter, the pale road dust on the black plastic dashboard, the overflowing ashtray.

'Amphetamine psychosis,' I said. I opened my eyes. The dash was still there, the dust, the crushed filter-tips. Very carefully, without moving my head, I turned the headlights on.

And saw them.

They were blond. They were standing beside their car, an aluminium avocado with a central shark-fin rudder jutting up from its spine and smooth black tyres like a child's toy. He had his arm around her waist and was gesturing towards the city. They were both in white: loose clothing, bare legs, spotless white sun shoes. Neither of them seemed aware of the beams of my headlights. He was saying something wise and strong, and she was nodding, and suddenly I was frightened, frightened in an entirely different way. Sanity had ceased to be an issue; I knew somehow, that the city behind me was Tucson—a dream Tucson thrown up out of the collective yearning of an era. That it was real, entirely real. But the couple in front of me lived in it, and they frightened me.

They were the children of Dialta Downes' '80-that-wasn't; they were Heirs to the Dream. They were white, blond, and they probably had blue eyes. They were American. Dialta had said that the Future had come to America first, but had finally passed it by. But not here, in the heart of the Dream. Here, we'd gone on and on, in a dream logic that knew nothing of pollution, the finite bounds of fossil fuel, or foreign wars it was possible to lose. They were smug, happy, and utterly content with themselves and their world. And in the Dream, it was *their* world.

Behind me, the illuminated city: searchlights swept the sky for the sheer joy of it. I imagined them thronging the plazas of white marble, orderly and alert, their bright eyes shining with enthusiasm for their floodlit avenues and silver cars.

It had all the sinister fruitiness of Hitler Youth propaganda.

I put the car in gear and drove forward slowly, until the bumper was within three feet of them. They still hadn't seen me. I rolled the window down and listened to what the man was saying. His words were bright and hollow as the pitch in some Chamber of Commerce brochure, and I knew that he believed in them absolutely.

'John,' I heard the woman say, 'we've forgotten to take our food pills.' She clicked two bright wafers from a thing on her belt and passed one to him. I backed on to the highway and headed for Los Angeles, wincing and shaking my head.

I phoned Kihn from a gas station. A new one, in bad Spanish Modern. He was back from his expedition and didn't seem to mind the call.

'Yeah, that is a weird one. Did you try to get any pictures? Not that they ever come out, but it adds an interesting *frisson* to your story, not having the pictures turn out . . .'

But what should I do?

'Watch lots of television, particularly game shows and soaps. Go to porn movies. Ever see *Nazi Love Motel*? They've got it on cable, here. Really awful. Just what you need.'

What was he talking about?

'Quit yelling and listen to me. I'm letting you in on a trade secret: really bad media can exorcise your semiotic ghosts. If it keeps the saucer people off my back, it can keep these Art Deco futuroids off yours. Try it. What have you got to lose?'

Then he begged off, pleading an early-morning date with the Elect.

'The who?'

'These oldsters from Vegas; the ones with the microwaves.'

I considered putting a collect call through to London, getting Cohen at Barris-Watford and telling him his photographer was checking out for a protracted season in the Twilight Zone. In the end, I let a machine mix me a really impossible cup of black coffee and climbed back into the Toyota for the haul to Los Angeles.

Los Angeles was a bad idea, and I spent two weeks there. It was prime Downes country; too much of the Dream there, and too many fragments of the Dream waiting to snare me. I nearly wrecked the car on a stretch of overpass near Disneyland, when the road fanned out like an origami trick and left me swerving through a dozen mini-lanes of whizzing chrome teardrops with shark fins. Even worse, Hollywood was full of people who looked too much like the couple I'd seen in Arizona. I hired an Italian director who was making ends meet doing darkroom work and installing patio decks around swimming pools until his ship came in; he made prints of all the negatives I'd accumulated on the Downes job. I didn't want to look at the stuff myself. It didn't seem to bother Leonardo, though, and when he was finished I checked the prints, riffling through them like a deck of cards, sealed them up, and sent them air freight to London. Then I took a taxi to a theatre that was showing *Nazi Love Motel*, and kept my eyes shut all the way.

Cohen's congratulatory wire was forwarded to me in San Francisco a week later. Dialta had loved the pictures. He admired the way I'd 'really gotten into it', and looked forward to working with me again. That afternoon I spotted a flying wing over Castro Street, but there was something tenuous about it, as though it were only half there. I rushed into the nearest news-stand and gathered up as much as I could find on the petroleum crisis and the nuclear energy hazard. I'd just decided to buy a plane ticket for New York.

'Hell of a world we live in, huh?' The proprietor was a thin black man with bad teeth and an obvious wig. I nodded, fishing in my jeans for change, anxious to find a park bench where I could submerge myself in hard evidence of the human near-dystopia we live in. 'But it could be worse, huh?'

'That's right,' I said, 'or even worse, it could be perfect.'

He watched me as I headed down the street with my little bundle of condensed catastrophe.

THE TIME DISEASE

Martin Amis

Undoubtedly one of the most remarkable imaginative novels of the Nineties has been Martin Amis' Time's Arrow *(1991), which has proved as significant to the career and fame of its author as* The Time Machine *did a century ago for H. G. Wells. The extraordinary story of time's 'arrow' being put into reverse and the twentieth century going backwards, it has been widely acclaimed for its grim ironies. Amis has admitted that two other time novels were primary sources of his inspiration: Philip K. Dick's* Counter-Clock World *(1967) and* Slaughterhouse-Five *by Kurt Vonnegut Jr (1969). His interest in future societies and time displacement can also be seen in his other novels,* Dead Babies *(1975),* Other People *(1981) and* London Fields *(1989), and his short stories such as 'The Time Disease' which he wrote for* Granta *in 1987.*

Martin Amis (1949–) is the son of Kingsley Amis, who was one of the main proponents of sf as a serious literary form back in the Fifties and the author of the landmark survey of the genre, New Maps of Hell *(1960), as well as the editor throughout the Sixties of the influential* Spectrum *series of anthologies. The younger Amis shares his father's interest, and his use of sf elements in his work coupled with his forthright and often controversial style has put him at the forefront of contemporary British authors. 'Something seems to have gone wrong with time— with modern time,' he has said recently; 'the past and the future, equally threatened, equally cheapened, now huddle in the present. The present feels narrower, the present feels straitened, discrepant, as the planet lives from day to day.' Amis has acknowledged his debt to J. G. Ballard in the writing of this tale of a technological near-future in which attempts are being made to control disjointed time. It makes a fitting and salutary finale to the whole collection.*

*   *   *

Twenty-twenty, and the *time* disease is epidemic. In my credit-group, anyway. And yours too, friend, unless I miss my guess. Nobody thinks about anything else any more. Nobody even pretends to think about anything else any more. Oh yeah, except the sky, of course. The poor sky ... It's a thing. It's a situation. We all think about *time*, catching *time*, coming down with *time*. *I'm* still okay, I think, for the time being.

I took out my handmirror. Everybody carries at least one handmirror now. On the zip trains you see whole carloads jack-knifed over in taut scrutiny of their hairlines and eye-sockets. The anxiety is as electric as the twanging cable above our heads. They say more people are laid low by *time*-anxiety than by *time* itself. But only *time* is fatal. It's a problem, we agree, a definite feature. How can you change the subject when there's only one subject? People don't want to talk about the sky. They don't want to talk about the sky, and I don't blame them.

I took out my handmirror and gave myself a ten-second scan: lower gumline, left eyelash count. I felt so heartened that I moved carefully into the kitchen and cracked out a beer. I ate a *hero*, and a *ham salad*. I lit another cigarette. I activated the TV and keyed myself in to the Therapy Channel. I watched a seventy-year-old documentary about a road-widening scheme in a place called Orpington, over in England there ... Boredom is meant to be highly prophylactic when it comes to *time*. We are all advised to experience as much boredom as we possibly can. To bore somebody is said to be even more sensitive than to be bored oneself. That's why we're always raising our voices in company and going on and on about anything that enters our heads. Me I go on about *time* the whole time: a reckless habit. Listen to me. I'm at it again.

The outercom sounded. I switched from Therapy to Intake. No visual. 'Who is it?' I asked the TV. The TV told me. I sighed, and put the call on a half-minute hold. Soothing music. Boring music ... Okay—you want to hear my theory? Now some say that *time* was caused by congestion, air plague, city life (and city life is the only kind of life there is these days). Others say that *time* was a result of the first nuclear conflicts (limited theatre, Persia v. Pakistan, Zaire v. Nigeria, and so on, no really big deal or anything: they took the heat and the light, and we took the cold and the dark; it helped fuck the sky, that factor) and more particularly of the saturation TV coverage that followed: all day the screen writhed with flesh, flesh dying or living in a queer state of age. Still others say that *time* was an evolutionary consequence of humankind's ventures into space (they shouldn't have gone out there, what with

things so rocky back home). *Food*, pornography, the cancer cure . . .
Me I think it was the twentieth century that did it. The twentieth century
was all it took.

'Hi there, Happy,' I said. 'What's new?'

'. . . Lou?' her voice said warily. 'Lou, I don't feel so good.'

'That's not new. That's old.'

'I don't feel so good. I think it's really happening this time.'

'Oh, sure.'

Now this was Happy Farraday. That's right: the TV star. *The* Happy
Farraday. Oh, we go way back, Happy and me.

'Let's take a look at you,' I said. 'Come on, Happy, give me a visual
on this.'

The screen remained blank, its dead cells seeming to squirm or hover.
On impulse I switched from Intake to Daydrama. There was Happy,
full face to camera, vividly doing her thing. I switched back. Still no
visual. I said,

'I just checked you out on the other channel. You're in superb shape.
What's your factor?'

'It's here,' said her voice. 'It's *time*.'

TV stars are especially prone to *time*-anxiety—to *time* too, it has to
be said. Why? Well I think we're looking at an occupational hazard.
It's a thing. True, the work could hardly be more boring. Not many
people know this, but all the characters in the Armchair, Daydrama and
Proscenium channels now write their own lines. It's a new gimmick,
intended to promote formlessness, to combat sequentiality, and so on:
the target-research gurus have established that this goes down a lot
better with the homebound. Besides, all the writing talent is in game-
conception or mass-therapy, doing soothe stuff for the non-employed
and other sections of the populace that are winding down from being
functional. There are fortunes to be made in the leisure and assuagement
industries. The standout writers are like those teenage billionaires in
the early days of the chip revolution. On the other hand, making
money—like reading and writing, come to that—dangerously increases
your *time*-anxiety levels. Obviously. The more money you have, the
more time you have to worry about *time*. It's a thing. Happy Farraday
is top credit, and she also bears the weight of TV fame (where millions
know you or think they do), that collective sympathy, identification and
concern which, I suspect, seriously depletes your *time*-resistance. I've
started to keep a kind of file on this. I'm beginning to think of it as
reciprocity syndrome, one of the new—

Where was I? Yeah. On the line with Happy here. My mind has a tendency to wander. Indulge me. It helps, *time*-wise.

'Okay. You want to tell me what symptoms you got?' She told me. 'Call a doctor,' I joked. 'Look, give me a break. This is—what? The second time this year? The third?'

'It's different this time.'

'It's the new role, Happy. That's all it is.' In her new series in Daydrama, Happy was playing the stock part of a glamorous forty-year-old with a bad case of *time*-anxiety. And it was getting to her—of course it was. 'You know where I place the blame? On your talent? As an actress you're just too damn good. Greg Buzhardt and I were—'

'Save it, Lou,' she said. 'Don't bore me out. It's real. It's *time*.'

'I know what you're going to do. I know what you're going to do. You're going to ask me to drive over.'

'I'll pay.'

'It's not the money, Happy, it's the time.'

'Take the dollar lane.'

'Wow,' I said. 'You're, you must be kind of serious this time.'

So I stood on the shoulder, waiting for Roy to bring up my Horsefly from the stacks. Well, Happy is an old friend and one of my biggest clients, also an ex-wife of mine, and I had to do the right thing. For a while out there I wasn't sure what time it was supposed to be or whether I had a day or night situation on my hands—but then I saw the faint tremors and pulsings of the sun, up in the east. The heavy green light sieved down through the ripped and tattered troposphere, its fissures as many-eyed as silk or pantyhose, with a liquid quality too, churning, changing. Green light: let's go ... I had a bad scare myself the other week, a very bad scare. I was in bed with Danuta and we were going to have a crack at making love. Okay, a dumb move—but it was her birthday, and we'd been doing a lot of tranquillisers that night. I don't happen to believe that love-making is quite as risky as some people say. To hear some people talk, you'd think that sex was a suicide pact. To hold hands is to put your life on the line. 'Look at the *time*-fatality figures among the underclasses,' I tell them. They screw like there's no tomorrow, and do they come down with *time*? No, it's us high-credit characters who are really at risk. Like me and Danuta. Like Happy. Like you ... Anyway, we were lying on the bed together, as I say, semi-nude, and talking about the possibility of maybe getting into the right frame of mind for a little of the old pre-foreplay—when all of a sudden I felt a rosy glow break out on me like sweat. There was this clogged inner heat, a heavy heat, with something limitless in it, right in the crux of my being. Well, I panicked. You always tell yourself you're going to be brave, dignified, stoical. I ran wailing into the bathroom. I yanked out the triple mirror; the automatic scanlight came on with a crackle. I opened my eyes and stared. There I stood, waiting. Yes, I was clear, I was safe. I broke down and wept with relief. After a while Danuta helped me back into bed. We didn't try to make love or anything. No *way*. I felt too damn good. I lay there dabbing my eyes, so happy, so grateful—my old self again.

'You screw much, Roy?'

'—Sir?'

'You screw much, Roy?'

'Some. I guess.'

Roy was an earnest young earner of the stooped, mustachioed variety. He seemed to have burdensome responsibilities; he even wore his cartridge belt like some kind of hernia strap or spinal support. This was the B-credit look, the buffer-class look. Pretty soon, they project, society will be equally divided into three sections. Section B will devote itself entirely to defending section A from section C. I'm section A. I'm glad I have Roy and his boys on my side.

'Where you driving to today, sir?' he asked as he handed me my car card.

'Over the hills and far away, Roy. I'm going to see Happy Farraday. Any message?'

Roy looked troubled. 'Sir,' he said, 'you got to tell her about Duncan. The new guy at the condo. He has an alcohol thing. Happy Farraday doesn't know about it yet. Duncan, he sets fire to stuff, with his problem there.'

'His problem, Roy? That's harsh, Roy.'

'Well okay. I don't want to do any kind of value thing here. Maybe it was, like when he was a kid of something. But Duncan has an alcohol situation there. That's the truth of it, Mr Goldfather. And Happy Farraday doesn't know about it yet. You got to warn her. You got to warn her, sir—right now, before it's too late.'

I gazed into Roy's handsome, imploring, deeply stupid face. The hot eyes, the tremulous cheeks, the mustache. Jesus Christ, what difference do these guys think a *mustache* is going to make to anything? For the hundredth time I said to him, 'Roy, it's all made up. It's just TV, Roy. She writes that stuff herself. It isn't real.'

'Now I don't know about none of that,' he said, his hand splayed in quiet propitiation. 'But I'd feel better in my mind if you'd warn her about Duncan's factor there.'

Roy paused. With some difficulty he bent to dab at an oilstain on his superwashable blue pants. He straightened up with a long wheeze. Being young, Roy was, of course, incredibly fat—for reasons of *time*. We both stood there and gazed at the sky, at the spillages, the running colours, at the great chemical betrayals . . .

'It's bad today,' said Roy. 'Sir? Mr Goldfather? Is it true what they say, that Happy Farraday's coming down with *time*?'

Traffic was light and I was over at Happy's before I knew it. Traffic *is* a problem, as everybody keeps on saying. It's okay, though, if you use the more expensive lanes. We have a five-lane system here in our county: free, nickel, dime, quarter and dollar (nothing, five, ten, twenty-five or a hundred dollars a mile)—but of course the free lane is non-operational right now, a gridlock, a caravan, a linear breakers' yard of slumped and frazzled heaps, dead rolling-stock that never rolls. They're going to have a situation there with the nickel lane too, pretty soon. The thing about driving anywhere is, it's so unbelievably boring. Here's another plus: since the ban on rearview mirrors, there's not much scope for any *time*-anxiety. They had to take the mirrors away, yes sir. They got my support on that. The concentration-loss was a real feature, you know, driving along and checking out your crow's-feet and hairline, all at the same time. There used to be a party atmosphere out on the thruway, in the cheap lanes where mobility is low or minimal. People would get out of their cars and horse around. Maybe it still goes on, for all I know. The dividing barriers are higher now, with the new Boredom Drive, and you can't really tell what gives. I *did* see something interesting, though. I couldn't help it. During the long wait at the security intersect, where even the dollar lane gets loused up by all the towtrucks and ambulances—and by the great fleets of copbikes and squadcars— I saw three *runners*, three *time* punks, loping steadily across the disused freightlane, up on the East Viaduct. There they were, as plain as day: shorts, sweatshirts, *running*-shoes. The stacked cars all sounded their horns, a low furious bellow from the old beasts in their stalls. A few dozen cops appeared with bullhorns and tried to talk them down—but they just gestured and *ran* defiantly on. They're sick in the head, these punks, though I guess there's a kind of logic in it somewhere. They do vitamins, you know. Yeah. They work out and screw around; they have their nihilistic marathons. I saw one up close down at the studios last week. A security guard found her *running* along the old outer track. They asked her some questions and then let her go. She was about thirty, I guess. She looked in terrible shape.

And so I drove on, without incident. But even through the treated glass of the windshield I could see and sense the atrocious lancings and poppings in the ruined sky. It gets to you. Stare at the blazing noon of a high-watt bulb for ten or fifteen minutes—then shut your eyes, real tight and sudden. That's what the sky looks like. You know, we pity it, or at least I do. I look at the sky and I just think . . . *ow*. Whew. Oh, the sky, the poor *sky*.

Happy Farraday had left a priority clearance for me at Realty HQ, so I didn't have to hang around that long. To tell you the truth, I was scandalised by how lax and perfunctory the security people were becoming. It's always like this, after a quiet few weeks. Then there's another shitstorm from section C, and all the writs start flying around again. In the cubicle I put my clothes back on and dried my hair. While they okayed my urinalysis and X-ray congruence tests, I watched TV in the commissary. I sat down, delicately, gingerly (you know how it is, after a strip search), and took three clippings out of my wallet. These are for the file. What do you think?

Item 1, for the news page of *Screen Week*:

In a series of repeated experiments at the Valley Chemistry Workshop, Science Student Edwin Navasky has 'proven' that hot water freezes faster than cold. Said Edwin. 'We did the test four times.' Added Student Advisor Joy Broadener: 'It's a feature. We're real baffled.'

Item 2, from the facts section of *Armchair Guide*:

Candidate Day McGwire took out a spot on Channel 29 Monday last. Her purpose: to deny persistent but unfounded rumours that she suffered from heart trouble. Sadly, she was unable to appear. The reason: her sudden hospitalisation with a cardiac problem.

Item 3, from the update column of *Television*:

Meteorological Pilot Lars Christer reported another sighting of

'The Thing Up There' during a routine low-level flight. The location: 10,000 feet above Lake Baltimore. His description: 'It was kind of oval, with kind of a black circle in the center.' The phenomenon is believed to be a cumulus or spore formation. Christer's reaction: 'I don't know what to make of it. It's a thing.'

'Goldfader,' roared the tannoy, scattering my thoughts. The caddycart was ready at the gate. In the west now the nuked heavens looked especially hellish and distraught, with a throbbing, peeled-eyeball effect on the low horizon—bloodshot, conjunctivitic. Pink eye. The Thing Up There, I sometimes suspect, it might look like an eye, flecked with painful tears, staring, incensed . . . Using my cane I walked cautiously around the back of Happy's bungalow. Her twenty-year-old daughter Sunny was lying naked on a lounger, soaking up the haze. She made no move to cover herself as I limped poolside. Little Sunny here wants me to represent her someday, and I guess she was showing me the goods. Well, it's like they say: if you've got it, flaunt it.

'Hi, Lou,' she said sleepily. 'Take a drink. Go ahead. It's five o'clock.'

I looked at Sunny critically as I edged past her to the bar. The kid was a real centrefold, no question. Now don't misunderstand me here. I say *centrefold*, but of course pornography hasn't really kept pace with *time*. At first they tried filling the magazines and mature cable channels with new-look women, like Sunny, but it didn't work out. *Time* has effectively killed pornography, except as an underground blood sport, or a punk thing. *Time* has killed much else. Here's an interesting topic-sentence. Now that masturbation is the only form of sex that doesn't carry a government health warning, what do we think about when we're doing it there, what is *left* for us to think about? Me, I'm not saying. Christ, are *you*? What images slide, what spectres flit . . . what happens to these thoughts as they hover and mass, up there in the blasted, the totalled, up there in the fucked sky?

'Come on, Sunny. Where's your robe?'

As I fixed myself a vodka-context and sucked warily on a *pretzel*, I noticed Sunny's bald patch gently gleaming in the mist. I sighed.

'You like my dome?' she asked, without turning. 'Relax, it's artificial.' She sat up straight now and looked at me coyly. She smiled. Yeah, she'd had her teeth gimmicked too—by some cowboy snaggle-artist down in the Valley, no doubt. I poled myself poolside again and took a good slow scan. The flab and pallor were real all right, but the stretch-marks seemed cosmetic: too symmetrical, too pronounced.

'Now you listen to me, kid,' I began. 'Here are the realities. To scudbathe, a flop out all day by the pool with a bottle or two, to take on a little weight around the middle there—that's good for a girl. I mean you got to keep in shape. But this mutton routine, Sunny, it's for the punks. No oldjob ever got on my books and no oldjob ever will. Here are the reasons. Number one—' And I gave young Sunny a long talking-to out there, a real piece of my mind. I had her in the boredom corner and I wasn't letting her out. I went on and on at her—on and on and on and on. Me, I almost checked out myself, as boredom edged towards despair (the way boredom will), gazing into the voided pool, the reflected skyscape, and the busy static, in the sediment of sable rain.

'Yeah, well,' I said, winding up. 'Anyway. What's the thing? You look great.'

She laughed, coughed and spat. 'Forget it, Lou,' she said croakily. 'I only do it for fun.'

'I'm glad to hear that, Sunny. Now where's your mother?'

'Two days.'

'Uh?'

'In her room. In her room two days. She's serious this time.'

'Oh, sure.'

I rebrimmed my drink and went inside. The only point of light in the hallway came from the mirror's sleepless scanlamp. I looked myself over as I limped by. The heavy boredom and light stress of the seven-hour drive had done me good. I was fine, fine. 'Happy?' I said, and knocked.

'Is that you, Lou?' The voice was strong and clear—and it was quick, too. Direct, alert. 'I'll unlatch the door but don't come in right away.'

'Sure,' I said. I took a pull of booze and groped around for a chair. But then I heard the click and Happy's brisk 'Okay' . . .

Now I have to tell you that two things puzzled me here. First, the voice; second, the alacrity. Usually when she's in this state you can hardly hear the woman, and it takes an hour or more for her to get to the door and back into bed again. Yeah, I thought, she must have been waiting with her fingers poised on the handle. There's nothing wrong with Happy. The lady is fine, fine.

So in I went. She had the long black nets up over the sack—streaming, glistening, a cot for the devil's progeny. I moved through the gloom to the bedside chair and sat myself down with a grunt. A familiar chair. A familiar vigil.

'Mind if I don't smoke?' I asked her. 'It's not the lungburn. I just get tuckered out lighting the damn things all the time. Understand what I mean?'

No answer.

'How are you feeling, Happy?'

No answer.

'Now listen, kid. You got to quit this nonsense. I know it's problematic with the new role and everything, but—do I have to tell you again what happened to Day Montague? Do I, Happy? Do I? You're forty years old. You look fantastic. Let me tell you what Greg Buzhardt said to me when he saw the outtakes last week. He said, "Style. Class. Presence. Sincerity. Look at the ratings. Look at the profiles. Happy Farraday is the woman of men's dreams." That's what he said. "Happy Farraday is the—" '

'*Lou.*'

The voice came from behind me. I swivelled, and felt the twinge of tendons in my neck. Happy stood in a channel of bathroom light and also in the softer channel or haze of her slip of silk. She stood there as vivid as health itself, as graphic as youth, with her own light sources, the eyes, the mouth, the hair, the dips and curves of the flaring throat. The silk fell to her feet, and the glass fell from my hand, and something else dropped or plunged inside my chest.

'Oh Christ,' I said. 'Happy, I'm sorry.'

I remember what the sky was like, when the sky was young—its shawls and fleeces, its bears and whales, its cusps and clefts. A sky of grey, a sky of blue, a sky of spice. But now the sky has gone, and we face different heavens. Some vital casing has left our lives. Up there, now, I think, a kind of turnaround occurs. *Time*-fear collects up there and comes back to us in the form of *time*. It's the sky, the sky, it's the fucking *sky*. If enough people believe that a thing is real or happening, then it seems that the thing must happen, must go for real. Against all odds and expectation, these are magical times we're living in: proletarian magic. Grey magic!

Now that it's over, now that I'm home and on the mend, with Danuta back for good and Happy gone for ever, I think I can talk it all out and tell you the real story. I'm sitting on the cramped verandah with a blanket on my lap. Before me through the restraining bars the sunset sprawls in its polluted pomp, full of genies, cloaked ghosts, crimson demons of the middle sky. Red light: let's stop—let's end it. The Thing Up There, it may not be God, of course. It may be the Devil. Pretty soon, Danuta will call me in for my *broth*. Then a nap, and an hour of TV maybe. The Therapy Channel. I'm really into early nights . . . This afternoon I went walking, out on the shoulder. I don't know why. I don't think I'll do it again. On my return Roy appeared and helped me into the lift. He then asked me shyly,

'Happy Farraday—she okay now, sir?'

'Okay?' I said. 'Okay? What do you mean, *okay*? You never read a news page, Roy?'

'When she had to leave for Australia there. I wondered if she's okay. It'll be better for her, I guess. She was in a situation, with Duncan. It was a thing there.'

'That's just TV, for Christ's sake. They wrote her out,' I said, and felt an abrupt, leaden calm. 'She's not in Australia, Roy. She's in heaven.'

'—Sir?'

'She's *dead*, God damn it.'

'Now I don't know about none of that,' he said, with one fat palm raised. 'All it is is, I just hope she's okay, over in Australia there.'

Happy is in heaven, or I hope she is. I hope she's not in hell. Hell is the evening sky and I surely hope she's not up there. Ah, how to bear it? It's a thing. No, it really is.

I admit right now that I panicked back there, in the bungalow bedroom with the chute of light, the altered woman, and my own being so quickly stretched by fragility and fear. I shouted a lot. *Lie down! Call Trattman! Put on your robe!* That kind of thing. 'Come on, Lou. Be realistic,' she said. 'Look at me.' And I looked. Yeah. Her skin had that shiny telltale succulence, all over. Her hair—which a week ago, God damn it, lay as thin and colourless as my own—was humming with body and glow. And the mouth, Christ . . . lips all full and wet, and an animal tongue, like a heart, not Happy's, the tongue of another woman, bigger, greedier, younger. Younger. Classic *time*. Oh, classic.

She had me go over and lie down on the bed with her there, to give comfort, to give some sense of final safety. I was in a ticklish state of nerves, as you'd imagine. *Time* isn't infectious (we do know *that* about *time*) but sickness in any form won't draw a body nearer and I wanted all my distance. *Stay out*, it says. Then I saw—I saw it in her breasts, high but heavy, their little points tender, detailed, *time*-inflamed; and the smell, the smell of deep memory, tidal, submarine . . . I knew the kind of comfort she wanted. Yes and *time* often takes them this way, I thought in my slow and stately terror. You've come this far: go further, I told myself. Go closer, nearer, closer. Do it for her, for her and for old times' sake. I stirred, ready to let her have all that head and hand could give, until I too felt the fever in my lines of heat, the swell and smell of youth and death. This is suicide, I thought, and I don't care . . . At one point, during the last hours, just before dawn, I got to my feet and crept to the window and looked up at the aching, the hurting sky; I felt myself grey and softly twanging for a moment, like a coat-hanger left to shimmer on the pole, with Happy there behind me, alone in her bed and her hot death. 'Honey,' I said out loud, and went to join her. I like it, I thought, and gave a sudden nod. What do I like? I like the love. This is suicide and I don't care.

I was in terrible shape, mind you, for the next couple of months, really beat to shit, out of it, just out of it. I would wake at seven and leap out of the sack. I suffered energy attacks. Right off my *food*, I craved thick meat and thick wine. I couldn't watch any therapy. After barely a half-hour of some home-carpentry show or marathon darts contest I'd be pacing the room with frenzy in my bitten fingertips. I put Danuta at risk too, on several occasions. I even threw a pass in on little Sunny Farraday, who moved in here for a time after the cremation. Danuta divorced me. She even moved out. But she's back now. She's a good kid, Danuta—she helped me through. The whole thing is behind me now, and I think (knock on wood) that I'm more or less my old self again.

Pretty soon I'll rap on the window with my cane and have Danuta fetch me another blanket. Later, she'll help me inside for my *broth*. Then a nap, and an hour of TV maybe. The Therapy Channel. I'm happy for the time being, and willingly face the vivid torment, the boiling acne of the dying sky. When the sky is dead, will they give us a new one? Today my answering service left a strange message: I have to call a number in Sydney, over in Australia there. I'll do it tomorrow. Or the next day. Yeah. I can't make the effort right now. To reach for my stick, to lift it, to rap the glass, to say *Danuta*—even that takes steep ascents of time. All things happen so slowly now. I have a new feature with my back. I broke a tooth last week on a piece of *toast*. Jesus, how I hate bending and stairs. The sky hangs above me in shredded webs, in bloody tatters. It's a big relief, and I'm grateful. I'm okay, I'm good, good. For the time being, at any rate, I show no signs of coming down with *time*.

ACKNOWLEDGEMENTS

The editor would like to record his special thanks to Steve Miller, Brian W. Aldiss, William F. Nolan, Donn Albright and W. O. G. Lofts for their help in the research and compiling of this collection. He and the publishers are also grateful to the following authors, their publishers and agents for permission to include copyright stories in the book: the Estate of Philip K. Dick and Victor Gollancz Ltd for 'A Little Something for Us Tempunauts' by Philip K. Dick; Peters, Fraser & Dunlop for 'Mr Strenberry's Tale' by J. B. Priestley; Scott Meredith Literary Agency for 'All the Time in the World' by Arthur C. Clarke; The Observer Newspaper Group for 'The Instability' by Isaac Asimov; Curtis Publishing Company for 'Time Has No Boundaries' by Jack Finney; David Higham Associates for 'She Caught Hold of the Toe' by Richard Hughes; the author for 'The Reason Is with Us' by James E. Gunn; Curtis Brown Literary Agency for 'Man in His Time' by Brian W. Aldiss; Galaxy Publishing Corporation for 'A Gun for Dinosaur' by L. Sprague de Camp and 'The Deadly Mission of Phineas Snodgrass' by Frederik Pohl; William F. Nolan for his story, 'Of Time and Kathy Benedict'; Orion Publishing Group for 'Flux' by Michael Moorcock; Ziff-Davis & Co., Inc. for 'I Hear You Calling' by Eric Frank Russell and 'Time Bum' by C. M. Kornbluth; New American Library Inc. for 'The Men Who Murdered Mohammed' by Alfred Bester; Abner Stein Literary Agency for 'Time Intervening' by Ray Bradbury; A. P. Watt Literary Agency for 'The Grey Man' by H. G. Wells; Random Publishing Group and Jonathan Cape for 'The Greatest Television Show on Earth' by J. G. Ballard; Mercury Press Inc. for 'Production Problem' by Robert F. Young and 'Through Time and Space with Ferdinand Feghoot' by Grendel Briarton; International Scripts for 'All You Zombies—' by Robert A. Heinlein; HarperCollins for 'The Gernsback Continuum' by William Gibson; Jonathan Cape and Peters, Fraser & Dunlop for 'The Time Disease' by Martin Amis. The illustrations in this collection